Gifts

By The Same Author

From a Crooked Rib
A Naked Needle
Sweet and Sour Milk
Sardines
Close Sesame
Maps

Gifts

Nuruddin Farah

Serif
London

First published in 1993 by
Serif
47 Strahan Road
London E3 5DA

Published in association with Baobab Books, Harare

British Library Cataloguing-in-Publication Data.
A catalogue record for this book
is available from the British Library.

ISBN 1 897959 00 1

Typeset by Baobab Books, Harare
Printed and bound in Great Britain by the Bath Press

To
Monique Lortie,
Axmed Sr., and
Abdulqaadir, my elder brother, and his family
and in memory of
My mother, and
Angela Carter
With warmest love.

In writing this novel I have incurred many debts, the most important of which is owed to Marcel Mauss, author of *The Gift*, translated into English by I. Cunison. I am also indebted to many friends, including Paul Doornbos, Professor Mohamed Omar Beshir of Khartoum University, and Dr Mechthild Reh: to whom my thanks.

Part I
A Story is Born

Chapter One

In which Duniya sees the outlines of a story emerging from the mist surrounding her, as the outside world impinges on her space and thoughts.

Duniya had been awake for a while, conscious of the approaching dawn. She had dreamt of a restless butterfly; of a cat waiting attentively for the fretful insect's shadow to stay still for an instant so as to pounce on it. Then the dark room lit up with the brightness of fireflies, agitated breaths of light, soft, quiet as foam. Faint from heat, Duniya watched the goings-on, supine. The butterfly flew here and there, movements mesmeric in its circling rainbow of colours. As if hypnotized, the cat's eyes closed slowly, dramatically, and it fell asleep.

Fully awake, Duniya got out of bed.

Knowing she had to walk to work, she left home long before her children were up. She had timed herself on previous occasions: it would take forty-five minutes at a luxurious pace, allowing time for exchanging elaborate morning greetings and yesterday's gossip with any neighbours or colleagues she might meet.

In the event she only nodded a few times, acknowledging salutations without pause as if she did not know those who spoke them. She averted her eyes from several men in the side street, men in sarongs, towels draped round naked chests, men gargling gregariously, chewing on *rumay* sticks to clean their teeth. Duniya needed no reminder that the half-mud, half-brick houses in front of which these men stood had no running water, no wash-basins, no proper toilet facilities. She lived in one of the few houses in this district of Mogadiscio that boasted such amenities.

Wherever one looked, people were pouring out of opened doors. The streets were alive with activity: women chatting volubly with neighbours; groups of uniformed children on their way to school; infants, too small to carry their satchels, being led to kindergarten. Here and there someone was busy siphoning petrol from one vehicle into another. Most cars had an abandoned look, their bonnets up, engines cold. Occasionally one was driven past and everyone would stare, first at the vehicle as if seeing a miracle, then at the person at the wheel, perhaps hoping for a lift. The one time a taxi stopped, crowds converged on it and there was a scuffle, whereupon the driver sped off, safe in his securely locked car.

Contrary to expectation, there was a touch of gaiety in the air, with total strangers willing to engage in conversation on any topic, though uppermost in everyone's mind were the scarcity of fuel and the increasingly frequent power cuts. Some people spoke knowledgeably about the politics of commodity shortages, guessing how long this would last. A man claiming to be in the know spoke of a government delegation going on a mission to the oil-producing Arab countries in the hope of returning with tankerfuls of petrol.

Duniya crossed an asphalt road which, though not signposted as such, was the boundary between two districts, one poor, in which she herself lived, the other middle-class if not well-to-do. From the nature of the conversation and the accents, she knew she was in Hodan. She entered a dirt road linking two tarred streets, a broad road that was quiet as a cul-de-sac. Suddenly, she felt violently upset; the surrounding silence disturbed her, making her breathing erratic. Seized with inexplicable fear, she sensed a chill in her bones, as if she had ventured into dangerous territory. She halted, not wanting to go further.

It was then that she spotted a cat resembling the one in her dream, crouched fearlessly before her, waiting to be picked up and cuddled. But Duniya did neither. She and the cat stared at each other and this increased her awareness of inner stress.

A few seconds later she saw in the hazy distance what at first seemed to be a butterfly with colourful wings revolving like spinning-tops. To her delighted surprise, it turned out to be a red-and-yellow-striped taxi, empty.

She got in, speaking not a word, and made herself comfortable in the back seat. Something told her not to interrogate her luck lest it should flee, but she did wonder if hiring the cab on her own might prove an exorbitant affair on a day like this. A discreet look in her wallet reassured her. But why wasn't the man moving? Had he spotted other potential passengers wanting to share? Then she realized she had not closed the taxi door. She clicked it shut and the car moved.

The driver touched the peak of the golf cap he wore, asking, 'Where would you like me to take you, Madam?'

'Maternity Benaadir Hospital, please.'

'At your service, Madam.'

Duniya tried to dismiss a lurking suspicion: the man didn't talk, act or look like a taxi-driver. Phrases like 'At your service, Madam' pinched his tongue in the way that new shoes press tightly on one's toes. He drove hesitantly, cautious with the controls, as if more accustomed to automatic transmission than manual gears. He reminded her of an inexperienced rider in the saddle of an unbroken horse. Several times the car stalled and he got out, apologizing, opened the bonnet, pulled at its wiry intestines, then got back in, only to repeat the process. He did not appear anxious, nor behave like a professional driver whose livelihood depended on the vehicle functioning. Rather, he was like a man condescending to cook for you while his maid and wife were both away: not wanting to be remembered for the ill-prepared result but for the humility with which he served you, the effort put into the task.

Moving at cruising speed, he said, 'As you may have gathered, I'm not familiar with the idiosyncrasies of this taxi.'

Then Duniya saw her face and his framed in the mirror, as if they had both waited all their lives for this one instant when their visages shared the space, sealed in a common fate. He was grinning, his jaw strong, his face shaven smooth as oilcloth, shining a friendly smile. It gave her an eerie sinking feeling, as if the earth were falling from under her. All of a sudden she did not want to be alone with him. Concurrently a realization came to her that she knew this man, knew his name.

'Why pretend to be someone you're not, Bosaaso?' she asked him.

'I'm afraid I've no idea what you're talking about,' he replied.

'Disguise comes in handy to you men as soon as you run out of your natural masks. Men,' she trailed off, as if the word described a species for which she had nothing but disdain.

She looked up at the sky. The sun seemed held in place by thin stilt-like strands of cloud, white as the branch of a deciduous tree without bark. Below the sun were two tiny dark clouds resembling foot-rests.

She and Bosaaso knew each other all right. She had been on night shift when his late wife spent a few laborious days in intensive care at the maternity hospital where Duniya was a senior nurse. Besides, they had a mutual friend in Dr Mire, principal obstetrician at the hospital and a boyhood friend of Bosaaso's.

'If I had known this was not a taxi I wouldn't have flagged it down, I promise you,' she said.

'But it isn't a taxi when *I'm* driving it,' Bosaaso said.

'Why are you driving it anyway?'

'Because my own car is being serviced, that's why.'

'None of this makes sense to me.'

Bosaaso tried to explain: 'I bought this taxi for a poor cousin of mine, who drives it so he can raise money. All income from taxiing is his, though the car remains mine and in my name.' He sighed, sensing that he had been long-winded.

'In that case, I'd like to pay.'

'Pay?' He sounded offended.

'You may choose to give the money to your cousin.' She paused. 'Would a hundred and fifty shillings be enough for a town trip, given today's fuel shortage?'

'Sure,' Bosaaso said.

But she sensed that he did not take her offer seriously. To counteract her hurt feelings, she gave a theatrical chuckle, pretending to be amused.

'What's so funny?' he said.

'The thought that one defers to money,' she replied.

He hung on her words like an angler to a rich catch. But he couldn't frame her face in his mirror, however much he adjusted it. She had gone very quiet in the back. He looked over his left shoulder and then his right, but saw no Duniya. Impervious to what he was doing or that he might meet other vehicles, he impulsively turned his head right around. Still he could see only a small part of her; her body was bent over – maybe she was picking up something from the floor. Then he lost control of the steering-wheel. The car swung, its tyres bumping against one kerb and then another, nearly colliding with the bumper of a vehicle that was parked off the road. Finally he came to a safe halt.

Suddenly the two of them were exaggeratedly conscious of each other's presence, aware of their physical proximity for the first time. Disregarding a small crowd that out of curiosity had gathered around the car, Duniya and Bosaaso touched, marvelling at having shared a life-and-death experience, at having stopped in good time before crossing a threshold.

Without him suggesting it, Duniya got out of the back of the taxi and went to sit with him in the front. He removed his golf cap and threw it out of the window. They started to move.

Duniya noticed how his smile emphasized the handsomeness of his features. And he had a habit of tilting his head to one side as though leaning against something; and he wrinkled his forehead, like someone in private trouble.

Duniya remembered the night she and Bosaaso had been together longest. While his wife, then in labour, was asleep in the private ward, they tiptoed outside for some fresh air. He didn't say much; and his head, she recalled, had inclined like the tower of Pisa.

He was now saying, 'About your paying for this journey, if I may . . .,' and he fell quiet.

'Yes?' she said, and waited.

'Do you ever go to the cinema with your daughters and son?' he asked tentatively.

'Now and then,' she lied.

'What kind of films do you see?'

Wondering where it was all leading, she said, 'The odd spaghetti western, or an Indian or kung fu film; there isn't much choice. Why do you ask?'

He didn't say anything immediately. Entering a difficult lane he concentrated on his driving. His indicator was not working, so he stuck his arm out of the window to show that he was turning right. However, first he braked in order to let a pedestrian cross the road. Duniya noted he was a careful man, considerate too.

Changing gear smoothly, he said, 'I suggest you take me to a film with you and your children, instead of paying anything today.'

'But I don't know when I'll next be seeing a film,' she said.

'There's no hurry,' he replied.

Was this some sort of male trap that would be impossible to undo at a later date, like links of an invisible chain?

'Perhaps you don't have time,' he said, 'what with grown-up twins and a young daughter to look after.' He added as an afterthought, 'And your work at the hospital. It must all be extremely demanding. Plus other engagements, I'm sure.'

Surprising them both, she said, 'I have plenty of time.'

He didn't speak for a while. Then: 'Perhaps I'm too slow. Or is there a catch? Is there something you haven't told me yet?'

'To be frank, I'm not sure I want to take anyone to a film.'

'Fair enough,' he said, as he turned a corner.

She hoped she hadn't been unnecessarily off-putting. From the corner of her eye, she watched him switch on the car's hazard light which blinked red, in time with her heartbeart. He was looking at her intently, wondering if he dared interrupt her thoughts.

In fact she spoke first. 'I hope I haven't been rude.'

'You'll be forgiven the instant you invite me,' he said.

'I've no way of reaching you anyway.'

'On the contrary,' he said. 'You're a very resourceful woman; you'll know how to get in touch if you want to.'

Too tense to think clearly, she remained silent.

'One way of reaching me,' he went on, 'is through Dr Mire at your hospital. I see him a great deal, almost daily.'

'Wouldn't he be put out by being asked to carry messages?'

'He'll be only too delighted, I assure you.' He grinned, dividing his attention equally between Duniya's face and the road, which was full of pot-holes and pedestrians.

He brought the vehicle to an abrupt stop. 'I am afraid I can't go beyond this point. There's a sign that says "No taxis". I forgot I'm not driving my private car. I'm sorry.'

Sitting up, she prepared for the difficult task of saying something wise or neutral, managing, 'You've been very kind.'

'My pleasure,' was all he said.

Murmuring something that was a cross between a "thank-you" and a "see-you", she stepped out of the car, confident they would meet again. She closed the taxi door without looking at him.

Having arrived early, Duniya conversed affably and at length with the three cleaning women, even offering to help them tidy the Out-patients' Clinic where she was to work that day. But they wouldn't hear of it. She did all she could to keep her mind busy.

But when the cleaners left and she was alone in the echoing hall, her mind kept replaying scenes from the chance encounter with Bosaaso. To while away time, she unearthed an old newspaper in which she discovered an item of interest:

MOGADISCIO (SONNA, Tuesday)

The Secretary of Agriculture and Livestock today warned of impending disaster and famine in Somalia unless immediate action is taken to terminate the breeding cycle of the desert locust. Mogadiscio residents recently witnessed huge swarms, 25 km wide and 70 km long. He said the government is launching a campaign to eradicate the pests but this can only be achieved with the help of insecticide and light aircraft for spraying, which are not available. A grant towards the campaign has been promised by the governments of the USA and the Netherlands. However, this was not enough.

The Head of State, Major-General Mohammed Siyad Barre, has invited the ambassadors of the Federal Republic of Germany, Britain, France and Italy to consider what assistance their governments can offer Somalia to cope with the disaster.

Last night five light aircraft belonging to the East African Locust Organization were grounded in Addis Ababa through lack of spare parts and fuel.

Quoting a senior official of the UN Food and Agriculture Organization, the Secretary of Agriculture and Livestock said efforts to fight the plague throughout Africa had cost at least $100 million and that additional funds of over $145 million will be needed in the coming year.

Chapter Two

At work Duniya meets her colleagues, including Hibo, a senior nurse, and Dr Mire. The morning brings troubles and joys. Duniya meets Bosaaso on her way home.

An hour and a half later Duniya came out of the courtyard clutching a crumpled sheet of paper from which she intended to call the roll of the women out-patients who had registered for the clinic and been issued numbers scribbled on paper tokens. She stood in the porch, half in the shade, half in the sun, more impressed than ever with the resilience of these women who had risen maybe as early as four in the morning in order to be here. She couldn't dismiss Bosaaso from her thoughts and she felt put out by that.

The instant they saw Duniya, the patients stirred, sighing like a theatre audience reacting to the curtain rising. Anxious for the list to be called, they stared up at Duniya as though examining her thoughts. She wondered how many of them noticed a slight tremor in her face, like the twitching flesh of a horse anticipating the sting of a fly. 'Number Fifteen, please!' she called.

A woman got up from her crouched posture, lifting from the ground the weight of an advanced pregnancy. Other women opened a door for her to pass through, looking on with envy as she presented her numbered token to Duniya, who checked it against the list. Telling the woman to go into the waiting-hall, Duniya turned to the crowd of women and shouted, 'Number Sixteen, please!'

Some of the women urged Number Sixteen to kindly hurry, because they had been up very early, had walked all the way here on exhausted feet and hadn't a chance in a million of finding transport home. Number Sixteen shaded her eyes from the dazzle of the morning sun, took her time getting up, then walked in a leisurely way towards Duniya. When the other patients suggested she hurry, the woman mumbled something to the effect that since the doctor hadn't arrived, there was no point in rushing. Did they want her to lose her baby? Many displayed irritation by shaking their heads and saying unkind things about the region of the country the woman came from, whose people they described as slumberous. Duniya, for her part, stared sunnily, squinting as she explained to Number Sixteen where to go, and then called: 'Number Seventeen.'

Silence. Then snatches of disturbed whispering broke out. Some of the women stared myopically at the tokens they had been given. Unable to read, they sought help from those who could.

Duniya called the number a second and a third time, whereupon a woman squatting at her feet said, 'Why not call another if Seventeen is either deaf or no longer here?'

'We must give her a chance,' Duniya insisted. She called the number as if everything depended on it, her eyes moving from one lethargic face to another. She might have been the teacher of a huge class, half of whose students had raised hands to answer an easy question.

Duniya was staring intently at a spot, now vacant, where earlier had been a young woman to whose face she could put no name but whom she was sure she knew. Or was she hallucinating?

The women had become impatient and there was a stirring in their midst. A very large woman got up to push her way to the front and said to Duniya, 'Number Seventeen has gone; I saw her leave in a taxi. Why don't you call the next number?'

'Eighteen must be her number,' another woman said sarcastically.

Duniya's eyes scoured the area in front of her, now left, now right, now centre, until her gaze ended where the young woman with the elusive name had been. Even before speaking, Duniya knew she was being stupid; nevertheless she asked, 'But why did she go?'

And there was a riot. The women out-patients raised their voices in complaint, some getting to their feet and others trying to calm things, making them sit down again. During an instant of respite, one of them asked someone else to come and help speed up the number-calling exercise, since this woman (meaning Duniya) had her head in the clouds.

Hibo, a senior nurse, together with a junior nurse, came out to the porch and quickly consulted with Duniya, who at first looked at them with incomprehension, perplexed about what had made her behave that way. All she managed to say was, 'Yes, please.'

Questions throbbed in her forehead where her veins were fast swelling. Before long she regained her calm, watching the patients shove and kick one another while trying to get closer to Hibo and the junior nurse. The large woman was indeed Number Eighteen; Duniya kept her curiosity in check, resisted asking her to describe the young woman with Number Seventeen. By the time the big woman was told where to wait, the two nurses who had replaced Duniya had conjured the riotous women into peaceable entities.

After finishing this part of the formalities, the nurses asked one another, 'What's the matter with Duniya today?' Lost in noontime reveries, Duniya sat by herself, uncommunicative.

In all there were eight female nurses in the hall adjoining the principal obstetrician's cubicle: six junior nurses and two senior ones, namely Duniya and Hibo. Two junior nurses shared a small table and the senior nurses had one each. They talked while copying details given to them by the patients, who withdrew once they had provided the required information. The card thus filled out would be taken to either Duniya or Hibo for initialling.

Duniya sat by herself, sucking in her cheeks; her body seemed to have undergone changes since morning, like a newly pregnant woman's physique adjusting to the condition. Her mind drifted as she half-listened to the other nurses' voices. Every so often she caught words that were as distinctly familiar as her own name, but most went past her, unheard. The nurses conducted their conversation in low voices, their movements sharp and weirdly frenzied, yet they went about their respective businesses with the participatory routine of ten people undertaking a job intended for fifteen.

Of Duniya the nurses made kindly, inquisitive overtures as to what might be bothering her, and asked if they could be any help. She assured them nothing was amiss; she was all right, really. When some insisted she confide in them because as colleagues they had the right to know, Duniya hinted that it was a matter of a slight indisposition, nothing to worry about. Honest. They said no more, for fear of upsetting her. After all they were fond of her.

Out of reach of her ears, the nurses agreed among themselves that Duniya's troubles must be bound up with one of her children or with personal frustrations arising from the fact that, although pushing thirty-five and already married twice, she had no prospect of finding another man, but had to raise her three children alone. The nurses concurred that Duniya gave the impression that secret-keeping was a luxury for which she was willing to pay handsomely. Except for Hibo, the others kept their respectable distance.

Approaching, Hibo said something Duniya couldn't catch. Hibo had the habit of talking conspiratorially, as if plotting the overthrow of an African dictator. Now her lips trembled, first the upper one, then the lower one, after which she scratched them one at a time as if an insect had stung them.

After a pause Duniya asked her to repeat what she had said. Duniya knew very well that Hibo's mercurial brain was capable of inventing something new altogether instead of repeating what she had said; she might even refuse to speak, full stop.

Hibo held on to every syllable, as if letting them go meant allowing a part of her privacy to leave her as well; hesitantly she said, 'Is it Nasiiba who's causing you so much worry?'

'Why should she?' asked Duniya, thinking it absurd that her daughter would cause her any concern.

'I only asked,' Hibo said rather sheepishly.

'No,' said Duniya firmly.

Hibo's eyes became a darker shade of brown as she considered what to say next. Then: 'I meant to ask if Nasiiba is well?'

Worried but also displeased, Duniya half-sighed. 'As far as I know, yes.' But she was not satisfied with her own answer.

'When did you last see or speak with Nasiiba?' Hibo asked, her tone imbued with the importance of a secret only she knew.

Duniya was annoyed by the question. She was alarmed to think that Hibo could know something about Nasiiba that she, the girl's mother, didn't. She said, 'Tell me what you know that I don't.'

Hibo's lips twitched again, disturbance dancing at the fringes of her mouth. Gaining confidence, she said, 'Nasiiba called at our place yesterday afternoon, looking pale, quite sickly. I asked what was ailing her. She wouldn't say, but later she told my daughter she'd been to the blood bank in our district to donate blood.'

'Why?' was all Duniya could think of saying.

Hibo shook her head.

Duniya's expression became stiff. Her mouth opened without emitting a single sound. Then she remembered being disturbed by Nasiiba's coming home late last night, visibly tired, yawning and telling her brother Mataan to leave her in peace.

Duniya was on the verge of saying something when a deferential silence fell on the hall. From Hibo's movements, she deduced that Dr Mire had arrived at last.

Dr Mire M. Mire, principal obstetrician of Benaadir Maternity Hospital, had barely come into the hall when he noticed Duniya's expression. He stood still, confirming to himself at a second glance that his favourite senior nurse wasn't her usual ebullient self. He remained where he was, tall, thin and shy in his white coat with the missing button. Silently, he observed changes in her, abrupt as nightfall in the tropics.

Duniya rose to her feet, conscious of everyone staring. She struggled with a custom-made smile; she finally managed to produce one which in its genuine freshness she offered to Dr Mire. He seemed pleased as if he had collaborated in manufacturing it. Instinct told him not to ask what was the matter with her today.

He greeted the other nurses in turn by name and indicated that he was ready to get to work immediately. He moved in the direction of his consulting cubicle, with Hibo and Duniya on either side of him and a junior nurse in tow.

Dr Mire was a man of strictly observed habits; he was fond of developing a more intimate relationship with rituals than with people. He was easily upset if small things went wrong, which in a place like Somalia occurred with annoying frequency. If irritated in a big way, he was depressed. To ensure the world didn't fall to pieces about him, Dr Mire depended on Duniya, who was never clumsy in her faithful observance of the details of these rites. He couldn't imagine working in Mogadiscio without her by his side, she who helped him understand his personal short-comings, who taught him to be tolerant, forgiving and forgivable.

'What have we here?' he asked, receiving the patient's card from the junior nurse.

There were five of them in his small cubicle, seemingly occupying every single inch of it. Duniya stood away from everyone else, her back to his desk, and Hibo and the junior nurses crowded in on him, catching every word he uttered. After studying the history of the woman's pregnancy, he turned to put a number of questions to the patient, who sat up to answer them, maybe as a sign of respect.

And then it happened.

Duniya's clumsiness ran amok. Her hand hit a bottle in which were kept pens, pencils and spare thermometers, knocking it over. Very noisily. Hibo and the junior nurses bent down together with Duniya to retrieve the scatter of objects. But having done so Duniya stood apart, idle in an indulgent manner. And silent.

Ill at ease, Dr Mire resumed his routine questions and was the more irritated to discover that the woman's responses contradicted what the card had told him. He looked to see who had initialled the card. Duniya. Dr Mire chose to examine the patient. As he bent to do this he appeared to relax, his body inclined like a worshipper at a shrine. Pregnant women had that effect on him.

In an instant his head shot up, his back straightened. His stethoscope hung down, knocking against the buckle of his trouser belt. He took his reading-glasses out of his breast pocket and with his outstretched hand received a biro from the junior nurse. Then he looked from Duniya to the patient, and from the patient back to Duniya, as if deciding whom to address first.

The woman said, 'I am to blame, Doctor, not the nurse. I lied.'

'And this is not your card either?'

'That's right.'

Dr Mire waited for the woman to explain.

'I know I'm infected with gonorrhoea, Doctor,' said the woman, her voice tearful although her eyes were dry. 'I lied because I couldn't say the truth in the presence of the other women outside.'

Dr Mire remained silent.

'It is because of my baby that I've come, Doctor,' she said.

Dr Mire had recovered his calm; it seemed that no consuming temper was likely to impose its will on him, although flames of rage had earlier appeared in his eyes, flames which the other nurses imagined would set his whole body ablaze.

'What about your baby?' he asked the patient.

The woman's voice cracked as she said, 'It is my lawful

husband who gave the gonorrhoea to me, Doctor. I've known no other man, Doctor, I swear. I was shocked to the marrow of my bones when I spotted the unhealthy stains on his underwear.'

Embarrassed, Hibo appeared too perturbed to look at the woman. Duniya's features assumed an amused indifference, as if to say she had her own worries. The junior nurse's eyes grew misty. Dr Mire was angry with himself for not having seen the woman a while back.

'You see, Doctor,' she said, 'it's my husband who brings things into our house, good and bad things. Please help me and my baby.'

Dr Mire nodded.

'Will my baby go blind, Doctor?' She was in tears.

Dr Mire hushed her. He let his half-moon spectacles rest on the bridge of his nose and after a moment's thought wrote on a pad that had the hospital's logo and name printed on it in Somali, Chinese, Arabic and English, in that order. He scribbled something short and essential as a postscript, initialling his remarks with a large M whose middle leg was shorter than the two on either side of it.

And then it happened a second time.

This time there was a mind-boggling noise, like something heavy falling to the floor and breaking instantly. Everyone turned, all eyes were focused on Duniya, whose innocent grin pointed her up as the culprit. A thick glass paper-weight had dropped, along with a full cup of water, water running in every direction like fleeing ants in a scatter of panic. Hibo and the junior nurse removed Dr Mire's papers as fast as they could, and Duniya helped, but not as though she had done anything wrong. There was no hostility in Dr Mire's eyes. He treated her as though she were a member of the family who had behaved in an unsteady manner; there was only enough anger in his look to fill a thimble.

After helping the pregnant woman to her feet and giving her Dr Mire's prescription, the junior nurse and Hibo considerately left the room, confident that the principal obstetrician would want to have a word with Duniya.

When they were alone Dr Mire said, 'Would you prefer to take the day off, Duniya?'

Her lips trembled as she said, 'Why?'

Mire raised his eyes, then pushed his spectacles towards

where his hairline had begun to thin. He seemed older than his forty-five years, emptied of all energy. He had returned to Somalia after twenty years' sojourn abroad, mainly in West Germany, where he had trained, and the USA, where he did his post-doctoral qualifications and then ran his own pharmacy and practice. He came home to donate his services to the government and people of his country, accepting no payment, only an apartment, conveniently located and modestly furnished. He was a childhood friend of Bosaaso's and it was rumoured that the two men had offered the same conditions of service to the respective ministries to which they were attached, Health and Economic Planning.

Duniya said, 'Why is everybody asking me if I'm all right?'

'When a number of people ask you if you're all right, perhaps it's a roundabout way of telling you you're not all right.'

'But I am all right,' she said.

In the eighteen months he had known Duniya, Dr Mire could not remember a single occasion when he was dissatisfied with her performance of her duties or her general behaviour. He preferred her to any other nurse, believing that she had the strength of mind to do what her conscience told her. She handled emergencies well, and like Hibo, didn't panic; he could rely on her to remain calm and professional. Whether he admitted it to himself or not, the fact that he was a friend of Duniya's elder brother, currently living in Rome, had a positive bearing on their working relationship.

'Be my mirror for a change,' she said, 'and tell me what I can't have seen.'

He said, 'You hurt easily today.'

'How do you *see* that?'

'I sense you are open sores all over,' he said.

'On the contrary,' she smiled, 'today I don't hurt at all.'

'I'll be specific,' he said.

Her eyes wouldn't focus. 'Are you psychoanalysing me?'

'Why haven't you changed into your uniform, for instance?' No longer defiant, Duniya was angry with her colleagues. 'But why didn't anyone tell me?'

'Do you usually need someone to tell you?'

Duniya fell silent. She didn't want to talk about her dream; or about her chance encounter with Bosaaso who had driven her to work.

Dr Mire went on, obviously misunderstanding the vacant look in her eyes lapsed into jargon, 'About uniforms – I don't want you to misunderstand me. I am quite aware of the class nature as well as the gender politics of hospitals in which uniforms assume a hierarchical significance, in particular, hospitals where all the doctors are male and all the nurses female. You weren't making a point out of this, were you?'

She thought for a second and her eyes brightened with mischief as she remembered her meeting with Bosaaso. 'Maybe.'

'Shall we talk about it now or some other time?'

'Some other time,' she said. 'There's all the time in the world, isn't there?' She grinned to herself.

'In that case, shall we resume work? And will you please steady your hand, prevent it from knocking the universe over?'

She went out without being instructed to do so and informed Hibo and the junior nurse that Dr Mire was ready to continue consultations. But she didn't change into her uniform.

She vowed to herself that her hand would knock nothing over from then on, and it didn't. Having assured Dr Mire that all was well with her, she had to do whatever it took to prove it.

It was such an arduous responsibility *not* to think about Bosaaso, given that Dr Mire reminded her of him. She also found it almost impossible whenever she came into contact with Hibo *not* to ask herself self-reproaching questions about Nasiiba. Since one thing led to another, Duniya recalled to mind the out-patient who spoke of her husband giving her gonorrhoea, a husband who brought into the house both good and bad things, the woman had said.

Stubbornly, Bosaaso came to her, assuming different shapes, mysteriously clad in all sorts of disguises. All the same her hand remained steady and she worked beside Dr Mire and her colleagues without knocking anything else over. Nevertheless, she still stood out because she wasn't wearing uniform. Agile and moving fast, she was compared by one of the junior nurses to an agitated butterfly, hopping from one pollinated flower to another. Also, Bosaaso's name was on the tip of her tongue when one of her friends asked her how she was getting home later that day since there was no public transport. No sooner had the first syllable of his name teased her lips than she closed her mouth, silencing it.

The rest of the day was taken up with routine work, pregnant women inquiring after the health of their foetuses, this one complaining of sleeplessness, that one about loss of appetite. Dr Mire would glance at the card, then at the woman in question, and with reading-glasses decorating his forehead like a devout Muslim's prayer-scar, he would now and again ask what the bed situation was in the event of an emergency. Glasses and gloves now off, now on, his hands now rubbery and now dry from constant contact with soap and alkaline-treated tap water, Dr Mire was ever prepared to undertake another examination. Duniya behaved like a truant pupil with whom the headmaster had had a wise word.

Only once was she near to knocking something over, feeling the hot wind of her rage cross her face like the shadow of a travelling cloud. This was because in her opinion Dr Mire humiliated an patient by insisting she come back next week accompanied by her husband, mother or mother-in-law, 'someone responsible', as he put it. Why? The woman had been re-infibulated each time she gave birth. Now what might he achieve by talking to a husband? The poor woman had come on her own to consult Dr Mire about a complication arising from the physical outrage meted out to her. Barely in her mid-twenties, she had been married three times, twice to the same man, who loved his women re-infibulated. This barbarous activity had turned the woman's private parts into an overmined quarry. After Duniya spoke her mind, Dr Mire revised his instructions to the woman, 'Come back next week, alone,' he said.

Soon it was closing time and the nurses were alone in the hall, after Dr Mire and all the out-patients had gone. Conversation reverted to how bad things were, and the immediate question that was the day's refrain: 'How do we get home if there's no transport?'

One of the nurses said, 'As I see it Mogadiscio is like a city preparing for an early evening curfew, with the odd car on the streets, and rivers of pedestrians breaking at the banks, at times flooding the main roads.'

Another, 'No electricity, no water, no bread baked, no papers.'

A third said, 'Does anyone remember the time Mogadiscio

had a power shortage that lasted several days? I happened to have graduated just that week and had been assigned here. You know what? The lights went out when we were in the middle of a delivery. We were just two nurses both recently graduated, and no doctor on call. A miracle that the mother and baby survived because my colleague and I pulled at the wrong limb.

In the silence that followed, Duniya suddenly felt an empathy with the Chinese, remembering it was the People's Republic of China that built and donated the Benaadir Maternity Hospital to the people of Somalia. The modesty of the Chinese as a donor government was truly exemplary. No pomp, no garlands of see-how-great-we-are. Somewhere in the hospital grounds was a discreet plaque announcing the day, month and year in which it had been commissioned and by whom. And you would meet the Chinese doctors, who came as part of the gift, as they did their rounds, soft of voice, short of breath when they spoke Somali, humble of gesture. Unlike the Italian and Dutch doctors on secondment from their governments as an overpriced aid package from the European Community, the Chinese did not own cars. They arrived at work in a van, in which they returned to their commune in the evening. And unlike other doctors (including Dr Mire) who ran their own vehicles, the Chinese gave lifts to nurses working the same shifts as themselves. So Duniya suggested that the other nurses try their luck with the Chinese.

A fourth nurse said, 'Petrol shortages, power failures or the unavailability of public transport can only be defined as a double curse for women.'

The nurse who had spoken first said, 'How do you mean?'

'On the one hand these give unheard-of advantages to men harbouring wicked intentions towards us; on the other, by refusing to be seduced with lifts, a woman exposes herself to the perils of being raped in a dark alley.'

Duniya's left eyebrow lifted slightly and her head leaned towards Hibo who wanted to whisper something in her friend's ear. 'Would you like my husband to give you a lift home?' she asked. Whenever Mogadiscio's city electricity failed, Hibo and her husband turned on their portable generator, a handy light-providing gadget and a status symbol nowadays, helping to keep muggers and burglars at bay.

'Are you offering just me a lift?' Duniya asked.

Hibo nodded.

'In that case, thank you no,' said Duniya.

The other junior and student nurses had overheard Duniya and Hibo's exchange. One of the nurses who lived near the hospital said, first to no one in particular and then singly to every nurse save Hibo, whom she deliberately excluded, that her grandmother would be more than delighted to have them come and camp with them, 'I offer our hospitality to those of you who live far and prefer not to walk.'

Three of the junior nurses and one of the students gratefully accepted her offer. 'What about you, Duniya?' asked the happy hostess of the community of nurses.

'No thank you, I'll walk,' said Duniya, running her words together, maybe because part of her thoughts were engaged with memories of meeting Bosaaso.

Two of the nurses said that they would try their fortune with the Chinese doctors. Would Duniya join them?

'Very kind of you, but I will walk,' she insisted.

When they had all gone, Duniya changed into her uniform. Even to her it was a mystery why she did something as odd as that.

It was almost five o'clock when she walked out of the hospital gates. She had been the first to arrive at the clinic today, it was proper that she was the last to leave, she told herself. But now there was a question nearly as obstinate as thoughts of Bosaaso: Why had she decided to change into her uniform when she was leaving work? Duniya needed no one to remind her that African men often viewed nurses as easy-going flirts, who were considered fun and were invited to orgiastic parties. Or did she think naively that men would be uninterested in pestering a woman in her working-clothes?

She had hardly walked three hundred metres beyond the hospital wall when a man driving a sports car said to her, 'I reckon you and I are going in the same direction.'

Luckily there were a number of other people around and she was in no danger of being pestered. None the less she was livid. She wanted to say, 'And where would that be?' but in the end chose not to lower herself to his level of thinking.

He said, 'Why don't you come with me?'

'Why?' she asked, curious to know what his answer would be.

'Because I wish to do you a favour.'

'Why?'

'I'll give a lift, then reward you with further gifts.'

'But I haven't asked you to do me a favour, or give me a lift or reward me with presents, have I?'

'You are a fool if you don't,' he said.

'Let me be,' she said in such a hostile voice that he drove off.

She was one of a crowd of pedestrians, crossing roads, avoiding roundabouts where motorists were inclined to park, waiting to ambush and rape women.

Then Duniya found herself staring at a relief of circles and dots, like small coloured light-bulbs shining full beam. Was she having visions? Before she could answer, Bosaaso was there, calling her name and opening the taxi door for her. At first she took no notice. Part of her was convinced that she was imagining it all, conjuring it out of her feverish desire to be with Bosaaso. Then the man came out of the car and bowed. Before getting in, Duniya felt the solidity of the vehicle with her open palms, preparing her mind for a future instant when she might have to ask herself if Bosaaso had come for her and she had gone with him. How strangely the human brain functioned. She got in.

'I just happened to be driving past when I saw you,' he said.

She wished she could shoo away her angry thoughts as one drives away early evening insects. 'Why lie to me, Bosaaso?' she asked.

He drove with silent punctiliousness, like a driving-instructor setting an example for a pupil. And she intercepted a smile perhaps intended for her but which faded before maturing, maybe as a result of her unexpected question. 'Why do you say I lie to you?' he replied.

Duniya disappeared into a deep silence that contained her for a long time. When she surfaced again she said, 'Why do you give me these lifts, Bosaaso? Please tell the truth.'

'Why do you accept lifts from me?' he asked.

'That's a foolish question, since your giving precedes my acceptance or rejection. My accepting your gift of a lift is itself a reciprocal gift. So may I now ask why you accept my gift?'

'Why are you hesitant about receiving things from others?'

'Because unasked-for generosity has a way of making one feel obliged, trapped in a labyrinth of dependence. You're more knowledgeable about these matters, but haven't we in the Third World lost our self-reliance and pride because of the so-called aid we unquestioningly receive from the so-called First World?'

A fluid smile finally broke on his face with the speed of an egg-white in motion. All he said was, 'I am drawn to you.'

Only after he parked did she realize they were in front of her place. How did he know where she lived? She did not invite him in, nor suggest meeting again. Stories pursue audiences to their hiding-places, she told herself. Bosaaso had become her narrative.

'Thank you,' she said.

He switched the headlights on full-beam, drawing early evening moths to dance frenziedly before them, tossing in mad agitation against the head-lamps.

'Goodnight, then,' he said, reversed his car and left.

She didn't wave goodbye.

MOGADISCIO (SONNA, Thursday)

Over a dozen Third World countries have refused to accept dairy products from the European Community as part of a development donation. These products, which include butter and milk, have been sent back to the donor nation because they are suspected of being contaminated by radio-activity from the nuclear plant accident at Chernobyl. The Somali Democratic Republic joins the list of countries returning these products. EC ministers, however, reiterate that the radioactivity level in these dairy products is so low as to cause no worry or danger to lives.

Chapter Three

Duniya eats a meal prepared by her daughter Nasiiba and they reminisce. The young girl remembers when she was small, before Duniya married Taariq, her ex-husband; and Duniya tells of her marriage to the father of her younger daughter.

A faint echo of Bosaaso's voice lingering in her ears, Duniya pushed open the front door. At that moment electricity returned and she felt a ripple of joy. But she stood at the threshold, cautious as a pedestrian about to cross a hazardous thoroughfare. Then she heard the music pick up speed and volume after a hesitant start. Nasiiba must be home; the smell of garlic emanating from the kitchen confirmed to her that her daughter was indeed there, busy cooking.

In her excited rush, Duniya shuffled one foot out of a shoe. This made her move unevenly like a hyena with hind legs shorter than front ones. She switched off the turntable, certain that silence would bring Nasiiba instantly to the room. She sat, waiting, unapologetic.

Slim and, Duniya thought, anaemic-looking, Nasiiba rushed in, ready to pick a quarrel with her twin brother whom she suspected had switched off her turntable. The look in her eyes softened and she grinned when she saw it was her mother. Nasiiba wore an over-sized garment, kimono-style. Duniya could see the curves of her breasts and her belly.

'So it's you!' said the young woman.

Duniya's face broadened with a smile.

Nasiiba walked over to adjust the turntable's dials now that power was back. That done, she replaced the record in its sleeve. Duniya knew well how protective her daughter was of her treasured gadget, bought from her savings at about the same time her twin acquired his bicycle, of which he was equally protective and proud.

The room where they were and which they shared was referred to as 'The Women's Room'. It had two big metal-framed beds with springs, Nasiiba's being the one by the larger of the windows; lying on it now was a greasy-toothed comb, and underneath it a shoulder-bag bearing the Somali Airlines legend. Duniya's bed, nearer the door, was neatly made and covered by a white bedspread; stored below it was a collapsible bed on which Yarey, her younger daughter, slept when she came to stay for weekends.

Only Mataan had the key to the other room, which he had fitted with a Yale lock. The Women's Room had one of those cheap locks a burglar could pick with a hairpin; Nasiiba had an unpardonable habit of losing keys and Duniya had tired of replacing Yales. As a result, all the family's valuables – documents, cash and jewels – were kept in the boy's room, which had a safe with a combination lock. But Nasiiba would not let her turntable out of her sight, wouldn't allow it to spend a night in her brother's room.

Now Duniya and Nasiiba stared at each other like children in a duel of will. Duniya felt her daughter had the eyes of a hypnotist, able to induce nervousness. She wondered if Nasiiba's *burchi*-power was the stronger, *burchi* being a mystical term for the overwhelming hold one individual has over another, regardless of their respective status – child over adult, offspring over parent, wife over husband. In this contest of stares Nasiiba's *burchi*-power was stronger.

Nasiiba shook her shock of tresses like a horse's mane, and the coloured beads plaited into her hair knocked against one another, producing a theatrical sound.

'Have you eaten, Mummy?' Nasiiba asked.

'No, I haven't.'

'I bet you haven't eaten all day,' Nasiiba guessed.

Duniya could remember only that she had met Bosaaso. This absent-mindedness was unhealthy. 'What's cooking?' she asked.

'Liver in garlic sauce, roast potatoes, rice and salad. And I'm preparing boiled milk with a dash of cinnamon and ginger to wash it down,' said Nasiiba.

Where did she get all this food? None of these items were available on the open market anywhere in the country. Deciding to pursue the question later, Duniya said, 'I'd love to eat with you, darling.'

Saying, 'I hope I haven't burnt the rice,' Nasiiba ran out.

In a few minutes she returned with a medium-sized tray on which were plates with the rice, liver and roast potatoes together with two mugs of heavily sugared warm milk. Duniya placed a mat on the floor, over the boundary dividing the living space from the sleeping space. (Years ago, Taariq, the then occupant of the room, had built a small kerb-high barrier of bricks to mark a frontier between the area with the bed and the area with the armchairs, low glass-topped table and his writing-desk.) Nasiiba noticed that her mother had changed into a dress, and her uniform lay strewn across the bed.

They ate in silence for a while, Duniya using her fingers and Nasiiba a knife and fork. Then Duniya asked, 'Where did you get all this food?'

Provocatively, Nasiiba said, 'Someone gave it to me.'

'Who?'

Daughter and mother were accustomed to each other's ways and intolerances. If there was one thing Duniya couldn't stand, it was her children bringing home unauthorized gifts of food, or money, given to them by Uncle So-and-so or Aunt So-and-so. She would half-cry, 'Are you trying to embarrass me? Don't I give you everything you need? Don't I give you enough? If you need more, why not ask me?' When the twins were smaller, it was the boy, not Nasiiba, who returned laden with what Duniya suspected were ill-gained presents and cash. He would retort, 'But he stuffed it into my pocket; I didn't ask for it, he gave it to me, folded, off his sweaty palm – Uncle So-and-so. What could I do?'

Duniya felt uncomfortable eating what was known in their household as 'corpse food', a term coined as a result of her saying to her twins that they could consume food gifts only if she, their mother, was dead, not before. But where did Nasiiba get this food?

Trust Nasiiba to change the subject to avoid answering a question. Trust her also to get away with it. She said, 'I've been thinking, Mummy, that we must get you some new dresses.'

And trust Duniya to fall for her daughter's trap. 'What's wrong with the ones I have?' But she was a step ahead of Nasiiba, thinking about a future day when she would need a new dress to go out in, if she were invited by Bosaaso.

'Not good enough.' As evidence, Nasiiba pointed out a brown stain on Duniya's dress, a smudge similar to the one you might spy on a breast-feeding mother's frock.

Duniya was in defiant mood. 'Who cares?' she asked.

They resumed eating. Nasiiba said, 'Next time you wear outdoor dresses, I suggest you take a sane look at yourself. We don't want potential in-laws to avoid looking you in the eyes.'

'What do you mean "potential in-laws"? Who?'

'You mean you don't know?'

Perplexed, Duniya said she didn't.

'I can't believe it. You mean you have no idea what your son might be up to?'

'What is he up to?'

Nasiiba was enjoying herself, prolonging the dramatic telling of her story to avoid getting back to the topic of food. 'Mataan has a woman-friend, a maths teacher, who's three years your junior, Mummy, and has never married. People say she's kept by a wealthy businessman, who pays the rent of her well-furnished flat and has given her a small car. You mean you *didn't* know?'

'How come *you* know?'

'You'd be surprised how many things *I* know but haven't told a living soul,' Nasiiba said matter-of-factly.

'For instance, that my son has a woman-friend?'

'Ask him when he returns tonight, if you don't believe me.'

Duniya didn't press the matter; Nasiiba derived a thrill from turning half-truths into embellished fictions, making each tale into exactly the story you needed to hear. 'Why did you donate blood you can ill-afford?' Duniya asked.

Unprepared for the question, Nasiiba was at a loss for words. She sighed, then replied, 'I felt like giving blood.'

'No other reason?'

'The blood bank was short of it and, being in a generous mood, I felt like donating some of mine.' She paused. 'Is there any law in this household forbidding its members to donate good, healthy blood when it's needed?'

Duniya was becoming impatient. Turning her head slowly towards Nasiiba, she said, 'I'm going to ask you two questions and I insist on straight answers. I mean it. Don't change the subject and, please, no long-winded explanations. Where did you get this food?'

'Uncle Taariq gave it to me.'

'Why did he give it to you?'

'He had to use up a lot of food from his freezer; he had half a ton of food to get rid of because of all the recent power cuts.'

'Why did you donate blood that you can ill-afford?'

'I can only repeat the reply I've already given.'

Duniya shifted in discomfort. Neither of them now had any appetite. Nasiiba gathered the plates into a pile, leaving Duniya the task of picking up rice grains from the mat. Nasiiba left the room, taking with her some of the tension that had been generated.

A dragon-fly flew into the room, slender of body, elegant of movement. Mesmerized, Duniya watched it. The dragon-fly flew out of the window just before the young woman returned.

Nasiiba changed the subject again. She had a way of springing surprises on her mother, over whom she undoubtedly had a certain *burchi*-hold. Obligingly, Duniya seemed happy to lose command, in her maternal element.

'You see, Mummy, we your children know precious little about your past and you know next to nothing about our present. Don't you think it's time we got to know each other better? Come with me for a swim at the sports club one day and meet my friends; and you could go for a ride on Mataan's bicycle, let him teach you. I'll teach you to swim. And get Mataan to tell you about his woman-friend, whatever her name is.'

Duniya smiled faintly, a commotion inside her head, noises pressing on her brain. She tried to remember the nebulous name of the young face she had seen at the clinic; but she couldn't.

Nasiiba was saying, 'I met Taariq today, for instance. I had a long chat with him. Yet there was a time when I hated the notion of him as my step-father. But what do I know about him when the two of you were married, or even before that when you were his tenant? Nothing. I want us to talk about these things – what I was like with him, what Mataan was like. Just to get things into perspective, if you see what I mean.'

'How was Taariq?'

'He's in top form, looking a decade younger,' Nasiiba said.

'That's good,' said in an amiable sort of way.

'He's getting his journalism published. Have you seen his article in today's daily?'

Duniya hadn't.

'And he's seeing a woman he's serious about,' added Nasiiba.

Mataan is seeing an older woman; Taariq, my former husband,

is serious about a woman he's seeing. What about me? Who am I seeing? Duniya reminded herself to avoid Nasiiba's traps.

'What was Taariq like, Mummy?'

Duniya didn't like what she remembered. Drunken bouts. Depressive days. She remembered the decisive night when she had walked in on him pouring out tots of whisky for himself and little Mataan, then eight years old. Mataan had barely taken a sip of his when Duniya entered. God, she was mad, so furious she threw Taariq out of his own house.

'Tell me, Mummy. Tell me about Taariq.'

It seemed strange to Duniya now that she had never talked to her children about the father of their half-sister. It was in this spirit that she consented to tell Nasiiba a little. She spoke slowly at first, undoing the knots of inhibition entwined round the telling. 'Taariq was wonderful with your twin-brother, not with you. He and you didn't get on well at all. He found you very demanding, a self-centred child. Being a newspaper columnist he worked at home, in his room all day at times, writing and rewriting. A perfectionist, he would submit his pieces at the last minute. When writing he drank a lot and ate little or nothing. Drinking gave him energy, a reason for exerting himself, some kind of self-coercion. There was pain on his face when he wrote, every word leaving its mark somewhere on his body.'

'Why does he bother then?' Nasiiba asked.

'I took a keen interest in Taariq's welfare,' Duniya continued, 'because he was marvellous with Mataan, like a father to him. I would cook larger portions and invite him over to our side of the house. He would accept the food but made it clear he preferred eating alone, "like a dog with its bone" as he put it. He had a sense of humour, and the uncanny ability to laugh at himself, which many Somalis are unwilling to do.'

'I don't recall any of that,' said Nasiiba regretfully.

Duniya returned to her theme. 'I was on night duty once, and, because I had asked him, Taariq tried to put you to bed. In your rage at the thought of him even touching you, you called him all sorts of wicked names, including one he didn't like: alcoholic. It was obvious you hated him, hated him so much that you woke up if he entered the room you were sleeping in, as though you had smelt him. Your contempt for him was pathological.'

Nasiiba said, 'I must apologize to him one of these days.'

'To please you, Taariq drank less,' said Duniya. 'Also he fetched two girls your age, his nieces, to be your playmates. He did all this with fatherly patience, and because he was fond of you. I was pleased that you got on fine with his nieces.'

'And Mataan?'

'I never saw my son happier than when in Taariq's company, running errands for him, delivering his idol's late copy to the editor in person. Taariq became so dependent on Mataan that he even trusted him with personal messages.'

'What do you mean?'

'Taariq had a woman-friend whom he'd known for years and to whom he was very close. Mataan, maybe because he didn't like the woman, decided to give her the wrong meeting-places and times whenever Taariq asked him to deliver message to her. This happened several times, with neither suspecting Mataan of sabotage. When they wised up to his tricks, it was too late to mend matters.'

'How very wicked of my brother to do that!'

'Anyway,' Duniya paused, 'During this period I returned home unexpectedly one evening, having swapped shifts with another nurse, I don't recall why. You were in bed asleep, cheeks tattooed with dried tear-stains, alone in the bed the three of us shared. And where was Mataan? The light in Taariq's room (the very one we are in now) was on and his door half open. I shouted a greeting from the courtyard and apologized for disturbing him, but had he seen my son? "He's sleeping here, on my bed," he said. We chatted briefly when I went to fetch Mataan. Well, things aren't that easy when, as Somalis say, donkeys are giving birth to calves.'

'I know,' Nasiiba said wisely.

With a strained look, Duniya asked, 'Do you see this barrier of bricks? I tripped on it and fell forward, nearly hurting my teeth when I hit my head against the bedpost. All because I hadn't minded the bricks. I was in excruciating pain.'

'What did you do then?'

Duniya chuckled. 'I got up to take Mataan away when the dizziness no longer impaired my vision. Then guess what? As I bent to lift him off the bed, the smell of Mataan's urine made my head turn in whirls of shame, call it guilt, or whatever.'

A smile touched Nasiiba's lips. 'And since Mataan had wet

his bed, you decided that you and Taariq would share the one I hadn't peed on. Result, this corpse of a heavy sleeper, that is me, was transferred to the bed on which her brother had emptied his day's intake of liquid.'

'How do you know?'

'Because I remember waking up in the bed of the man I hated,' said Nasiiba.

'You remember that?'

'Oh, yes.'

'But you've never mentioned it.'

'There are a million things I've never told a soul.'

Duniya said, 'How could you still remember that?'

'For one thing, I hated Taariq so. For another, it was my brother who wet the bed, not me. Someone else's urine always smells different from one's own, but that's beside the point. I woke up. I'm not sure you want to hear this.'

The older woman sat up, alert. 'What?'

'Well, I heard your voices, yours and Taariq's in lusty whispers. I came closer to eaves-drop, then watched. I saw everything through the keyhole and heard everything, every single groan, every no and every yes.'

'Everything?'

Nasiiba nodded.

There was amusement in Duniya's voice. 'If you saw and heard everything, then what's the point of my telling you anything? You probably remember things better and know more than I.'

Nasiiba shook her head. She leaned forward. 'How did you come to be Taariq's tenant in the first place?'

Duniya's heart wasn't in the story-telling any more but she knew Nasiiba wouldn't leave her in peace. So she said, 'Someone in the neighbourhood, an elderly woman, misdirected me.' She sounded bored and tired.

'I don't follow you.' Nasiiba was plagued by a desire to be told more.

'Until Taariq saw me and I asked if he had a room to let, the thought of renting it hadn't crossed his mind. But when I insisted that a neighbour had mentioned he had a place going, he looked puzzled at first, and to a certain extent offended. The misunderstanding was cleared up soon enough, however, and I turned to leave. Then he changed his mind.'

'Why?'

'I've never inquired.'

'Maybe you were destined to become husband and wife.'

Duniya let her thoughts wander a little.

'Go on,' Nasiiba said.

'It seemed to me that he reasoned that he and I were kindred spirits; I could see it, and he could too. Anyway. After his instant decision to rent the room, he asked when *I* could move in? I mentioned the existence of children, just in case. I had seen lots of landlords who didn't want a single woman with children. He asked the sex and ages of my children and I told him. Twins were a blessing, his voice beamed with rejoicing: "Bring them."'

'You moved in the same day?'

'We did. We brought everything we owned, a mattress, a few burnt pots I'd been given second-hand and all our clothes in a single tea-chest. He lent us a bed, then introduced me to the owner and keeper of the local general store, who consented to open a credit account, bills to be settled at the end of the month. And I never looked back from then on.'

'You got on well, Taariq and you, didn't you?'

'Except for the one huge fight, the one before the final splitting up, we seldom quarrelled in the years we lived first as tenant and landlord, then as husband and wife,' said Duniya.

'It's good that you've remained friends,' said Nasiiba, 'because such friendships are rare after a divorce, especially when children are involved.'

'That's right,' Duniya agreed.

'He still loves you; he told me that today,' Nasiiba said.

Duniya had barely time to react when she noticed that Nasiiba had got up to put on jeans and a T-shirt with the Band Aid logo printed across its front. 'Where are you going?' she asked.

'I won't be long,' said Nasiiba, consulting her watch.

'It's after nine o'clock,' said Duniya, as though mentioning the time might deter her daughter.

'I won't be long.'

'It's late,' Duniya said, helplessly.

'I said, I won't be long.'

Duniya had the power to stop her, but what was the point? Traditionalists would describe Duniya's offspring as *hooyo-koris,* children growing up in a household with a woman as head.

Going out Nasiiba shouted, 'I love you, Mummy,' clearly emulating American girls whom she had seen in films. There was no doubt in Duniya's mind that her children loved her.

NEW YORK (Reuter)

Millions of people in the developing world have starved to death as a result of the policies of Western creditor nations, a United Nations Development Programme spokesman said. In a gloomy annual assessment, the spokesman argued that the finely woven economic tapestry could be unravelled at any time, causing calamitous suffering in the Third World. It was unfair, he added, that poor countries have been made to depend totally on what happens not in their own economies but in those of richer, more economically developed countries, whose debts they are unable to service, let alone repay.

Chapter Four

In which Duniya remembers how her dying father promised her hand in marriage to his friend and peer.

A high-pitched whistle was what Duniya heard. She looked around. Beds. Window-ledges. Door-sills. Sure enough, she spotted it: a frightened half-collared kingfisher with cinnamon breast, dark blue patch on either side of its neck, bill shining black in the electric brightness. The bird perched on an arm of the ceiling-fan. Another shill whistle, then out through the window by which it had entered.

Power was abruptly off and Duniya was in the dark.

Her memory of her first husband Zubair, father of her twins Nasiiba and Mataan, dated back to a day when she was four years old. Abshir, her full-brother, had recently won a place in the country's most prestigious secondary school in Mogadiscio and to celebrate took his beloved younger sister to Galkacyo shopping-centre to buy her a present by which to remember the occasion. Unable to find anything she fancied, he promised to send something special from Mogadiscio. But he bought her an ice-cream, a newly introduced luxury.

While passing the house of Zubair, a friend and neighbour of their father for many years, she and Abshir noticed a handsome horse in the old man's barn. An in-law of Zubair's had presented the Arab stallion as part of the bride-wealth for the young woman he wed. Zubair overheard Abshir's remark to Duniya that he'd do anything to be allowed to ride this most beautiful horse he had ever set eyes on.

Abshir, a timid eighteen-year-old, was embarrassed, stammering, 'It's *Dunya* who wanted to ride the horse, not me,' pronouncing his sister's name gently as he often did, without an *i* after the *n*. 'I wanted to look, that's all. I knew you wouldn't mind.' Then Abshir held his only sister's hand encouragingly. 'Take a look at the horse, this is probably the only time you'll see him,' he said.

'Can I touch him?' she asked. For a moment Abshir wasn't sure whether she meant Zubair or the horse. She repeated her request: 'Please let me touch him.'

Zubair turned his unsighted head with the slowness of a lighthouse beam. 'Would you like to ride this beautiful horse, Duniya?' he asked.

'If I say yes, will you give him to me for keeps, Uncle Zubair?'

'Sure. Just ask your brother to receive the horse on your behalf.'

'He's teasing you,' Abshir said. 'No one would give away such a handsome horse to a baby girl your age.' His tone was decidedly envious. 'But you may touch him.'

Speechless with excitement, Duniya nodded vigorously.

'Come and touch him,' encouraged Abshir. 'Don't be afraid.' And he lifted her off the ground, something which she resisted at first because she was now frightened.

Touching him, Duniya said, 'Uncle Zubair gave him to me. Tell Abshir the horse is mine, Uncle.'

'He is yours,' confirmed the blind old man, who had been lavishing unrequited love on the good-looking beast.

'He's teasing you,' Abshir insisted.

With childish insistence she said, 'The horse *is* mine.'

'Mind the ice,' Abshir admonished, 'and behave yourself.'

Upset, she let the ice-cream drop to the ground in a moment of uncontrollable rage. 'Never mind,' Abshir said placatingly, 'I'll get you another, but be careful, don't dirty your dress.'

'I don't want an ice,' she said angrily. 'I want *my* horse.'

Zubair pointed with his walking-stick in the direction of where the horse's tackle was kept. 'Take him for a ride, Abshir, will you?' And as Abshir bent down to pick up the saddle and bridle, to bring them over, he asked, 'Have you ever ridden a horse, Abshir?'

'Never a horse like this king here,' said Abshir.

'I am sure you will be all right,' Zubair reassured him.

'I want to ride him too,' pleaded Duniya.

'Only if you behave yourself,' her brother said.

'But this is my horse and I behave how I please,' she said.

Zubair gave a guffaw. Then he said, 'I offered you this handsome horse, Duniya, and it seems you've accepted him. But what have you given me in return, my little one?'

'I will marry you,' she said.

When she was a little bigger Duniya heard the story of how Zubair's former wife fell in love with a jinn, whom she bore several children. Zubair had been married to her for almost twenty years, with grown-up sons and daughters who had by then given them grandchildren; and he was busy courting the affections of a much younger woman. When his wife was gone for a few days, everyone assumed she was visiting her children and grandchildren – no one at first had any idea of her affair with the jinn. But as Zubair's sumptuous wedding to the young woman approached, people began to show interest in his first wife's reactions to the goings-on, only to discover she wasn't there to answer their queries. When the story of her jinn-lover was told, the townspeople's initial attitude was more or less dismissive, rationalizing that such tales were bound up with the understandable sentiments of a jealous, hurt woman.

So Zubair's first wife lived her life undisturbed, vanishing when she pleased, reappearing without explanation. One day, two young men, one of them her cousin, the other Zubair's, decided to get to the bottom of it and followed her right into the bushes. Later they reported that they had never known anyone, male or female, who walked as fast as her. Reaching her destination, she built a fire and began to prepare a meal. While doing so she held a conversation presumably with jinns, whom the young men couldn't see and whose language they couldn't comprehend. Inferring that the woman and her jinn-lover were preparing to make love, the young men withdrew discreetly.

Zubair married the younger woman, his dream, his virgin. He was a wealthy man, reputed to own ten thousand camels divided into various herds, in the care of distant cousins and hired hands. As many as twenty head of cattle were slaughtered to feast the invited and uninvited wedding-quests.

But on the first night with his young virgin, Zubair felt unmanly. Also he kept hearing voices, as if a drone of jinns were speaking to one another, inside his head, in an alien language. Just before dawn, his young bride died, untouched, a virgin.

When his wife reappeared after a few days, Zubair had a serious talk with her, alone. In their frank confrontation he told her everything that had taken place.

'I've given you five sons and two daughters, what more do

you want from me?' she said. 'I had never known nor desired any other man until I saw that your lusty eyes had fallen on a younger woman, with firm breasts, healthy skin and a handsome body. Imagine then,' she went on, 'when less than a week later I met a man as good-looking as an angel, who declared his love to me. It was only afterwards that he revealed his identity to me, that he was a jinn, not human. But this didn't bother me, in fact it made my affair more romantic, requiring more courage. I bore him children, half-jinn, half-human, and we are happy together.'

'Did your jinn-lover kill my bride on our wedding night?'

'Are you mad?'

'Was it he who interfered with my erections?' he asked, desperately humiliated.

Her lips began to move. She seemed to be whispering to someone in the room whom Zubair couldn't see, only sense. She turned to him after her low-voiced consultation. 'Could it be that you killed your virgin bride to hide your shame?'

'This is preposterous,' Zubair said.

Again his wife entered into a whispered debate with invisible parties. She chuckled, then said, 'Perhaps next time something disastrous occurs to you, you'll blame my jinn-lover for it too.'

Not long after this conversation with his estranged wife, Zubair was in the midst of dawn prayers when a curtain of darkness suddenly lowered upon his sight, rendering him totally blind. It wouldn't lift, no matter what he did; nothing would restore his vision.

Asked how he felt, he would respond, 'It is as if two wicked, playful little jinns are mounted on the unlit rays of my pupils, depriving me of my vision. Maybe they'll tire of playing their vengeful games one day and dismount.'

But they did not alight. Instead, his wife was taken ill. Meanwhile, Zubair stopped saying his prayers altogether. Finally Zubair's wife died a quarter of an hour before Duniya was born.

Nearly seventeen years later: a gesture of kind violence!

Duniya's father was on his bed, awaiting death. Zubair was his constant visitor, coming and going, Zubair whose stick kept tapping the unseen wall separating their houses, a sadly omened sound. When together, the two friends talked of death, agreeing that only Allah knew who would join Him first.

An intimation of his imminent death that day made Duniya's father speak his last feverish words. He decided to offer, as he put it, 'a gesture of kind violence' to his friend and peer Zubair. Would Duniya please take him as her lawful husband?

The curse of it was that no one else was there, only Duniya's mother. And Duniya accepted to do her mother's bidding, for one cannot argue with the wishes of the dead and the elderly, people said. Either one does as the dead say, or one doesn't, but one has to face the consequences of one's actions. Duniya didn't wish to look over her shoulders in anticipation of the moment when she might spot the evil of her parents' malediction lurking in every depression, every valley or shadow. 'Let's get on with it,' Duniya said courageously. And to Zubair who had never seen her with his own eyes but who had known her all her life, Duniya, his new bride and virgin, said, 'Go and prepare for my coming.'

Family friends and relations tried to convince Duniya not to grant her father's dying wishes. Zubair, for his part, lest he be accused of offending her pride, pretended to have grown a numb set of toes. But Duniya's mother, speaking loudly as people with hearing difficulties do, reiterated that her late husband had suggested their daughter marry Zubair, there was no question about it, she had *heard* it; the young woman might as well comply.

Then Duniya's half-brother Shiriye, a lieutenant in the army, arrived unannounced. When told what was afoot, he vowed to put a stop to this nonsense, arguing that Duniya's mother was virtually deaf. But by late evening Shiriye had changed his mind. And Zubair would not confirm or deny the rumour that he had made the customary overtures a bridegroom makes towards the bride's blood brother. And Shiriye left in haste the following morning.

Years later Duniya would write to her full-brother Abshir that their half-brother had departed from Galkacyo like a man with something to hide. The truth was that Shiriye had secretly accepted a gift from Zubair.

'Do you remember that I offered to marry you when I was four, giving you my hand in exchange for a handsome horse?' Duniya asked Zubair when her father's funeral rites had ended.

'Yes, I do,' he replied.

'Now where is that horse?'

'Times have been hard,' he replied.

'Let's get on with it then, without pomp and show, without the beating of a single drum, or a trill of ululation.'

'Yes, let us.'

'Go forth and prepare for my coming,' Duniya said.

Several nights later, Zubair admitted her to the room prepared for their honeymoon. On the floor was a large mattress decked with cushions and pillows (on one was Duniya's name embroidered in green, for luck). The most prominent item was a rocking-chair, a gift from Zubair's seaman son. It dominated the room from its vantage point. They sat in it together, they made love in it, and now and then they even fell asleep in it, holding each other in a loving embrace.

Given the difference in age and temperament, Zubair and Duniya got on better than either had imagined possible. For the young bride, the responsibility of looking after a blind old man was daunting, a wearying task, like learning a new language one had no real interest in. She had to master a limited vocabulary and a body-language that was efficient and precise. She got used to his being given everything, got accustomed to the fact that she could never ask him to pass her the salt, the sugar or to switch off the light, though he might have coped were it absolutely necessary.

He made several adjustments to accommodate her. And when he resumed praying, Duniya took up a position in such a way that she became his point of reference, and so it was before her that he prostrated himself in his worship of Allah, and to her that he addressed all his devotions.

He was a huge man, physical, loving. He had frequent naps, putting Duniya in mind of an overgrown child who collapsed exhausted in the midst of play. There was something child-like about his mouth, with which he seemed forever preoccupied, like a toothless old man who chews his own saliva, biting the inside of his cheeks. But Zubair had all his teeth: and he was healthy, considering his age.

She bore him twins, Mataan (meaning the twin) looking very like him, and Nasiiba the spitting image of Duniya's brother Abshir. (Once, albeit in a light-hearted manner, Duniya asked Dr Mire if it were possible for a woman to carry in her womb two-egg twins emanating from two different sources, when one of the men had never made love to the woman in question.)

One evening Duniya wanted to know if the jinns in Zubair's

eyes were still on sentry duty, guarding the door to his sight. Zubair described them as two immobile beings, supposing his blindness to be born of his former wife's vindictiveness. He explained to Duniya that although they still blocked the entrance to his vision, the jinns nevertheless appeared to have tired of their spirited pranks since his marriage to her.

He died in his sleep, aged sixty. At the time Duniya had the twins at her breasts. His voice, thick, mumbled something like, 'Do you mind if we switch off the light?' just before he was called away by death. In retrospect she regretted not asking if the jinns had dismounted briefly, letting him see. Otherwise why ask that she turn off the lights? She was in the rocking-chair, breast-feeding her two hungry monstrosities and anything she said would have sounded awkward. Angry that the dazzling brightness of the electric light had made sleep unthinkable, she turned to say something. But he expired before she managed to speak her piece. A fortnight later she was on a plane to Mogadiscio.

So many years later in Mogadiscio, reminiscing!

Just before she was ready for bed, having showered and brushed her teeth, power returned and so did the half-collared kingfisher. Duniya hadn't made up her mind if it was the same bird, when it flew away without alighting. Duniya got out of bed to switch off the lights that had come on in the kitchen, the toilet, the courtyard.

No sooner had she done so and returned to the darkened room than she heard a car door open and then close. Half-kneeling behind the partly drawn curtain, she watched as Mataan, her seventeen-year-old son, got out of a car with a woman at the wheel. They were talking in low voices, no doubt arranging future assignations. But where was his bicycle? Had it been stolen? Or had he felt unsafe riding it home because it had no lights?

The woman drove away before Duniya managed a good look at her face. Mataan waved enthusiastically until the car disappeared around the corner. What mattered, Duniya told herself, remembering what Nasiiba had said, what mattered was not whether the woman was older than he but whether they were comfortable with each other.

Mataan moved in the direction of their door, to let himself in.

Tall, he walked with his back straight, like a man returning home to a waiting wife, a man who must remove all traces of his other life, in which another woman figures prominently. Mataan wiped his face and gave his hair a soft pat, touching his recently combed hair. As he came closer, his mother could see that he had his bicycle-chain in his left hand and his books in his right. From where she was, his bicycle-chain resembled a hunting-crop.

When the key turned in the outside door, Duniya tiptoed away from Nasiiba's bed on which she had been kneeling, thinking: Shall I call his name or wait until he has hung his talismanic bicycle-chain on the nail above the entrance to his room?

In the event, she did not call his name. She let him shower, let him wash off the impurity of sex (Islam is very particular about a man's body coming into contact with a woman's and both must wash after love-making). But when she heard his steps going past the Women's Room door, she spoke his name.

'Who is it?' his startled voice asked.

'It is I,' Duniya replied.

He made it clear that he didn't want to talk.

'Good night then,' she said.

'Dream well, Mother,' he called.

Duniya did not wake when Nasiiba sneaked into her own bed. Once she fell asleep, Bosaaso came to her to tell her his story.

MOGADISCIO (Agencies)

Plans are under way for a huge relief operation in the war-torn drought-stricken north of the Somali Republic, where the rains have failed for the past four years. The airlift of emergency food aid will begin in about a week, a senior government official said. A regional official confirmed that between 300 and 500 people were dying daily in some of the larger localities and many more would starve to death unless emergency airlifts reached the affected area soon.

Chapter Five

Bosaaso, at first dreaming then awake, relates aspects of his life history to Duniya, who is asleep and perhaps dreaming him *too.*

Bosaaso had been up for some time, turning and tossing in his bed, eager for dawn. He had dreamt of a brightly-coloured eagle soaring high, unprepared to alight on any of the tall eucalyptus trees in the vicinity. Below, where he waited for the handsome bird to descend on a branch so he could take aim and shoot it, was a long-legged red plover, chattering its customary oaths, repeating its standard vow in the ugliest sequence of notes ever sung by a bird.

In his dream, a small boy carrying a kilo or so of uncooked meat on an uncovered platter walked into view, and the alert eagle came down in a sudden swoop, going not for the blood-dripping raw flesh but for the child's brain. The boy fell to the ground in fear, dropping the meat. Several women emerged from behind the acacia bushes and formed a mournful circle around the prostrate boy. One woman stood apart, a woman wearing a patchwork of peacock-coloured clothes, with feathers in her hair. The others hushed when she beckoned. She took from the folds of her clothing a talismanic pebble which she placed near the boy's nostrils. The child jerked with life-returning spasms. Then he rose and, unafraid, walked away, taking with him the platter of meat, now dusty.

Anxiety in Bosaaso's chest stirred up a dusty cough and, still asleep, he sneezed. He diverted his mind by telling himself (and Duniya in her dream, of which he was part) the story of an only son of an only parent. The boy's given name was Mohamoud.

He was a most fortunate child. He had a mother who sang well, being endowed with a beautiful voice, who cooked wonderfully and was an excellent seamstress. These three assets made her a frequent and welcome guest at weddings and all manner of events at which her services were in demand. She was Mohamoud's single parent, his father having stowed away on a ship – everybody thought – never to be heard of again.

The boy and his mother lived in the small coastal town of G., not far from Cape Guardafui, on the east of the Somali peninsula. They were a feature of the locality, always together, colourful as the clothes she stitched herself, like itinerant gypsies, ready at the drop of a hint to entertain an audience. There was something decidedly ambivalent about the boy's attitude to his mother. He loved her to sing her songs and he loved the food she prepared; on the other hand, he felt it degrading that he should accompany her everywhere, tagging along at the feasts where she performed.

She was paid mostly in kind: mutton, beef or camel meat, a choice portion to cook at home for herself and her son. Mohamoud loathed crossing town with the fly-inviting raw meat wrapped in a sooty cloth. He hated being near the improvised cooking sites, four-stone arrangements on which cauldrons were placed, under which fire was lit. He was equally embarrassed by his mother's habit of calling him and giving him food in front of all the women, with none of the other boys being asked to join him. He would scamper away somewhere, like a dog seeking a quiet place to chew a bone, unobserved. It embarrassed him to eat when no one else was doing so.

Mohamoud felt more relaxed when his mother wore the singer's mask and chanted ballads praising the virtues of a bride or groom at an auspicious wedding. His mother would be clothed in her best and would smell of the charming scent of sandal and other *cuuds*, which he loved. He didn't have to go with her on such days. She brought back cooked food herself after she performed.

She had an impressive rich voice and a gift for improvisation. She dressed well, far better than any other woman in the town, in fashionable frocks which she designed and sewed. It was agreed that the town's male tailor was not as skilled as her, so the women brought along dresses he had made for her to reshape. Having no sewing-machine (she couldn't afford to buy one), she did everything by hand. In matters of taste, the townswomen sought her opinion and when she gave it, they held it in high esteem. She led a very busy life, receiving and entertaining visitors.

The townspeople knew little about the woman's past. It was her husband, not she, who hailed from G. She had come with him, already pregnant. They arrived in the back of a lorry, brown with dust of mysterious provenance. The lorry deposited them, leaving in its wake questions no one picked up from the dust-laden footpaths of the town. She was the wife of a son of the town, and suffice it to say the man had a disreputable history, as a famed gambler. He was a restless soul, of a breed and temperament that a sleepy town in the backwaters of Somalia could hold little interest for; and no work be found for him. The tailor, who held a grudge against the woman, was reported to have said that the son of the town had brought a witch there.

The day after she gave birth to a son, the boy's father left, to stow away on the first ship that called at this abandoned littoral. His parents were kind to the poor woman and the boy, named after his grandfather. Until he was five, Mohamoud shared an *alool*-bed with his mother, who was an asset to her in-laws, boasting a variety of talents unusual in a town like G. She showed no interest in other men, most of whom were fishermen down on their luck and surviving on remittances from relatives slaving away in petrodollar Arabia.

The town's womenfolk displayed unlimited affection and trust for her. To show her gratitude, she taught their daughters how to knit, held free reading and writing classes for older women in her in-laws' compound in the evenings. Her restlessness, which she put to good use, reminded people of the boy's departed father. It made her in-laws wary, worried that she, too, might pack her meagre belongings and vanish for ever with their grandson. But she offered them no reason to suspect her of that.

His mother's fame preceded Mohamoud at school, and some of the bigger bullies teased him incessantly. A cruel boy named Ali described her as 'an itinerant kitchen'. Trading insults with him, Mohamoud mentioned that Ali's mother lived on the town's welfare, virtually a beggar surviving on charity. Now who deserved to be heaped with scorn, a woman who was hard-working or one living on hand-outs? They got into a fight and Mohamoud hit the bully so hard he hurt his hand, but the other boy lose a front tooth. He might have been expelled had it not been for the testimony of a classmate named Mire, whose father was the district judge, a man worthy of the headmaster's high respect. Mire placed the blame squarely on Ali, accusing him of provoking Mohamoud in the first place. The headmaster expelled Ali. And Mire and Mohamoud became friends.

Mire gave his new friend an assortment of clothes he had outgrown; these the boy's mother altered or mended, as necessary. As a gesture of appreciation, Mohamoud would bring to school the *bursaliid* doughnuts his mother prepared for him, sharing them with Mire. The two ate together often, Mire out of a sense of adventure, Mohamoud out of loyalty to their closeness and also because he hated eating alone. The other boys bought inedible cakes, hard as rocks, and bread from a zinc kiosk situated at a corner where the school's dirt road met the town's only thoroughfare. Mire's father's house, one of three stone houses, was in the government residential area. Mohamoud's grandparents' place was the end-house in a cul-de-sac. Because Mire read a lot, he encouraged his friend to borrow books.

A lorry arrived one day and a letter was delivered to Mohamoud's mother, giving news of her husband, who had apparently been sighted in Mogadiscio having a ball of a time like a sailor on leave. A week later, a telegram arrived bearing his name and a message that she should come to the metropolis, bringing the boy. The first missive enclosed a photograph of a man with a deformed lower lip; no one doubted the authenticity and source, since it contained bits of gossip known exclusively to members of the family. The grandparents grew suspicious, uncertain that they would ever set eyes on their grandson again. It was Mire's father's intercession that made them concede that she could take the boy away.

On the eve of their departure, Mire, together with his father, came to wish them a safe journey. Mire's father had arranged a lift for them in a government Land Rover returning to Mogadiscio. Not knowing how much help she would need on arrival in the capital, Mire's father gave her letters of introduction to friends of his. The two young friends looked anxiously forward to their reunion, something of which they seemed certain.

The boy and his mother lodged with her people in the capital. There was no sign of the man who had sired him. The first few months were miserable for young Mohamoud, who missed his friend Mire, missed his grandparents, the small-town air and the house in which he had lived. Moreover, now that they were in

Mogadiscio there was nothing special about his mother, for there were thousands of women like her. Seldom invited to be the honoured guest or to cook at weddings, she attended college to qualify as a teacher, and later found a job in a school.

Two years later, Mire and Mohamoud were reunited in Mogadiscio, but they lived at either end of the sprawling city and could not visit each other as much as they wished. When term restarted, Mohamoud transferred to Mire's school, consenting to walk four kilometres there and back every day.

It came to pass that there were three other boys who bore the same first, second and third names as our friend Mohamoud, which proved confusing. One day a teacher who was calling the roll wondered how on earth one was supposed to distinguish them. Being unusually full of mischief that day, Mire gave his friend the nickname 'Bosaaso'. And, although Mohamoud insisted he did not come from the town of that name but from G., the nickname stuck.

Certain that Duniya was with him and had enjoyed hearing the story of his childhood, Bosaaso postponed the instant when he opened his eyes. Somewhere in the echoey two-storey house where he lived alone, a door opened and banged shut, a bath-tub was run and a toilet flushed. His face tightened in the sad expectation of finding her gone or that she might not hear him or answer his call. Yet with his eyes still closed, his outstretched hand informed him that in his bed there was a depression to his right, where she had slept; and his cheeks felt stroked, touched by her lips, kissed.

He had the air of a contented man, even when he opened his eyes and didn't meet her in his house, in any of the rooms he entered. He gave a start when he heard a high-pitched whistle and then saw a half-collared kingfisher in the kitchen, settled in the very chair where Duniya might have been.

The kingfisher, exempt from giving explanations, flew out.

Smile-shy, Bosaaso moved quietly about his kitchen, as if not wishing to disturb a guest still asleep somewhere in the building. He waited for the water in the kettle to boil. He caressed the teapot's spout, as if fondling a cow's teats to make it yield more milk, the to-and-fro movements of his hand gentle and elegant. Gradually he indulged the memory of a scene from the past, remembering the world he had shared with his late wife. Current obsessions intruded into his mind only when he noticed he had set the breakfast table for two, placing plates, mats and cutlery in front of the chair where the kingfisher had sat.

Bosaaso had bought the china set from a Danish woman returning to Copenhagen after a three-year stint with a Scandinavian voluntary aid organization. The woman insisted she was selling the set 'dirt cheap', more or less 'giving it away'. He paid a token sum, ten US dollars, since Ingrid demanded that he pay something, anything. Being African, he felt uneasy offering a meagre five dollars for a set of china that had survived nine years in Mogadiscio (the woman had herself bought it from an Englishwoman who worked with another voluntary aid outfit, War on Want, and had paid in sterling).

In his memory, as he sat down to breakfast facing 'Duniya's' chair, Ingrid the Danish woman was pale, with lipstick so bright red he couldn't look at it without squinting. She had a heavy accent and spoke fast, spraying forth missiles of saliva that darted from her mouth with worrying speed. Her front teeth were artificial, the top halves white, the bottom very dark.

Bosaaso and Yussur, his late wife, had gone to Ingrid's to see what second-hand items they could buy at a discount. The idea of calling on her was Yussur's and the two women turned the session into a discussion about the philosophical and cultural aspects of giving and receiving gifts. Bosaaso listened, fascinated. They addressed the winning points of the debate to him. Ingrid generalized about the exchange of gifts in Europe, saying, among other things, that in her continent one might offer a hand-me-down to a friend or a poor relation who was hard up; but the notion of giving for its own sake was alien, and not as habit-forming as in Somalia. Occasions were important, not the gifts, she said. Christmas was a season in which everyone participated in an orgy of giving and receiving.

Yussur listened, shaking her head, hackles rising, whenever Ingrid made a condescending remark about Africans. Bosaaso found it rewarding to analyse the crop of the Danish woman's generalizations; it was when she came to specifics that her logic began to crumble.

At one point Ingrid said, 'This china, for instance, has survived for almost ten years in the caring hands of Europeans who knew how to appreciate such a treasure.' Then, injecting disappointment into her voice Ingrid added, 'It makes me sad to think that you, Yussur, may behave like these *Apfricans* all over the place who have no idea how to take care of sensitive gadgets with souls, like a car, a computer with software sensibilities or a set of china with as fragile an anima as a bird's. To my mind *Apfricans* haven't got what it takes to appreciate the cultural and technological gifts that are given to them.' And she smiled at Bosaaso, whose left cheek had been the target of a flying ball of saliva.

Yussur's hand had given a caressing touch to her own pregnancy, as if offering an encouraging pat. Turning to Ingrid, apparently not angered by these derisory remarks about Africans, but taking them in her stride, Yussur had asked, 'Now is this china that you've sold to me and my husband dirt cheap almost a gift?'

'More or less a gift, yes.'

'Tell me, Ingrid,' Yussur went on, 'if you sell your gifts for ten US dollars, equivalent in local currency to more than a senior civil servant's salary, what on earth do you call the donations your government or charitable organizations give to my government and famine-stricken, alms-receiving people?'

'We call it "aid". It may be in the form of emergency food or technical aid or as grants to be written off later, or soft loans. There are different designations, depending on the specific situation.' Ingrid remained confident.

'We receive,' Yussur said very clearly, 'and you give.'

'In a general sort of way, yes. That's right.'

'Why give, Ingrid?'

Ingrid fell silent, puzzled, and Yussur asked, 'What's in it for your people to give my people things?'

'Because we have certain things that you *Apfricans* need.'

Yussur said, 'But that is ridiculous.'

It was Ingrid's turn to feel offended. 'What's ridiculous about what I've just said?'

'Surely you don't give something of value to yourself simply because someone else does not have it or is in need of it?'

Silence. Yussur sought Bosaaso's gaze and was met with an appreciative nod of his head. But Ingrid was of a different mind: 'Aid is aid, good or bad, whether there are strings attached and whatever its terms of reference. You say one thing but want another, you *Apfricans*. I am fed up listening to this nonsense. Why ask for help if you don't like it? The headlines of your newspapers are full of your government's appeals for more aid, more loans. Nonsense.'

Yussur's legs had gone to sleep. To make the blood return to them, she rose to her feet, moving back and forth as she spoke:

'My husband told me only recently that the United States, the world's richest country, between 1953 and 1971 donated so-called economic assistance worth ninety million dollars to Somalia, one of the world's poorest. Over sixty million of this so-called aid package was meant to finance development schemes, including teacher-training and a water supply system for the city of Mogadiscio. But do you know that nearly twenty million dollars were accounted for by food grown in the USA by American farmers, given to us in sacks with the words DONATED BY THE USA TO THE REPUBLIC OF SOMALIA written on them? And of course from that we have to deduct the salaries of Americans working here and living like lords in luxury they are not used to at home. Why must we accept this intolerable nonsense?'

'Don't ask me,' Ingrid retorted and shrugged her shoulders.

'Who do I ask?'

'Ourselves.'

Bosaaso had nodded thoughtfully, saying nothing.

Yussur continued, changing her tone of voice, 'The other day I was reminding Bosaaso of a Somali proverb: "*Qeebiyaa qada.*" Would you render that in English for Ingrid?' And both women looked at him.

He had reflected for a while, then said, 'I would tentatively translate it like this: He who distributes the offerings of fortune receives little as his personal share.' Smiling, he told himself that this had been his only contribution to the conversation.

Yussur said, 'What I'm trying to say, my dear Ingrid, is that a language is the product of a people's attitude to the world in which they find themselves. Now can you understand why it irks me to hear you describe the china for which we paid ten US dollars as a gift?'

'You're entitled to your opinion and I to mine,' Ingrid replied.

At that instant Yussur felt the pangs of labour and her features contorted with pain, her body with groans. As she groped for a chair, her body swung round. The tragic irony of it was that in her dolorous blindness she broke a china cup.

Bosaaso rushed her to hospital. It was an arduous labour, Yussur's first, lasting several days, and Bosaaso and Duniya made each other's acquaintance then. Yussur gave birth to a bouncing boy named for Dr Mire, but her milk yield was insufficient and had to be supplemented. Now this might not have bothered her were it not for her traumatic memories of being weaned from her own mother's breasts. Incidents Yussur had clean forgotten returned to haunt her with frightening clarity, including overhearing her mother confiding in a woman neighbour that she enjoyed her milk-heavy breasts being sucked by Yussur, then four, more than she relished making love to her husband, the child's father.

Depressed, Yussur did not bear her anxieties well. She exaggerated this small failing, predicting nothing but a gloomy future for the baby whom she adored. Her maternal ego was hurt and she became morose, lacking in will-power.

Because Yussur had a feeble constitution and did not wish to meet anyone, she asked Bosaaso to seek Dr Mire's advice. Drugs were prescribed and bed-rest advised. Mire brought a psychiatrist who had a long chat with Yussur. All these steps helped. For a while she behaved like anyone with normal needs, happy to be alone with her baby and her husband, and demanding to be discharged from the hospital where she was in the private ward. Since Mire was not in Mogadiscio, other doctors agreed to sign her papers.

No one realized that Yussur was prone to depressive moods deep as death. To overcome the stress, she would lock herself in the master bedroom where she felt safe and also isolated from her mother and her younger sister who dropped by often to visit. Her mother talked, asked questions, suggesting absurd remedies for Yussur's ills, worrying that the golden-egg producing daughter might die or something might happen to her baby: for in that event Bosaaso would cease providing for the mother and sister. Yussur wanted to see no one except her baby, her Bosaaso and the maid.

In a rare peaceful moment when she was less melancholy, Yussur asked Bosaaso, 'You don't mind being alone with me or the baby in this huge house, shut off from the rest of the world, do you, Bo?'

'Of course not,' he had said.

'And you don't think I am insane, do you?'

'Of course not.'

Quietly efficient, the maid attended to Yussur and the baby's needs. Herself a mother of several grown children, the maid gave cautious counsel in a gentle voice, acted sensibly whenever Yussur snapped at her, discourteous as only the young can be.

The doorbell rang day and night, at all hours. Yussur's mother and younger sister wished to be let in. When no one answered the bell, the two women took the mechanism to be faulty or the current to be off, so they resorted to banging on the door so hard one might have mistaken them for police officers preparing an assault. Unadmitted, they camped in the fore-yard, under a tree by the gate.

Dr Mire returned a couple of days later; he was let in immediately. Bosaaso came out of the house and left in Mire's vehicle. Three hours later they arrived accompanied by a neurologist and were surprised to find all the doors open and to hear women's wailing. Three women mourning the death of Yussur and baby Mire.

The versions of what had happened given by the maid and by Yussur's mother disagreed in essentials as well as substance. Apparently the maid, out of motherly kindness, admitted the old woman and sister directly after the doctor's car had gone.

In both versions there is a balcony overlooking the garden, with Yussur standing on the balcony. And in both, Yussur held the baby in her tight hug, saying, 'Will you be a darling boy and fetch me that lone flower in our garden and then give it to me?'

But from here on the two versions differ. In the mother's telling, Yussur would walk back, bend to put the baby in its cot, then change her mind and return to her position on the balcony from where she would request her baby to fetch her the flower. Here the mother's story ends. In that of the maid, no time elapsed between the moment Yussur made this most unusual demand of a baby not a week old and the instant she threw him down to get the lone flower. The maid told of a flash of insanity brightening Yussur's eyes between her speaking the word 'give' and death from the fall. Where was Yussur's younger sister? Well, she had gone to her sister's wardrobe to try on a dress because she had been invited to a party – and she missed it all.

All versions agreed in one fact: Yussur and baby Mire died.

MOGADISCIO (SONNA, 1 August)

Liv Ullmann has been recently appointed a special UNICEF Ambassador and in this new role has been visiting several countries in Africa south of the Sahara.

As part of her commitment, Ms Ullmann will travel rough on aircraft transporting grain, medicines and other emergency aid being airlifted to areas affected by famine and malnutritional ailments. Ms Ullmann has said that she is happy whenever she sees a smile breaking and then spreading on these children's faces, happy when she notices them regaining hope in their own survival.

On her mission of mercy, Ms Ullmann will visit a select number of feeding centres and refugee-related projects in the continent, which is said to contain the world's largest war-displaced population.

Chapter Six

Duniya wakes from a dream in which Bosaaso tells her a story. She has morning conversations with Nasiiba and Mataan. And she is lent an article from yesterday's national newspaper.

Duniya woke to a door being unbolted loudly. An instant later she heard a jaw-breaking yawn, then footsteps approaching and going away. Then the window overlooking the road was flung open, and the heat of the morning sun strode into the room. A blast of warmth licked the exposed part of Duniya's face, scorching it.

'Time to get up, Mummy,' Nasiiba said.

Now why was Nasiiba up and about so early, earlier than her twin brother who had earned for himself the nickname 'household alarm'? And why was she insisting that the rest of the world wake up?

'Shake off the sloth of sleep, Mummy. Up,' Nasiiba sang.

Duniya did not stir.

'What's the matter with everyone today?'

The sun felt hot, no longer in its infancy. Duniya wished she could cling to the comfort of sleep a little longer and resume her interrupted dream. But that wasn't to be. Nasiiba was making a noisy point of the fact that she had risen before either her mother or brother, though she had been the last to go to bed. Duniya wondered if her daughter had butterflies in her insides about something – was this the reason?

'Mummy?'

'No,' Duniya replied. The word came out of its own accord.

'What are you talking about? No what?' Nasiiba asked.

How inconsiderate of the young to think only of themselves, Duniya thought. She recalled the Somali proverb that says your offspring are not your parents – the children's thoughtfulness is a shallow well whose bounty runs out fast.

'I want to tell you something,' said Nasiiba, sounding urgent.

Duniya wasn't interested in being told anything.

'It won't take long, I promise.'

Duniya wasn't interested.

'Open you eyes and listen to me.'

'No,' Duniya replied.

'You are in a negative mood today.'

Duniya said nothing.

'It's very important that I tell you something, Mummy.'

Duniya lay quiet and unmoving. One of her ears was beginning to fill with air, causing a little pain; the other ear failed to hear anything as though suffering a momentary attack of Meniere's disease. Her body slipped briefly into that ambiguous zone between sloth and sleep as she remembered her dream, in which Bosaaso told her how his late wife was resurrected from the dead, and she saw a baby clutching a lone flower tightly in its long-nailed fingers. The baby had been born without an anus and, there being no experienced surgeon in the city to perforate one for it, it had died, with no one mourning it.

Nasiiba was saying, 'Aren't you going to work today, Mummy?'

Duniya's decision was sudden. She said, 'No.' There was a brief silence. 'What about you? Aren't you going to school ?' she asked.

'I am not,' responded Nasiiba.

'Why not?'

'Because I will not,' said Nasiiba, typically.

Duniya uncovered her face and her eyes blinked, hurting for a while, until they were used to the dazzle of the bright sun.

Both women now turned towards their door, which was open to the central courtyard. A rush of wind blew past Duniya's face and out of the window. Heralded by a clumsy footfall, Mataan spoke a greeting. Nasiiba did not return it. Duniya imagined her son's open-mouthed expression. She could see him now in her mind's eye, staring at his sister, nonplussed.

'Good morning, Mother,' Mataan said, raising his voice.

Duniya's thoughts were busy elsewhere, determining whether she had seen a sparrow fold its wings and drop from the sky towards the earth. Because Duniya didn't respond to her son's salutation, Nasiiba took the opportunity to say, 'Our mother is behaving strangely this morning, Mataan; she's acting like a child refusing to take its food and saying no to everything.'

'Have you no respect for your elders, Twin-sister?'

'What do you know about respect, you?' Nasiiba retorted.

'All I'm suggesting is that you respect your mother,' he said.

'All I am saying is that it's none of your business,' chanted Nasiiba.

'One would think . . .,' he began, but abandoned the thought in mid-sentence. He walked away making hardly any noise, like a burglar tiptoeing out of a place he has broken into mistakenly.

'Mataan?' Duniya called him back. She remembered that the night before he had come home not on his bicycle but in a woman's car.

'Yes, Mother?' He was discreetly out of her eyes' reach. He would never think of entering a room without knocking, even if the door were wide open.

When she didn't speak, he said, 'I meant to tell you when I got in last night, Mother,' and his voice trailed off.

She waited, hoping to hear about the woman he had been with.

'It's about my bicycle, Mother,' he continued. 'I was riding it last night and a man reversed into me and knocked me down. I meant to tell you when I got back.'

She sat up, her voice worried, 'Are you hurt?' She wrapped a sheet around herself. 'Come closer, let me see you.'

Mataan was tall and very thin. At school his nickname was Lungo, Italian for 'long'. He touched his elbows where there were bruises, his knee-caps and a slightly bluish spot on his skin and rib-cage. 'I wasn't hurt much,' he said.

'I wish you wouldn't ride your bicycle without lights at night.'

'But I had them on, Mother,' he said.

'Then why didn't he see you?'

'Because he didn't have his lights on.'

'Did you see the man who bumped into you? Did you take down his insurance details and all that?' Duniya asked.

Mataan nodded.

'Where is the bicycle now?' inquired his mother.

'At a friend's place,' he said.

Nasiiba, who had held herself in check until now, said, 'Ask him to name the friend at whose place he left his bicycle, Mummy.'

Mataan and Duniya both looked at her censoriously.

'Why are you looking at me like that, as if I slaughtered your favourite she-camel? I'm talking to *my* mother.'

'You're being ludicrous,' he said, half-choking on the last word.

Duniya appealed to her children, 'Please, no fighting.'

Nasiiba was livid. 'Mother, could you explain why you won't talk to me yet you chatter away to Mataan like a gossiping market woman?'

'Because he has been hurt in a bicycle accident.'

'You wouldn't have taken any notice if I had been.'

'Now why is that?' asked Mataan.

'Because you're a boy and I'm a girl,' said Nasiiba.

The twins' exchanges reminded Duniya that for several nights Nasiiba had been grinding her teeth in her sleep, perhaps out of genuine stress over something.

In obvious fury Nasiiba was putting on a pair of jeans.

'Where are you going?' asked Duniya.

'Somewhere someone will talk to me when I speak to them.'

'I've made breakfast, aren't you having any?' Mataan asked.

Nasiiba left the room, as if late for an appointment.

After breakfast Duniya read Taariq's article in the day before's paper:

The Story of a Cow

This is a true story. It happened in a village in Lower Juba in Somalia and involves two families related by marriage and by blood. I shall be vague about their identities, though precise enough to say that it took place during the middle months of the worst famine in the Horn of Africa this century.

These were difficult months, in particular for anyone vowing not only to survive the famine, but also to outlive it with their integrity untarnished. Many a person yielded to hunger and other forms of pressure, many who thought of themselves as good, honest and incorruptible discovered to their dismay that famines make aspiring to such ideals either foolhardy or at least questionable.

In this village lived two large families whose compounds entrances faced each other, whose children played together, whose young men and women danced with one another and intermarried. Before the famine, no one recalls a quarrel, light-hearted or serious, ever taking place between members of these compounds without it being stopped instantly. Disagreements likely to create friction were ended before anyone had time to comment on them, suspicions were allayed before they sowed seeds of hate in anyone's mind, child or adult, male or female.

Then came the famine. The first nine months of it decimated the cattle, reducing their number to a handful of skinny beasts. Meanwhile the earth produced but little. One saw skinny cows whose bones stuck out so visibly that crows, mistaking these for dry eucalyptus twigs, alighted on them.

To quicken the pace of the story, let us concentrate on two representative household heads, who in accordance with the ethos of the day we shall assume to be men. Let's call one Musa and the other Harun. We'll skip unnecessary details and pick up the tale when there is only one surviving cow, and after all other families have left the area for foreign-run feeding centres. The remaining cow belonged to Harun.

For several days, the two families shared the small amount of milk produced by the famished cow, supplementing it with desert fruits collected by Musa, which he offered as his contribution. To the suggestion that he and his family trek to the nearest UNICEF-organized feeding place, Musa retorted that they would rather die than accept hand-outs of grain grown elsewhere, given by infidels for whom he had little respect, whose ways of worship and manners he either disagreed with or disapproved of, and whose humanity he doubted.

The land has ways of supporting those who trust in its bounty. It never ceased to surprise Musa how much there was to be had. He would go for a walk and come upon a rabbit crouching in the shade of a dust-laden acacia tree, or find a fat pigeon cuddling in the warmth of a nest of fortune, as if waiting for him; now and again a dik-dik would run after him, making of itself an offer. In exchange for the meats, Harun gave Musa's baby daughter enough milk to wet her dry throat. Musa, however, divided everything with which nature supplied him in two equal halves, one his, the other Harun's. One day, nature ran out of gifts with which to surprise Musa. And the cow yielded so little milk that Harun declared he could no longer spare a drop for Musa's baby. The second day dawned, another night fell; the cow produced even less milk than before, insufficient for Harun's family's immediate needs. Musa prayed to God, who is said now and then to take from the rich to give to the poor. He prayed and waited.

On the third day, something unusual happened. The cow walked into Musa's compound and refused to be driven away. No amount of cajoling or caning would convince it to return to its lawful owner. Being of generous spirit, Musa conceded that the beast be milked where it was, in his compound, though Harun made it clear he would get not even a drop of milk.

All that night Musa listened to his children's hungry cries and his wife's curses. But just after midnight, they heard a gentle knock on their door. With a mixture of anxiety and hopeful anticipation, Musa answered. He was most surprised to find the cow wanting to be milked. What was he to do? His wife remarked that fortune favours the weak among men, who know not how to take advantage of it. For his part, Musa had made a vow never to steal. He pushed the door shut, leaving the cow where it stood, unmilked.

The next morning, he explained to Harun what had happened, but Harun accused him of theft and lying. Musa's wife said, 'What did I tell you?' But when Harun tried to milk the cow that day, everyone was in for another surprise. The cow would not submit to being touched by him.

Not knowing what to do, Harun appealed to Musa, who offered to milk the cow for him. But what would be in it for him?

Harun said: 'A third of what the cow yields is yours.'

Musa approached the cow with caution. It remained placid, eyes large as onions from a fertile land. And it didn't kick, but submitted to his elaborate caresses, its udder getting heavier and fuller by the second. Although he couldn't explain why even to his wife, Musa called the cow by a name: he had designated the cow *Marwa*! In short, it offered thrice as much as it had done during the pre-famine days. Two-thirds went to Harun, a third, as agreed, to Musa.

But Harun was displeased. He argued: 'If Musa is a magician and calls the cow Marwa, to which it responds favourably, so can I.' However, when that evening Harun called the cow Marwa, it kicked him so hard in the shin that he dropped the receptacle, breaking it. Musa again indicated his generous willingness to try his hand. He milked the cow, which gave four times as much milk as before and now he called it *Safa*. Yet he swore to his wife that on neither occasion had he had the slightest idea what to call the animal until the moment he spoke the correct name.

That evening, a group of travellers paid the two families an unexpected visit. It was the Night of Qadr, believed to be the most blessed night of the year, and the men from the other hamlets commented on the abundance of the cow's milk. All night Musa remained silent. Not so Harun; he talked a great deal, boasting that the cow was his. One of the men wondered why, if it was his, it was in his neighbour's compound. Harun responded that it preferred lodging with his friend; 'You know how cows are,' Harun said, trying to be humorous, and then laughing uneasily.

The following morning the cow was gone. The travellers testified on oath that they saw coming out of Musa's compound not a cow but a man, handsome and tall, adorned in the saintly robes of Friday-mosque white.

Then it began to rain in abundance, and for a while there was respite from the famine, although not immediately. The other families returned to their homesteads, reduced in number, for some had starved to death on their way to the feeding centres, and some decided to remain in the cities where the famine had driven them.

Harun and Musa listened to their stories. When their turn came, Harun told his version of their story, but Musa would not open his mouth to say anything. Someone asked Musa if it was true that Khadr, the miracle-performing saint, Elijah's alter-ego, had turned himself into a cow to test them?

Musa wouldn't comment.

Taariq Axmad

Somehow Duniya became restless directly she finished reading the article, and in an instant she was turning the whole room upside down, emptying cupboards and drawers. Yet she didn't know why she was doing this, had no idea what had got into her, or what she might be searching for.

She opened her daughter's drawers, one at a time, meticulously replacing things where she found them. In the second drawer she came across an Iranian magazine for Muslim women,

Mahjouba, tucked away and hidden under an unwashed pile of the young girl's underthings. Duniya suspected the copy of the radical Islamic magazine to be there for unholy purposes, and wasn't surprised when her search rewarded her with wads of cash, in Somali notes, tied together with a rubber band. For a moment Duniya appeared so disheartened, she did not know what had struck her.

She recovered from her shock only after counting the money and remembering that she had herself given it to Nasiiba, to settle the family's outstanding monthly bills with the owner of the district's general store. Did it mean Nasiiba had forgotten to clear last month's debts?

In a fit of annoyance, Duniya changed into outdoor clothes and walked the few hundred metres to the general store. Speechless, incapable of returning her neighbours' greetings, her tongue lay inert inside her mouth. But the shop was closed for the day, because its owner was out of town.

Duniya returned home, angrier than before.

Part II
A Baby in a Rubbish-bin

Chapter Seven

Duniya returns home to discover that a baby, apparently abandoned by its mother, has been found by her daughter.

Duniya tripped and nearly fell forward, regaining her balance just in time. She was entering her house when her foot, residing loosely in open-toed sandals, kicked the tips of her exposed digits sore against the lintel of the door. Calling down Koranic curses on wicked jinns lying in her path to cause her stride to falter, Duniya bent to touch the chipped nail of one big toe. What was making her so blundering and unsteady? She stumbled at the memory of knocking things over in Dr Mire's cubicle yesterday. She also remembered tumbling headlong over Taariq's brick barrier onthe night they decided to marry. And there was no avoiding recalling the image of Zubair, her first husband, wobbling his way about, toppling things with a blind man's walking-stick. Duniya solemnly vowed to herself to keep her balance and not fall.

Just then her giddiness climbed to a plateau, and she sensed the presence of a spirit paying her home an ethereal visit. She could not explain even to herself how she arrived at this conclusion, yet she was sure that she was bearing witness to something extraordinary. And then she heard the distinct whimper of a baby asserting its existence, a whimper coming from the direction of the room she shared with Nasiiba. Perhaps she was imagining being at the hospital, where perhaps such an infant had just been delivered, issuing a cry soft as the touch of afterbirth. She moved toward the open door, postponing self-questioning. At the doorway she stayed still for a couple of seconds, she saw a baby draped in a towel and lying on Nasiiba's lap. One instant Duniya was going to say something terrible, and the next her tongue abruptly turned turtle and she was saying, 'Isn't it cute?' She was stretching her hand out to receive it, but Nasiiba seemed reluctant to part with the baby.

'I found him,' the young girl said.

'Give it here,' Duniya requested.

'It's a boy,' Nasiiba said as she handed over the baby.

Duniya toiled with her breathing as she took the baby in her arms and sat down with the deliberate slowness of one troubled. Did this baby in any way resemble the one of her dream? Nasiiba was eager to tell her something, but she displayed no interest.

As she sat, a flexing of muscles reminded Duniya of the pain of labour, more than seventeen years ago. She also remembered that of late she had been hostess to several mysterious calls from birds and other beings. She made up her mind not to be the proverbial bad swimmer who, drowning, seeks support from the foam on the surface of the water which is killing her. No, she wasn't going to ask Nasiiba any questions, was uninterested in establishing the foundling's identity or where it had been found. The time would arrive soon enough when everything would begin to make sense.

She half-listened to Nasiiba's pedestrian explanations as to where she had come upon the baby and in what state of filth, but couldn't help remembering Harun and Musa's story published in the newspaper, a story in which Elijah's alter ego, the Prophet Khadr in Islamic mythology, had metamorphosed himself into a cow, perhaps to test their endurance. Had Khadr now chosen to enter her house in the guise of a baby abandoned near a rubbish-bin?

No sooner had her cursory examination confirmed that the foundling had an anus than they heard a man's voice shouting the Somali greeting formula. The new caller was Bosaaso, and so Duniya said, 'Please come on in.'

Nasiiba sat up in nervous tension as if the man had come to lay claim to the foundling and take him away. As far as Duniya was concerned, too many fresh thoughts were making demands on her; she had to deal with one at a time. She wished she knew if every isolated event was part of the same chain of incidents fettered to a common fate, hers and Bosaaso's.

Bosaaso presently stood in the doorway. He looked from Nasiiba, who had risen to her feet, to Duniya, to the baby. His hesitant frame gained confidence the moment he decided the baby belonged to neither Duniya nor her daughter. It must be connected with Duniya's work, but he couldn't determine how. He had been to the hospital and Dr Mire had guessed that the reason his senior nurse hadn't reported for duty today must be that she couldn't find transport.

Nasiiba said to Bosaaso, 'We found him.'

'Did you?' he said as casually as if he had known about it all along. He nodded at Nasiiba, and she nodded back, acknowledging each other's presence. It was hard to believe that they had not met before and that Bosaaso had never set foot in this room. Presently he paid close attention to the baby at whose tightly closed fist he stared, and he asked Duniya, 'Where did you find him?'

'Nasiiba did,' she said, with the formality of someone presenting one in-law to another. Bosaaso and Nasiiba smiled at each other.

'Where?' Bosaaso asked, crossing to sit in the armchair beyond the brick-barrier, and facing Nasiiba.

She told him where.

Silent, he held his head inclined. He looked about the room with the sensuous approval of somebody who knew it well. He was at home there, his body totally relaxed.

It was into this quietness that Mataan wheeled his bicycle with its wobbly tyre, his face pinched with the surprise of discovering his twin-sister and his mother in the company of a man he had never met before. Then he saw the baby. In the brief time he had to think he decided that the man and the baby belonged together.

He mumbled an 'I'm sorry,' turned and was about to push his bicycle with the buckled wheel away when his mother called him back, explained about the foundling, then introduced him to Bosaaso.

Someone named the foundling *Magaclaawe,* meaning 'The Nameless One'. Nasiiba and Mataan did not agree as to who had given it the name although they concurred on the time of day it had been bestowed: early afternoon, after Duniya had said, to Nasiiba and Bosaaso's delight and Mataan's surprise, that they would keep him. Nasiiba put no pressure on her mother to make this decision; she knew better, for it would have been counter-productive. Mataan would admit later that he hadn't considered the question at all, whereas Bosaaso, who had mulled it over, felt that he hadn't been close enough to Duniya for his counsel to be heeded. But everyone was clearly excited. When Nasiiba brought out a cot for Magaclaawe, Bosaaso was tempted to offer them all the baby things that had once belonged to his now dead son, but didn't for fear that Duniya might resent it.

The foundling's feeding noises, touching as a famished animal's, put Duniya in mind of the Somali notion 'ilmo jinni', the offspring of jinns. This brought with it a motley of memories, including of Zubair's first wife, who had been suspected of having an affair with a jinn. Although Duniya tried to disregard them, these thoughts came to her every so often. For instance how was it that Nasiiba had forgotten to settle the family's debt? And why had she donated blood? Duniya decided to wait for the appropriate time, not confident of getting a satisfactory answer out of Nasiiba.

There was something else. Had she not always looked forward to the day when her children had grown up so that she could do what she desired with her own time and freedom? And had she not boasted to Bosaaso, on the day he gave her a lift in a taxi, that she had plenty of time? The foundling was now a reality. It remained to be seen if Duniya would now have more time to herself, more physical space and liberty.

Bosaaso cleared his anxious throat, 'I suppose we have to start worrying about the bureaucratic part of the foundling's affairs. I suggest we register his existence with the authorities.'

Duniya noted he included himself in the 'we'. She was pleased.

'But do we know enough about him, enough even to fill a single sheet?' Mataan asked.

'That's one of the major points,' said Bosaaso. (It amazed Duniya how familiar all this was sounding: Mataan conversing with an adult male-friend of his mother's.) 'We report that we have no information about its ancestry, no inkling who his parents are.'

Duniya nodded her agreement.

'Somebody must know,' Mataan said. 'Know a little more than we,' he added as an afterthought. Duniya looked from her son to her daughter and her face tightened; she prepared for a quarrel between the twins. In a sense she looked forward to it, wondering how Bosaaso would handle it.

She busied herself by feeling the foundling's cheeks, then undoing the knots of the towel that served as a nappy. They all watched her. Now she felt the baby's small feet, one at a time, now its knuckles; she did all this with the professional touch of a nurse, as if she meant to enter the details in a ledger. The midwife in Duniya ran far ahead of the mother and woman.

The air was so anxiety-ridden that Bosaaso couldn't inhale any more. He said, 'Perhaps Mataan and I should go to the local police station and report the foundling's presence here.' He got up.

Duniya smiled and waited.

Mataan then said respectfully to Bosaaso, 'Before going I suggest Nasiiba tells us how and where she found the baby.'

Duniya looked from Mataan to Bosaaso, her eyes avoiding Nasiiba's altogether. The clouds on her mind's horizon were dark with the gathering of a storm about to break.

Mataan, who tended to be cautious, addressed Bosaaso, 'At least she'll give us a clearer picture than we have so far, and that will surely make our task easier.' He sounded very reasonable.

Nasiiba said, 'There was this small crowd of women surrounding the baby when I got there, and he was in a basket. I tell you I've never seen such frightened faces – the women's, I mean. They wouldn't go near the Nameless One and wouldn't let anyone else either.'

Eyes ferried to and fro. Everyone was at sea, but the storm hadn't broken.

Nasiiba went on, 'First, the women warned me not to touch him. Then one of them said she was going to report the baby's condition to the police – that's right, she used the phrase: the baby's condition, as though it were an ailment. She walked away, angry, you might say offended. Then the others engaged in a debate about how bad things were and so on, you know how people talk these days, complaining about food and petrol shortages. You know how this type of women talk,' and Nasiiba changed her voice in imitation of the woman's, 'she said: "Do you think young women nowadays would bat an eyelash before fornicating with any man in a car who was willing to give them a lift and a gift?" Well, I challenged her, telling her she should blame the men, not the young women. That got them all going, arguing among themselves, though they were agreeing a lot of the time. One of them claimed there's a link between urban squalor and the absence of a good moral code in a city like Mogadiscio. Another disagreed, but a third agreed with the two previous speakers, adding that there was indeed a link between urban drift and young people's disrespect for their elders, and she quoted a variety of examples, some her own.' Nasiiba paused, enjoying the attention she was receiving and, like the good actress she was, decided to bring her statement to a close before anyone interrupted her. 'While they were all engrossed in this sort of talk, I stole the foundling away, unseen, and brought him here.'

'Why?' Mataan asked.

Nasiiba pretended not to hear his question and turned to Bosaaso, who in turn asked, 'You say no one saw you?'

'I mean no one followed me here, not that it matters anyway.'

Mataan had another question. 'Did you bring him away in a plastic carrier-bag in which you made holes, or what?' He was clearly being wicked. 'And why steal him in the first place?'

'What business is it of yours to ask me these questions?'

'It is as much my business to ask as it is yours to bring home a foundling without seeking anyone's opinion.' Mataan was calm. 'It is my business because if he stays here to share what little space we have or cries at night and we lose sleep, well, then, you see, my darling twin sister, it is my business and Mother's as well.'

A smile darkened Duniya's eyes. Bosaaso was impressed by Mataan; unthinkingly, he touched the young man's elbow, as if congratulating him on the delivery of a long speech. Nasiiba stood at an angle to them, her body leaning towards the wall in a rather unbalanced manner. 'What if I refuse to tell you any more?' she said to Mataan.

'You won't because that won't do.'

Nasiiba was defiant: 'You can't make me say more than I want.'

Mataan looked in the direction of his mother, seeking her

guidance. Several expressions spanned Duniya's face, partitioning it into segments of sadness and exaltation. She said nothing.

Nasiiba spoke to Bosaaso, who was most attentive, 'It was very exciting coming home, bringing him with me. He only weighs a few pounds. I felt as if I were taking illicit notes into an examination hall despite the presence of suspicious invigilators.'

'Where did you get the nappy and feeding-bottle?' asked Mataan.

'A neighbour gave them to me.'

'A lie has a short leg, Naasi,' Mataan said, 'and it doesn't run as fast as a truth, which will catch up with it sooner or later. I suspect there is little truth in what you are telling us.'

At that point Duniya said, 'I wish we could take him to the hospital, have him seen by a paediatrician.'

Nasiiba was worried. 'Is anything the matter with him, Mummy?'

'We all have visible and invisible wounds,' said Duniya, applying penicillin-cream on the child's navel area, 'and some wounds are curable, some not.'

That the foundling's navel was infected had been noticed by everyone in the room, for Somalis associate the area with the she-camel that parents allot to new-born baby boys, in a sense the first potlach a male child receives. Somalis tie the umbilical cord at both ends with a hair plucked from the gift-camel's tail. No such present had been offered to the Nameless One.

'We can take him to the hospital, can't we?' Nasiiba inquired. She turned to Bosaaso. 'You have a car – you don't mind giving us a lift, do you?'

Mataan said, 'There's no point.'

'Why not?' Nasiiba challenged her twin.

'We can only take him after we've registered his existence with the police authorities,' Bosaaso explained.

'That's typical men's logic,' said Nasiiba, 'ridiculous!'

'It's in the nature of bureaucracy to be self-propagating.' Bosaaso continued, 'first the Nameless One must exist. To exist he requires papers. To acquire these he must have names. To have these he must have parents, to whose identities he may be traced. Only then will the bureaucracy of a hospital deal with him.'

'We must do something,' Nasiiba said, and appealed to her mother: 'Please make someone do something.'

'Off you go then, you men,' Duniya said to Mataan and Bosaaso.

Mataan and Bosaaso left. When Duniya looked up she realized that Nasiiba was preparing to leave. Did she not want to be alone with her mother for fear of being pressed to tell all she knew about the foundling? Duniya asked, 'Where are you going, Naasi?'

'I won't be long.'

She nearly asked her daughter to pass on her best regards to the baby's mother and assure her that he would be taken very good care of. But she didn't speak; her stare was fixed on a dragon-fly that had come into the room. And Nasiiba left.

The dragon-fly flew out of the window by which it had entered, but not before paying its respects to the foundling, above whom it hovered for a few moments and whose forehead it touched with its feet – in a gesture of blessing him?

Nasiiba and the dragon-fly had not been gone a minute when the Nameless One began to cry so heartily Duniya wondered if he were missing her daughter's odour or the fly's presence. The foundling cried as if possessed, dominating Duniya's consciousness as no other baby had ever done before, not even one of her own. He threw into his performance all that he was capable of, coughing, sneezing, burping and wetting himself into the bargain. For the first time in her life, Duniya did not want to be alone with a baby. She wished someone else were present to lend a hand, to share her agony, to bear testimony to what was happening.

Her prayer was answered. A woman was shouting, *'Hoodi-hoodi'*. Duniya kept repeating the customary welcome, *'Hodeen,'* but no voice was loud enough to drown the foundling's passionate fury. An elderly woman, stooped with advanced years, entered. Duniya was pleased to see her. She remembered the woman as a neighbour, but not her name.

The old woman said, 'So here you are, Little One,' touching the baby's tear-wet cheeks and smiling. 'Everyone in the neighbourhood is talking about you and how generous Duniya is, considering the times we are in and all, and you cry when you have no reason to.'

The foundling fell silent, listening to the old woman's teasing remarks as though he understood every word. Something was becoming obvious to Duniya: the Nameless One missed human voices, not bodily contact. Was it possible that there had been the uninterrupted hum of human talk from the instant he was born? Duniya did not recall Nasiiba mentioning him crying when the curious old women talked to one another; certainly, he had not cried when there were four adults in this room debating what to do about him.

'He is all right,' the old woman said, 'isn't he?'

'Yes. He is.'

'You are very generous,' she told Duniya, 'God bless you.'

Duniya felt awkward and self-conscious. It was then that she noticed that the old woman had a long hair on her upper lip, a singular hair looking out of a mole, dark as the most fertile of earths. Duniya couldn't help focusing on the hair, active as an insect's antennae, as the old woman spoke, 'My grand-daughter goes to the same school as your twin-daughter, so that is how I know you. Maybe you know my grand-daughter, the one with the non-Somali name – Marilyn. You won't believe it, but she was named for me, and my own is Maryam. She tells me that Marilyn is the name of a famous actress who's now dead. You know the young these days, bringing mysteries and foreign ways into our lives.'

'Yes, I know Marilyn,' said Duniya.

The old woman sat on the chair Duniya indicated. 'I have come to offer our house's blessing. I have come ahead of the others to tell you not to hesitate to ask if you need someone to look after the baby when you go to work and your children to school,' said the old woman.

'It's very kind of you to make such a welcome offer, which I am glad to accept.' And Duniya saw the old woman eyeing the baby with understandable anxiety.

'We have lots of help,' said the woman. 'There are a number of young girls in our house; we can always raise a couple more hands if necessary. So please do not hesitate to come when you need somebody to relieve you.'

Duniya assured her, 'I won't hesitate. Thank you.'

Then the old woman stretched out her hand to touch the baby. On the back of her wrist there was a ganglion, prominent as a hump. 'You have not gone to work today, have you, for instance?'

'My not going to work had nothing to do with the baby,' said

Duniya.

'I mean, you may not be able to go to work tomorrow?'

The old woman was anticipating quick decisions, things Duniya had not given thought to before. This was because a lot had not been thought out, and no one knew what would happen, least of all Duniya.

'Your daughter knows where we live, not very far from here,' the woman was saying to Duniya, 'remember, my grand-daughter's name is Marilyn,' and she shook her head sadly. 'Mind you, it is not that I begrudge this American actress anything, but I always wished my grand-daughter to remember that she was named for me, and not after some American nude embellishing frustrated men's fantasies and rooms; besides, I will not live for ever. But there you are.'

Unceremoniously, she got up to leave, taking each step as though it were an ordeal. She stopped in the doorway to say, 'Remember not to hesitate. We can help provide a baby-sitter.'

'Yes, I'll remember the name Marilyn,' Duniya promised.

A man was saying *Hoodi-hoodi* and another was talking non-stop, trying to make a point. Bosaaso was announcing that he and Mataan were back, and the young man was eager to impress the older one. When the old woman walked past them, on her way out, in deference to her age they stepped out of her way and fell silent.

Then Bosaaso said anxiously, 'The inspector, who sends his best wishes, says no one has reported a missing baby, nor has anyone else reported seeing one near a rubbish-bin. He says he is grateful to be informed and glad to know the foundling is in your capable hands, and he trusts that his presence won't create inconvenience.'

Duniya nodded her head silently.

'But bureaucracy being what bureaucracy is,' Bosaaso continued, 'the inspector suggested you and I register as co-guardians, since it was I who reported the case in person and signed the statement.'

'You and I as co-guardians of the foundling?' Duniya said, asking herself what, in the future, this would mean. She also wondered whether or not he had taken her for granted.

'The inspector wondered if Bosaaso was willing to put down his name as co-responsible – that's the word he used – just to be on the safe side,' Mataan said, 'and that's what we did, put your names down as co-responsibles for the foundling.'

There was something she did not like about the whole thing, but she was not sure what. Could it be that an unmarried woman, in her mid-thirties, with school-going teenagers would not be able to look after another baby, a foundling at that? Could it be that the inspector who knew her thought putting down Bosaaso's name as co-responsible would look good on paper?

'The inspector confessed,' Bosaaso said, 'that he had no idea about the legal status of such foundlings and those who happen to find them, since all this is a recent phenomenon, as he put it, part of this permissive society's reward to itself.'

Mataan added: 'I quoted to the inspector the Somali proverb: whoever finds an unclaimed item, let that person appropriate it.'

'The inspector took us to task, asking lots of questions we had no way of answering,' explained Bosaaso. 'Frankly it didn't help matters when Mataan said Nasiiba knew a lot more than she'd told.'

'What made you make such a stupid remark?' Duniya said to Mataan.

'I'm sorry, Mother,' said Mataan, 'but the truth is Nasiiba knows a lot more than she has told us, and she must be made to tell it.'

'Why?'

'For the good of everybody concerned.'

Duniya placed the sleeping baby gently back in his cot, turned on Mataan, 'Do I ever ask you to tell me all you know about . . . everything and everybody? Aren't there areas of your life that remain your private affair? Do I ever ask you how you spend your time or who your friends are, Mataan?'

'No,' he agreed, 'but this is different.'

'Suppose she says she won't tell us anything. What am I to do? Beat her up? Throw the foundling back into the rubbish-bin? I won't press Nasiiba to tell me anything she doesn't want me to know,' said Duniya. That dealt with, she said to Bosaaso, 'How did the two of you manage to register the foundling?'

'I made a statement, which I signed,' said Bosaaso. 'Because you weren't with us, Mataan countersigned it. We gave as much detail as we had. The inspector opened a file labelled ABANDONED BABY CARE OF DUNIYA. He told us he would release word to the press, especially Radio Mogadiscio. We have to report back to him once we have taken the baby to the hospital for a thorough medical examination, at our own expense, which I didn't object to. The idea is to allow time for the foundling's parent or parents to have a change of heart; and because a paediatrician might find reasons why the parents abandoned him in the first place. In other words, is the baby well or ill?'

'And then what?' Duniya asked.

'A board will decide whether to entrust us with responsibility for raising the foundling, since we are in effect co-responsibles.'

'You and I?' Duniya said, feeling amused, humoured.

'And then following an appearance before a board, it will be decided if we are fit to be his parents.'

'On the condition that we are married?' Duniya asked.

'Maybe.'

'Enough of that,' Duniya said.

They fell silent and no one spoke for quite a time. Then the baby's lungs exploded with a most furious cry, surpassing in tension the one he emitted earlier when left alone with Duniya. As everyone began to fuss over him, their voices silenced him, comforted him.

To help quiet the foundling, Mataan told an Arab folktale:

> One day Juxaa, the wise fool, invited a number of friends for a meal but discovered that he didn't own a large enough cauldron to cook in. He borrowed one from a neighbour, promising he would return it.
>
> The following afternoon Juxaa returned the huge pot he had been lent, but he put a smaller cauldron inside it. The neighbour reminded him that he had loaned him only the big one. Maybe the small pot had been borrowed from another neighbour?
>
> 'Your large cauldron, come to think of it, gave birth to a small one overnight,' said Juxaa. 'I thought it unfair to conceal this miraculous birth from you. Given the situation,' Juxaa assured him, 'both the big and the small pot are yours, and you may keep them.'
>
> The neighbour was highly impressed and described Juxaa as a very trustworthy gentleman of rare breed. The two men parted, each praising the other and Allah as well.
>
> A month or so later Juxaa borrowed the great cauldron from the same neighbour for a similar purpose, to give a feast. When

Juxaa didn't return the huge pot on the promised day, nor even a week after that, the neighbour went in person to Juxaa's house, asking to be given back his property.

Juxaa hung his head, saying, 'I'm sorry I forgot to come and commiserate with you, for your huge pot died and we buried it.'

'Died?' asked the neighbour in utter disbelief.

'That's right. It died and we buried it.'

The neighbour burst into a wicked laugh. 'Now whoever heard of a brass cauldron dying and being buried?'

'Come to think of it,' retorted Juxaa, 'neither had anyone else ever heard of a large brass pot giving birth to a smaller one.'

Defeated, the neighbour went away, bothering Juxaa no more.

Chapter Eight

In which Duniya's half brother turns up and the old animosity between them is revived. Duniya's younger daughter from her second marriage visits. But it is Bosaaso who comes first thing in the morning.

For Bosaaso the foundling served as an excellent pretext to call at Duniya's place whenever he pleased. The previous evening he had come as late as ten o'clock and, seeing the lights on and the windows and doors open, had presented himself, half-apologizing. Asked to join them, he had eaten with them an ill-prepared meal. No one stood on formalities. Nasiiba had had the youthful bravura to say to him, 'Would you like us to offer you a bed, given how often you are here?' He took the statement in the light-hearted spirit in which it had been made, replying humorously that it would be his honour to accept such generosity, especially from Nasiiba. The elderly woman was there, a welcome participant in the fun and games, and said to him, 'But of course she is teasing you.'

The gathering turned into a party, with more people arriving later than Bosaaso and not leaving until after midnight. He was enchanted to make the acquaintance of Marilyn, who bore a definite likeness to her namesake. She, Mataan and Nasiiba took turns preparing and serving kettles of tea, while other neighbours who had come to see the foundling and visit Duniya alternated between despair and optimism, winning or losing their card game. Old Maryam made herself useful by holding the baby or changing his nappy when his stomach ran a mile of diarrhoeal anxiety, as it had done rather frequently, to everyone's alarm. Duniya was asked her trained opinion as to whether they need worry; she suggested they wait a day.

A group of people consisting primarily of curious neighbours sat in open-air congregation outside their badly ventilated houses, chatting among themselves while watching Duniya's visitors' comings and goings with keen interest. Some of them commented on the harmonious fellowship between Duniya's twins and Bosaaso, and between Duniya herself and Bosaaso.

At about a quarter past midnight Bosaaso had left in his car, returning less than half an hour later with something in a carrier-bag. The onlookers could not tell from where they were if he brought medicine for the baby or food for the adults. But those inside would report that more tea was drunk, more losing or winning hands of cards dealt. In the laughter one might have heard as well as happiness perhaps a touch of tension too. Those present in the foundling's room might even have caught the quiet looks Duniya and Bosaaso exchanged.

Now he said, shielding his eyes from the sun, 'Good morning, Duniya.'

She seemed pleased to see him though, from her red eyes, he guessed she had hardly slept. The house was so quiet, Nasiiba must have gone out already, and Mataan, whose door was shut, must be asleep. A young girl whom Bosaaso had not seen before was washing nappies and towels. Was this the help Marilyn's grandmother had promised, the loan of a maid, as a stop-gap measure?

'Did you manage to close your eyes at all?' he asked.

'Not long enough to dream,' she said.

His eardrums throbbed with the excitement of his heartbeat. 'I wish I could relieve you.' A thoughtful pause. 'Why don't I?'

'Did you get home all right?' she asked.

'I don't know how, but I did. The car took me home,' he said.

They fell silent, looked at each other, smiled, looked away. Something was making them feel ill at ease. It was apparent in the way they stared, then avoided meeting one another's gaze.

He said, 'Before I forget. What are you doing tonight?'

Her eyes were unfocused, her grasp of time vague. She found herself staring at his long-fingered hands, wanting to touch them. She said, 'I'm *doing* him,' meaning the foundling. 'Why? Do you want me to take you to the cinema?'

The radio had been on since before his arrival, and he stared at it now, not listening to its jabber, but as if being reminded of an incident from his past. Duniya explained why she had the radio on: the foundling seemed to have a perverse need to hear uninterrupted, continuous noise; otherwise he burst into a worrisome cry.

'When I got home after two,' Bosaaso said, "I found a note from Mire inviting me to dinner. In a postscript, he wondered if you might like to honour him with your presence – in plain language, if you would like to join us.'

'Why in a PS?' she asked, smiling.

'I suppose he's not sure about our relationship or if you would accept his invitation. Besides you might think him presumptuous to suggest I bring you along, just like that.'

'Why is that?' she said.

'Maybe if he'd extended a formal invitation to you and you turned it down, he would feel hurt. But if, despite being invited in a PS, which is an afterthought, you still come, then he will feel honoured. I don't know.'

'What if I don't go?'

'It will be boring, just him and me.'

'What would you like me to do?'

'It would please me if you came.'

'Then I will.'

They both moved forward as though to embrace, but did not. They felt uncomfortable being alone with each other and wished someone else were with them. Maybe if somebody else joined them, the nervous anxiety would be minimized and the tension generated by their being alone would then assume a certain nobility, bestowed with its own beauty.

Bosaaso appeared eager to leave, and she said, 'Please don't.'

She called to Mataan, who emerged from his room ill-clad in a sarong with a towel draped round his neck and a book in hand. He disappeared on seeing Bosaaso, to reappear shortly thereafter, decently trousered and wearing a UNICEF T-shirt a few sizes too large for him. What would Bosaaso like to have?

'Tea, please. And, Mataan,' Bosaaso said, more at ease now the young man had come on the scene, 'I brought some sugar. It's in a milk-powder tin, on the front passenger seat of my car.' He proffered his car keys, adding, 'Could you fetch it?'

Taking no notice of the keys, nor the offer of sugar, an item not easily available in the country, Mataan said, 'We have sugar, don't we, Mother?'

'I believe we do,' she said.

Mataan's eyes were on her, solicitous. He didn't wish to offend anyone, not least his mother, remembering previous occasions when he had brought into the house gifts of which she disapproved.

She said, 'Could you find a cake of soap for the young help so she can wash her own robe? You know where we keep laundry-soap, in the top cupboard of your room; and on the shelf directly below that you'll find sugar, if there's none in the kitchen.'

'Yes, Mother,' Mataan replied, and turned to leave.

Bosaaso displayed slight disappointment at his gifts being rejected. He was at once anxious and relaxed, both happy and unhappy. 'Mataan?' he called.

'Yes?'

'I'll come and give you a hand.' He didn't want to be alone with Duniya. At least for the time being, he preferred her son's company to hers.

'It's not necessary,' Mataan said.

'I'll come all the same.' And the two men walked away side by side, towards the kitchen, a small cubicle, resembling an out-house, and next to it, a shower-place whose walls, Bosaaso noticed, had water-stains, dark as silver.

Duniya thought that marriage was a place she had been to twice already, but love was a palace she hadn't had the opportunity to set foot in before now. If what she and Bosaaso were doing was the beginning of a long courtship that might eventually lead to such a many-roomed mansion of love, so be it. So far she had only seen glimpses of it, in a rear-view mirror, in the eyes of a driver who wasn't a taxi-driver. Prior to that she had seen signs of it, in a dream, fuzzy in shape as a butterfly in zig-zag motion. Granted, she had since then feasted on moments full of rejoicing, in glances furtively delivered and withheld from public recognition. There was no rush, she said to herself. They had all the time in the world to explore the depths of their feelings for one another.

The foundling began to stir in his cot. Because of the fluctuating voltage of the city's electricity, the volume of the radio had gone very low, to the point of almost fading completely. As the power stabilized, so did the volume of the radio transmission, and the baby went back to sleep.

Duniya was telling herself: People will say wicked things about my motives, probably accuse me of being after the man's wealth. But what do they know about the motives of a woman like me? Let them bad-mouth her; she didn't care what people said. One would have to wait; one couldn't predict where the tale would lead. When she had accepted to honour her half-deaf mother's request to marry Zubair, she had said it was an aberration. If that was a lapse, and Taariq only a stop-gap, could Bosaaso be the conflux of their river of souls, flowing into one another, together, for ever and ever?

Bosaaso came in. 'Here we are,' he said, placing on a low table a tray on which were three cups, each filled to the brim with tea. Mattan arrived with slices of home-made cake, which Nasiiba had baked.

The three of them were sitting in the courtyard, sipping tea and nibbling cake, when Nasiiba joined them. As usual the young woman was full of stories and the excitement her tales generated, full of rumours. While telling snippets of some and narrating fragments of others, Nasiiba helped herself now to Duniya's tea, now to untouched cakes, and now Mataan's glass of water, like a pollinating butterfly going from one flower to another.

'Oh, what rumours!' she exclaimed.

Just before noon, a man angered by such a rumour came to call. He had come directly he was given news about the foundling. He was Shiriye, Duniya's half-brother, her senior by twelve years. His ugly voice announced his arrival.

Entering, he shouted Duniya's name angrily, not a greeting. Fat-bellied, he met their hostile stare with indifference. He stared back longest at Bosaaso, whose face he couldn't place, a man who, as far as Shiriye was concerned, was not-family.

Soon he too felt uncomfortable as he inhaled the discomfort in the air and as his gaze met with inimical stares. His Adam's apple moved fast up and down as if he were choking on his own saliva, and he wiped sweat from his forehead with the intensity of someone concealing a thought best unspoken. Bosaaso, feeling very uneasy, got to his feet to shake the man's proffered hand. Mataan stood up, not only to surrender his seat to his uncle, but also to receive a gentle pat on his shoulder, while Nasiiba, like Duniya, remained seated and watched the unfolding drama with amused detachment. Before seating himself, Shiriye said to Bosaaso, 'I have no memory of ever meeting you and doubt if anyone will bother to introduce us. My name is Shiriye.'

'People call me Bosaaso,' he said, heels together in military fashion, as if it was expected of him when saluting a senior army officer.

Shiriye said, 'I am Duniya's half-brother, a vocation I would not choose for myself, I assure you.' He fell silent but stayed as erect as he could, considering the tension surrounding him.

Silent, but never standing still, because Shiriye's body was incapable of being still. He was like a huge animal whose tail was swishingly busy chasing away flies; or the wide nostril of a hippopotamus twitching of its own accord; or the jaws of a cow munching last night's cud; or a German shepherd dog airing its oversized tongue. Duniya had these beastly thoughts about her half-brother who was not a handsome man, if the truth was to be told.

He was short, fat and almost totally bald. His belly spilled over his tucked-in shirt and tight army belt like the triple chin of an overweight man with blood-pressure trouble, and he wore a cravat. He breathed like a heavy snorer. He had short hands and stubby fingers, one of which was busy picking his nose and pulling at hairs in his nostrils. 'What is all this I hear, Duniya?' he said, taking a step towards her as though he might strike her. Trained to cover his back, like a guilty man expecting to be stabbed from behind, he relaxed his body only when Nasiiba got up and stood out of his way, so he might sit with no one's chair behind his.

'Now what is this you have heard?' Duniya said.

'I've heard about a baby. Where is it?' But he appeared not in the least interested in the baby's whereabouts, 'A foundling, sex male, that is what I have heard.'

'I thought you liked baby boys,' she replied.

'Only if they are mine or if they are genuinely my sister's,' he said, and burst into laughter, as though this were funny. He fell quiet, embarrassed that no one joined his laugh. Then he spoke slowly, intending to hurt Duniya. He said, 'I have heard it said that you have been entrusted with the destiny of a bastard.'

'A what?'

'The destiny of a bastard has been entrusted to you,' he said, deliberately.

Nasiiba and Mataan grinned conspiratorially, like clowns at a street-theatre performance, and waited for their mother's reaction, hoping she would somehow wrong-foot Shiriye and win this round. Bosaaso, however, decided that Duniya and Shiriye were staring like two people who had hurt each other many times before and were unwilling to forget or forgive the hatred this had engendered. And he thought of other quarrels involving his late wife Yussur and her mother. He would not have believed it possible to communicate so much hate in a single, concentrated look as Duniya was then giving Shiriye.

Shiriye was saying, 'Bringing up a bastard is sin, the wages of which are the fires of hell and Allah's anger.'

'How do you know the baby is a bastard?'

'Isn't he?'

'I said, how do you know he is?'

'We don't know his parents, do we?'

'Could he not be an orphan, both parents dead?'

'A bastard is a bastard is a bastard. What difference does it make if one parent is known or neither? Where did you find him anyway? In a rubbish-bin?'

Not wanting to get angry, she said, 'Nasiiba found him.'

'She is trouble, this Nasiiba of yours. She finds nothing but trouble, is involved in nothing but trouble.' His glower met her grinning eyes. They had nothing but hate for each other, Nasiiba and Shiriye, who appeared in her nightmares to whip her for disobedience. 'Look at you,' he now said to his niece. 'Your twin-brother has never brought any dishonour into your household.'

Nasiiba said nothing. But Duniya contradicted him, 'Don't you remember predicting Mataan would be an alcoholic before he was ten?'

'I made a big thing out of a small incident,' he said.

'Mataan is no alcoholic, as you can see,' she insisted.

'How do you know?'

Duniya said, 'We do things openly in this household, not behind each other's backs.' They stared daggers at each other. '*I* don't collect bride-wealth behind a younger half-sister's back, nor do *I* write letters weighed down with falsehoods describing Duniya as a whore, and Mataan as an alcoholic before reaching his teens.'

Shiriye got up, angry. Bosaaso looked away. The twins stood to one side, whispering in a corner. It was obvious that Duniya had not forgiven her half-brother who, she once said, had never made her a single gesture of kindness, not one; with whom she had never shared a single instant of joy, not a second of fellowship. She now said to him, 'Sit down. Where are you going? Haven't you come to visit your sister Duniya? Make yourself at home.'

'How can I?' he said, shaking his head ceaselessly.

'We once agreed, you and I,' said Duniya, 'that buried bones must not be dug up. But you never stop, like a hungry dog digging by feel and smell. And when I put on display the ugly skeletons you've dug up, you rise and are ready to depart.' She paused, and was sarcastic again, 'Now what in your elder half-brother's wisdom had you in mind to do for me when you decided to pay me a visit?'

Shiriye shifted in his seat, ill at ease. Bosaaso, like an asthmatic leaving a room a smoker has entered, got up. Duniya motioned to him to sit and he did so obligingly.

'I've come intending to bring only goodwill,' said Shiriye, 'and to inquire if I may be of any assistance. I have not come to unbury bones whitened by death. Nor do I like being compared to a dog.'

'Tell me specifically what you've come to offer,' said Duniya.

'I have arrived to proffer the advice of an elder brother,' he said. 'We won't get into semantic questions about whether the foundling is a bastard or an orphan. My question all along has been: how will you manage to feed yet another mouth?'

'God gives to whom he pleases,' Duniya said.

Bosaaso averted his eyes, letting them dwell on an eagle above.

Shiriye asked, 'Does Abshir know what use you're making of his highly valued monthly gifts in hard currency?'

'What do you think our brother will do if he's told I'm running a mini-orphanage?' said Duniya harshly. 'Do you think he would disapprove and so discontinue his remittances?'

'If I were Abshir, I would discontinue.'

'Abshir is my full-brother,' said Duniya, 'my mother's son.'

'Thank your fortunate stars I am not Abshir,' said Shiriye.

'I do, I do,' said Duniya.

They both remembered their respective mothers' quarrel in which Duniya, then only a foetus, was hurt as the two women hit each other with pestles. Duniya also recalled accusing Shiriye of writing a letter to Abshir in which he described her as a street-walker. She claimed she had been sent a photocopy of the missive. Added to this was the fact that Duniya had never forgiven her half-brother for his secret acceptance of bride-gifts from Zubair.

Shiriye said, 'Without digging up more skeletons decayed with years of hate and distrust, could you answer my question and tell me why you want to keep the foundling?'

'Would it make sense to a man like you, who has never known the meaning of a kind gesture, that *we* are keeping him out of pure kind-heartedness, motivated by goodwill, an act of mercy such as one might extend towards a blind man crossing a dangerous road?'

'Did I hear you say "we"?' Shiriye asked.

She said, 'Yes, you did.'

Bosaaso made his first and only contribution to the discussion, 'Duniya and I are co-responsibles for the foundling.'

'There's nothing to worry about, in that case,' Shiriye responded.

'How do you mean?' Duniya challenged him.

Shrugging his shoulders, Shiriye smiled first at Bosaaso, then turned to his half-sister, 'I needn't worry any more, since there is a man involved in helping you raise the foundling, and I trust that you won't encounter financial or social difficulties.'

Duniya's explosive rage was sudden. 'Are you telling me, Shiriye, that just because a man has registered his name together with mine as co-guardian of the foundling, everything is fine?'

'I'm saying there's no cause for worry with a man like Bosaaso sharing responsibility. A woman needs a man by her side, for people to take her seriously and for the world's doors to open so she may enter with her head raised and her person respected.'

Duniya rose to her feet, her voice angry, 'I want you to get out of my sight this instant.'

Shiriye made a friendly overture to Bosaaso, who decided to side with Duniya. Then Shiriye appealed to his nephew and niece, 'What on earth has got into her?'

She repeated, 'I want you to leave this house *now*, Shiriye.'

'But . . .!'

'Otherwise I will not be held responsible for what happens.'

Shiriye saw hate in the eyes of all whose reaction he sought. In Bosaaso's the sun's rays were mixed with scorn. A trained army man, Shiriye knew when to retreat. He did so quietly.

No one spoke for a long time, not even Nasiiba; nor did the

foundling wake or cry in the prolonged silence. However the young maid, finding all this incomprehensible, made a furtive departure, maybe to report to the outside world on what had happened.

Mataan then told the story of how the dik-dik, a small African antelope, took vengeance on the elephants: 'One day a dik-dik was minding its own business, passing along a narrow path in a dense forest, when an elephant in a hurry tried to overtake it. After several attempts, the irate elephant hit the dik-dik with his trunk, and it fell into a huge pile of elephant dung. On recovering from the shock, the dik-dik called a gathering of its clan, at which the dik-diks decided to become territorial and to shit always at the same spot in an attempt to make a huge mountain of their dung in which an elephant would get stuck, trunk and all. And it came to pass that one evening a cow-elephant did.'

A quarter of an hour after Mataan told his unappreciated story, everyone heard a primeval scream. Bosaaso saw Duniya raise her head in the attitude of a she-camel scenting the approach of one of her young. A series of welcoming groans came from the twins, followed by an increasing spiral of noise, culminating in a final yell, which brought forth a young girl who hurled herself into Duniya's open embrace. There was absolute joy in their getting together, animal rejoicing. Bosaaso thought again of a she-camel's reunion with one of her own after months of suckling a straw-filled dummy calf.

The twins joined in the hug, but Bosaaso did not feel excluded. He was happy to bear witness to so happy an encounter, on the heels of such hate between a half-brother and half-sister.

'Come, come,' Duniya patted her children on their backs. 'Let us introduce Hibo-Yarey to Bosaaso.'

Mataan and Nasiiba would not let go at first. And Yarey was saying, 'Where is *he*? Where is *he*?' No one was any the wiser, even when the twins let go, whom she meant: Bosaaso or the baby.

Duniya restrained Yarey by taking hold of her hand, dragging her towards Bosaaso, to whom she intended to introduce her. But the little girl wanted to be shown the baby, and was repeating her question, 'Where is the baby, Duniya?' (Not living with her, Yarey called her mother Duniya, not Mother or Mummy as the twins did.)

Now each twin took one of Yarey's hands and brought her to

the room where the baby lay in a cot, asleep. 'Will one of you please bring him out of the cot and give him to me to hold?' she said

Mataan lifted the Nameless One from the cot and handed him to Yarey, who received him as a fragile item. Her chest seemed about to explode with her excited breathing.

'Sit down if he's too heavy for you,' Duniya suggested.

The twins sat on either side of her, balancing the baby on the little girl's lap. The three of them chattered uncontrollably, Nasiiba summarizing the foundling's history so far.

'How come you're here without your overnight bag, Yarey?' Duniya asked.

'Because Uncle Qaasim didn't have petrol in his car, so he couldn't bring me. Someone else gave me a lift to a place not far from here, and I ran the rest of the way.'

'Who told you about the baby?' Nasiiba asked.

'I was running home, you see, when Marilyn stopped me to tell me about it. I ran faster to get here because I so was excited.' Despite having one deformed tooth and another that was lifeless, dark, dwarfish-looking, Yarey none the less had a sweet smile.

Duniya now took the opportunity to introduce her to Bosaaso, 'Yarey, this is Bosaaso.' And to him, 'This is Hibo-Yarey.'

'I guessed as much,' said Bosaaso.

Yarey's smile was as disarming as a gypsy's charm. 'Has the baby been given a name yet?' she asked Nasiiba.

'His name is Abshir, after Mummy's brother,' Nasiiba lied.

Mataan corrected his twin, 'No, Yarey. The baby has not yet been given a name.'

'But he must be given one,' insisted Yarey.

'We've been calling him the Nameless One,' said Mataan.

'Why don't we give him a proper name, his own?' Yarey asked.

'First we must know we can keep him,' interjected Duniya.

'But we found him,' Yarey rationalized. 'Nasiiba was the one who found him, so he's ours.'

'There are legal problems to solve before we can name him,' said Duniya. She was trying to drown out Nasiiba, who was telling Yarey about Bosaaso, saying that he lived in a house larger than Uncle Qaasim's, had a TV set, the most recent make of Japanese video recorder and an extremely varied collection of video cassettes; and that he would eventually return to the USA where he had lived for over twenty-five years. If he and Duniya married, which was likely, then they all would move to America.

Suddenly, Yarey said, 'I'll take the baby to Uncle Qaasim and Aunt Muraayo's house and leave him there for them to raise him. Is that all right, Duniya?'

'Why?' replied a surprised Duniya.

'Then I can come home, to live here.'

'But. . . !'

'If Uncle and Aunt have another child to replace *me*, then I won't feel so terrible leaving them, you see!'

'But you can come home whenever you like,' said Duniya.

Nasiiba whispered more secrets in Yarey's ear. Yarey looked from her mother to Bosaaso, and back to Nasiiba, who nodded encouragingly. For a second or so, Yarey remained quiet.

'What did Nasiiba whisper to you, Yarey?' Duniya asked.

'Nothing.'

Mataan moved away from his sisters, distancing himself from what was happening. Bosaaso, self-conscious, fell under Yarey's intense stare as she pondered what was going on between him and her mother. But Duniya appeared ecstatic, and the house had a festive air, because of a foundling who made them all new friends.

'Can I come home then, Duniya?'

'Of course.'

'Will *Uncle* Bosaaso let me watch his video?' said Yarey.

Duniya could not think of how to reply. She looked at him, then at Nasiiba, then focused on the horizon, too embarrassed to speak.

'Yes, of course,' Bosaaso said.

But Yarey sensed she had upset Duniya. She motioned to Nasiiba to take the foundling. She then went to where her mother was sitting and knelt by her, kissing her hand. 'I am sorry, Duniya. I shan't listen to Nasiiba any more, I promise.'

Bosaaso rose to leave. 'We're expected at Dr Mire's at seven-thirty. I'll come for you,' he said.

'Stay well,' Duniya replied.

'You too,' he said.

MOGADISCIO (SONNA, 30 July)

The average Somali household cuts down (and uses fully or partially) as many as 150 trees or shrubs annually, according to a study published last week by the Ministry of Agriculture and Livestock. A vast number of shrubs or trees are uprooted for one purpose or another and a great many of these are burnt as fuel or used as construction material for fencing or walling compounds.

This loss of woodland has in part caused a decrease in rainfall, in the availability of water *per se*, and in the presence of wildlife over large areas of the Republic. The report, compiled by Somali experts and the first of its kind, adds that overstocking of camel and cattle herds strip more and more tracts of land of trees, shrubs and grasses, thus contributing to drought.

The report commends the Somali government, aid agencies and friendly nations that have attempted to minimize the country's disaster, which can be understood in the light of similar environmental crises occurring in Africa and throughout the Third World.

Chapter Nine

In which Duniya, in a dress borrowed at Nasiiba's insistence, goes with Bosaaso to Mire's home for dinner.

While taking his siesta, Bosaaso saw a handsome-feathered, heavy-footed bird, a cross between a hawk and an eagle, for which he had no name. The bird remained quiet and contemplative, perched on a telegraph pole at the edge of a park where he and his late wife Yussur were picnicking with their son in his cot, a portable radio playing nearby.

At some point the bird took off and was gone from sight for a good while. When next they were aware of its presence, it was descending threateningly from a great height, coming closer as though it meant to do the baby harm. Both parents were relieved to see the bird fly away, clutching in its beak not their child but a flower.

Bosaaso woke up, disturbed. Immediately he recalled that he and Duniya had a dinner engagement with Mire. He showered in haste, drove as fast as was safe, and was parked in front of Duniya's place on time. He rushed into the Women's Room breathless with worry and relaxed only after making sure that the foundling was unharmed.

On their way to Mire's, they both sat like tailor's dummies – Bosaaso because he had decided not to talk about his siesta nightmare, and Duniya because the dress which she had put on at Nasiiba's insistence was beginning to feel tight round the waist, making her breathing difficult. Both smiled anti-septically, saying nothing for a long while.

Bosaaso, uneasy at the silence, said, 'I envy Mire; living alone, he has a self-preserving quality about him. I guess I envy you too, mainly because, like my mother, you are yourself an activity. That is to say *you* happen, and the rest of the world happens.'

It occurred to Duniya how little she knew Dr Mire, and although she did not say so in as many words, she said circumspectly, 'A balloon with air in it flies where there is wind.'

Bosaaso did not understand her meaning, but said, 'If you get to know him better, you'll appreciate how much he enjoys the company of people who interest him. You'll be surprised to know that he speaks a great deal more than me, for instance.'

'Does he ever talk about himself?'

'He does.'

'But you don't?'

He smiled, and said, 'Don't I?'

'Hardly,' she said.

'Maybe there is little to speak of.'

'Are you hunting for praise-songs like the ones your mother used to improvise as lullabies when you wouldn't sleep?'

It struck her how tense they both were, and how aggressive she was being. The need for self-restraint was becoming too much to bear. It was easier to discuss Dr Mire than their own feelings for each other. Neither had spoken a single loving word aside from the one occasion when Bosaaso had said that he had been drawn to her. It wasn't that there was little closeness between them. On the contrary, there was a great deal of physical attraction. But both were cautious, perhaps feeling they couldn't afford to fail each other in their expectations.

'You've never been to Mire's place, have you?' he asked.

'No.'

Silence. The headlights parted the darkness of the night as a comb does the hair of a bushy head.

'But you get along fine, the two of you?' he asked.

'I've never been in touch with him socially, so I don't really know the man. As a matter of fact, this is the first time he and I are meeting outside the hospital grounds. He often reminds me that he's a friend of Abshir, but then so are you.'

Bosaaso didn't know what to make of the throw-away last phrase. Tension welled up inside him, his lungs billowing in action. The words surged out of his mouth, 'What do people say about Mire?'

'They speak of his reserve, his reticence, and the nurses can't help comparing him to the other foreign doctors who work with us at the hospital. Personally I have no difficulty imagining what he's like deep inside, but I draw a blank when I try to think of him not working. My elder brother once described him in a letter to me as "the Prussian" – in a positive sense, mind you.'

'It is interesting how the nurses perceive him,' commented Bosaaso.

'If they're holding a loud conversation in the hospital corridor they hush on seeing Mire approach,' Duniya said. 'He himself has told me that his nephews and nieces, playing noisily in their parents' compound, fall quiet the instant they spot him.'

'So the nurses say unkind things about him?'

'Not terrible things, no.'

Bosaaso remembered how much his late wife's mother had hated Mire. Yet Mire behaved as though none of this touched him. He was obviously at peace with himself and nothing else mattered.

Duniya volunteered, 'People here are informal, no wonder he strikes some who come into contact with him as anti-social. Strange, but that isn't how I perceive him.'

'No?'

Duniya looked at her unsteady hand which had knocked things over the very morning Bosaaso had come into her life disguised as a butterfly in a dream. She remembered how kind he had been, how touched she was by what he said. She couldn't recall his precise words, only his kind gesture, a trace of his fondness for her.

'I perceive him as a timid man, shy like a child among adults he doesn't know how to deal with. I've watched him in situations where he's withdrawn into himself, showing nothing but his exterior self, like a turtle under attack.'

'That's nice,' said Bosaaso, smiling and thinking aloud. 'A moving description, very poetic.'

'In a letter, my brother Abshir reported to me how Mire himself had described his reticences being as prominent as the dimpled deformity of a mirror.' Why did Abshir's name keep coming to her? Was it because of the ugly fight with her half-brother Shiriye?

Bosaaso was now slowing down. Had they already arrived? Duniya thought how much she would have loved the two of them to talk about personal matters that were of great concern to them. For instance, what about the baby? The subject of the foundling was bound to come up with Mire over dinner. She wished she had asked Bosaaso what his views were; wished she had told him hers. But he was already parked in a plot of undeveloped land alongside other vehicles, among them Mire's Mini, which squatted midget-like next to the bigger cars.

Mire's smile as he greeted them, Duniya thought, was the gesture of a man whom you happen to encounter at the very instant he has transferred a valuable treasure from one hiding place to another: secretive. The smile lingered, finally thinning to the size of Mire's evenly trimmed toothbrush moustache. He stood a couple of inches shorter than Bosaaso, with a heftier physique than his childhood chum and a sonorous voice that was a delight to listen to. He now stepped aside, his posture erect, head showily bowed, his hand motioning them in saying, 'Welcome.'

Entering, she thought she saw an inelegant expression on Mire's face, of slight hesitation, of a man vacillating between two extreme moods, one formal, the other less rigid. Duniya grinned inwardly, remembering another occasion when she had noticed such a sudden change of mood in him: the morning her hand ran amok, knocking over his pens, thermometers and pencils.

Bosaaso led them into the spacious living-room, which Duniya was delighted to note wasn't extravagant. It was sparingly furnished, the decor simple, every item locally made. No loud colours, nothing the *nouveaux riches* associate with being chic, modern; no TV, no video machine, none of the sophisticated gadgets in which the computer age abounds, save a cassette-deck and a short-wave radio, the latter with its antenna up. Wallpaper and curtains matched harmoniously. Was Bosaaso's living-room in his two-storey palace as plain as this? Or was it distastefully exhibitionist? Duniya was delighted she had come to Dr Mire's first.

The two friends stayed half a pace behind her, like professional waiters seating a VIP client. Reaching the sitting section of the room, Dr Mire encouraged Duniya to take the larger chair.

'Please,' he urged, guiding her gently towards the prominent armchair upholstered in green.

As yet neither of the men sat down. 'To start with, what will you have, Duniya?' Mire was asking.

'Something non-alcoholic, if I may,' she replied.

Bosaaso meanwhile kept the civil distance of a head waiter, standing with hands behind his back, his whole body at the ready to be of help.

In response to their host's list of what he could offer, Duniya said, 'Orange pressé, please.'

'Certainly,' said Mire.

Suddenly there was too much movement. Mire left, walking backwards half the way, deferential. Bosaaso went to sit in the small armchair nearer Duniya. Mire halted just before entering the kitchen, did an about-turn and asked, 'What will you have, Bosaaso?'

'The same as Duniya, please.'

'Keep it simple, keep it natural?' teased Mire.

Bosaaso nodded. But why wasn't Mire leaving? Anxious, Duniya crossed, recrossed and uncrossed her legs, conscious of the eyes that were *not* focused on her. She was uncomfortably aware of the moisture of her armpits and the tightness of the dress at the waist. And Mire was walking away, promising to return shortly.

Alone, Bosaaso shifted closer to say, 'Are you all right?'

She didn't want to think of the immediate cause of the distress: her dress. 'I'm fine, thank you,' she replied.

'Has either of us said something to upset you, Duniya?'

She wrenched her thoughts away from what had been distressing her. She said, 'What have you told him about us?'

'Nothing.'

'I don't believe you.'

'Not much really.'

'That's not telling me a lot,' she said, keeping her voice low.

'I haven't said much to him; only generalities.'

'What about the foundling?'

'I gave him the facts as I know them,' he responded.

'Such as what? What facts?'

'I've told him who discovered the foundling, where and how. Those sort of facts. And how we've registered him in both our names, as his co-responsibles. The bare facts, no embellishments.' He paused. 'Now what has upset you?'

'I hate it when men take me for granted, as a woman,' she said.

It was his turn to say, 'That doesn't tell me a lot.'

They fell silent and apart, because Mire made his well-timed entrance, clearing his throat. He approached, bearing the tray. He carefully placed a small square table-napkin before each person. Duniya thought his flat had something dry-cleaned about it. Hardly any dust anywhere. She couldn't work out how he isolated himself and his flat from Mogadiscio's sandstorms or the rust and weight of its humidity. She received her drink from him with both hands, saying, '*Mahadsanid*,' her head bowed in gratitude.

Mire served his friend, joking, 'I've never known Bosaaso to drink anything non-alcoholic. I hope you realize what you are doing to him, Duniya.'

She said, 'Special occasions impose certain restrictions on the will of those wishing to remember. Maybe that's why he is having this sort of a drink, don't you think?'

There was a light touch of annoyance in Mire's voice, in the attitude of an elder brother preparing to reprimand a younger one. 'You mean he's already told you?' he said to Duniya.

'Told me? What?'

She sensed both men staring at her with engaging attentiveness. What were they talking about? Were they saying that Bosaaso had reformed and given up drinking alcohol altogether, this being an oblique reference to Taariq's excessive use of this most poisonous substance?

Mire asked, 'He hasn't told you about Abshir?'

'My brother Abshir? What about him?' It couldn't be bad news, since their faces opened up with smiles. 'Tell me, I can't wait.'

'It's possible he may be coming shortly, to visit.'

She half-rose from the armchair, 'Visit me?'

'That's right.'

She felt tongue-tied, unsure how to react to the news. She would never forgive herself if she said something ridiculous, and nothing wise seemed to come to mind. She listened to the music with only half her brain, music that was consciously oriental, not Arabic. No, it had a whining tune, far eastern. She leaned forward and said eagerly, 'Has he written to you, Mire, that he will come shortly?' And in her heart she hoped that Abshir hadn't.

'He's vacationing in Greece and met a friend of mine whom I spoke with on the telephone today – it's my friend's birthday. It was she who told me that he said he was planning to visit you,' said Mire.

Suddenly they were toasting, her brother's name occurring in the brief wishes of *caafimaad*. Her hand unsteady, she dropped her drink and spilt some of it on her dress. She got up, in discomfort; she would have been grateful for the privacy of a bathroom, or some room with a door that she could bolt from inside. It had become difficult for her to breathe, this sudden excitement was much too much. She was hot behind her ears, her armpits wet like a peed-on mattress. Bosaaso showed her where the washroom was.

She didn't emerge until she heard, 'Dinner is served, Mada!'

Good breeding whispered in Duniya's ears for her not to confess openly that she did not have a name for the dish she was eating, anathema to devout Muslims who insist they identify every ingredient of the foods they touch or consume. Mire was sensitive enough to suspect that Duniya's traditional reserve might account for some of the unease on her face. However he didn't speak either to her or Bosaaso: he looked from one to the other, hoping, maybe, that his friend would assure Duniya that she wasn't eating pork.

Meanwhile Duniya was thinking about something that worried her: her knocking things over, spilling drinks, kicking her toes sore. The fact that this was becoming routine with her, almost boringly predictable, rankled in her mental picture of herself. Had she lost control of a certain brain nerve, causing imbalance both in mind and body? She did not like being associated with leaving falls, crashes and wreckages in her wake. Why, shapes were becoming vague in her vision. Walls at times retreated. Her hands would bend athletically at the wrist, strong like a javelin thrower's. She reminded herself that in Somali mythology the cosmos balances on the horns of a bull, a beast that is forever staring at a cow tied to a pole right in front of him. It is said the bull's body loses equilibrium whenever his love, the cow, turns its eyes elsewhere, and this physical shift is responsible for the earthquakes around the world. Was she, Duniya, subduing the universe by breaking things into bits?

'Do you know the name of the dish we're eating?' Bosaaso asked.

It took time for the words to reach her mind and make sense. She felt the weight of their stares and knew she had done something that displeased them. She hadn't touched her food. She decided to turn it to her advantage decided to draw perverse pleasure from showing her ignorance: this usually went down well with the generality of men who received with delight any confirmation that women did not know as much as them. But it might also help her regain her misplaced self-confidence which she would then show off, like wounds sustained in a battle. She said, 'What's it called, this dish?'

'Moussaka,' said Mire.

And immediately Bosaaso interjected, 'These, as you can see,' using his fork to demonstrate, 'are layers of minced meat, that is aubergine, topped with a layer or two of parmesan cheese.'

Duniya then said, abrasively rubbing her recovered self-confidence, 'Moussaka is such a beautiful name that I bet if the dish ever became popular in Somalia some mother would name her daughter Moussaka.' She might have been setting the future theme of a conversation on the subject of name-giving.

'Would you name your daughter Moussaka, Mire?' asked Bosaaso.

'*I* wouldn't,' responded Mire, 'but I am sure some women might.'

Bosaaso said to Mire, 'You recall the girl in our town who was called *Makiino* – the bastard form of the Italian *macchina*? I remember thinking how weird for a mother to name her daughter after such a contraption. But, in retrospect, I can see it made sense. For one thing, the machine did the job faster and more efficiently than any person. For another, it reduced the hours of labour, minimizing exhaustion. In addition, it made the woman forward-looking, since the notion introduced her to a larger universe where machines were scientifically and culturally an integral part of one's daily life.'

'There was this other girl, wasn't there?' Mire said. 'Her mother had named her *Aasbro*, do you remember? Another called her daughter *Omo* after the detergent powder, in recognition perhaps of the usefulness of such an item; or *Layloon*, a corruption of "nylon", maybe because she had very smooth skin.'

'We know a man, don't we, Mire,' Bosaaso said, 'who presented his bottom first at birth and was given the name *Daba-keen*, a descriptive phrase of the breech position in which he had been born?'

Duniya ate in silence, remembering her mother's reasons for naming her only son Abshir. He had been a blessing, she would say, in boastful recall of how well he had done at school and university. Now Abshir was planning to visit her, Abshir whom she hadn't seen for years, whom she had last called on during a brief trip to Rome.

Mire said to her, 'Do you have any idea why you were given your name? Let me tell you that I was named for my grandfather, and of course you know the story behind Bosaaso's nickname.'

Duniya hoped Mire could see in her eyes the pleasure that news of Abshir's arrival had given her. Self-conscious and half-choking on her emotions, she said, 'I was my mother's only daughter and the last-born, so I presume I meant the world to her.'

Bosaaso might have been a parent ladling out encouragement to a shy child. 'Which is what Duniya means: the world,' he said.

'The cosmos,' said Mire, with interpretative exactitude.

Then they talked at length of traders, Arab and European, wandering the African continent, propagating their faith, making gifts of their deities and beliefs (like present-day foreign aid), presents that the Africans accepted with little question.

Bosaaso asked of no one in particular, 'Can you think of a Somali concept comparable to the modern notion of cosmos, in Arabic "Dunya"? You see, there's the Arab contention that they gave us the notion of cosmos by offering us not only their Islamic belief but sharing with us their world-view on which we've constructed our subsequent understanding of the workings of the globe.'

'What was in it for the Arabs to *give* us their world-view, together of course with an Allah-created cosmos, which contradicted our traditional belief systems?' asked Duniya.

Bosaaso's face darkened as he tried to think of what to say.

'Duniya does have a point,' said Mire, 'although to my mind the essential difference between African traditional beliefs and the Judaeo-Christian and Islamic credo is bound up with mystic proportions of a centrally created cosmos. The starting-point is this: *who* or *what* do we worship? In the case of the Somali who deifies crows, the answer is clear: Somalis defer to death, crows being associated with the ending of life, a termination of this existence. What the Judaeo-Christian and Islamic systems offer is a forward-looking, reward-offering, life-after-death rationalization, a credo in which you are guaranteed paradiasical delights after death.'

'What does all this mean, in plain language?' Duniya asked.

'It means,' Mire said, 'that, on the surface of it at least, you invest your efforts in your daily activities of self-worship (in Judaeo-Christian as well as Islamic systems God is recreated in the image of man elevated to a higher plane, whereas in Somali thought, crows are unlike man's idea of himself), and are promised heavenly dividends worthy of your trust in a god who gives and takes away life.'

'God gives, man gives!' Bosaaso said, not sounding very serious.

And silence fell. It had become obvious to Mire that he was not making sense to Duniya, who appeared to have given up listening to his theorizations. It was time for the fruit salad.

When they had finished their dessert and the espresso coffee had been served, Duniya vanished into the bathroom for a while, in need of the quiet that comes of being alone in a room with a door to lock. She also thought the two friends would appreciate a few moments to themselves in which they could lapse into their masculine idiom. In fact she had the feeling that they were like two people forced to speak in a foreign language for the benefit of a third person. After almost a whole evening of it she decided to give them a little time in which to speak in their own tongue.

From the bathroom and without undue effort Duniya was able to hear their conversation, the first half of which was mainly about the foundling, that he had not as yet been given his innoculations or a name. Bosaaso answered Mire's questions with apparent reserve, mumbling some of his responses. At one point Mire asked, 'Tell me, why are you keeping him, the two of you, I mean?'

'Who said we are keeping him?' Bosaaso replied.

'Aren't you?' said a puzzled Mire.

'I have the impression,' explained Bosaaso, 'that he is keeping us, in the sense of cementing my and Duniya's friendship and strengthening it, day by day, minute by minute.'

'In what way?'

'The foundling has become the principal focus of our worries and pleasures, the central focus of our affections. We take care of him as though he were our own flesh and blood.'

'So what does that mean to you?' Mire asked.

'I can only speak for myself, because Duniya and I haven't discussed this aspect of our relationship.'

'What does he mean to you personally then?'

'Until our relationship is more solid,' said Bosaaso, 'and maybe even after that, the foundling will have been the symbol of our being together.'

'I'm not sure I'm with you,' Mire said.

'Look at it this way: he has been the central activity for her, me and for her children with whom I get on very well.'

'So you foresee a day soon when your relationship will take off so to speak, with no help from the foundling?' asked Mire cautiously.

'Especially now that Abshir is coming.'

'Why is that?'

Voice low, Bosaaso said, 'Can we talk about it another time?'

'I see what you mean,' said Mire.

They fell silent.

Joining them, Duniya was given a tour of the flat. She was taken to Mire's workroom, which felt quite like a hermit's, a place where ideas were developed and where minds grew. There was a chaos of books, piles and piles of them, heaped upon one another on tables, spilling off the edges of a bookcase. Whereas Bosaaso had acquired two vehicles, one to give to his cousin as a taxi, the other for his own use, and in addition to a two-storey house for himself, another house for his community of cousins – Mire had invested his wealth in the acquisition of knowledge.

The workroom had its own comforts. There was a huge reclining chair, a custom-built chaise-longue, with inscriptions in German (Bosaaso explained that it was a gift from Claudia, Mire's German woman-friend). There were lots of undusted corners in this room, and a number of half-drunk cups of coffee lying uncollected where they had been forgotten a day or so before. For Mire, Bosaaso said, the world outside his workroom had to be orderly, but not here. He couldn't impose order on the growth of ideas. Here he was a human being; here he was not embarrassed by his own emotions.

He was private here too. There was a life-size photograph of Claudia Christ, his German woman-friend, overseeing everything in the workroom, from the vantage point where the portrait hung, high enough and in a way Duniya felt the European woman was looking into the mind of whoever stood anywhere in the room. The woman had thin lips, short hair, a tiny nose, projecting chin and prominent jaws. She made Duniya feel as if one were visiting a shrine.

Bosaaso served as her guide. He showed her translations into Somali of great European classics, including Shakespeare, Goethe and Dante, of which Mire had done drafts, with notes and introductions, each of them dedicated to Claudia. Mire translated directly from the originals, languages with which he was familiar. One day he hoped to publish this work of a lifetime.

He also pointed out Claudia Christ's books, four of them, all in the original German and dedicated to Mire. Very noble of the woman to devote her life's work to a man who hadn't married her, not yet, thought Duniya.

The tour ended, she thanked Mire for a most pleasant evening and requested that she be taken home. As she left, she wondered how she was going to return Mire's invitation. She would have to find a way of having him come for a meal at her place when it wasn't crowded with noisy children. Her brother's arrival would serve as a good pretext. 'You must come for a meal when Abshir is here,' she said.

Eyes mischievous, Mire replied. 'I hope for more than a mere meal.'

Bosaaso and Duniya were silent all the way to her place, where they noticed coming and going. Duniya didn't encourage him to enter the house. They said their goodbyes outside. She got out of the car, but not before giving him a light kiss.

'See you tomorrow,' he said.

'Good night and thanks for everything,' she replied.

MOGADISCIO (SONNA, ANSA, 7 January)

An Italian government Aid Protocol was signed the day before yesterday at a reception held at Caruuba Hotel, Mogadiscio. The aid package has many applications to a number of development-related areas, ranging from the rehabilitation of rice-farming in Jowhar and environs, the extending of the capacity of beds of several general hospitals throughout the Republic, as well as the strengthening of relations between the two countries.

In this connection the Italian government has promised to increase the number of professors on secondment from Italian institutions of higher learning to the National University of Somalia. The Somali university is the only one outside Italy where all subjects are taught in Italian. As part of this programme, Italian scholars of Somali are helping their counterparts to complete an Italian-Somali dictionary and a linguistics project on which the team has been engaged, under the supervision of the University of Rome and of the Somali Language and Literature Academy.

The Protocol was signed by the Secretary of Foreign Affairs on behalf of Somalia and on behalf of Italy by its Charge d'Affaires.

Chapter Ten

In which Duniya and her three children play host to a number of visitors, including Muraayo. And as usual Bosaaso calls.

The morning was silver bright and a slight chill had blown into the room together with a dragon-fly which in fidgety movements up and down seemed to write a name in code. To read this, Duniya wiped away dewy humidity from her eyes, unsure of the result at first. The baby stirred on account of the cold wind in the Women's Room and Duniya got out of bed to cover him with one of her *guntiino*-robes. When this proved insufficient, she picked him up and held him in the warmth of her embrace, cooing until he ceased to howl. She put him back in his cot and, having closed the window, returned to her bed.

Then she saw in her mind's eye the dragon-fly's coded writing and was confident she read a name written in tattoo-blue, fringed with water clear as ice. It was the name of the young woman Duniya had seen at the Out-patient's Clinic on the morning Bosaaso had given her a lift in his butterfly-taxi.

She woke up, her mind cluttered with unrelated memories.

'You know, I'm serious when I say I won't be returning to Uncle Qaasim and Aunt Muraayo's home,' Yarey said.

Duniya hushed her nine-year-old daughter. The radio was on. They listened to the news for a while, but before long Yarey lost interest in her mother's preoccupation with happenings in the world outside, insisting that Duniya pay heed to her.

'Did you hear what I said?' Yarey asked raucously.

Duniya wouldn't be dissuaded from listening to an item about the Head of State receiving a combined North American and EC delegation visiting to discuss Somalia's foreign-aid requirements. Immediately afterwards came an item about a baby boy, a couple of days old, found near a rubbish-bin in Duniya's district. But no other details were given – only that the baby was abandoned, not even that it had been given a home and two co-responsibles, Duniya and Bosaaso.

'Will you hear me out now?' Yarey asked.

'Yes?'

'I want my things brought here, in Bosaaso's car.'

Duniya did not like being rushed. She preferred dealing with problems one at a time. Besides it was too early for her to know what Yarey might be talking about. She had too many other things on her mind, including preparing for Abshir's visit, plus all the other matters she must talk to Nasiiba about.

'Can it wait until later, Yarey darling?' she said.

'I want my things brought here. Today.' It was a command.

'Why?'

'Because I don't want to return to Uncle and Aunt's place.'

Duniya reminded her daughter that Uncle Qaasim and Aunt Muraayo had been chosen as compromise guardians since she, Duniya, and Taariq, Yarey's father, couldn't agree who should keep her. Naturally they did not want to go to court. Taariq at the time was weighed down with drink-related depressions, Duniya with financial difficulties, since she couldn't support three children on her own. As part of the understanding reached it was decided that Duniya stay on in the two-bedroom house where they now lived paying only a token rent, and Yarey would grow up in Taariq's elder brother's household, considering also that his wife Muraayo hadn't a child of her own. All this had been delicately negotiated (Duniya tried to make Yarey understand the complexities of the situation), and had taken several protracted sessions. That way, Taariq had easy access to his daughter, who spent weekends with Duniya.

'Let's give them the foundling, that'll solve everyone's problem,' Yarey said.

'What problem?'

'And then I can come home.'

Duniya clucked her tongue to register her dissent. 'Your returning home has nothing whatsoever to do with the foundling. That's altogether a different matter. And as I said before, you may come back and live with us any time you like. But I'll have to talk over the terms with your father, Uncle Qaasim and Aunt Muraayo.'

'But it's not fair.'

'What's not fair?'

'You see, if I come to live with you then Aunt Muraayo and Uncle Qaasim won't have a child to consider their own, whereas there'll be four of us children here, all yours,' Yarey reasoned.

'Your uncle has children from his previous marriages,' Duniya reminded her.

'But his current wife Aunt Muraayo won't have them in her house.'

Duniya did not comment.

'By the time the foundling is my age, he'd have accepted Aunt Muraayo as his mother. Have you thought about that?' said Yarey insistently.

'I suggest you stay with Aunt Muraayo who's accepted you as her own child,' Duniya said, her tone teasing, cajoling. But no sooner had she uttered it than she wished she had not.

'You mean you prefer him to me?' Yarey said.

'God forbid, no.'

'Why's this ugly foundling so important to you?' challenged Yarey.

'He has no other home, you have at least two. Be fair, Yarey.'

'Yesterday you had a nasty fight with Uncle Shiriye over him.' Yarey went on in a hostile tone, 'And now you say these cruel things to me, your own daughter. Why is he so important?'

In a moment's concentrated rush, it dawned on Duniya that there was a way to pacify Yarey. She would set the young girl a baited trap. She would make her feel important, confide in her.

'Are you big enough to keep a secret to yourself, Yarey?'

'Of course I am,' said Yarey, all ears.

'Can I trust you not to tell Nasiiba or Mataan or anyone else?'

'Sure!'

Duniya said, 'Uncle Abshir is coming shortly.'

Yarey couldn't contain her joy. 'When?'

Pleased that she could manipulate the mercurial moods of her youngest daughter, Duniya said, 'I'm not sure exactly when.'

'Have you had a telegram or letter from him?'

'A friend of Dr Mire's had breakfast with him yesterday,' Duniya volunteered. 'You've never met, Abshir and you, have you?'

'No, never.'

'You'll have to keep this a secret though.'

'I will,' promised Yarey.

Meanwhile Yarey had completely forgotten about the foundling or her plans that they be swapped. She was bubbling over with excitement.

'Do you think there's still time for you to write to him before he comes?' she wanted to know.

'Why?'

'Because I want him to bring me something from Italy.'

'I don't know about that,' Duniya wasn't encouraging.

'That Somali Airlines stewardess what's-her-name can take a letter to him. Let's find out when she's flying to Rome and we'll give her a letter or something, a message.'

Duniya's body stiffened at the reference to the stewardess.

'What's wrong?' Yarey inquired.

'What would you like Uncle Abshir to bring you from Italy?' Duniya said, frowning.

'I want a Walkman.'

Duniya smiled limpidly. 'We'll try to get a message to him.'

'And there's something else,' Yarey was too thrilled to be still.

Patience diminishing, Duniya asked, 'Something he can carry easily through customs?'

'A film called *ET*.'

'A film?'

'A video, then I can watch it on Bosaaso's machine.'

'We'll try to reach him somehow.'

'Promise?'

'And you promise not to talk about his coming to a living soul?'

Yarey nodded.

'If you don't keep your end of the deal, I won't keep mine,' said Duniya.

'I will,' said Yarey. 'I'm grown-up now.'

Nasiiba, who had just showered entered the room. When Yarey and her mother kept conspiratorially quiet, Nasiiba suspected they had been discussing her. Otherwise why would both avoid eye-contact with her? She looked from her young sister to her mother, from her mother to the foundling and then finally at the radio, which was jabbering on, but words failed her. And Duniya said girlishly to Yarey, 'Shall we go and shower together?'

'That'll be fun, Duniya,' said Yarey.

They left the room, convincing Nasiiba that either they had been talking about her or knew something they wouldn't share with her.

After showering, which they both enjoyed, Duniya borrowed Mataan's room to change. In the mirror her face looked soft like the earth after spring rains: brown, whole, supple. For a while she listened to the young people's chatter in the courtyard: Mataan, Marilyn and her friend and another whose voice she couldn't place. Nasiiba and Yarey were feeding the baby. The curtains drawn, the door bolted from inside, with enough sunlight to see herself in the looking-glass, Duniya took a studied interest in her body for the first time in many years. And what she saw depressed her.

She had neglected her own body while she took care of others' physical needs, as a nurse, as mother of three children, and now as co-guardian of a foundling. She hadn't realized she had grown so fat that she had a belt of it round her waist.

Somali men are said to be turned on by the mound of flesh round a woman's navel. But what kind of women did Bosaaso like? Did he prefer them slim, young-bodied, with not an extra ounce anywhere? For a woman of her age and background, Duniya knew her body was still in good shape. Surely, she thought, it wasn't a body to turn up one's nose at. It had served her faithfully all these years, giving of itself all it possibly could, and it had known only two men, one of them sixty-odd years old. In the two years she had been Zubair's wife, they could not have made love more than thrice a month. Yet she had not felt sexually dissatisfied; most traditional couples did not make love often, and no one made such a big deal about sex anyway.

Her second husband Taariq wanted it nightly. Nor did the calendar of her period deter him from demanding that she oblige. However his stamina was short-lived and he came at the very point when she started to climb the ladder of her own sexual pleasure. When he was drunk, she would push him away like an infant breast-feeding playfully. He would without a fuss fall asleep, snoring instantly so she would have to shake him awake in order to have a quiet night.

By leaps of logic she found herself considering the women Bosaaso had known, who might have left indelible influences on him. His mother. The Afro-American with whom he had cohabited for several years. And Yussur. Duniya made a mental note to find out as much as she could about these women, not as rivals, just as people. Would Nasiiba know anything about the Afro-American, Nasiiba who knew such things?

Getting into a dress belonging to what Duniya referred to as one of Nasiiba's moods (Nasiiba had the expensive habit of buying clothes she never wore, dresses bought when they took her fancy and which she then forgot), she now felt let down by her own weakness. Why, she had never thought the day would come when she, Duniya, would rack her brain about male likes and dislikes or would dress to please a man! She was being silly falling in love and admitting it; stupid borrowing a dress of Nasiiba's when the one she had worn the night before had made her feel so uncomfortable, tight at the waist, itchy and moist at the armpits.

Someone was knocking on the door. Urgently.

'Who is it?'

'Open the door, Mummy.'

'What is it?'

'Open and I'll tell you.' Nasiiba was breathless as though all the jinns in the cosmos had formed themselves into a union to chase her to this door.

'What is it, Naasi? Tell me,' Duniya said, opening the door.

'It's about the baby.'

For a moment Duniya couldn't think whom she meant. 'What baby?'

'The foundling.'

'What about him?'

And Duniya remembered the name of the young woman whom she had seen at the Out-patient Clinic – Number Seventeen. Fariida was the girl's name. Sister to the Somali Airlines stewardess whom Yarey had wanted to contact so she would take a letter to Abshir. Heavens, what complications!

Duniya told her daughter to calm herself, 'Whatever it is you have to say, remember the universe is two hundred million years old and won't come to an end before you've spoken your piece. Now what's bothering you?'

'Muraayo is here,' said Nasiiba, chest palpitating with anxiety.

Duniya was not moved by this news. She turned, asking

Nasiiba to zip up the back of her dress. This done, Duniya walked over to the standing-mirror to take an appreciative look at herself. She was amazed she had accomplished all this without tripping or knocking things over in clumsy gestures of lost equilibrium. Then: 'Now why should Muraayo's being here frighten you so?'

'It's about the foundling.'

Duniya calmed herself down. 'What about the foundling?'

'Promise you won't give away the foundling to Muraayo?'

Duniya decided that Yarey had been naughty and had threatened not to return to Muraayo's household but to stay here where, because of Bosaaso and the baby, a lot of late-night fun was taking place, more than at Uncle Qaasim's. 'Why shouldn't we give the foundling to Muraayo?' she said to Nasiiba.

'He's not meant for them,' Nasiiba said.

'I may not be the most intelligent woman in the world, but I'm not that stupid and none of what you've said so far makes any sense to me.' Duniya paused. 'Tell me, when did you last see Fariida?'

Nasiiba acted strangely, looking about suspiciously as though Fariida were hiding in the shadows of the darkened room. Then she swallowed hard, and her eyes popped as if she had by mistake eaten her own Adam's apple. She recovered quickly enough to say in her characteristically defiant way, 'What has Fariida got to do with what we're talking about?'

'You're the one who *found* the baby,' said Duniya. 'Not me.'

Duniya could sense because of Nasiiba's stillness of breath she had hit a target. But the feeling lasted only briefly. What made her feel triumphant was that it was Nasiiba who knocked her great toe on Mataan's doorsill, not Duniya.

'Tell Aunt Muraayo I'll be with her in a moment,' said Duniya.

Fariida: the mother of the foundling? Who was the father then?

Muraayo gave Duniya a light kiss on the cheeks and a cursory embrace. She was a huge woman, standing five foot nine and nearly twice as wide as Nasiiba. Her bare arms were of the enormous size that filled the sex-starved fantasies of some Somali men. She had very shiny, dark skin, and frequently went to her favourite coiffeuse to have her hair done in different styles, wearing it uncovered. She called at the tailor's just as often, never failing to bring him fashion magazines from which to copy, in the belief that her dresses resembled no one else's in Mogadiscio. With equal enthusiasm and panache, Muraayo visited silversmiths and goldsmiths with whom she haggled relentlessly so she would receive favourable trade-ins for her wares. Muraayo's build was such that people stepped aside, willing to surrender to her as much space as she wished to take. What was more, people simply couldn't help obeying her commands.

The twins did not like it that she treated them as though they were infants. Mataan, with unusual frankness, had once said, 'Aunt Muraayo pampers her huge body with an overdose of self-adulation.' In Nasiiba's opinion 'to think of Muraayo is to recall fiery moods and self-indulgence'. Duniya concurred with both her children, adding that Muraayo was a woman to have as a friend, not an enemy.

Duniya and the twins had known her in the days when she had been slim, just married to Qaasim, Taariq's elder brother. A life-force, that was how Duniya described her then. Muraayo had emanated womanhood. When a number of years went by without her being blessed with a pregnancy, this did not bother or sadden the couple. She was supposed to have said that her husband Qaasim had as many children as he was likely to want. 'What I give him is what his former wives never offered him: life and love.' No one doubted her word. Rumour had it she was not infibulated. It was also a known fact that the walls of their house cracked with the primeval screams of their love-making, thereby giving birth to the gossip that one of her neighbours described the whole thing as a fake show, meaning that Muraayo wasn't enjoying love-making but acting. Some of these women wondered if she was not infibulated.

Some of the men thought of Qaasim as a cuckold; for it was said that Muraayo had the habit of entertaining male visitors in the wing of the house furthest from the main entrance and in which their bedrooms were, when her husband was not at home.

Muraayo now pinched Duniya's cheeks in the Italian style, using the middle joints of the index and middle fingers. And as she effected this with elegance she said, 'And what have we here, Duniya dear? A small foundling, retrieved from a rubbish-bin, already famous enough to be a news item on the radio's morning bulletin. Imagine? And what else have we here?' Words emerged from Muraayo's mouth with the speed of a newscaster running short of time and so cutting and improvising all at once. 'A new dress, Duniya, all peacock feathers, figure excellent, every hair in place, plus flowers in the hair. Quite a finished job! A union sealed? Have you already taken the vows till death pull you assunder and all that?'

Duniya racked her mind to work out the meaning of all that Muraayo was saying. She was obviously talking about Bosaaso and the baby. But what about the flower in the hair? Where was such a flower? In whose hair?

Muraayo then said, 'How are *you* anyway? Happy?'

'We are well, thank you.'

'But there is a man after all these years, Duniya, a man – my God, what is happening to you?' Annoyingly, Muraayo wouldn't let her say anything, speaking as fast as she did, and non-stop. 'I mean: are *you* happening, Duniya dear, in the sense of burgeoning into a late blossom of a woman-flower – love and love, imagine – is that what we are witnessing the beginnings of, my dear?'

Bracing herself, Duniya said, 'Would you like to sit down and make your statements from the comfort of an armchair?' And she was pleased she could talk just as fast as Muraayo and still make sense. Would she be able to keep pace with Muraayo's accelerated jabber?

'I've been here quite a while,' said Muraayo.

Now what did that mean? Trouble? Did Muraayo feel offended, being made to wait for Duniya to join her, while the younger ones were busy with one another and the foundling?

'Come and have some tea,' suggested Duniya. 'It will calm our nerves.' She knew she would have to take hold of the reins of the conversation lest it get out of hand. She never liked the drift of Muraayo's chatter but somehow was able to control its ebb and flow, and if need be turn its tide anywhere she pleased.

'No tea,' Muraayo said, her tone that of an annoyed child.

Yarey readied to go to the general store, a few hundred metres away, to get Aunt Muraayo a soft drink of her choice. It was not lost on anyone that at Muraayo's place no one went out to get an ice-cold soda or something from a retail shop, but to one of three fridges, whereas at Duniya's there was no fridge. For such services as keeping drinks chilled the owner of the general store charged a little extra.

'Don't go anywhere, Yarey,' commanded Muraayo. 'I haven't seen you for almost twenty-four hours and don't want you out of my eyes. Let someone else get a Coke for me or whatever they have chilled.'

Nasiiba told Mataan to go and get it; Nasiiba who felt that a lot was at stake that might affect the foundling's future. Duniya noted in her mind that Nasiiba hadn't spoken a single word since their encounter in Mataan's room, when the young woman had been incapable of responding to the question about whether she had seen Fariida, Fariida whom Duniya imagined to be the abandoned baby's mother.

Something was happening. Was the baby happening? The atmosphere was getting heavier and heavier. Not since the morning Shiriye called had Nasiiba known a half-hour so tense. Marilyn and her companion, another girl, both felt redundant and left; their hostess, Nasiiba, did not even see them to the door. Duniya sensed that her house was emptying like a town fearing to be sacked.

No one said anything until Mataan returned with Muraayo's cold drink. Delivering it as though he were ducking a bullet meant for someone else, he too left for the securer shelter of his room, whose door he pushed half-shut. Yarey stayed because Muraayo wouldn't let go of her hand, whereas Nasiiba remained not only because she felt that the foundling's destiny was at stake, but also because (she would say later) she adored family quarrels of this kind. Nasiiba switched off the radio at some point and the baby did not stir.

After taking a sip of her Coke, Muraayo said, 'Fancy finding a foundling near a rubbish-bin. Other people find treasures or other forms of pot luck. Not you, Duniya. You find a baby, a live one, healthy, unclaimed, in a basket, already waiting to be brought home, pampered with love and put on display. The story has a Moses-touch to it, almost myth-like, don't you think?'

Duniya didn't say anything.

Muraayo went on, sounding triumphant, showing off, reminding everyone that she was educated. 'When a nation is going through a crisis similar to ours, God produces a trump-card of a miracle and he plays it into the hands of someone whom He chooses for that purpose. Is this foundling a baby born to save the Somali nation from imminent disaster? Fancy, in addition to finding a baby, fancy unearthing a man, at your age, Duniya, an Idris come down in his chariot, one of the best of his kind, an American-educated Bosaaso, prosperous as the green currency of which he is rumoured to have plenty. Fancy that, Duniya dear – wealth, education and a foundling, all at a single stroke. What a sweep of fortune; the tarot cards will carry a bust of you from now on, I assure you.'

Muraayo held her audience captive, confident that she could get away with anything. Duniya was the nervous one, because she was thinking to herself that maybe Muraayo knew the father of the foundling, a hand she would play when and only when pressed. Who might the father be?

Presently Muraayo was saying, 'Yarey has told me she wishes to remain here with you and wants all her things brought from our house. Have you been told that?'

Nasiiba shifted in her chair, excited as if watching a cock-fight.

Duniya was calm. 'I don't share Yarey's opinion and I told her so when we spoke about it earlier this morning. We'll have to talk, I've explained to her, Taariq her father, Uncle Qaasim, you, we'll have to sit round a table and discuss it.'

Muraayo took a tighter grip of Yarey's wrist to whom she turned and said, 'Now why would you want to leave us and come here?'

There was pain on Yarey's face; the little thing did not speak.

'Haven't we been kind to you? Haven't we treated you like our child?'

'You've always been kind to her,' Duniya said.

'Let the girl speak for herself,' Muraayo said to Duniya.

Duniya's face wore a tawdry expression, threadbare rags of anger, but she let it pass unchallenged, saving her guns for other matters of greater strategic significance.

Muraayo made Yarey stand apart from everybody, like an errant pupil being questioned by a teacher insisting that she confess a wrong-doing. It was humiliating to Duniya, but she bore it.

Muraayo said, 'Have Qaasim and I not given you all the love you require? Have Qaasim and I not bought you all the modern toys you fancied and more? Haven't we bought you whatever you demanded?' And so on and so on. Give. Buy. Receive.

Grateful. Key words to do with giving and receiving. What had the little girl to do with all this?

Yarey nodded silently.

And then Muraayo said, 'Do you realize that here, at Duniya's, there's no TV, no video, and you won't have a room of your own, not even a bed you can call yours, only a collapsible one that tucks away under someone else's, a bed bought second-hand, which gathers dust under a bedroll in an overcrowded corner, not fit for human habitation, but beasts!'

Duniya said, 'All right, Muraayo, that's enough!'

Muraayo turned to her, staring, as if she didn't understand her. 'Enough what? When you don't talk to your silly, ungrateful girl and make her see sense, Duniya?'

'You've said more than my patience will tolerate,' Duniya said, 'certainly more that my pride will accept.'

'The poor thing doesn't know what's good for her,' delivering this in a breathlessly hyphenated tone of voice, as if the statement were one single long-winded word.

'I won't discourage my daughter from wanting to come home to me.'

Muraayo disregarded Duniya's comment, saying to Yarey, 'You've been our daughter for almost six of your nine years, haven't you?'

Yarey nodded.

Now Muraayo turned to Nasiiba, 'And you and your twin-brother: do you remember that Qaasim and I gave you a place and a home when your mother went away on a few months' refresher course to Ghana, when her own brother Shiriye wouldn't have you? And this was long before we were related by marriage, long before Taariq married her?'

Nasiiba remained unmoved.

Addressing no one in particular, Muraayo continued her monologue, 'Children don't mean much to me but a house without a child is a place in which ghosts and jinns congregate.' Then to Yarey, 'You've mattered to me because I watched you grow right before my eyes and I would like you to have the opportunities of being educated abroad, in the USA or Canada.'

Duniya said, irritated, 'You're doing it again, Muraayo.'

'What am I doing?' asked Muraayo, puzzled.

'Let's talk of something else, change the subject. As it is you're offending my sensibilities and my self-esteem. "We can offer you this, we can give you America and Canada on a tray, and the world's TV, video and toys at the push of a button." That's no way to speak to my daughter.'

'How do you want me to speak to her?' Muraayo sat up.

'I suggest we change the subject.'

'Whether you like it or not, Yarey knows who bought her the clothes she's wearing this very instant!' Muraayo said bitterly.

Duniya was shocked beyond recognition. Her mouth opened, only to make an O sound, then her lips pouted, speechless. She had unseeing eyes, hollowed out like key-holes. Duniya's self-control was amazing today, decided Nasiiba. 'I suggest we postpone talking about all this till we're in a more receptive mood.'

'There is nothing to talk about or to postpone,' Muraayo said.

'In the meanwhile we'll both have spoken to Taariq, the girl's father and Qaasim her uncle and your husband, since they too have a stake in this. Let's not insult each other any more.'

Muraayo scratched her head cautiously with a fingernail. As she did so, everyone could see her hairy armpit. Duniya thought about Somali women growing armpit and pubic hair – features of modern times, Amen!

'I want the foundling, then,' said Muraayo, in keeping with her habit of never making any commonplace demands.

'What did you say?' asked Duniya incredulously.

'Either Yarey or the foundling.' It was not a request politely spoken, but a command in an either/or tone. And mortals like Duniya had no choice but to obey such orders.

'I have to consult the foundling's co-responsible.'

'Who is that?' wondered Muraayo.

'Bosaaso,' said Duniya, drawing delight out of saying the name.

There was an odd mixture of sarcasm and bitterness in Muraayo's voice. 'So that's who he is, the man who is happening in your life, making ours impossible to live.'

'What do you mean?' Duniya said.

'Never mind,' Muraayo said, dismissively.

The silence was a strain on everyone's nerves, save Muraayo, who sat majestically confident, overspilling with the noises her bangles, silver and gold-bracelets made. Nasiiba's eyes lit with a wicked grin. Mataan had come too and stood on the periphery, with the air of a football fan watching a cup-final. Yarey had plonked herself beside Nasiiba, sharing her armchair. The children, in short, remained quiet and conspiratorial as if they secretly knew what was about to happen.

Muraayo stammered uncharacteristically, saying, 'All I meant to point out to you is that raising four children will present you with a heavy financial burden unless this Bosaaso man is willing to give you a hand. Let's face it, you can't even meet all Yarey's expensive tastes.'

Duniya was too annoyed to respond.

'I know Yarey can't be without her video and TV,' Muraayo continued.

Yarey said, 'Uncle Bosaaso has a more sophisticated video-machine.' No sooner was it said than she realized she had annoyed her mother. She hid her head behind Nasiiba.

'Remember too that this house in which you live virtually rent-free belongs to my husband,' boasted Muraayo. 'Be reasonable, Duniya. Use your head. Either give me the foundling or let Yarey come back with me right now.'

Duniya got up, hotly. She did not know what was coming out of her mouth. She said: 'We'll keep the foundling in order to give him to you, how about that?'

With a superior air, Muraayo said, 'That doesn't make sense.'

'It does to me,' argued Duniya.

'What about Yarey?'

Duniya's eyes were aflame with rage she could no longer contain. 'Get up on your heavy, fat feet, Muraayo,' she said, standing as if preparing to fight it out, woman to woman, fist to fist.

Muraayo stood up, perplexed.

The twins moved towards each other and Yarey joined them, forming a three-person club of spectators to applaud their mother. It was as if Duniya and Muraayo were two little girls quarrelling over the ownership of a doll, which they would tear apart, limb from limb, until it was no longer a doll but something else, something much bigger, placed on a symbolic level.

'Do you know where the door is?' asked Duniya, still calm.

Muraayo was not intimidated; she stared at Duniya, daring her to take the next step.

'I want you leave this instant, Muraayo, and fast too.'

'You'll regret this.'

'I've heard enough nonsense for one day,' said Duniya. 'Leave.'

Muraayo said, 'You're not a good mother to your own daughter.' She pointed to the girl's chin, 'Look at this. It's eczema. Yarey's been here only twenty-four hours and her skin-irritation has returned. You call yourself a nurse. Why don't you apply the medicine the girl brought with her? You have no time for her, only for the new man in your life and the foundling.'

Duniya shouted, 'Get out, of here, out of my sight!'

'This is my husband's house,' Muraayo stood her ground, defiant.

'I'm the tenant and I have the right to throw you out,' Duniya threatened.

'Wait until I tell Qaasim what you've done to me.'

To everyone's surprise, including hers, Duniya said, 'Give Qaasim my compliments and tell him to find a new tenant for this place. We'll be moving out shortly.' And suddenly Duniya knew who the foundling's father was. She didn't know how she arrived at her conclusion, but she *knew* it.

Speechless, Muraayo let go of Yarey's hand and left.

Then Duniya ripped open her dress, as though she were a person who was now sane, breaking the manacles of her insanity. Yarey and the twins sat in silence, sharing one armchair, and holding hands.

The whole place was electric with tension. Everyone stayed out of Duniya's way. The foundling kept quiet, fed well, slept. He didn't wake or cry even when Nasiiba had switched off the radio.

And Duniya? She had her feet up literally, contemplating her toes. Not alive to the world, not paying it attention, she stayed where she was, silent, thinking. She felt relieved. She knew she would have had to move out of Qaasim's house sooner or later. The problems confronting her now that she had served the quit order on herself were of a different nature: she must find a place soon enough, to welcome Abshir into.

Somebody prayed, *O God, let Bosaaso come!* Then they heard running feet, light as raindrops on zinc-sheeting. Nasiiba said, 'Here he is, in plimsolls, jogging,' and they all waited. When he came in, they felt like soldiers who were relieved to learn they were among friends at last. They welcomed Bosaaso and started to tell him in whispers everything that had passed. He looked in Duniya's direction like someone waylaid by bandits, but he remained with the children. Nasiiba urged Mataan to tell them a Juxaa-story. Both Yarey and Bosaaso encouraged him too, with Nasiiba adding that Duniya would also love to hear one.

A hunter who was an acquaintance of Juxaa's one day brought him a pheasant as a present, which Juxaa's wife prepared for the two men. A couple of months later a man unknown either to Juxaa or his wife knocked on their door. 'Who are you?' they asked the man.

'I am a friend of your acquaintance, the hunter,' the man introduced himself, 'who gave you a pheasant as a present which your wife prepared and on whose meat the three of you feasted.'

Juxaa and his wife welcomed the man in and they fed him generously. The visitor left, promising to let the hunter know that a feast had been given him in his honour,

A few weeks went by and another man knocked on Juxaa's door. To the question 'Who are you?' the man responded that he was a neighbour of the friend to Juxaa's acquaintance, the hunter, who had brought them a pheasant as a gift, upon which they had all feasted.

'Welcome,' said Juxaa to the man, letting him in.

Half an hour later Juxaa placed before the man a very large cauldron, with the lid still on. When the man removed the cover, he discovered to his surprise that there was nothing in the large pot, except water, turning and boiling hot. 'What's the meaning of this?' inquired the caller.

Juxaa said, 'The bubbling water before you has been boiled in the very cauldron as the pheasant that my acquaintance, the hunter, has presented us with; what is more the cauldron is the same pot in which your friend's food has been cooked. Welcome. Eat.'

Saying nothing, the man left Juxaa's house.

Half an hour later, Duniya sat alone in the armchair where they had left her. A voice was urging her to get up, go to the foundling's cot and find out why it hadn't stirred for so long. But another voice, equally convincing, was encouraging her to concentrate on the handsomeness of an eagle flying high in the heavens and refusing to land anywhere. And this second dreamy voice said, 'The foundling has done whatever it came into this life to achieve. It arrived unheralded and will probably leave unannounced. A mythical child, if you like,' the voice went on. It did not sound at all like Bosaaso, more like Nasiiba, 'a baby whose beginning shared the timelessness of fables, expiring in the inexactness of legends. Think of Moses in a bullrush basket floating down a river, think of miracle babies, think of myths,' the voice concluded.

But I want to get up! Duniya said to herself, although she hadn't the urge within her to stand up. It was as if a weight heavier than she was holding her down, forbidding her to rise.

Then a dragon-fly alighted on the tip of her nose.

But Duniya was too sleepy to chase the dragon-fly away. She thought she heard a knock on the outside door, and maybe someone stumbling in. Or was that the noise of the foundling moving in its cot? Duniya saw an eagle descend, watched it enter the baby's room, saw it emerge, holding clasped in its beak as it flew out towards the heavens not a baby but a dragon-fly.

Everything was so dreamy and still, Duniya thought she too was *not* among the living.

Chapter Eleven

In which Taariq and Qaasim call on Duniya. Mire comes to call later in the afternoon.

Duniya woke up to a cabalistic quietness in which she was not sure if she imagined Taariq's voice asking if she would like a cup of tea. But what about the foundling? And where was Taariq? For a sleepy instant, everything was real as a dream being dreamt.

Noises came from the kitchen: a kettle being rinsed, then filled with tap water; matches being struck, gas flames smelling blue and nauseating. Someone was pacing up and down, whistling. These hints strengthened her suspicion that Taariq had come, that it was his voice she had heard. She arched her back, her neck a little stiff. She had fallen asleep in an armchair just outside Mataan's room, as if guarding his door. She had his bicycle-chain in one hand and the dress Nasiiba had given her in the tight grip of the other. She must have fallen into the shallow well of siesta just as Bosaaso and the others left. Again, the question: what about the baby?

She would ask Taariq to take a look, she thought drowsily.

He had visibly aged since she last set eyes on him, only God knew how long ago. Now he looked like a man at peace with himself. A mutual friend by the name of Cige, himself an excellent journalist, one of Somalia's best, had once said to Duniya, 'No sight is uglier than a journalist not writing any more. All that unemployed energy is so sad. It's like a river running to sand, wasting itself.' Cige and Taariq and Duniya had been standing in front of the government printing press where the country's only daily newspaper, *Xiddigta Oktoober*, was printed. Duniya had gone to seek Taariq's assurances that Yarey would not be made to undergo the torture of infibulation. Both Qaasim and Muraayo had given their word, but Duniya wanted to be absolutely certain. Only that morning Hibo had brought to the hospital her youngest daughter who had been circumcised without her knowledge by her visiting mother-in-law, Gallayr's mother. To set Duniya's mind at rest, Taariq pointed out that Muraayo had not herself suffered such an amputation. Her worries allayed, she accepted that Yarey stay on in Uncle Qaasim's and Muraayo's household.

At last the meaning of the noise became clear, as Taariq arrived carrying a tray of tea and a jug of cold water from the clay water-pot. Awake, Duniya saw him hesitate, wondering where to place the tray. Suddenly she lumbered to her feet, full of energy. This filled him with vitality too. Duniya took in all that met her eyes, noting the state of disrepair the house was in – was it appropriate that she quit without giving consideration to that? Nothing to regret, she told herself, no sins to repent. The floors would be whitewashed, the walls too; all would be well.

He had found a low table for the tray, and said, 'Where has everyone gone? Where are the children?'

Marriage is one way of forming ugly or good habits. Taariq knew her preferences; he knew how she liked her tea, how much sugar she took, that she seldom drank it with milk. She also noticed he had brought her a jugful of water so she could get rid of the taste of sleep. He poured out two cups of tea.

She took a mouthful of water, gargled, then spat. She wasn't sure if it was sleep or blood that she tasted in her saliva as she gargled. She rinsed her face with the cold water, then sat down. No formalities between them. On second thoughts, she wished she had done all this gargling and face-washing in the privacy of her bathroom. She felt self-conscious suddenly, as though her behaviour was something picked up from constant association of late with Bosaaso.

'The girls have gone to a film, I don't know where,' she said.

'Do you know what they've gone to see?'

'*Nosferatu*. I think that's what Nasiiba said.'

'Not *Profumo di Donna*?'

Duniya pondered. She remembered seeing and liking it in Rome in the original, with Abshir. She was sure the girls had not gone to watch *Profumo di Donna* at a friend's. But they were civil with each other even in their disagreements, not tearing into each other out of a sheer desire to pick faults, as they had done the last seven months of their marriage. He took a sip of his tea.

'And Mataan?'

'Bosaaso asked him to keep him company.

He was silent, which afforded her time to take a closer look at him. He had come dressed for the occasion, in a faultlessly ironed shirt, decent trousers, with a belt – imagine Taariq wearing a belt! And he had proper shoes, with matching socks. She had known him to wear odd socks, his shirt buttons to be of different sizes, shapes and origin. And his eyes were open, and he was no longer dwelling in the mistiness of his drunken stupor.

Duniya reminded herself that he had abandoned drinking and smoking, and was writing and publishing again. God, whatever had happened to her Taariq! Waving her hands in front of her, as if removing a web her imagination had woven in front of her, Duniya asked, 'Why are you here, Taariq?'

'I've come to visit you,' he said.

'You have always been a liar, Taariq.'

'What makes you say that?'

'Has Muraayo anything to do with this unexpected visit of yours?'

'Probably.'

'Am I right to assume that you are heralding Qaasim's visit later today?'

'That's right.'

All this time, her hands were caressing the kettle's spout. She filled her cup to the brim; he extended his towards her and she poured more into his too. 'So you've come because two women – one your former wife, the other your current sister-in-law – had what might be called a women's fight? You've come,' she raised her hand in the gesture of someone not wanting to be interrupted, 'you've come, wise and male, because two stupid women have had a petty fight. I'm afraid you're late. These women have done whatever damage they are capable of. Your tardy arrival as the wise male mediator of women's irrational quarrels will not mend things either.'

He said nothing. He knew well not to interfere with the smooth flow of her talk. She had her temper and he knew this was no time to speak. He waited.

'As it happens,' she continued, 'my father did the same, years ago when his two wives, one of them my mother, the other Shiriye's, were involved in a fight of which he was the cause, and in which one of them was hurt. My father came, as wise men do, late after the event. He came to instruct the two women to shake hands in front of him and other male witnesses. Make peace, he commanded. Shake hands, he ordered. Shut your mouths, he instructed.'

Taariq remained still and silent. 'I've learned to be suspicious of men presenting themselves as peace-makers between women,' Duniya went on, 'when they, the men, are the cause of the quarrel, the initiators of the enmity and rivalry between women-folk. Tell me then, Taariq, my dear former husband and father of my youngest daughter whom I love dearly, tell me why you are here.'

'Actually, I've come to see the foundling, out of curiosity.'

'I don't believe you,' Duniya challenged him.

'As if you ever have.'

Turning away, she said, 'Get on with it then. See him and be off.'

'I've already seen him.'

'You have?'

Taariq nodded. 'He's asleep.'

'Does he look like anyone you know?' she asked.

'It's much too early to be able to tell accurately.'

'Have you taken a good look at him?' she asked.

'Asleep, with his fists covering part of his face, as though he were defending himself against a coming blow. Yes, I took as good a look as I could, in the circumstances.'

'Why?'

'Answer my question first, Duniya.'

'Go on and ask.'

'Whom should he look like?'

'Tell me why you took a thorough look at him and I'll tell you whom he's said to resemble,' Duniya bargained.

'I'm a journalist and the foundling was a news item this morning, so it's professional interest on my part,' Taariq justified himself.

She decided Taariq did not suspect that Qaasim may have fathered the foundling. Or was she herself in fact wrong in assuming that, since all Nasiiba had said was: the baby is not meant for them, meaning Muraayo and Qaasim.

He said, 'Do you remember saying more than once that most men have no idea how to react to babies before the newly-born's faces break with smiles of paternal recognition?'

'I don't recall saying that precisely, but the words carry my stamp.'

'Well, today I've met two men who've been affected by the foundling's presence here in your house: Qaasim and Shiriye.'

'It's Qaasim who interests me, not Shiriye. What did Qaasim have to say?'

'We were in the living-room when Muraayo returned, after your fight. You know how she is, a river of words breaking at the banks, regardless of the seasons. Well, she abandoned us in the middle of a swamp of words. I, for one, could hardly grasp what the quarrel was all about. Of course, the aspects of the fight regarding Yarey were clear enough, but nothing she said about the foundling made any sense to me. I had heard of a baby being found near a rubbish-bin, but the radio didn't say who had given the foundling a home. Then Qaasim interrogated her about the baby in such an intimate way, he got me interested. Who had brought the baby home? Who was there at your place? Did Muraayo know any of the young girls at Duniya's? Was there a young woman, Nasiiba's age, who was minding the baby as well? Muraayo remembered a girl Nasiiba's age helping with the baby. Sitting up, very alert, Qaasim asked for her name. Only when Muraayo gave the girl's name as Marilyn did he begin to relax. But by then, I was hooked, and I had to come.'

'I'm looking forward to seeing Qaasim,' Duniya said.

'Who is this Marilyn?' Taariq asked.

'She isn't the baby's mother, if that's what you think.'

He shook his head, 'I mean, does this Marilyn have a grandmother called Maryam and do they live in this neighbourhood? If you don't jump the gun, but give me a straight answer, I'll tell you a story.'

'I love stories,' Duniya said.

He decided to go in quest of her good-will and talked about the night she threw him out of the house, sodden drunk and sleepy. This was the first time he had talked about it.

'I fell asleep in the shade of a tree,' he said, 'not knowing if it were day or night, when out of the silver brightness of a full moon, the figure of an old woman bearing the gift of a blanket emerged. She covered me with it, tucking me in like a motherless baby. But she didn't leave me all that night. She sat by, on a low stool, guarding me against thieves and dogs whom she shooed away whenever they approached. You see, when I woke the next morning, I had a vague recollection of an old woman's voice telling a young girl whom she called by the unusual name of Marilyn to go back to sleep, because there would be school on the morrow.'

'Did you ever meet the old woman?'

'For weeks afterwards, I would come in a borrowed car, park within sight of the family door, hoping to see her, thank her and return the blanket. When I had mustered enough courage, I knocked on the door and asked if there was a woman who would meet my drunken description of her or a young girl called Marilyn, the man of the house reacted negatively both to my visit and my queries, telling me to leave. You won't believe it, but I still have the blanket, as a souvenir by which to remember the night you threw me out.' There was no bitterness in his memory of the night.

'It must be the same old woman,' Duniya said.

'How come she's in your life too?'

'She turned up one morning, to offer us the loan of a young maid, to help us look after the foundling,' Duniya explained. 'She came first, solitary like *Khadr*, a genuine comfort. Come to think of it, I used to see the old woman off and on. It's such a pleasure to know them, they are such delightful company, she and Marilyn. They arrive at all sorts of odd hours, to mind the baby. They get along well with everyone, the two of them, including Bosaaso, co-responsible of the foundling.'

Taariq was now jittery, unable to decide which of the many strands worked into his or Duniya's yarn he should pursue. He had an orderly mind, in which thoughts were instantly catalogued, given a sub-heading, ideas were divided into paragraphs as if he were writing them down in a systematic order. Working another strand into the yarn already spun, Taariq said, 'Shiriye, who was at Qaasim's today, thinks you're mad to want to keep the foundling.'

'What was Shiriye doing there?' Duniya said suspiciously.

'He was eager to have a private word with Qaasim,' said Taariq, giving away nothing. 'Maybe he wanted to make more money on the side, selling watches or buying them at a discount from Qaasim, I don't know.'

'What reasons did Shiriye give you when he thought I was mad to keep the baby?' Duniya asked.

'Shiriye doesn't give reasons. He spouts opinions, crude prejudices and unlearned pontifications.'

'What's your opinion, your refined, learned opinion?' Duniya asked.

He wore that distant smile of his, like a mirage, promising water to the thirsty, and giving the traveller hope of an oasis beyond the hill. The water of Taariq's smile finally rose muddy and grey. He said, 'It's such a difficult thing to advise people on these matters. It's like getting married, a decision best left in the hands of the two persons involved, not third, fourth or fifth parties.'

'But what would you do if you were in my position?'

'I'd have to know a lot more than I do now before making up my mind.'

'But even if you did know, the beat of your mind and the path mine walks are so different that I doubt if we would arrive at the same conclusion.'

'I could not agree with you more,' he said.

Nagging at her mind, all this time, was the unfulfilled desire to get up and find out why the foundling had not stirred or cried for so long. But a voice whispered in her ear, assuring her that all was well with the baby, there was nothing to worry her.

'Tell me how you see it,' she said.

'I wouldn't give him to Muraayo, for instance.'

'Why not?'

'Muraayo – and mind you I am very fond of her – has little in-depth understanding of symbols. What she does is to live on the surface of things, in the glitter of false beauties, easily contented with the superficiality of things. A baby like this foundling requires parents who will treat him as if he were of special standing, not reminded of his earthy beginnings, or God forbid, that his ancestry is unknown. Imagine if Jesus were jeered at by his peers, scornfully telling him that he did not have a father like them. The strength of the Jesus myth is that we are not told much. In the case of Moses, we first see him a floating foundling, in an ark, sucking his thumb. Then we meet him as an adult, God's messenger. We don't see mythical babies growing up, because it deprives them of that magical credibility that is the essence of all myths. So to remain faithful to the incredible task before him, this foundling has to grow up in an environment away from the likes of Muraayo and Qaasim, grow up in an incubated area of the world, unexposed to the day-to-day realities which surround most of us.'

'Suppose we believe that he has known parents?'

'It doesn't mean much.'

'How is that?'

'Jesus had a known parent,' Taariq said, 'his mother, so did Moses, or the African Sunjata or Mwindo – all these mythical children had known mothers. Maybe they were half-gods, half-human.'

'What if he dies young, say, even tomorrow, or ten years from now, or if something incurable kills him or if tetanus claims his life? Will all this talk about myths have been mere babble, mere words, no more?' she said.

'He'll have assumed a different kind of motif in our story; everybody will get something different out of him.' He paused. 'At worst, he'll have served to make some of us think seriously.'

'What if Qaasim comes asking for him?'

It was amusing to see him hesitate, like a wary Huda afraid to stumble on the consonants of her discomfort. For this was closer to home, this was not a Judaic, Christian, Islamic or Mendink myth, this was more real, touching on fraternal realities and truths, on the relationship between elder and younger brother. And Taariq knew it, and he knew that Duniya knew it too. He was frank in his opinion.

'Qaasim doesn't know the value of gifts. I've known him to give away some things even before taking possession of them himself.'

'Tell me why I should keep him.'

'Because you are most worthy of him.'

'In what way?'

He wore his far-away smile and Duniya knew what that meant. None the less, she listened to him respectfully. 'I don't wish to sound religious,' he said, 'but I'm increasingly beginning to think that humankind must have faith in abstractions, and on this foundation we must reconstruct the world as we know it from the myth we have faith in, but not know, really know. There's sustenance in myth, of an enriching kind.'

Duniya did not understand what he was talking about, but thought it unnecessary to ask him to explain. The light in his eyes dimmed, like the blue of a pilot-light of a gas-cooker going out because the gas-bottle it had been feeding on has run out. Had a sudden feeling of exhaustion descended on him? Could it be part of the withdrawal syndrome, unpleasant reactions to the absence of nicotine and alcohol at the same time? She changed the subject with considerable haste.

'I enjoyed reading your "Story of a Cow",' she said.

He searched for words with the clumsiness of a man with very fat fingers trying to undo a subtle knot. He did not manage to speak a full sentence she could follow. His eyes narrowed to a slit.

Duniya was sure he was asleep, and she let him. She remembered the number of times he had come home, devastated. Or when she had returned from work to find him all over the floor and beds in the shapeless position drowsiness had called on him and her three children. She would take them to their respective places of sleep.

Now Duniya was certain she heard vague noises. Because she had her back to the door, she turned to see who it was that had come and decided to leave. Not meaning to, she kicked Taariq awake, and, startled, he cried something that sounded like 'Who?'

The voice of an equally worried woman answered, 'It is I.'

'Please come back,' said Duniya, recognizing the old woman's voice.

In the meantime, Taariq sat up, eyes bloodshot, rubbing them sore and redder. She apologized for waking him; he, for napping.

And Duniya got up to welcome Maryam, Marilyn's grandmother with the words, 'The children have all gone with Bosaaso and they have left me in charge today.' Then she introduced Taariq.

It was weird, but the old woman would not look at Taariq, who had risen to shake hands with her. Looking intently at Duniya, she said, 'I am sorry to drop in on you like this, but I was actually looking for Marilyn, hoping I would find her here.'

'No, I am afraid she is not here.'

'Did she go out with your children?'

'I doubt it.'

She turned round and said to Duniya, 'I must be on my way then.'

At which point, Taariq said to her back, 'Have we not met, you and I?'

A smile dirtied the old woman's clean features. 'Have we?' she asked.

'You gave me a blanket one early morning, and kept vigil so that my drunken figure would not be pestered by stray dogs, hungry cats and midnight thieves, for which I've never thanked you.'

Marilyn's grandmother shook her head, 'I don't recall any of that.'

'I have kept the blanket as a souvenir of your kindness.'

'It must be someone else you are confusing me with,' insisted the old woman.

'I meant to return the blanket, but didn't for a number of complicated reasons, and therefore kept the episode as a private memory of an old woman's kindness.'

'In that case,' the old woman said, 'why devalue the significance of the act by mentioning it in public? Why must you speak of it?'

Taariq reflected on what the old woman said.

'She has a point,' Duniya agreed.

The old woman, her voice now confident and her eyes prepared to meet Taariq's, said: 'Is anything the matter with the baby? Why is he so quiet?'

No sooner had Duniya thought of what to say than the outside door opened, admitting the pot-bellied, perspiring figure of Qaasim. Like Shiriye, Qaasim had the eyes of a man who wanted to be somewhere else. He was very fat, like Shiriye, his body round like the lower part of a baobab tree, with stubby, short-nailed fingers. Qaasim's eyes were small, his teeth tobacco-stained. His belly, it occurred to Duniya, had the shape of a cement-mixer. Qaasim, unlike Shiriye, spoke little. He let his money speak for him. Like an emperor with a full coffer to distribute, Qaasim gave and gave and gave. He left before people, praising or blessing him, got to the 'Amen' of their prayers.

'Where is the little devil?' he said, in haste.

'What little devil?' asked Duniya.

'The little jinn that has created all this discord?'

The old woman looked as if she wished she had gone away earlier.

Duniya said, 'When you come to someone's home, you greet them first, you take a seat, you remain polite.'

'I said where is he?'

'Where are your manners?'

'Manners, listen to her talk of manners to me?' he addressed the old woman. 'Where are your manners, Duniya? I'd like to know where your manners have gone, deciding to sever all relations with us, at a stroke. Don't talk to me of manners.'

As the old woman prepared to leave, Qaasim said to her, 'Do you know where the little devil is?'

'Of course, he is no devil – an angel maybe.'

'Where is he?'

'You know there are only two rooms here, since you own the place,' said the old woman angrily. 'Find him yourself.'

He gave heed to her advice and went to the Women's Room. When eventually he re-emerged, he was not saying a word and was in no haste either. He took a seat, mournfully. A blanket of sadness covered every inch of his large body, including his pot-belly, which appeared to have shrunk like a burst balloon.

Without being told so, Duniya knew the foundling had died.

As though he were a waterhole and all the others thirsty animals that had come to drink from it, everybody sat round Qaasim. Only Nasiiba and Duniya did not and they knew why. Yarey, in her restless mood, sitting astraddle his knees, kept asking, 'But why?' Yarey looked from Nasiiba, who had been the first to find him living, to Uncle Qaasim, who was the first to see him dead. Duniya, in a sad instant, did not put it past Qaasim to have strangled 'the little devil who has created so much discord'.

The foundling's death shook Duniya profoundly. She could remember nothing that had ever touched her so deeply as his death. Nor could she be as philosophical about it as Taariq who had quoted the Somali proverb in which it is said that death saddens you less if it strikes a homestead far away from your own, or a camel herdsman whom you do not know. She asked herself what would become of Bosaaso and her myth-construct?

Bosaaso was the first to move away from those sitting round Qaasim's waterhole. Agitated, his memory replayed a couple of sequences from two other deaths, his late wife and son. He stood still, rocking on his heels. He said, 'Now we have to think of his burial and the bureaucratic rituals surrounding it.'

For a moment, Duniya hated him. How could a man so

sensitive be so down-to-earth at the same time? She wondered if anyone had told him about the quit-order notice she had served on herself. And what was he likely to say when he had the opportunity to speak?

Taariq, on the other hand, had tear-stained cheeks and kept looking clumsily for a clean handkerchief, only discovering a crumpled tissue, dry with the holes of previous uses and mucuses, whenever he put his hand in his trouser pockets.

'I suppose we will have to submit the baby's body to the mortuary for a post-mortem,' continued Bosaaso, 'to find out why he died, and then submit six copies of the death certificate to the district police station where we registered him in the first place.'

The old woman was the only person who went into the Women's Room where the corpse was, keeping vigil, saying a few Koranic verses. She closed the window overlooking the road and covered the dead body with a sheet from Duniya's cupboard.

Duniya wondered what would become of Bosaaso and her? Would something irrational like the foundling's death demolish the symmetries they had constructed together?

At the foundling's wake, anecdotes about death and creation myths were told. Present were a number of friends, including Mire, and all of Duniya's immediate family. Mire told the first anecdote.

'A child dies in his sixth year and finds himself allotted to a lower berth than that occupied by a much older man who had died at sixty. The young boy says to God. "Why is it, Lord, that I have been offered a lower berth in heaven's hierarchy than the grey old man here above me, when I haven't lived long enough even to sin?" And God responds: "Because this old man not only reached and lived beyond the age of reason, but he withstood all temptation without committing a single sin. That is why he has been rewarded well." Unconvinced, the child then says, "I beg Your divine patience to tell me why I had to die young and wasn't given the opportunity either to prove myself worthy of your rewards or that of sinning to deserve this punishment?" God replies, "Because We knew you to be a sinner, and We spared you, for you would surely have earned Our disfavour if We had allowed you to live a moment longer. God is All-knowing, and Merciful." And so the child prostrates himself before the Almighty,

Whose pardon he seeks, repeating the litany: God gives, He is All-knowing and Merciful.'

In the silence that followed this, Duniya got more drinks for those who wanted them. It was Bosaaso who had brought a crateful of ice-cold soda to the wake. For once, Duniya did not raise objections to receiving something from him. Now, she came back to where they all were, to hear Taariq tell a creation-myth.

'God, to while away His time, decided to create human beings, although not in his image, as the Bible says, but in the image of an Ethiopian. So He gives orders that clay be moulded in the shape of humans and fires be built to bake them. Then God stands to the side, watching His angel-assistants at work, and they bring to Him, with understandable excitement, a clay model as soon as one is ready to be shown to Him. The first one is overdone, too dark. No good, says God. Allot this very dark creature to a forsaken place in the continent of Africa. The fire is lit afresh, another clay model is thrown in and then brought out, and God commands it to be assigned to Scandinavia, His comment being that it was too pale, no good either. The angels obliged. The same process is repeated again and again and again, until God finally gets what He wants: a model of handsomeness and of virtue, the right colour of skin, the right texture of hair, the right human intelligence and pride, everything. After viewing this special creature, God assigns him to Ethiopia. Gives to this creature the best of lands, the best weather, the best fruits the seasons offer. Makes him the envy of his neighbours, in short, the envy of all the races. And there came into being an Ethiopian.'

More stories were told. Duniya plied back and forth, providing drinks and snacks and Bosaaso helped her. She heard only parts of some of the other myths that Mataan and Qaasim retold, including a cynical Nigerian myth of creation in which God sits one whole day watching the Nigerians misbehave, and He just laughs. Then a Somali and a Chadian, both in tatters of threadbare famine, present themselves before God and ask why He had been so unkind to them while He had given all kinds of wealth to Nigeria. To which God replied, with tongue in cheek, 'Take a good look at the people I gave to that country. You are better off where you are, I assure you.' And the Somali and the Chadian leave, gratified.

Duniya thought that at the centre of every myth is another:

that of the people who created it. Everybody had turned the foundling into what they thought they wanted, or lacked. In that case, she said to herself, the Nameless One has not died. He is still living on, in Bosaaso and me.

Part III
Duniya Loves

Chapter Twelve

In which the foundling is buried and formalities with regard to the rites of burial are dealt with quietly. Later that day Duniya is invited out to a restaurant.

Duniya awoke with a start and she remained restless for some time, turning and tossing in her bed, in utter discomfort. She had dreamt of a dog, of indistinct breed, ugly and short-muzzled like a bulldog; and of a rowdy lot of teenaged boys and girls teasing him, the dog barking, his frightened tail timidly glued to trembling legs, and the teenagers having fun tormenting him.

At a handsome distance from the noisy youths, as though trying to separate herself from them, stood a woman bearing no resemblance to anyone Duniya had ever met, a woman who in some inexplicable manner appeared to share an atavistic bodily and spiritual closeness to the hound, in that she had a feral stare and sharper canine teeth than any Duniya had seen in the mouth of a human. At any rate, Duniya's attention rested on the woman who, with an expectant air, kept looking to her right. Was she waiting for someone coming from that direction? Duniya picked out the figure of a man lying on his back on the bare ground and out of whose middle a tree with a single leaf sprouted. The dog barked now at the bullying youths, now at the woman who seemed totally unaware of him, then again at the man who stayed impervious to all around him, and finally at the twiddly leaf, easing his nervous cries at the appearance on the scene of an eagle, quiet as its folded wings, an eagle which alighted on the tree: the tree forfeited its one and only leaf, its wholeness, its life.

Silence fell.

Meanwhile, the woman seemed to search her head for clues to the significance of what was taking place. The eagle focused his powerful eyes on the dog, now silent. The dog fixed on a snake whose arrival created a troubled stir in everyone, save the woman. But there were agitated movements all round. And there erupted a gust of wind enveloping everyone and everything in its mysterious activities, a whirlwind gathering dust, spiralling upwards; whereupon the woman's eyes were touched for an instant by happiness. Also, doubt stole over her hard stare, softening it into the sweetest of smiles.

And the snake bit the woman.

And the skies were awash with the colours of seaweed.

Her gait eloquent as a sleepwalker's, the woman strode away from the scene, the rowdy youths and the dog following, stopping only when they came upon the cot in which a baby's corpse lay.

At this Duniya woke.

Burying the foundling was a quiet affair, attended only by family, friends and the priest invited to minister a simple religious ceremony. Bosaaso's cousin's taxi provided transport for those without their own who wished to join the procession. Mire could not come, Taariq could not get away from work, whereas Qaasim arrived very late, just as they were leaving the cemetery. When the corpse was interred and all formalities done with, Bosaaso and Duniya drove straight to the district police station to inform the authorities of the baby's death. The inspector was deeply saddened by the news, saying, 'Why, it was only yesterday the foundling was in the news, a living testimony to Duniya's generous spirit.' The inspector doubted if the media would be interested in carrying the news of his demise.

From the district police station Duniya and Bosaaso went to the hospital, where they discovered she had been assigned light duty for the day. Her colleagues expressed their full sympathy, one and all, and she remarked to herself how touching it was that they spoke to her as though she had lost a baby of her own flesh and blood, not a foundling. All the while, tributaries of tears worked their way up from her chest, her nose snorting, eyes blinking, their lids closing and opening on their own accord: this ended in her larynx bursting into an explosive sobbing, her mouth slobbering with the spermy saliva of slovenly secretions. But her eyes remained absolutely dry.

Even so, some inner worry drummed in the ears of her heartbeat. And she yawned ominously, feeling she had been emptied of her natural strength, and that a change had taken place inside her. A mantle of mystery hung over why the foundling's death should affect her in ways she hadn't imagined possible. She felt dissipated. Worse, she felt emptied of possibilities of what to do with herself, her time, what to say about *him* who had come and gone, what to think, how to think clearly. Sadness showed itself in her look now and again. Her posture ungainly, her legs a little shaky, the soles of her feet riddled with thorn-stings sharp as needles, Duniya sat down, sensing the state of her weightlessness. Indeed, the fear that she might fly off was so over-powering that she held on to the back of the chair, incapable of gauging its effects on her bodily behaviour. Only when she thought about Bosaaso did it seem worth her while to stay put.

Again she was won over by the memory that their house appeared emptied of life too, the radio silenced and every single door securely locked. Duniya was glad to be moving, in anticipation of happier days. Her children, in the meantime, had gone their different ways, Yarey opting to spend the day with Marilyn, Mataan with Waris, and Nasiiba – who knows what surprises she might spring on her mother when she finally re-emerged. An empty house is a sad thing, Bosaaso had said, but a vacuous life is a sadder one.

He gained courage and began taking more and bolder decisions, speaking of filling their evenings and empty late afternoons with activities. *We* would do this, he would say, *we* would do that. *We* would learn to swim. *We* would go out to restaurants. *We* would learn how to drive vehicles, in the hope of becoming independent, no longer in need of being given lifts, or even pestered by terrible men. *We*, it turned out, was a composite person, (Duniya + Bosaaso = we!), able to perform miracles, capable of filling days and nights with delightful undertakings worth an angel's time.

When the baby had been alive neither Duniya nor Basaaso had thought of inventing things to occupy them: he had made life take shape around them. And people came, visitors arrived in hordes, to play cards, to consume tea, to tell each other stories and to become friends. Duniya couldn't help taking account of the fact that the foundling's death imposed a compulsory set of grammatical alterations on their way of speaking, producing a *we* that had not been there before, a *we* of hybrid necessities, half real, half invented.

The light duty which Dr Mire had assigned to her today consisted principally of receiving the in-patients' X-ray plates and registering their names against the spaces alloted, only that. She would stare for an endless number of minutes at the negatives of the X-rays, fascinated, dreamy-looking, her fingers absently tracing the multi-wrinkled reproductions, thinking (how weird!) of a dead foetus preserved in a jar filled with clear vinegar – my God, how very shocking, she said to herself sadly, Part of her imagined the blank emptiness of the cryptographic plates to represent the baby's death and the filled spots to stand for those occupied by Bosaaso.

And then Bosaaso came to fetch her. It was early afternoon.

On meeting him she said that she felt hungry all day and yet had not really wanted to eat, for she had no appetite. Or maybe she wasn't expressing herself well? Bosaaso surmised that eating was an undertaking for its own sake. He cited as an example the weeks following Yussur's and his son's tragic deaths when he gave up smoking. He also remembered how empty he had felt as soon as he finished defending his PhD thesis. He had been so restless he could only fill the vacuity he sensed in his soul with work, more work. It was then that the idea came to him.

'We're going out to dinner tonight,' he said.

Smiling condescendingly, she said, 'Who are *we*, may I ask?'

'You and I, of course.'

A long instant passed before she realised that his presence had a pleasant effect, and she was not feeling all that vacuous; rather she felt as if she were filled with aspects of him. 'And where are *we* going?' she asked.

'I know a good restaurant.'

'See you shortly,' she said.

He offered to come for her at about seven.

Duniya's feeling of weightlessness returned directly she was alone, so that she had to lean against the outside door once she opened it. She remained where she was until her chest rose with her breathing, her heart beating faster in anticipation of self-hatred, a notion which nauseated her. Or was it love? Whichever it was, she wished to have nothing to do with it. Surely to be affected by such a nebulous sensation of sickness is no love, or is it? Her self-questioning inspired courage in her and she was able to walk through the entrance, her gait uncertain, her whole body numbed by worry.

She unlocked the door to the room she shared with Nassiba and brought out a chair; perhaps is she stayed still, the fog in her mind would clear. But she couldn't remain at peace with herself; it was as though her brain carried with it seeds which suddenly broke, bringing forth a baobab tree in full bloom. She thought that the previous week's events had planted seedlings sown to germinate, something that would happen sooner or later, but the foundling who had been the seedsman was no longer there.

Duniya's thoughts were chaotic and in a state of upheaval until the door opened, letting in someone with steps soft as weak applause. The tense look in her eyes as she welcomed Nasiiba with a smile belied her true feelings. Contradictory emotions were disguised by the defiant grin that defined Duniya's features as she and her daughter touched, as they kissed. As usual the young woman was full of life, bursting with the desire to make something happen. She was visibly sad that the foundling had died, but that didn't deter her from investing her energies either in herself or her mother. 'What's happening, Mummy?' she asked.

Duniya felt very restless today and she got up, her cheeks feeling warm. She couldn't decide what to tell Nasiiba and what not to; a great deal was happening, and not all of it was good or bad, or even easy to explain. Love was happening, for instance. Nausea was taking place, for example. She gave as reassuring a smile as she was capable of and then said 'We're going to dinner, Bosaaso and I.'

Nasiiba said, 'We're going out to restaurant, are we?'

Duniya decided that Nasiiba's use of the first person plural was essentially different from her own, realizing, as though for the first time, that the pronoun had such a wealthy set of associations. It was like learning a new language. Presently, Duniya was attended by the pleasant remembrance that at the mention of Bosaaso's name all her vertiginous sensations were gone. She felt anchored, her soul cast in its intention to pursue its destiny, its happiness.

'We must dress up, mustn't we then?' said Nasiiba.

Duniya stood in the sadness of a shock she hadn't anticipated. The truth was she hadn't thought of dressing up for the occasion, she hadn't the calmness of mind to prepare herself for the changes that were taking place around her, as well as inside her. She now gripped the chair nearest her, glancing at Nasiiba's direction, and recognizing the need to put herself in her daughter's hands; in essence, admit that she was in love.

Her tone of voice not unlike a very young girl trying on her mother's high-heel shoes, Duniya said, 'How about if I shower first? Don't you think that's a good idea? In the meantime you may choose the dress you want me to try on.'

'What a wonderful idea,' said Nasiiba rather excitedly.

Sunlight glared wickedly on her eyes, and she grinned. Things were much more complicated than she imagined, and no giving was innocent. What was it Nasiiba had said? That she would help dress her? Duniya was distressed at the thought of her daughter asking her to undress, to stand naked in front of her, to pirouette before deciding how she should dress. She now stood in a posture of intense self-questioning, wondering what to do. She was wrapped in the folds of a robe, fully clothed, save for her head whose curls shone from being hastily shampooed but fully rinsed.

Nasiiba said, 'I've shut the outside door and we're as private as we are likely to be. What I want you to do is to step out of your puritanical robe so I can take a good look at what you've got by way of a body. We haven't much time, so please hurry.'

Staggered, Duniya said, 'You can't be serious?'

'I am,' Nasiiba assured her.

'I am your mother,' Duniya reminded her.

Nasiiba looked in the general direction of the door to the room they shared, 'I'm your daughter, need I remind you, and in any case, I've seen you naked or part-naked many times. So what's the fuss? Let's get one with it.'

Duniya's memory was haunted by the thought that Nasiiba had seen her totally naked and making love to Taariq, as she had learned a couple of nights before. Her voice laced with pauses of self-doubt, she inquired, 'What's that on the back on the chair?'

'The dress I want you to try on.'

If she knew how, Duniya would have brought the whole charade to an end. Did Nasiiba think that because she had presented her with a dress or because Duniya had accepted to be dressed up, the young woman could request that her mother undress?

'You're no shrine,' said Duniya, 'and I'm not making an offering of my body. So saying, she turned her back on Nasiiba but she failed to take one single step away, as though incapable of understanding the significance of her decision. She was weighed down by a sadness of heart because all loving thoughts were for the instant absent from her. She was close to making an appeal to let her be when Nasiiba suggested anew that she undress.

Somehow Duniya came to realise there was no turning back and what had to be done had to be done, reminding herself that the twin's father, being blind, had never set eyes on her body, and that it was ironic now that his daughter was undressing her. She also drew strength from the memory that she, as a midwife, had seen many a woman naked, women whose bodies she had handled, whose most private parts she touched with panache. Her gaze worried, her body trembling, she flung aside the robe with which she had been covered, saying, 'There you are,' speaking the words with flamboyance.

Nasiiba's judgement came quickly: 'Not bad at all.'

Duniya, for her part, was too tongue-tied to say anything. The one good thing this humiliation was achieving for her was that she was becoming heavy like a club-foot, no fear of flying away from weightlessness. This caused a kind of acrimony to grow within her, but she was certain the feeling would vanish and she and Bosaaso would once again be united – and in love.

Meanwhile, Nasiiba was formidably excited, her speeches a mixture of half-understood and fully-comprehended ideas, throwing freely into the air a wonderous set of words meaning nothing to her. There was a sub-pattern in her language, something earnest and humourless too, like a mother readying her daughter for a children's party given in the house of an in-law with whom the woman is uncomfortable. It was an effort for Duniya to stand naked and still.

Nasiiba was saying, 'You will wear your hair up, in a crown of a bun. But first we'll comb it, and before doing so, we'll apply some sort of brilliantine-conditioner. A very upright bun will suit you fine. And no head-dress.'

'May I put on something in the meantime?'

'In a moment, no need to panic.'

Duniya reached for a headscarf, with which she covered her embarrassment in the attitude of an Eve hiding herself with Freudian fig-leaves. Her face was undeniably that of a humiliated person, but she remained silent, although not still.

'Here is an underbodice, a pair of underpants and a brassiere,' Nasiiba said to her mother. 'Now put these on and no fuss please.' The young woman might have been a mother giving two stop-gap mouthfuls to a child crying for food.

'I should never have asked you to help me dress,' regretted Duniya.

To this Nasiiba retorted, 'Parents seldom remember the million embarrassing moments their children live through, being dressed in clothes they would rather not wear, being fed on food they would rather not eat, being washed when they would be all too delighted to remain dirty, their private parts being fingered, mutilated, massaged. Not only have you done these and worse to me, but do you realize Mother dear, that as a Somali mother and a Muslim one at that, you have the legal, parental right to check if I am virgin.'

Having put on the underpants, the brassiere and the underbodice Duniya asked, 'What would you like me to do now?'

Nasiiba grabbed a straight-backed chair and placed it in such a way Duniya would face east, where the light was better. Then she walked back and took a good hold of her mother's hand, and her mother followed her, timid like a bride entering her new home. 'Sit and stay still and don't say a word,' Nasiiba commanded.

Duniya did not like it when someone else held sway over her, she hated the feeling of powerlessness, of not knowing what was being done to her. 'The reason why I rebel against the authority of men,' she once said to a friend, 'is that they tend to make decisions affecting women's lives at meetings at which women are not present.' Was Duniya now seeing Nasiiba as 'male'? Had she not stripped her, as men had, had she not rendered her powerless as men had? 'What are you doing to me, Nasiiba?' she asked.

'Have faith in me,' was all Nasiiba was willing to say.

She began twisting and turning plaits of hair on Duniya's crown. Both were relaxed enough; Nasiiba was the more pleased with the outcome of her artistic effort, though Duniya was less tense, her body less rigid. As if this displeased her, she went out of her way to say, 'Incidentally, Nasiiba, did I see wads of money tacked and hidden away in an Iranian Islamic women's magazine called *Mahjouba*?'

Duniya might have put a pet cat, well-fed and pampered, which had brought into one's living-room the corpse of a dead lizard when one had guests. 'I won't stand for this nonsense,' Nasiiba raged, having in anger thrown the comb which, in somersaults of fury, hit the furthest wall in the courtyard. 'What were you doing rummaging in my drawers, through my private things?' All combing, plaiting and bun-shaping came to a sudden stop. Nasiiba was livid.

'I believed *I* had misplaced something.'

'I hate you sometimes,' said Nasiiba.

'No, you don't,' Duniya said.

Like someone appreciating an artwork, Nasiiba took a couple of steps backwards. She placed her hands on her hips in a defiant gesture and said, her voice mimicking her mother's, 'By any chance, did *I* see Fariida at the clinic today? Or: in aid of what did you donate blood, Nasiiba? And now what?' And then, in her normal voice, 'What were you doing rummaging in my things?'

'At times I wonder if it's your place or mine to lose tempers? Now come,' Duniya said, 'don't let's waste more time, for the truth is I suspect I know where the money came from. Come and finish what you've started, and be quick.' Duniya was very firm.

Before long, and without so much as a word, Nasiiba resumed building a castle of a bun. And neither talked until Nasiiba said she was done. And when she saw discomfort on her mother's face, the young woman brought out a mirror for Duniya to take a look.

Duniya said. 'I've never worn my hair uncovered, since my seventeenth year, Nasiiba.'

'You're modern-looking when it is uncovered,' suggested her daughter.

'And it sticks out like the red of a semaphore in an otherwise darkened street and the whole world can see it from a mile away.'

'You will get used to it, and Bosaaso will love you all the more for it,' ventured Nasiiba.

At the mention of Bosaaso's name Duniya relaxed.

Meanwhile, Nasiiba's tone of voice had lost its distinctiveness. She was saying, 'Your face needs a touch of make-up, a thin coat, that is all.' And she was coming menacingly in Duniya's direction, carrying a variety of brushes and bottles.

'No make-up for me, thank you.'

A moment later Nasiiba was back, carrying a pair of ear-rings. 'Whose are these?' wondered Duniya suspiciously.

'They are yours actually, given to you by Uncle Abshir.'

Duniya nodded her head, acknowledging the truth of the statement.

'If you believe that your ears stick out like the flagposts of a football stadium, perhaps this pair of ear-rings will correct that.' They were very pretty, a circular shape with a five-cornered star fitted into the frame, and painted blue.

By the time they heard Bosaaso's car-horn announcing his arrival, Duniya had the chance to give her head a few touches here and there, and was feeling comfortable in the dress she had chosen and which Nasiiba had approved. It was just as she was joining Bosaaso who remained in the car that Duniya said to Nasiiba, 'Please give my condolences to Fariida, who I understand is the foundling's mother, and tell her to come and visit us whenever she feels like it.' And Duniya left the house in haste, eager not to be interrogated by her daughter.

And *we* went to a restaurant.

The moment the waiter who came to take their order left them alone in the half-dark, they kissed, with only a paraffin-lamp providing a semblance of light. The desire to kiss had caught them unprepared, with the suddenness of a hay-fever sneeze: it was brain-clearing. They embraced a long time, their breath merging, and each had what it took to make the other comfortable and vulnerable.

Silent, not kissing, they now sat on a straw-mat on the ground, under a thorny tent of acacia bushes, a paraffin-lamp hanging down from a branch in the tree, its light not interfering with their privacy. Any Mogadiscian wanting undisturbed quiet, or in search of the city's best lamb and rice, indeed any resident of Mogadiscio desiring to taste the romanticized image of untamed jungles: such people came here, men and women in love, foreigners in need of local colour or visitors seeking meal-souvenirs to remind them of Somalia. Needless to say, these entrepreneurial kitchens attracted Mogadiscio's local motorists and for a very good reason.

The waiters carried lanterns, adhering strictly to codes of behaviour guaranteeing absolute privacy to the clients patronizing the establishment. They moved quietly, they cleared their throats or coughed as they approached a tree-tent in which a couple nestled intimately against one another or in each other's embrace.

Duniya got to her feet, which were wobbly, once she caught her breath, after what amounted to the longest kiss, the most passionate one to date. Maybe, giddiness made her lose the sense of where she was, with whom or why. Her head spun, her legs were not stable enough to support the weight of her swaying body, and yet she was on cloud eleven, remembering no joy comparable to this. Had the long, passionate kissing dazed her so that she had taken hold of Bosaaso's car keys as she scrambled to her feet, something of which she had been unaware? He was now saying to her, 'And where are we driving off to, may I ask?'

'But I don't even know how to drive!' she replied.

'In that case, I will teach you how to,' he said.

And she sobered up instantly.

She sat down away from him, recalling her conversation with Nasiiba who had offered to teach her to swim. Was she, Duniya, being prepared for a higher state of completeness, as it were, being taught to swim and to drive too? She pushed the car keys towards him.

As though in response to her unfriendly gesture, the heavens thundered threateningly, and a mad wind blew. Bosaaso rose to transfer the paraffin lamp from the place higher up in the tree to a spot much lower, out of the current of air. While looking up at him Duniya saw comets flying earthwards, falling, as the Somalis say, on jinns and non-Muslims. She gave a start when a bolt of lightning struck the skies, making her think of the three-thronged whip farmers crack to chase away birds feeding on their crops.

As he sat down beside her, he said, 'What fireworks!'

'These are merely falling stars dropping on jinns: isn't that what Muslims say?' she asked, taking hold of his outstretched hand and fondling it. She didn't know what she was saying or why.

'The Koran informs us that these fiery comets are hurdled at nosey jinns eaves-dropping at the gates of heaven,' Bosaaso commented.

'Very naughty of them!' said Duniya.

When the heavens stopped thundering and the shooting-stars dropped no more, Duniya told herself that maybe the jinns, having become less inquisitive, had come down to earth and were whispering sweet nothings in her ears, which she touched on impulse.

'Is one of your ear-rings missing, or did you come out wearing only one?' he asked.

'You couldn't have lost it in the car?'

'My ear-rings?' And she felt her ear-lobes, one at a time. 'I arrived wearing a pair of them,' she informed him, but made no move.

'I am certain I didn't.'

He was immediately on his knees, searching for the missing ear-ring by feel, in the half-dark, because he was sure she wouldn't want him to bring down the paraffin lamp. The uneven roughness of the straw-mat pricked his palms. Nevertheless he remained undeterred even when she displayed little interest in recovering the missing item. 'When do you think you lost it?' he asked.

She decided to frame the moment of their passion in her private memory, choosing not to speak of it lest she should devalue it. And yet she was definite the ear-ring had dropped then, a few moments prior to the instant when the heavens let go a fireworks of falling stars. 'I can't recall when,' she said.

He went nearer her. 'I remember the shape of the ear-ring's star, painted light blue, enclosed in an all-encompassing circle of silver.' He was so close to her she could hear his breathing, and could feel the warmth of his body. He took hold of her hand; she let him. 'They were beautiful on you.'

She said nothing, because his head was moving upwards, towards her mouth, and their lips were preparing to encounter in a kiss of insane passion. She sensed a tremor running through her: what flames, she thought to herself. Supporting his weight, which was lighter than she had imagined, he returned again and again and again, asking for more and more. Finally she gave him a gentle push, saying, 'Please do not rush me.'

He breathed loudly and explosively as if he had been under water for a long time and had just come back to the surface. He sat up, his face spreading with an understanding grin. She would have thought him coarse if he had spoken a single word of explanation or of apology. And both were glad when neither said anything.

She studied the shadow his head cast, a head tilting to the side. He sucked his lips in silence. Looking at the night outside, beyond the paraffin lamp's moving shades, Duniya could see the silhouettes of lantern-carrying figures swinging in and out of her sight, like falling stars taking an eternity to reach the earth before exploding.

Silent, they watched an approaching, gyrating light. The footsteps of the waiter were followed by the noise of an idling diesel engine probably the vehicle of a client being escorted to a tree-tent. Then they heard low voices, that of a man and a woman placing their orders. Then quiet.

Bosaaso said, 'If it were my mother who had lost an ear-ring, she might have hummed a tune and danced a sad song about such a wasteful loss. If it were my Afro-American friend who had misplaced it, then the song and dance would have assumed a rhetorical dimension. And if it had been Yussur, she would have given a moan of regret, and would somehow have brought her mother into the talk, to blame her for it. But you? You say nothing, and show no worry in the world.'

A lantern came into view, and its carrier shouted a number from a decent distance. Since it wasn't theirs, they ignored the waiter's cry. When everything was quiet, she asked 'What's your Afro-American friend's name?'

'Zawadi is her African name, Sarah her American given name.'

'Is Zawadi a Hausa name?'

'Swahili.'

'And how long did the two of you live together?'

He pondered for a long moment.

'You don't have to answer if you do not want to.'

He shook his head vigorously. 'It's not that I don't want to answer your question, it is that our living together had two phases, the first being simply flat-sharing, in that I was her tenant, then half a year or so later we began sharing more and more of the responsibilities of house-keeping and emotional aspects of our lives, including her two children.'

'What age were they?'

'They were much smaller then, of course, the girl eight, the boy six. This was thirteen years ago, when I first started working with a UN agency, based in New York, a year after taking my PhD.'

'And what work did she do?'

'She's a community worker,' he said, pausing only to continue a second later. 'You see, I don't mind living by myself, but eating alone is something I cannot bear. As it happened I would cook larger portions and would invite the children to share the food with me, given that their mother would seldom come home to feed them. The children would play with the neighbourhood kids, and all I did was ask them to take a break, come and eat, and they would do so.'

Duniya was reminded of her own situation with Taariq, just before they married, with Taariq looking after her twins and her hospital assignments frequently keeping her out of the house. She was about to ask him if he had considered marrying her, when she saw a lantern approaching quietly. A waiter shouted their number, to which they responded simultaneously. The tall waiter entered their acacia-tent with his head bent, smiling. He placed the food before Duniya, and pushed the bill, 'which must be paid before consumption of item', as he put it, in front of Bosaaso. Duniya insisted that they each settle half the bill, but Bosaaso wouldn't hear of it, saying he was taking her out this evening, and requesting her not to spoil a pleasant night out by debating about petty sums such as these – after all, he had always accepted her generosities.

The bill settled, the waiter left. Duniya wondered if Bosaaso had been generous with the tip

Silent, they took turns rinsing their fingers in the warm water the waiter had brought for that purpose. In the half-dark, she thought that Bosaaso was smiling like someone about to make a mischievous remark. She has the calm confidence to wait, and he the good breeding not to interrupt her eating.

'If Zawadi had said yes, I would have married her,' he said.

Duniya took a deep breath, but said nothing.

They ate in silence, Duniya affecting disinterest in the reasons why Zawadi wouldn't marry him. She took care not to munch noisily, lest this interfered with their quiet thinking. Once or twice, their fingers collided, and each apologized to the other. When this happened a few more times Duniya chuckled. Bosaaso went on, 'Basically, Zawadi mistrusted men as husbands, not as lovers, or even platonic friends. She loathed being taken for granted, which, she said, was how black men behaved, no matter where in the world they lived, the USA, Africa, the West Indies, men who considered women their rightful property. Some of the black men she knew came into a woman's place with their flies bulging with unfulfilled lust. It was as though they were entering a urinal, she would say, their trouser fronts undone, at the ready, prepared for action.'

He gave himself time to eat a morsel in silence.

'Will you tell me how someone like Kaahin has entered your life?' she asked. 'It seems to me that he doesn't belong in your years of childhood spent in the town G. Or does he?'

'Zawadi brought him into my life.'

'How's that?'

'In one of her community work projects, Zawadi stumbled upon Kaahin, living in commune off Harlem, with no papers authorizing him to be in the US, and not doing what he had gone to do, take a degree. She took him into her able social worker's hands and within a year he was straightened out, capable of going back to Harvard.'

Duniya said with feeling, 'What an amazing woman, this Zawadi.'

'She is a gift. You should meet her.'

They fell silent, both thinking that Zawadi and Duniya would get along splendidly.

Then Duniya said, 'What I don't understand, after all this, is why Zawadi is not here, living with you or paying you occasional visits. Surely there's the Afro-American myth and wish on the part of many of them to return to their mother-continent. Or did you discourage her from joining you?'

'On the contrary. When Mire came to pay us a visit in New York and he and I began toying with the idea of returning home and volunteering our services, Zawadi made encouraging remarks about the project we were embarking on, that's all. Of course she was only too ecstatic for us, but she wouldn't come. It was she who contacted Kaahin, convincing him that his lot lay with ours.'

All this remains a mystery to me,' she confessed.

'Zawadi quoted a variation of an English proverb, giving it a slight twist: "It is at home that charity is bred like a stallion of Arabian nobility." She urged that there was no point to her coming to Africa to do volunteer work when her home-grown people, the Blacks in the USA, needed her just as desperately. "Besides," she added, "Africa is not ready for my Black American way of life, and I am too old to unlearn all I've learned." But she promised that one day she would pay Africa a deserved visit.'

Neither spoke for a good while, and they ate quietly and self-consciously. When both had eaten enough, each helped the other to wash and rinse their hands by holding the soap, giving the towel and pouring out the water.

Anxious, their conversation travelled no further than immediate, mundane questions responded to with short answers. Somehow Abshir's name came into their talk, and Bosaaso remembered that a friend of his was leaving for Rome on the Somali Airlines flight in a couple of days. Would she want him to carry Abshir's letter?

'Let's find out is Miski is on that fiight,' suggested Duniya, 'because she has always been our courier and she and Abshir have an established way of reaching each other.'

BRUSSELS (AFP/Reuter)

After economic and political pressures (and no doubt some delicate negotiations), the European Community has finally imposed its mighty will on the Ethiopian President Mengistu Haile Mariam by making him accept that a team of EC officials oversee the distribution of food aid in the country's northern provinces of Tigray and Eritrea. The Ethiopian government has communicated its acceptance of these conditions to the EC

Development Commissioner based in Addis Ababa. The European Community has been preoccupied over the possibility that food aid might not reach the two northern rebel-held provinces. Preparations are presently under way for the team to fly to Addis Ababa.

To date, the Community has granted food aid worth 260 million dollars. In addition, it has also given some long-term development aid amounting to about 100 million dollars for the Marxist-led government of Ethiopia to carry out reforms in its land and agricultural policies.

Chapter Thirteen

In which Duniya is given her first driving lesson.

A woman lay asleep in the scanty shade of a fig tree, dreaming. She heard a weak whistle, that of a kestrel, then the shrill cry of a kite calling her name, a call she refused to respond to. When the woman imagined that the hawk had tired of shouting her name, she opened her eyes and to her amazement saw a hat drop from the clutch of the kestrel's claws, a hat which she caught with her alert hands. When next the hawk spoke her name, the woman prepared to get up, but couldn't bring herself to do so, given that she was absolutely naked. Again the kestrel's claws let go another surprise gift, this time a garland of leaves, thus providing her with something to cover her embarrassment with. That done, the woman rose to her feet, putting on the hat, too.

But the woman was on a footpath going south towards a marshland. With the sleepy look of a dreamer, she spotted the figure of a man in an upright position, a man dwelling within the confines of a pearl-shaped framework of wires serving as a cage. Further ahead, there was a three-storey house with a large fruit garden surrounding it. Rather suddenly, the hawk chanted its message, 'Befriend me, Woman, and I will be yours for ever; have faith in me and I will give you what is due to you.'

Frightened, the woman let go both the hat and garland of leaves, upon which she now trod. The hawk's cries ceased, night became day: and the woman woke up.

Duniya and Bosaaso met later that day in front of the hospital. It was a little after two in the afternoon. One could see how much they had looked forward to their reunion, having been separated by sleep as well as work. They had had a serious talk about what Duniya referred to as her family's total dependence on Bosaaso's lift-offering generosity, something that would have had to come to a stop sooner or later. They had arrived at an alternative arrangement mutually acceptable to both: from tomorrow morning, Bosaaso's cousin's taxi would take Nasiiba and Yarey to and from their respective schools, in return for a token sum to be paid by Duniya monthly. She was content, the children were, and so was Bosaaso.

They were in his car now and he was driving her home. 'And how has your day been?' he asked.

'It's been difficult,' she said, leaning forward and buckling up, a must for any passenger in Bosaaso's vehicle. She was incapable of putting on her safety-belt, but nevertheless kept up the attempt.

He helped her with it, and both were conscious of their hands touching. 'Mine has been nothing but meeting after meeting after boring meeting without us achieving anything,' he said.

'The classical definition of bureaucracy.'

'I hate it.'

Her voice was unexpectedly curt, saying, 'Please let's leave quickly.'

He changed gear without questioning her or turning to discover whom they were avoiding. The screeching tyres raised dust and the eyebrows of a number of bystanders waiting for taxis and buses. Neither spoke until they were on the principal road leading to her house; and it was Duniya who found it necessary to do so. 'There is a strange mixture of possessiveness and a sense of guilt in my determination to be alone with you, and I don't like it; although I do not mind that you also give a lift to my colleagues, I really do not want anyone else to be around. I wonder if I am becoming mean, or jealous?'

His choked throat wouldn't clear of the joy with which it was clogged.

'How would you explain my behaviour?' she asked.

He was thinking exalted thoughts, the expression on his face became a smile. 'Maybe it's because of the early phase of our relationship – maybe that accounts for what one might call your "possessive behaviour". Is this partly why we've arranged for my cousin's taxi to pick up Nasiiba and Yarey from their respective schools, since we intend to be alone with each other?'

There was no point challenging his interpretation of the reasons why she had agreed to pay for her daughters' taxi fare monthly; not to be alone with him, although this gave her pleasure, but to depend less and less on his generosity. But never mind, she thought. 'But how do you explain why we wish to spend more time together, by ourselves?' she said.

'I suppose there isn't enough in the way of you and of me to go round, which is why we tend to appear possessive, appear to be unwilling to share,' he said. 'You. Me. Us. That's what it comes down to, ultimately.'

Duniya took note of the flourish of pronouns, some inclusive, some exclusive; pronouns dividing the world into separable segments, which they labelled as such. Apparently, the two of them were *we*, the rest of the world *they*. Together, when alone with each other, they in turn fragmented themselves into their respective I's. That is to say, they were like two images reflecting a oneness of souls, more like twin ideas united in their pursuit to be separable and linked at the same time. Is this the definition of love?

Aloud, she said, 'I cannot help feeling guilty turning my back on my colleagues whose eyes I avoid because my wish to be alone with you is overwhelming. I grant you the feeling awes me with a sense of shame and guilt.'

He slowed down. Traffic moved at a turtle's pace, crawling and honking. A lorry had levelled the trees separating the dual carriageway in an ugly accident, with half of the vehicle's huge body on its side and the cabin facing in the opposite direction to that in which it had been travelling. They talked about the incorrigible foolishness of some of the drivers not only risking their own lives but those of others. By the time they reached Duniya's home, Bosaaso was able to tell her that he had arranged for her to be given her first driving lesson.

'And who is to give me my first lesson?' she asked.

'We'll talk about it after lunch,' he said.

They were welcomed at the outside door by Yarey who was eager to see them. Nasiiba, for her part, had prepared a special meal for them. 'But why's the table set for only two?' inquired Duniya.

'We've eaten,' announced Mataan, 'the kind of a feast one starves oneself for.'

'Enjoy yourselves,' said Yarey.

'Bon appetit,' said Nasiiba.

Wearing her hair uncovered brought along with it a change of dress style, in a sense a change of personality. Bosaaso liked it a great deal, her children approved of it too, but were they the only ones who mattered? Obviously not. For some of her colleagues at work had commented on it adversely. She herself had often described a woman's bare head as being narcissistic, and requiring the use of mirrors and similar modern gadgets. After lunch, for instance, Duniya gave herself a few moments alone in the bathroom, absorbed in an act of self-regard, her attention totally engrossed in the three white hairs that wouldn't curl no matter what she did, three flimsy white thread-like filaments with a slender body, unhealthy and pale. She knew she shouldn't pull them out, otherwise they would multiply, a fact she had learnt from Taariq, her second husband whose once very dark beard was now laced with a great many grey hairs. She might never have taken notice of these emaciated hairs if she had been wearing her hair hidden in the prudence of an Islamic tradition which instructs women to cover their hair with scarves of modesty.

'Where are the children?' she asked.

'Maybe they think we would appreciate some privacy,' he said, getting up in an attempt to welcome her.

'Everybody is going insane,' she said, bending down to pick up a pair of plimsolls which Nasiiba had brought out for her to try on. She sat down to do just that, in silence. The shoes did not pinch, but neither were they comfortable. Duniya took a couple of steps backward, then forward, self-conscious like someone at a shoe-shop acquiring a pair. Then her eyes fell on a pair of slacks slung over an untaken chair, testimony to how much Nasiiba would commit her mother to, Nasiiba who knew no limits, and who would want her mother to change her style of clothing, and with it her modest personality. No slacks, Duniya told herself, dreading the thought of putting on a pair and discovering a front bulge where there had been none before, not to mention the prominent, fleshy hips; these imperfections worried her aesthetic sense of being.

'I've made some tea,' he said at last.

She was delighted at hearing this, delighted, above all, because he had felt comfortable enough to make them tea at her place. 'Where would you like us to have our tea?' she asked, satisfied with the canvas shoes.

'Out in the shade,' he said, and he shifted the chairs, one at a time.

As she accepted the tea he served her, she acknowledged to herself how he wished to assure her of his good intentions by inviting her first to Mire's, then out to a restaurant, before asking her to go with him to his place. So far, everything was going smoothly. Only, she thought, her reluctance to accept his gifts was making him tense, and this might, in the end, cause a strain on their relationship. But he did not insist that she receive everything he offered. And there were no indications of anxiety in him. In any case, she reasoned to herself, she did accept gifts from him in the form of lifts, in exchange for meals which he ate at her place. Fair was fair, and he was the kind of man who was fair.

'Did you say that you didn't know where the children went?' she asked.

He shook his head, no.

'I feel they are up to no good, and sense you aren't telling me something I ought to know,' she said teasingly. 'So where did they go? Or have you taken them somewhere yourself?'

Again he shook his head, no. Again.

Duniya abandoned the idea of pressing him to tell her secrets he didn't want to part with, certain that sooner or later one of her children would let her know what they had done, or where they had been to, and with whom. She had a sip of her tea reminding herself that the two of them had come a long way since they had first met each other in a taxi, he disguised as a cabby. Since then, they had become very close, and her children were fond of him. Although she had promised herself not to insist that he tell her where her children had gone, Duniya wondered what he would do if she had. Would he give in to make her content?

'About your driving lesson this afternoon?' he asked.

Oddly enough, this brought to her mind their passionate, long kiss the night before, when she had risen to her feet, unconscious of what she was up to, or of the fact that she had his car keys in her hand. 'What about my driving lesson?' she asked.

'I've taken the liberty of asking a friend of mine to give you the lessons,' he said.

'And where is he, this friend of yours?' She was sure it wasn't Mire he had in mind, but then she didn't know his friends; he often came to her home alone and never bothered to talk about others. 'Who is this friend of yours?'

'His name is Kaahin,' said Bosaaso.

He could tell that the idea of Kaahin giving her driving lessons didn't suit her. 'I don't know the man,' she said, which was true.

'But you don't like him?'

'What makes you say that?'

'That much is clear.'

She kept walking in the direction of the door, as if expecting Kaahin might come through it any instant. 'Where is he, anyway?'

'He's late, as usual.'

'The closest he and I got to each other was when he reversed into Mataan, nearly killing him, poor thing, and I would have murdered him if he had hurt my son, I swear I would have,' she said.

'The trouble with him,' Bosaaso said, 'is that he loves women.'

The anomalous word 'love' that Bosaaso had used in a wrong context shocked her, to say the least. She sat up. 'He what?'

'People say that Kaahin loves women,' said Bosaaso, backtracking.

'To my mind, Kaahin does not love women,' she said, 'in fact, he hates them, or rather he despises them.'

'People say he loves them,' Bosaaso insisted.

She was as quick as her anger. 'And what do *you* say?'

He felt pushed around a little and did not like whatever it was that she was doing to him, or to their friendship, but hoped he would somehow bring all this Kaahin-created fracas to a peaceful end by saying, 'There's really no earthly reason for you and I to have this kind of quarrel about someone neither of us cares about.' He paused thoughtfully and continued, 'Let's drop the subject altogether.'

But she wasn't prepared to do so and asked, 'Are you made of china, Bosaaso?'

At first he didn't understand her meaning.

'Do you fall to pieces like a china cup when you have an argument with me?' she went on. 'Do you smash into smithereens if someone shouts from the minaret of their rage to express their views?'

'Let's drop it,' he suggested.

'No, we will not, damn you,' said Duniya.

He winced, remaining silent.

'I want you to tell me what you think about Kaahin, not what people say,' she shouted. 'Give me your opinion, not other people's.'

Speaking his words with a glassy attentiveness lest they too should break, he obliged. 'He embarrasses me, and embarrasses Mire for bringing our names into disrepute, our names which he uses as though they were certificates of respectable contacts. And I agree with you, he hates women, in fact he hates himself, and his attitude towards women is testimony to this, a means by which he deceives himself.'

'What of the sticker pasted on the bumper of his car?' she asked.

'The one that reads "Kaahin: Women's Cain", is that the one you mean?'

'That's right.'

Saying nothing for a while, Bosaaso shrugged his shoulders, staring ahead, meditating. Finally he said, 'We all have our adequate share of friends and relatives who embarrass us. Besides, he's not really a friend of mine, only a friend of a friend. Even Zawadi is not responsible for his bad behaviour, I'll absolve her of that.'

'The man is a misogynist,' said Duniya, 'hiding behind fancy-looking cars and mountains of laundered money. It disturbs me to hear you use the word "love" in such a context as Kaahin's and the women whom he seduces with handouts of cash. He is unhealthy, chasing his lust without scruples.'

He could see the extinguished fire in her gaze. He moved in on her to exploit the peaceful mood, announcing, 'Kaahin isn't going to be your driving-instructor, given that he is almost three-quarters of an hour late. I am sorry I suggested it in the first place.'

Whereupon, Duniya began to undo the already threadbare laces of her canvas shoes with absolute caution lest they should snap. 'And what's it that you are doing?'

'Are we not staying at home?' She looked up at him.

'We're doing no such thing,' he said.

She stared at him, puzzled.

'I am going to teach you myself.'

She gave one of her famous chuckles.

'Or don't you have faith in my teaching ability?' he teased.

'It's not that,' she explained. 'But will you be able to snap at me and show your anger if I go into reverse when you ask me to move forward, or if I turn left when you tell me to turn right?'

'I promise you I won't overlook any grave errors you commit,' he said, pleased with himself.

'Keep one thing in mind, Bosaaso. 'I'm not made of china and won't break that easily. Speak up whenever you have good reason to, and never bottle up anger. Cry from the loftiest minaret of your rage, if need be. It may be divine to be forgiving all the time, but it is definitely not human. Even God punishes those who earn His wrath.'

He gathered the tea things, then said, 'Shall we go?'

'Let's,' she said.

Duniya was at the wheel, murmuring something to herself as taking a memory test. The car she and Bosaaso were in was parked in an open space, where many other learners were being given their driving instruction, and now they were facing an aged wall, at the rear of *Genio Civile*. Bosaaso had suggested she concentrate, but that was not what she was doing. She was asking herself why she was learning to drive when she had no car, and no hope of getting one. Was this going to be another nail hammered into the coffin of her dependence on him? Or was theirs simply another clichéd relationship, so to speak, in which women were the providers of food, shelter, peace at home and good company in exchange for the man's offer of upward mobility, security and cash.

Some people sweat when they are nervous. Others get upset stomachs. Some freeze. Others fidget. Duniya was tense all right, so her ears filled with the compressed air of her inner anxiety, and she couldn't hear a thing. Otherwise she was very calm and one wouldn't have suspected her of being under any strain.

'Concentrate!' Bosaaso repeated.

'That's precisely what I am doing, if you please,' she said.

He started from the beginning, naming the important parts of the car, one by one. It was as if he were giving each part he named a fresh lease on life, touching them where possible. He wanted her to know them by their names, he wanted her to remember their function, before moving the vehicle an inch. Now he touched the controls as he pointed them out, as he showed her how the gears operated. Presently he explained how the clutch functioned, and then he pressed the pedals; finally the brake and the accelerator.

Ideas were elbowing each other out, fighting for space in her head, a positive thought out-doing a negative one, or vice versa. She discovered to her surprise that Zawadi, was making her presence felt. To rid her mind of Zawadi, Duniya said: 'Did you know that my brother Abshir's nickname used to be *Scelaro*?'

'Because he learnt things fast?'

She nodded.

After a short pause he said half-censoriously, 'Concentrate!'

Duniya recited the names of the vehicle's parts as he touched them. He was impressed. She did all this with tremendous speed and precision. Then she changed the gears while not moving, and went through the motions of driving through traffic, clutching the steering-wheel, one foot pressing the accelerator, the other alert, and close to both the brake and the clutch.

'How do you put it in reverse?' she asked.

He hesitated and was about to say, 'Later,' but he changed his mind and showed her, the car not yet in motion. She repeated all he had told her, including his instructions about how to reverse. After a very heavy pause, she asked, 'Are you ready?'

'I am, if you are,' he said, smiling.

'Your safety-belt, please,' she said.

They moved very slowly and after an appropriate lapse she shifted gears, apparently comfortable, with the ease and confidence of someone who had driven for years. Her lips were moving all the time. Was she praying? Or was she rehearsing the sequence of moves she would perform? The truth was surprisingly different, for Duniya kept saying to herself, If Zawadi can, so can I; if lots of stupid men can drive, so can I. All the same, the rest of her body was still like a statue at the centre of a spirited storm.

She stopped the vehicle without being told to. Neither said anything, they listened to the engine idle. Again, without being instructed, she switched off the engine, only to start it again instantly, and to drive further and further away from the circle their car tyres had made. As she slowed down, Bosaaso could discern signs of fatigue on her face.

Maybe it was easy to impress Bosaaso: he was a man in love.

She stole a furtive glance in his direction and she thought she had caught his evasive look in the sieve of his gaze. Did he consider her to be foolhardy in taking all this head-on, without fear or worry? Why, Bosaaso had appeared preoccupied at the very moment when she had been most daring. What kind of a man was he? Cautious? Or was he likely to panic?

The car stalled now that she had lost her concentration. Some people cannot help smiling when a car, in which they are being driven by a learner, buck-jumps. Although unaware of it, Bosaaso smiled. To her, the smile was like a stab, and it hurt her. So she started running the engine faster, and then drove round and round until he was visibly worried, frightened. Then she cut off the engine.

Scarcely had he prepared to say something than she turned the key in the ignition and was off, this time reversing. The car buck-jumped. But she didn't despair. She tried it again, repeating the same process. The rear of the vehicle wouldn't obey her commands, swerving snake-like, going out of control, never straight as she had wanted it. Because Bosaaso didn't speak, anxiety welled up inside her, certain that he thought she was being foolish. Finally, she stopped the car.

A long silence.

She remembered when she was four or five, remembered riding Zubair's Arab stallion. She had taken a fright, for the beautiful horse's flanks had been too wide-backed. Abshir, her brother, had been with her and she had held on to him, certain that no harm would come her way.

Bosaaso wondered aloud if she would like to practice more.

'Sure,' she said, accepting his offer.

When the car was moving, Duniya recalled a story Zubair, her first husband, had told her about a horse that had gone mad and wouldn't stop running. The horse grew wings of madness and flew in an easterly direction, towards the sun, as though intending to reach its source. People said that jinns were in the saddle of such horses. Now what if the car refused to stop? What if one of Zubair's wife's relatives who are half-jinn and half-human were to take command of the steering-wheel? Not wanting to risk her life and his, she tested the brakes and was relieved to learn that they were in working order.

'Is anything the matter?' Bosaaso asked.

Duniya's lips gave a tremor of self-blame, and she looked away and at her lap with the apprehensiveness of somebody who didn't know how to apologize. Bosaaso didn't want to find out what had upset her and was pleased to swap seats with her when she suggested they do so. He held his curiosity in check, and came round to the driver's side of the car, touching her as she shifted over to the passenger's seat. Bosaaso put the vehicle into motion without saying a word.

When they were driving past Aw-Cumar's store, where Duniya's family had an account, she asked him to drop her off and to go ahead and wait for her at home. She gave him the key to let himself in, suggesting that he make himself comfortable if either Mataan or Nasiiba were not at home.

He promised her he would.

Aw-Cumar's shop was a small six-by-ten cubicle, criss-crossed with wooden counters running from one end of the wall to the other, with a fold-away counter serving both as table and barrier. Beans, corn, salt were visibly laid out in flat-bottomed boxes. The counter was as high as Duniya's navel. There wasn't anyone in the store today and she wondered where Aw-Cumar might be.

Then she heard his praying whispers, a sequence of sounds familiar to Muslims all the world over, consisting mainly of a stream of alliteratives in the letter S, as part of the Bismillaahis without which prayers are considered sacreligious. Oblivious to what she was doing, she leaned against a ramshackle structure into whose wooden frame Aw-Cumar had hammered nails, so as to discourage idle-talkers from supporting their elbows on it while they held forth, wasting his time. Duniya made a pained sound when the nails pricked her, and hoped she didn't irritate Aw-Cumar.

She discovered a moment later that she did not. He emerged from below the counter, issuing a salvo of Koranic blessings. When he rose to his full height, he was a mere five feet tall. Duniya didn't respond immediately, letting the cluster of prayer-consonants clash and explode in the finale of a Semitic cacophony, conscious of the smile framing his friendly face. Islamic etiquette demanded that a woman not come into bodily contact with a man currently in communication with his Creator, women being impure. She held her ground and waited.

He saluted her several times, albeit from a civic distance. Before long he was saying, 'Please accept my belated condolences for the premature passing away of the foundling. May God's blessing be on your house, Amen!'

She didn't know why she felt ridiculous, but she did. And she thanked him.

He uttered several more salvos, then touched his face with his forefingers, a little later his cupped hands moved down towards his chin, praying all the time, his lips astir with the letter S and on their heels a number of Arabic gutterals. Aw-Cumar proffered his hand at last, a hand which was soft and of an extraordinary roundness, no joints, no cartilage or bone anywhere. In fact he gave away his whole wrist as though he wished one to keep it for him while he dealt with some other business more lucrative than a hand-clasp. Duniya remarked to herself that he had a bracelet of extra flesh around what might once have been a wrist. And a circular expanse of finger-nails. 'What can I do for you?' he said, his hand in hers, and as though he wouldn't want it back.

'I've come to pay my respects, since I haven't called round for a long time, and also to find out the situation with my account,' she said.

'It's very kind of you,' he replied.

Meanwhile Duniya's eyes went past him to take in the shop. In these days of galloping inflation, famines, foreign currency restrictions and corrupt market transactions, shops like Aw-Cumar's had two opposing attitudes towards their clients. There were those whom they treated with special benevolence and to whom they sold hard-to-obtain goods. And there were those to whom they displayed empty shelves, to whom, shaking their heads, the store-owners would say that such and such an item had not been available on the market for months or years, whichever was the more credible. Duniya belonged to the category of customers whom he favoured. Moreover Aw-Cumar was attached to the twins, especially Nasiiba, with whom he often dealt, whose moods he could read, and from whom he occasionally bought some of Duniya's US dollars at a concessionary rate.

'Do you have sugar?' she said.

He said neither yes nor no but, 'Anything else?' while he was still in deep thought, maybe praying. She looked up at the gaping shelves in the hope that their emptiness might inspire her. 'What about rice?'

But then both of them fell silent when a neighbour, clearly not one of Aw-Cumar's favourite clients, came in and asked if there was any likelihood of his selling to her half a pound of sugar for any sum he wished to name. Aw-Cumar's head shook with actorly sadness, saying, 'I'm afraid I have no sugar, not even for my own family's consumption.'

When the woman-customer had been gone a good few minutes, Aw-Cumar called one of his daughters who rushed in through the back door, coming as she did from the inner compound at the rear of the store, a highly valued property belonging to the shop. Her father's hand lay on the young girl's coxcomb-hairdo as he turned to Duniya asking, 'How much sugar and how many kilos of rice would you like?'

'Three kilos of sugar, or is that too much to ask for?' she hesitated.

'Five?'

'All right, five.'

'And three kilos of rice, the best, imported from China?'

'Thank you,' she said.

And there he was, waiting for her to order anything her heart desired.

'Would you like some flour?' he inquired of her, when she couldn't come up with any orders.

'Do you have flour?'

'Would ten kilos do?'

'Thank you,' she said.

'Would you like a kilos of raisins?

'At times I wonder why you are so kind to me.'

'You've been kind, a mother to an abandoned baby,' he said, and after a pause continued, 'And don't think of thanking me, for what I have is yours and if I am in short supply myself then I cannot help it.' He scribbled something on a piece of paper, gave the chit to his daughter whose coxcomb he held onto as he said, 'Take this to your step-mother and bring back what is written here. All right?' But he wouldn't let go of the girl until he insisted that Duniya maybe ask for the universe and he, Aw-Cumar would serve it to her, right off his counter, heaven, hell and all.

'That's all for now, thanks,' she stammered.

And the young girl rushed out of the store through the door in the rear, with a shriek of childish excitement. There were repeated cries of anger as she interrupted her sisters' game of hopscotch.

'May I have the accounts book please?' said Duniya.

Aw-Cumar opened and closed a couple of drawers, looking for it. Duniya remembered an embarrassing incident when Mataan, thrilled at the arithmetic abilities of which he was proud, had taken it upon himself to do the totalling up of Duniya's debts, discovering an ugly discrepancy. This caused both Aw-Cumar and Duniya a great deal of distress, and he swore he hadn't done it deliberately. From then on, it was agreed that Nasiiba and no one else would enter in the accounts book any sum owed to Aw-Cumar.

'Here,' he said presently, giving her the accounts book.

The sum owed to him was entered in Nasiiba's hand in this exercise book, with one of its covers already torn off. Like a door hanging on a half-broken hinge, the other cover held, more or less, on the teeth of additional staples punched on the side. Nasiiba had scribbled in ink the words 'Duniya & Family: Accounts'.

Opening and turning the pages Duniya discovered that all the bills had been settled by Nasiiba, all until a week ago. Duniya's look was of a disturbed kind, noting to herself that perhaps the money in the Iranian Islamic magazine had a wicked story behind it.

Aw-Cumar said, 'Is something worrying you?'

'No, nothing.'

'Please tell me what's bothering you, because I can see your eyes going pale with preoccupation,' he said. 'Let me assure you that your accounts book is clean like the slates of a saint at Judgement Day, not a single stain anywhere.'

Improvising, Duniya said, 'I've come bearing sad news.'

'Oh?'

'We are moving out of the district.'

Aw-Cumar's features displayed a genuine sorrow. 'But we shall miss you!'

'The children and I will miss you too.'

He was a most discreet man. Duniya suspected that Aw-Cumar was in on the gossip being circulated in the neighbourhood, about a wealthy US-returned Somali who was infatuated with 'our midwife'. But he made no reference to it, not even when he inquired if they knew where they would be moving.

When Aw-Cumar's daughter brought back Duniya's provisions in a large carrier bag advertising a brand of cigarettes, Duniya asked, 'How much do we owe you for this blessed manna from the heavens of your kindness?'

His lips trembled with sums which he committed instantly to paper; finally he added the sums up in his head and gave her the total. Duniya entered and initalled it in the exercise book.

She was feeling ill at ease because she had lied to him. After all she had not come with the intention of buying any provisions, only to take a look at the accounts book. Was this why she was becoming garrulous? And why didn't she leave directly after she had received her supply of food? 'My brother Abshir is paying us a visit shortly and we are very excited at the thought and eager to welcome him,' she volunteered.

'How long has it been since he was last here in Mogadiscio?' One might have thought he was talking about somebody he knew. Maybe he remembered how often Abshir's name came up in Duniya or Nasiiba's conversations in a casual manner, particularly with regard to their provision of foreign currency, since he was the primary source.

'Long before the twins were born,' she said.

Aw-Cumar was a very kind man. 'I would certainly like to make his acquaintance, although he has been but a name to me all these years,' he said.

Aw-Cumar's daughter ran off to broadcast the news that Nasiiba's mother was moving out of the district to the others who were still playing some kind of hopscotch. A moment later another little girl was scampering away from her hiding-place with the exciting news that Nasiiba's uncle was coming to Mogadiscio soon. These took their toll of emotions and Duniya's throat filled with tears and this made her voice very hoarse. 'Thank you very much, Aw-Cumar,' she repeated, hardly able to say a word without pausing.

'Please don't move out of the district without letting us know your new address, as we would like to keep in touch with you and your children, of whom we are terribly fond,' he said.

She promised she wouldn't move without alerting them to the fact.

Entering her place which was a little under a hundred metres away, Duniya shouted *'Hoodi-hoodi'* and was expressly delighted to hear Bosaaso's 'Come in'. He joined her near the gate to help her carry in the provisions. Then he said anxiously, 'I must fetch Nasiiba and Yarey.'

'And where are they?' she said, hoping he might tell her out of absent-mindedness.

'Ask them yourself when they are back,' he insisted.

'You know I won't,' she said.

'Fair enough then,' he said, 'for I won't tell you.'

But she had the weird feeling they were at Bosaaso's place, watching something on his video. A hostile expression clouded her features briefly. Then she told herself that she should have a high-handed word with Nasiiba. After all, Duniya wanted to put her house in order before Abshir's arrival, and before making up her mind about Bosaaso.

'See you soon then,' she said, dismissing him that way.

And he was gone.

The meal that evening was a dull affair: red beans and rice, a commonplace dish, Mogadiscio's staple nightly diet. It was Nasiiba's garlic sauce that brightened things up, giving the food a sharper taste. Duniya wished she had made the meal more interesting, if only for Bosaaso's sake. No doubt she appreciated his willingness to share whatever they were eating. Very humble of him, indeed.

Once they had eaten, Mataan excused himself saying he had homework to do. He went to his room, pushing his door shut, and remained quiet, maybe working, maybe not. Yarey yawned and yawned, she was bored and tired. But Nasiiba and Bosaaso wanted to talk. It felt as though they intended to save the world with their chatter from its current crisis of civil wars, drought and intellectual bankruptcy.

Duniya got to her feet, ready to leave. Bosaaso, deferential, looked from Nasiiba to Duniya and back and didn't know how to act. 'You don't have to go. Let her. She's writing a letter to her brother Abshir,' Nasiiba said.

Neither Duniya nor Bosaaso could think of anything to say for a time.

'In that case I'll come for you in the morning,' he offered.

'There's no need,' she said.

He looked worried. 'Aren't you going to work?' Nasiiba asked.

'I've arranged an alternative form of transport for work,' she said, sounding mysterious.

He was desperate as he said, 'Won't you be taking your second driving lesson tomorrow afternoon?'

'Yes, but after Nasiiba and I have gone house-hunting.'

'How exciting, Mummy, to be looking for somewhere to live.'

'Can I come with you, Duniya?' said Yarey.

'Good night then,' Duniya said to Bosaaso.

'Good night.'

And to Yarey, 'Come, my dearest. Come with me if you're bored.'

Left alone, Nasiiba and Bosaaso talked and talked, whereas Yarey fell asleep the instant her head touched the pillow. Duniya read for a while and then wrote a letter to Abshir, her brother.

My darling brother:

I write to you with a sense of urgency and because Dr Mire has told me that you are planning to pay me and my children a long-awaited visit. I can't tell you how delighted I am to receive you, to welcome you with a pent-up love which has been treasured for you for years.

As I pen this I can overhear Nasiiba and Bosaaso's conversation about mythical and religious tensions present in the notion of 'return', and I think of you and how much I've missed you, and how much I long for the day when we'll be reunited, to share our happiness and our pains.

You will find me a changed woman. A letter such as this cannot tell you much. But I look forward to telling you everything myself. Please please please telegraph me care of the hospital where I can be reached, giving me the details of your departure from Rome and arrival here so we can come to meet you at the airport.

I've been made to promise to ask you to bring special gifts for your nieces and nephew. Attached please find a list drawn up by Nasiiba – but then again you may disregard them.

Your loving sister,
Dunya

Restless, Duniya could not sleep. Nasiiba and Bosaaso were still talking several hours later. Whereupon Duniya shouted to Nasiiba to take from her Abshir's letter and give it to Bosaaso, who knew someone leaving for Rome the following afternoon. Bosaaso saw this as an indication that it was time he left, which he did.

The night echoed with his and Nasiiba's good-night wishes.

Chapter Fourteen

Duniya is given a lift to work by Mataan on a borrowed motor scooter. Later that day, before her driving lesson, Duniya goes house-hunting and in the process calls on Miski, Fariida's sister.

A woman in her mid-thirties is watching a sunset in a dream setting. A younger woman, presumably her daughter, materializes from nowhere and blocks her view. The older woman turns the other way, as though uninterested, her gaze this time dwelling on several stray evening clouds migrating towards darkness.

Mataan had a beautiful mouth which was often open. His silences stretched long, like an unending road, straight, unbending, not at all desolate. He had a way of surrounding himself with wise silences and his eyes would have a remarkable vacuity behind them. One was tempted to comment on these when alone with him. Shy, quiet, tall and skinny, with his mouth ajar like a door pushed open by the breeze, Mataan might concentrate on a wart on one's face, waiting, saying nothing, forever patient. More than his one-liners, it was his silences one remembered.

His twin sister's silent pauses had in them blind curves and on encountering them one had to be on guard for fear of being ambushed. Thus would Duniya try to explain her different attitudes towards her children's quiet moments.

Mataan now said, 'I've borrowed a motor scooter, Mother, and can give you a lift to work. My classes today don't start till after ten-thirty.'

She had heard him leave the house at the crack of dawn, maybe to collect the scooter from its owner. Most probably he had decided to borrow it after having overheard her conversation with Bosasso the previous night, in which she had talked of arranging an alternative way of getting to work.

'Whose is the motor scooter, Mataan?' she asked.

'It belongs to the cousin of a friend, Mother,' he said.

It didn't require much for her to conclude that the Vespa belonged to Waris's cousin – Waris, Mataan's woman-friend. And though he was standing out of Duniya's vision now, she knew he was swallowing lumps of nerves. Nasiiba and Yarey had been gone for a quarter of an hour showering together, and in the intervening period Mataan had come to make his offer of a lift, knowing that his twin would be averse to his gestures. 'Come closer so I can see you,' Duniya suggested, and when he did, she said, 'I don't wish to interfere in your private affairs, but do you think it's wise of me to turn down Bosaaso's offer only for you to borrow a motor scooter from someone else to take me to work?' In the mean-time she wrapped herself in a bedspread.

He said humbly, 'I don't know,' meeting her eyes for the first time.

'Whose is it really?'

'The scooter is owned by an older man who likes to borrow my bicycle, so he can keep fit. I seldom make the exchange, Mother.'

'I wish you wouldn't borrow things for my sake,' Duniya said.

He looked away. After a while he turned and her eyes fell on his young face, and a thought crossed her mind, one she couldn't explain: that Mataan looked like a son. Whereas Nasiiba put her in mind of a young woman likely to become a mother one day, Mataan had the look of a sturdy young tree, firm and steadfast as somebody's young son. To be labelled 'Mataan: a son!' like a clothes dummy of a tailor's with a price tag on it. Duniya reasoned that he would surely eventually marry a woman older than him.

'How much does a new motor-scooter cost?' she asked.

'You can't get them because of foreign currency restrictions.'

'How much would a good second-hand one fetch?'

He was silent, then said, 'Let's first find a home to move to.'

Nasiiba and Yarey had come on the scene, so Duniya and Mataan adapted themselves to the new arrivals. Yarey was in a chatty mood. She said, 'You must go to see an Italian film called *The Tree of the Wooden Clogs*. Nasiiba and I saw it yesterday and we loved it, didn't we, Naasi?'

Duniya guessed that Yarey's lines had been given her by

Nasiiba and had been rehearsed to the last comma, question-and exclamation-mark. Mataan, too, suspected this to be the case.

Yarey went on, 'And you must see the big house Bosaaso lives in all by himself, Duniya, a big garden, a very large kitchen, larger than this place we live in, the four of us.'

Mataan left in haste, and this disturbed Nasiiba. 'What was he talking about, Mummy?' she asked.

To avert early morning confrontation between the twins, Duniya suggested that Nasiiba hurry, for it was impolite to make the taxi wait longer than absolutely necessary.

Nasiiba was of a mind to disregard her mother's advice, and she repeated her question, 'What was he talking about?'

'Mataan has borrowed a motor-scooter to give me a lift,' Duniya replied, regretting it the instant the words had left her lips.

Nasiiba was dismissive of the man who owned the Vespa, saying, 'Do you know what people say?'

'No, what do they say?'

'The man is a homosexual, an old man in his fifties who prefers the company of younger boys. Did Mataan tell you that?'

There was the clichéd silence of a pin-dropping quality.

The quarrel was cut short by the arrival of the taxi taking Nasiiba and Yarey to their respective schools. Nasiiba opened the windows overlooking the road and shouted something to the man whom she called Axmad. Meanwhile she and Yarey stumbled into their school-uniforms, each reminding the other to be quick. 'Remember we're going house-hunting this afternoon,' Duniya said to Nasiiba.

'Right-oh,' Nasiiba mimicked an American film heroine dashing out of a room.

Mataan and Duniya had breakfast together, Mataan making the omelette and tea, and afterwards clearing the trays and doing the washing-up, including his sisters'. Duniya was undecided whether to wear her hair covered or uncovered. Given that she would be on a motor scooter and not in a car, would her hair be a scatter of plaits, waving in all directions, like the hands of a bad swimmer drowning? Thinking of their safety (she was actually thinking about seat-belts as well as Bosaaso), she wondered if it was possible to find helmets at such short notice. It was too late in the day to worry about it.

'Tell me, do you like Bosaaso?' she said to Mataan.

Mataan hesitated, then said, 'I do – really.'

'What do you like about him?'

'I feel comfortable with him.'

'Comfortable in what sense?' He appeared to be having difficulty with his words; he stammered, every consonant proving a hurdle. The brown in his eyes darkened.

She had almost given up on getting any answer out of him as she asked, 'Do you like him as much as you liked Taariq when you were a lot smaller?' And she felt foolish saying this.

'As it happens, I always prefer having friends older than me, and Bosaaso is the sort of man whose friendship I would tend to cultivate, someone whose learning I would emulate. I don't regret my closeness to Taariq, and hold no resentful feelings towards him.'

'What would you do if you were me?' she said.

He sat forward, as though a gun had been pointed at his nape. 'In what regard, Mother?'

'Would you marry him?'

Mataan's tongue was active, not in the act of speech but scouring the inside of his mouth as if searching for a clue there. 'Knowing you, Mother,' he said at last, 'you'll make up your mind one way or the other on the spur of the moment. So I don't know what to say.'

Somewhere in the labyrinth of Duniya's mind there was a cul de sac. She said, 'People say that I'm after his money.'

'People say all sorts of wicked things,' he echoed.

'Doesn't that worry you?'

His lips swelled out in handsome protrusion as he thought about this. He said, 'I don't mean to be disrespectful, but what has Bosaaso got that you could be after by way of money, a Green Card or property? I doubt very much if his income is higher than Uncle Abshir's, who's prepared to give you all you need, and foot all our educational bills anywhere in the world.'

'All the same, people's tongues are busy, spreading evil gossip.'

'I wouldn't worry about them if I were you,' he said. 'They say terrible things about the man I borrowed the scooter from. It's his affair if he is homosexual; what makes his sexual taste their business I don't know. Some people say unkind things about

Waris on account of the age difference between us.' His lips might have been those of an infant who had just been breast-fed, and not sufficiently.

'You love her, don't you?'

An open mouth is like an open door: one is tempted to look in. Mataan's had a beautiful set of teeth, with a gap in the centre of the top row. Women never failed to comment on his *fanax*, wishing it was Nasiiba who had it, for it is commonly believed that girls look prettier when they have gaps in their teeth. Such good-looking features are an asset assuring women of men's attention and marriage. And Nasiiba would retort: Who wants to marry anyway?

'You don't have to answer my question,' said Duniya.

This was meant to prod him, considering that he was susceptible to her probings. 'I think I'm in love with her, yes,' he said, and he was immediately ill at ease.

'Shall we leave?' she asked.

He stood up, tall, slim and shy. 'Are you ready?'

She too got to her feet. She felt uncomfortable in the slacks she had on, her navel bulge an irritation. But she wasn't going to change into a dress or her uniform which she had stuffed into her bag; wearing either would be inconvenient on a scooter. Mataan was waiting for her by the Vespa, modest as the dull, brown and humble grey colours which he liked.

'Here we are,' he said, kick-starting the machine.

Duniya sat side-saddle. It was the first time she had ridden a motor scooter and it scared her. Mataan had to stop two or three times, to remind her that it was important to co-ordinate their bodily balance, otherwise they might tip over and hurt themselves. 'It's like a boat with an outboard engine,' he said, repeating what the owner had told him. But Duniya had no idea what he was talking about, never having been in such a contraption.

However, she enjoyed the ride once they got going, the wind blowing in her face, her ears filling with air, her head empty of all worrying thoughts, save the new pleasant sensation of being on a scooter and no longer scared. It was like a new-found freedom. She felt light. The roads were lined on both sides by people waiting endlessly for transport which never arrived. In her mind, these people had arrived to wave to the two of them riding past, like a presidential motorcade receiving a tumultuous welcome.

There was something scary about the experience. The sky was out of bounds and the earth appeared either too far below her or else too close to her feet, which hung down, almost touching it. There seemed many more potholes than she remembered encountering when in Bosaaso's car. On the other hand, they could be spotted well in advance, and be avoided. Duniya's eyes were active and registered the details of people's clothes. 'I feel wonderful,' Duniya shouted, 'It feels wonderful.'

'What?' shouted Mataan.

She repeated what she had said, adding, 'We must buy a scooter.' He didn't show any reaction; maybe he hadn't heard her suggestion.

Her sides began to ache and her muscles stretched with acute pain from having sat awkwardly, like someone holding back her weight away from another person sharing a limited space. None the less this was decidedly more fun than the humiliation of being in the company of somebody one didn't know. In another sense she was happy to make the point to Bosaaso that she had alternative ways of getting to work, wasn't totally reliant on his good-will and kind gestures, thank you.

'Look at them,' Duniya said.

He slowed down and asked, 'Look at whom?'

'Look at them dressed in these exquisitely tailored clothes!' and she pointed at the women and men on either side of road, potential passengers of buses that never arrived, thumb-raisers for lifts that were never offered. 'I wonder if they're on their way to a wedding or to a seasonal festivity in their office. How can they care so much about their appearances when they're penniless?' Her ribs pained from her long shout, her lungs ran out of the breath she could generate. She paused, then after a while continued, 'Both as individuals and as governments, we Somalis, better still, we Africans, tend to live beyond our means.'

They rode in silence until they reached the hospital entrance, and she got off, happy that the journey was at an end. Her feet had grown numb, but the rest of her body felt light, as though she had just descended the gangway-ladder of an aircraft. Mataan raised the scooter on its stand and got down to give her her handbag, although his satchel remained slung over the handle-bars.

Barely able to hear her own voice she said, 'I want you to

change three hundred and fifty US dollars for me, Mataan dear,' and she gave him seven fifty-dollar bills, recalling to her memory all that had taken place the previous few days, including the discovery of the foundling, her meeting with and falling in love with Bosaaso, and the wads of money which she found tucked away in Nasiiba's Iranian magazine. 'We'll need some cash when we go house-hunting this afternoon, in case a landlord insists on an immediate deposit. Don't go to Uncle Qaasim if you can help it.'

'But I can't think of anyone else,' he confessed.

'Ask around,' she suggested. 'Good rate, safe person. I'm sure one of your friends will come up with a name. After all, this is good money, what Nasiiba calls "Bosaaso-money" nowadays.'

'I'll see what I can do.'

She walked away, wishing him good day and advising him to take care.

Bosaaso came to fetch her after work, and after exchanging the formula greetings they remained quiet. The images pouring into Duniya's mind refused to cohere. Maybe it was to do with a nervous bug in the pit of her stomach, a worried reaction to a hasty decision to serve the quit-notice on herself. There was no going back, she would have to move out, find some other place. But where?

Where did one start? The city of Mogadiscio expanded right before her eyes, growing a thousand times in size, although somehow she convinced herself that she should not be easily discouraged. It was a pity that newspapers did not carry notices advertising small flats to rent, only large villas intended for foreign residents of the metropolis, who were willing to pay their Somali landlords in hard currency. For locals, news about the availability of vacant accommodation, like other information, was circulated primarily by word of mouth in this essentially oral society.

Her pride and instinct for self-preservation advised against involving Bosaaso in her search. She did not have her own means of transport and taxis were impossible to find. Besides, he was willing to take her anywhere. Or was this exploitative?

It was when she thought of herself as a woman and thought about the female gender in the general context of 'home' that

Duniya felt depressed. The landmarks of her journey through life from infancy to adulthood were marked by various 'stations', all of them owned by men, run and dominated by men. Did she not move from her father's home directly into Zubair's? Did she not flee Zubair's right into Shiriye's? There was a parenthesis of time, a brief period when she was her own mistress and the runner of her station, so to speak, as a free tenant of Taariq's, only for this to cease when they became husband and wife. Meanwhile, her elder brother Abshir's omnipresent, benevolent, well-meaning shadow fell on every ramshackle structure she built, pursuing every move she made, informing every step she took: Abshir being another station, another man. Now there was Bosaaso. *Morale della storia*? Duniya was homeless, like a great many women the world over. And as a woman she was property-less.

Over lunch, not speaking to anyone, not even Nasiiba (who had prepared today's meal), nor Yarey (who had attempted to drag her into their conversation), Duniya recalled how often she had postponed looking for her own home, away from her half-brother Shiriye's, where she and her twins had lived in virtual terror and humiliation. It was thanks to being misdirected by a neighbour (who might have been Marilyn's grandmother for all she could tell) that she had knocked on the wrong door, Taariq's. And he had taken pity on a homeless woman, with twins to raise. Would someone take pity on her today, being driven by a man in such a handsome car?

'Why, you look so miserable. Cheer up, Mummy!' Nasiiba said.

Her sadness long as her chin, Duniya replied, 'Give me one reason why I should.'

The twins exchanged glances, resting ultimately on Bosaaso. This was lost on no one, save Yarey, who was busy dismantling a Parker pen belonging to Bosaaso, with nobody telling her not to ruin it.

As if setting the theme of a discussion, Duniya said, 'The simple fact is that I am a homeless woman, and there is no getting away from it.'

Before long, the group began to talk at length of the notion of homelessness which, according to Bosaaso, had its origin in the myth of the displaced Adam, not Eve. This was challenged by Nasiiba, who argued that in Islam there was no such myth as the fall of man. There was the wandering figure of a migrant, in the Islamic notion of Hijra, which may also be interpreted as an act of a pious Muslim fleeing persecution. In an ideal Islamic society, the mosque is the place where the homeless go.

'Not homeless women, surely,' interjected Duniya.

Mataan affirmed, 'That's right.'

'In an ideal Islamic society . . .' began Nasiiba.

'In which case there'd be fewer homeless women,' said Duniya, 'perhaps because of the multiplicity of wives men are allowed to retain as their dependants or concubines.'

Sensing the tension building, Bosaaso changed the subject from the homeless in Islamic societies to the homeless in New York, men and women without shelter of their own, who slept under bridges, on flattened cardboard boxes serving as mattresses. Duniya remembered being shown such people in the environs of the Stazione Termini, the main railway station in Rome. Nearby there was a piazza called Independenza, the Somalis' and the Eritreans' meeting-place in the Italian capital. Duniya wondered why it was that foreigners and the homeless congregated round departure- or arrival-points in their country of economic exile. There was no denying that expatriates living in Mogadiscio were prone to go to the airport at the slimmest pretext to welcome or bid farewell their travelling compatriots. Somalis used to turn up in large numbers at Fiumicino, Rome's international airport, whenever a Somali Airlines flight arrived or departed.

In response to a question from Mataan Bosaaso said, 'There are more homeless people in the city of New York than there are official residents of Mogadiscio, Somalia's capital. The figure is shocking.'

'Truth is always embarrassing,' commented Nasiiba.

'In fact,' Bosaaso continued, 'there's recently been a controversy surrounding a United Nations film about the homeless in the world. You'd be surprised to know that some US Congressmen and Senators tried to prevent the public viewing of this documentary. And I take it, you've also heard about the Polish government's gift of blankets to the homeless in New York?' and he glanced in Duniya's direction.

Duniya admitted she hadn't heard of it.

Tentatively, Nasiiba said, 'Didn't it all begin with President Reagan dispatching tinned milk to Poland, after the Chernobyl disaster, a gift meant to pack an ideological punch? Poland versus the Soviet Union. It turned out to be an unfortunate joke against Reagan, apparently, because the milk was found to be bad when opened. In response – tell me if I'm wrong, anyone,' continued Nasiiba, enjoying everyone's attention, 'the Polish government shipped blankets to New York's homeless, but the parcels were addressed care of the White House. Ha, ha, ha!'

'And what did the Americans do?' Duniya inquired.

'Newspaper headlines,' said Bosaaso. 'That was all.'

Mataan said, 'And yet we are under the mistaken impression that being poor, famine-stricken and homeless are phenomena associated with underdevelopment, shortage of hard currency and so on. It's disturbing to think that we, too, will have a million homeless people in our cities if we become technologically advanced.'

'It's tragic,' agreed Duniya.

The discussion shifted from the specific to the general, then back to particular economic and social realities, and everyone agreed that the homeless were mostly people of colour, or old, that black women tended to have the strength to survive, despite their enormous burdens, better than their male counterparts.

Asking no one in particular, Mataan said, 'You know the Islamic concept, *xabs*?'

'*Xabs* is interpreted by Islamic scholars as the right of obedience,' explained Mataan, 'although the word shares its root with another understood to mean detention. The point is that women aren't permitted to leave their husbands' homes without their husbands' prior notification, and any woman who violates this right may be described as rebellious. The home, therefore, the veil and the fact that women can't go out of the house, say, to work in an office or as a nurse in a hospital: these come under *xabs*: the right of obedience. A homeless woman is one who has no husband or a male relation to provide her with shelter.'

There was a brief pause and Duniya, exploiting it, wondered aloud whether Yarey, who had fallen asleep, should be taken to bed where she would be more comfortable. At the mention of her name, Yarey's head rose like that of an infant not yet endowed with speech, who responds to the mention of its name in a conversation. 'Do you never tire,' she said, 'Nasiiba, you talk and talk and talk?'

'I wasn't talking,' Nasiiba came to her own defence.

'When I fell asleep you were speaking, and when I woke up you still were,' said Yarey. 'I thought you said you were going to Miski's?'

Duniya looked from Yarey to Nasiiba. 'What about Miski?'

Yarey was now wide awake. 'Naasi promised the two of you would go to Miski's and hand over to her a list of things I want Uncle Abshir to bring me.'

'What's all this?' asked Duniya of Nasiiba.

'Relax, Mummy.'

'How can I, with you around!' Duniya had the harassed look of a skinny dog in an African city, trotting around, its tail permanently between its legs, alert, ready to scamper away at the sight of any moving shadow, certain that someone would stone it.

'The reason why we should go to Miski's, Mummy,' said Nasiiba, 'is because Miski is planning to leave the two-bedroom apartment she's been living in with Fariida.'

No sooner had Duniya prepared to question her than she heard Mataan say that he had forgotten to give her the equivalent of three hundred and fifty US dollars in Somali shillings, and he returned from his room with a satchel of notes.

As they left in Bosaaso's car to call on Miski, Yarey and Mataan scooted off on his borrowed Vespa to Taariq's and maybe to Qaasim's. Nasiiba locked up the house, as if they were going away on a short holiday. Duniya had the sad feeling that, since the foundling's death, her place had the lonely look of an orphan.

Miski had just let herself in when they arrived. She hadn't even changed. Her body smelt of air-freshener, her cheeks, when Duniya kissed them, felt dry. They were pleased to see each other. Nasiiba led the way to the living-room when the formality of introductions between Bosaaso and Miski was over and done with.

There was a narrow hallway, then what served as the sitting-room. To get to the other two rooms, you veered left, past a toilet and a kitchen, and suddenly were in one of the rooms. Duniya didn't think this was her idea of a home; it would be a nightmare to wake in such a place if you were visiting a younger sister. Poor Abshir wouldn't know where his room was in relation to anyone else's. Maybe it wasn't so inconvenient sharing it with another sister, as Fariida and Miski were doing. Duniya would have a hard time convincing the twins to stop quarrelling.

In the living-room, now that they were all seated, Duniya turned to Miski, who was in her mid-to-late-twenties, of medium height, and with a rather formal general posture, perhaps the result of her being an air hostess. She noticed, however, that Miski's mouth was very agitated, her involuntary movements making one think of pain endured, bottled up, with no likelihood of ever being released.

Miski was holding a note her younger sister Fariida had left her, saying that she had gone to the physiotherapist, and didn't know when she would be back. Miski looked tormented.

Bosaaso took the seat Nasiiba waved him into, one separated from others by a small island of unoccupied space. He felt out of place, not only because he couldn't follow the meaning of Fariida's message, which Miski had read out loud, but he had never met Fariida and had no idea who she was.

The living-room had a musty odour. Maybe the windows had not been opened for at least a day. Someone had smoked, dumped ash carelessly, leaving cigarette-butts in a saucer; maybe the same person had eaten left-over rice, potatoes and ketchup out of the same saucer. The coffee table was covered in breadcrumbs, the couch on which Nasiiba was sitting had been slept in recently, and the cushions were brown with sweat. Everywhere were signs of youthful disorder. Miski, whom Duniya knew to be an orderly person, appeared ill at ease being called on by a stranger like Bosaaso before she had readied the flat for his visit.

There was a sense of fellow-feeling among the adults. Duniya was remembering vivid moments of embarrassment such as when Mataan wet Taariq's bed; or the number of times Nasiiba had embarrassed her; Bosaaso, for his part, was recalling the occasions when Zawadi's son stubbed out his cigarettes in a butter-cup.

'We're sorry to drop in unannounced like this,' Duniya said.

'I'm glad you're here. I would have come to see you if you hadn't,' Miski replied, searching for something in her handbag.

'Have you just got back?' Bosaaso asked.

'Literally,' Miski said.

'From where?'

'Rome.'

'When did you go to Rome?' Nasiiba asked.

'I stood in for a stewardess who couldn't go,' Miski explained to Nasiiba. 'And you'll be glad to know,' she turned to Duniya, 'I saw Abshir and have a letter from him.'

'How is he?' asked Nasiiba.

'He's looking forward to being here,' said Miski, giving Duniya two envelopes, one thicker than the other.

'When is he due here?' Duniya asked, not opening the envelopes.

'Everything's in the letter, Mummy,' said Nasiiba, impulsively snatching both envelopes from Duniya's clutch. 'Why can't you read?'

Bosaaso, sounding eager, asked, 'But when is he due here?'

Duniya's lips trembled as if saying a brief prayer.

In the meantime, Miski counted her days and nights, consulting her watch before answering Bosaaso's question, 'I'm flying back late tonight. That means we'll be on the same flight tomorrow afternoon.'

'I'm really looking forward to seeing Abshir,' said Bosaaso.

Duniya stared at Nasiiba who was engrossed in reading Uncle Abshir's letter. To make sure she would not be disturbed by anyone, Nasiiba sat apart from everybody, like a cat unwilling to share its food with others.

'You're moving out of here?' Duniya asked.

'That's the first I've heard of it. Where am I moving to?' Miski asked.

Duniya hoped Nasiiba would say something, explain where she had got the news from, since it had been she who had said Miski had decided to move. But Nasiiba's attention was totally devoted to Abshir's letter.

'Perhaps Fariida understands that you are moving out,' ventured Duniya.

'When does Fariida understand anything?' said Miski decisively. 'And pray where would I move to?'

Nasiiba interrupted her reading. She looked first at her mother, then at Miski to whom she said, 'Do you know if there's a vacant flat in the Mocallim Jaamac area, in the centre of the city, Miski?'

'Yes, there is,' said Miski.

'And doesn't the vacant flat belong to a relation of yours?'

'It belongs to my former fiancé's father, that's right.'

Certain that her mother and Miski could take it from there without her help, Nasiiba lost interest in the conversation. Returning to reading her uncle's letter, she sat as if impervious to the world around her, her feet tucked under her, and looking pleased.

After a long pause, Duniya asked Miski, 'Do you think we could take a look at that flat? We are very anxious to find one?'

'But why are you moving out of yours?' Miski asked.

'It's too complicated a story to tell you now,' said Duniya.

Miski was suddenly sad. 'I hope it hasn't anything to do with Fariida's baby?' she said. 'It wasn't my idea that she abandon it.'

Bosaaso sat up as if stung by a black ant, but he said nothing.

'Our moving out of Qaasim's house hasn't anything to do with Fariida or her baby,' said Duniya.

Nasiiba interrupted her reading to look from her mother to Miski and to say, 'Mummy's lying to you. The truth is Fariida's baby has everything to do with our moving out of Uncle Qaasim's house. But it is a long story, as Mummy said. I promise to tell you when we're alone and Mummy and Bosaaso are gone.' Then, as if nothing untoward had taken place, Nasiiba resumed her reading.

No movement, no sound, only a drift of disturbed eyes. Perhaps amused, Bosaaso could not tear his away from Nasiiba. To describe Duniya as embarrassed and leave it at that would be a distortion. Nevertheless, she wasn't angry with Nasiiba, if anything she was pleased. Uppermost in her thoughts was the prospect of his retaining faith in her, a prospect causing her great distress. What if the poor man thought Duniya had known about the foundling's identity all along and hidden it from him? Would he believe it if she had told him that she hadn't discussed the topic with either Nasiiba or Fariida, or for that matter Miski? Bosaaso meant a lot to her, and she didn't want him to lose trust.

Perhaps shaken by the revelation, Bosaaso's gaze evaded hers, dwelling on the floor ahead of him, dazed. But he didn't appear totally abandoned in the ship-wreck of new discoveries when he looked up and their eyes locked in an embrace of acknowledged grins. He had hope, Duniya thought, he still had love for her in his look.

Encouraged by this, she said to Miski, 'Do you believe that any initial interest in your relation's city flat is even justified?'

'It has enough space for you and the twins, if that's what you're after,' answered Miski.

'There are four of us, plus of course Abshir visiting.'

Wincing, Miski didn't ask why there were four of them, not three, and her hesitation left traces of a tremor on her lips. The young woman had weak knees, a meek heart that was as large as it was generous. Perhaps Fariida had been blamed wrongly for being the one who had introduced Miski's former fiancé, the son of the owner of the city flat Duniya was currently interested in, to the girl whom he had made pregnant and in that event married.

Now Miski collapsed into an armchair. This was turning into a difficult scene for anyone to handle; and as if this was the only action she was capable of undertaking, Miski grimaced. Then she said, 'The city flat has two rooms, facing a large courtyard, a small garden, with a kitchen and two outside toilets, meant as part of servants' quarters which never got built. The rooms are very big, each equipped with its separate bathroom-cum-toilet, bidet and other amenities, and they're airy, the ceilings high. Apparently they once belonged to the Catholic Mission's Holy See office in Mogadiscio.'

'Do you know how much the landlord is asking?'

'It's very expensive.'

'How expensive?'

'How much can you afford?'

Duniya mentioned a sum.

Hesitation made Miski's nose twitch. 'I'll try to get the keys from the proprietor for that amount, saying I'm moving in, or maybe I'll tell him the truth. I hope honesty pays generous dividends.'

'Let's pray to God I can afford it,' said Duniya.

As though on cue, Nasiiba said, 'Mummy, Uncle Abshir has sent you lots of cash, three thousand US dollars.' The young girl gave herself the luxury to pause, get up and walk over to where her mother sat. Standing over her, she went on, 'Here's the money in this envelope, I've counted it myself. And here in the thinner envelope is a long letter containing just one important piece of news: he's arriving the day after tomorrow, in the afternoon, on the Somali Airlines flight from Rome – not tomorrow afternoon, as Miski said.'

Duniya received the envelopes, thanked Miski for bringing them.

Whereupon Nasiiba urged her, 'I suggest you go now, Mummy, taking Bosaaso with you, poor man, who's been out of it all. Miski, after her shower, will take me to the landlord and I'll bring the key when I come home. If the flat has been taken, so be it; we'll have to think again, look again.'

Duniya could not ignore the wisdom of Nasiiba's suggestions. When as a bonus she was offered a young, stronger hand to help her rise to her feet, up and out of the sagging armchair into which she had sunk, she took it gratefully.

Bosaaso appeared relieved to be leaving and as she assisted him, Nasiiba teased him (calling him 'Old-bones'), adding, 'You two give each other your driving lessons and leave us to deal with the flat.'

Miski looked sad.

As they said their goodbyes, Duniya's anxiety showed all over her face. It was not going to be easy to convince Bosaaso that she had no knowledge of the foundling's identity before this afternoon.

Duniya had had only a quarter of an hour to practise her driving, when, with the suddenness Bosaaso began associating with her, she brought the vehicle to an abrupt halt. She said she wanted to talk, explain all that had happened, including the reason why she hadn't told him all that she suspected she knew about the foundling's identity. It was up to him to trust her or not.

She started the story from the beginning, omitting nothing, arguing that the foundling had become and would remain for her a symbol uniting the two of them. Would their affection for each other survive such self-questioning?

Nature had supplied Bosaaso with an accommodating spirit. He listened attentively, did not speak nor move any part of his body for a long time. Then his nose twitched involuntarily, as if overcome by a musky sexual odour or something as vital, as immediate. 'Will you marry me, Duniya?' he said.

The question did not surprise her; she had expected it for quite some time. Nor did its timing disturb her. Rather, it was the way he spoke it, as though it were an ordinary request, as pedestrian as 'Please pass the salt'. Silent, like someone determined to set a hurt bone, Duniya reasoned that he must have worked on the question so thoroughly that he botched it.

'Will you take me home, please?' she said.

'Of course,' he replied.

They swapped places and he drove her home.

GENEVA (UPI, AFP)

Foreign donors from more than 80 governments and relief organizations have pledged 300 million dollars to cover Mozambique's emergency needs for the next calendar year. More money is likely to be promised in the coming months to bring the total to 400 million dollars, the sum requested by the Mozambique government.

The International Donors' Conference gave its full backing to the Maputo government's argument that the chief cause of the country's economic crisis was the war being waged by the Mozambican rebel movement, assisted by the USA and South Africa.

Chapter Fifteen

In which Duniya meets Caaliya, the woman with the pseudocyesis problem, and learns of Caaliya's pregnancy. Later that afternoon, Duniya is given her first swimming lesson at the Centro Sportivo, where she meets Fariida.

It was clinic day for Duniya.

The beggars begged and chanted; and the poor pregnant out-patients gave what they could ill-afford in the hope of having uncomplicated deliveries. The women sat in close formation, facing in the same direction. Duniya moved to and fro, filling in forms, several other nurses helping her with the assignment.

Today there were not many patients and the nurses talked of taking a mid-morning break and maybe finishing the day's work by noon. The doctor on duty was an obstetrician named Cawil, who had a very high opinion of himself. He spoke of no one but himself, telling how many deliveries he had assisted, giving himself an extraordinary ratio of success. He didn't like Duniya, whom he made redundant on the days he was in charge of the clinic, assigning her the most boring jobs. She had the strength of mind to overlook his meanness.

Just before the mid-morning break, the woman Caaliya came wanting to speak. There seemed to Duniya a difference in her behaviour as well as her physical posture, although the exact nature of the change was indeterminate.

'I'd like you to take a look at this,' Caaliya was saying, and she offered Duniya a piece of paper, decorated with a doctor's illegible scrawl. Duniya received the indecipherable chit.

'That's Dr Mire's hand, believe it or not,' said Caaliya.

Duniya studied the coded mysteries. 'What does it say?'

'It confirms beyond any doubt that I am with child,' said Caaliya.

Duniya made as if to walk away, but didn't.

'You don't believe me?'

Duniya's face seemed to prepare for the onset of a sneeze,

though it was not a sneeze that made her twinge, it was the discovery of a fellow-feeling, a sudden closeness to Caaliya, at the thought that this woman might be truly pregnant. 'Have you seen any other doctor?' she asked.

Again Caaliya delved into her bag searching for the Chinese evidence of her incredible story: the story of a woman who had the persistent charm of collecting any piece of paper a doctor had scribbled on, who carried them as evidence of her motherhood, in much the way a mad person might show a document proving his sanity; Caaliya who had insisted for years that she was pregnant – now at last she was!

During the break, Duniya met one of the Chinese doctors in the corridor. It amused her to think what beastly appellation the Chinese might give to a year in which Caaliya did become pregnant, a year in which Duniya fell in love, a year in which Abshir confirmed he was coming to visit. On her way back to the clinic she ran into Dr Mire. Since neither seemed to be in great haste, they spoke for a while and she gave him news of Abshir's impending arrival. She invited him to dinner with them the following night. Then she asked if it was true that Caaliya was indeed pregnant.

'She is,' he answered.

Duniya said nothing for fear of sounding foolish.

'The human body has its inherent mysteries and one cannot always account for its behaviour, neither are all its self-expressions and manifestations an open book to medical practitioners. Maybe she wants to be a mother so much she will become one.'

'But why is it necessary to give her a To-whom-it-may-concern testimonial?'

'Well, she asked me to give her a document stating that she was pregnant. Something to show to her co-wife, I suspect.'

Duniya let a soft smile descend on her face, like a bird alighting on a leafless tree. Then without so much as a 'Good day', Mire nodded in her direction and walked away at the very instant she had prepared to allude to what was happening between her and Bosaaso. It was just as well, she thought, and returned to the clinic.

Soon it was noon and two hours later she was at home preparing lunch. Bosaaso came to take her and Nasiiba to the Centro Sportivo for her first swimming lesson.

Duniya had difficulty getting her feet off the bottom of the swimming-pool and was incapable of controlling her balance. She remembered her dream from the previous night in which she was a sparrow. She had stood guard at the entrance to a cave. Afterwards, a large bird arrived. This giant new arrival had an illuminated disc in its beak and this he gave to Duniya. She was squinting when she awoke and her tongue had been taken hostage by her own teeth, which bit into it until blood was drawn; and she was pale with fright.

When she jumped into the pool at the Centro Sportivo, it was late afternoon. Marilyn was her swimming-instructor, and Nasiiba was rather irritable, like a parent who had brought a child to an adults' party. Duniya attributed this tension to the peculiar situation in which they found themselves: she was the only woman her age, all the others being Nasiiba's peers. Some were training for an All-Africa swimming event scheduled to take place in West Africa, so Duniya was asked to keep to one end of the pool, to stay as far as possible out of the trainees' way.

Marilyn showed immense tact. She told Duniya for the nth time, 'It's really very simple, if you follow my instructions. Please concentrate and do as I say.' But Duniya soon lost concentration, and her eyes followed Marilyn's wandering gaze which unfailingly took in the breadth and width of the entrance to the pool. Marilyn and Nasiiba seemed to be watching out for a visitor. Who? 'Let's try again,' Marilyn suggested patiently.

Duniya couldn't trust her ability to stay afloat. Her feet would drop into a deeper hole in the water, and the water swallowed, as if gulping several mouthfuls of Duniya, whose eyes were of no use, whose ears of no help, whose splashing noises were scandalously loud and clumsy, like a child's.

Panic justifies flight, and one flees, thought Duniya. But her fear of drowning was heavier on the heart than anything she could imagine. And when least expected, her feet would fail to reach the ground. Whenever anyone laughed, she thought it was at her. She believed she was making a spectacle of herself, but began to relax only when they were at the shallower end of the pool, where she could support herself on her feet. 'Please give me a moment to catch my breath,' she pleaded to Marilyn.

'Take your time,' said Marilyn.

Duniya blamed herself for not having talked everything

through before hurling herself into the pool. Before her first driving lesson she had gone over the basics with Bosaaso, unrushed, so she understood the theory before she started the engine. Here, it was different. She felt humiliated by the despicable remarks some of the young boys and girls were making; felt unprotected from the onslaught of unabashed youth, uncared for by Nasiiba, who had vanished God knows where. Marilyn was a friendly and sweet girl, but Duniya couldn't depend on her totally; Marilyn was pretty, but with little depth and, in a certain sense, inarticulate when it came to explaining the theory of swimming, taking someone else through the first steps. Teaching Duniya was a secondary activity to both Marilyn and Nasiiba, it seemed to Duniya. For whom were they waiting, she wanted to know, why were their eyes focused on the entrance to the pool?

'*I* am not waiting for anybody,' Marilyn replied.

'Then why are you and Nasiiba looking up anxiously at the entrance all the time?' asked Duniya, curious.

Marilyn's shoulders shrugged as though of their own accord, 'Ask Nasiiba.'

She was that kind of girl, Marilyn. For her, Nasiiba was the leader, there was nothing else to it. She did what Nasiiba bid her do. Duniya was sure Marilyn knew whom they were expecting. Some secrets are more important than those in whom they are confided. In the ears of her imagination, the older woman imagined her daughter telling Marilyn a secret and then instructing her not to divulge it, adding, 'Just teach her to swim and be sweet to her.'

Earlier, in the changing-rooms, Nasiiba's adept hands had helped Duniya squeeze into a swimming suit borrowed from Fariida. Duniya had felt like a bride being given the ritual bath and scented massage. Nasiiba had said, 'You'll lose weight. You'll leave behind in the swimming-pool a minimum of two kilos today, I promise you.' Nasiiba and Marilyn had escorted her into the water, like bridemaids attending her at a wedding ceremony. As Duniya's feet had touched the water, she had been frightened. Nasiiba had said, 'There's nothing to be afraid of, Mummy, nothing to worry about. Close your eyes and jump in, and by the time you open your eyes, you'll be at the other end of the pool.'

Duniya watched young girls entering the pool with the ease

with which she had walked into her marriages. Hadn't she done just that: closed her eyes, and found herself married to Zubair, to Taariq?

And then her eyes fell on Fariida coming through the entrance. Fariida was walking with a waddle, her feet shuffling, like a senile person with a bad back. All activity seemed to cease and a moment of silence fell on the whole place. Some of the girls congregated round Fariida, noisy like summer flies at a halva party. Fariida's answer to the question 'Where have you been lately?' was that she had gone mountain-climbing in the north and had fallen off a cliff, ending up with a slipped disc, forced to lie on her back since. Fariida's friends left a pathway open for her, commiserating with her as she walked past them on her heavy feet. They had known her as an able athlete who twice had stripped the title-holder of the swimmer's crown. (Duniya would learn later from Nasiiba that when Fariida went to East Africa with Qaasim, the story was that she had climbed Mount Kilimanjaro.)

It didn't take long for the hubbub to die down. Some of the girls gathered in groups in order to exchange the latest gossip. Some said that Fariida had been pregnant and had aborted the baby; some insisted the tale was as tall as the mountain the young woman was credited to have climbed.

Then Nasiiba re-appeared and brought Fariida to meet her mother, who chose to stay in the water, at the edge of the pool. It was disconcerting to pretend that she had seen her recently. So they chatted, feeling awkward. For the first few minutes of their conversation, Duniya avoided looking Fariida in the face. Displaying signs of discomfort, the younger woman crouched by the pool, and Duniya dared not leave the water for fear that she would develop cold feet and abandon the idea of learning to swim. In the meantime, her costume tightened round her body like a boa constrictor.

It was then that Nasiiba, adept at organizing other people's lives, suggested, 'Why don't you join us later? Fariida and I will lie by the pool. You do what you've got to do, and we'll do what we must.' To Marilyn, Nasiiba said, 'Please go on teaching Mummy to swim.' Watching Fariida shuffle away, Duniya thought that she had lost weight, but not her long-limbed charm. She had lovely eyes, was taller than Miski and a great deal handsomer. She was several months older than the twins. Fariida had on a baggy frock, perhaps one she had worn when pregnant with the foundling.

Duniya now saw the water she stood in as that of afterbirth and innocence. She recalled Nasiiba purporting that Duniya did not know her children well, or what they were up to. Meeting Fariida was an eye-opener for her, an encounter worth remembering.

Now that Fariida and Nasiiba had receded into the darkening backdrop, Marilyn's anxious voice was saying, 'If you'll relax and follow my instructions, Duniya . . .'

'I sink like an anchor whenever I lift my feet off the floor of the pool,' Duniya said.

'Don't *think* about it,' Marilyn was getting into her stride, as if she had gained courage from the contact with Fariida and Nasiiba. 'That's the first thing about swimming. Let your body take care of itself, let it float when it will, let it drop anchor if it wants to.'

Duniya nodded her head, like a child who has been convinced that a measles injection will not hurt. It might have been the younger woman's tone of voice that finally did the trick, but Duniya felt hypnotized. Smiling sweetly and not thinking, she put her full trust in Marilyn.

'Now!' said Marilyn, meaning *start*. She placed her open palm, wide as a pitta bread, under Duniya's body, lifting it up, like an acrobatic skater on a rink vibrant with enthusiastic applause. 'That's superb,' she encouraged. 'Good, very good!'

There was silence, and Duniya thought everyone was watching her.

'This is a success story,' Marilyn was saying.

And Duniya was thinking, *I am the story, I am success.*

Duniya hated failure. She didn't want to cause Marilyn or Nasiiba any embarrassment. Finally, her body found its balance, and her feet made the right noises, her arms splashing in and out of the water. Under Marilyn's supervision she swam back and forth, becoming more and more confident, and urged on by the success story her body was telling.

Then Marilyn sensed a tremor of worry in Duniya's body. It was like a traveller coming upon a sudden bend in a road, a turning not signposted. Marilyn placed her outspread palm further up, closer to Duniya's chest. A little later, Duniya's body regained its lost balance. She told herself that to the one who had reached the summit of Everest, no mountain was high enough. She thought of herself as the axis around which the whole universe rotated, which was why she couldn't afford to go down, sink or abandon ship. She was glad Marilyn had corrected the small error in good time, and with tact. Then they swam together back and forth, staying out of the way of the other swimmers. Suddenly, Marilyn's guiding hand vanished like a magician's handkerchief and Duniya splashed with total abandon. Standing on the tip of her toes, she said, once she caught her breath, 'That was something, wasn't it, Marilyn?'

Marilyn made the immodest claim that she had taught Nasiiba and Fariida to swim.

Duniya did not speak her thoughts.

'Where are they?' Marilyn wondered. Then she pointed, 'There.'

Following where Marilyn's finger pointed, Duniya saw Fariida and Nasiiba lying side by side on the far edge of the pool. Seeing Fariida made Duniya eager to know what the young thing had been through. But would Fariida talk, would she tell her everything? 'Can you find your way to them?' asked Marilyn. 'Because I'd like to swim a little.' And without further ado, she swam away.

Duniya was wary of stepping out, seized by paranoid speculation that everyone would be staring at her as she walked towards Nasiiba and Fariida. She had just looked in the girls' direction, wanting to gauge the distance separating them, when she noticed that Nasiiba was smoking a cigarette. This shocked Duniya. But why?

This self-questioning had a positive effect on her own behaviour, suddenly making her feel indifferent, impervious to everything. She no longer cared who saw her over-exposed body. She stepped out of the pool and walked purposefully towards Nasiiba, whose cigarette became the beacon on which to concentrate. No sense of chill ran through any part of her as she walked up the stone steps and out of the pool; and she didn't swallow back nausea, as she had feared. Duniya reminded herself that theirs was a household where there was a semblance of individual freedom and problem-sharing, where there was no male authority: weren't freedoms like these to be taken? Mataan had his Waris, Nasiiba her smoking.

When she joined them, Nasiiba said, 'Sit or lie down, as you like.' Fariida grinned at Duniya welcomingly.

Shocks come and go, like layers of skin peeling. Duniya could now look at Nasiiba smoking, without the accompanying feeling of violated emotion, pretending not to be bothered by it.

From her vantage point, towering above the two prostrate figures, she decided that Fariida's choice of colours shared a faint resemblance with salad rinsed in fresh water. She lay down beside them on a towel, facing them both. Duniya said, 'What should I say to you, Fariida? Welcome back? I'm glad you're alive? Or why didn't you let me know right from the beginning?'

Fariida's prominent jaws moved, opening wider as she offered Duniya her profile. She looked at Nasiiba, as if for guidance, then said, 'We would be telling a different story if I had spoken to you that morning, wouldn't we?'

'We would indeed,' Duniya agreed.

Nasiiba got up. 'I'll let the two of you talk,' she said, and without waiting for their reaction, moved away, at a fast trot, until she reached the springboard, from which she dived into the pool.

'Where were you all this time?' Duniya asked Fariida.

'I had a small room in the Buur Karoole district,' Fariida said, 'less than two kilometres from your place. Nasiiba would cut classes to come and see me. For a long time no one knew where I was, no one, that is, except Nasiiba. It was a healthy pregnancy, physically, and being an athlete helped a great deal. I had no need to consult a doctor. To have blood, urine and similar tests or my temperature taken I contacted a friend via Nasiiba. That morning, however, I was feeling a bit down and had confused the dates and Nasiiba had not come to me.'

'What did you do the morning I caught a glimpse of you?'

'You called and called and caused me worry. So I went off in a waiting taxi, back to where I was staying.'

'I see,' said Duniya.

'But since my blood is the same rare group as Nasiiba's, you might say I owe my life to her. When I left you at the clinic, I took the taxi straight to a clinic I had been using, and the doctor said to admit me. Delivering a baby in such circumstances is an atrocious shame, but Nasiiba was an angel, donating blood, seeing to it that I was well taken care of. It was she who suggested I "abandon" my baby to her. So what does one say to you, I ask myself? "Thank you very much" to your "Welcome back"? Or "The experience has been worth it" to your "I'm glad you're alive"? Or "How could I let you know when I didn't know myself?" to your "Why didn't you let me know right from the beginning?"'

'You say you had a taxi waiting for you on a day the city of Mogadiscio had none plying its streets. How come?'

'Please don't rush the story.'

'I'm sorry,' Duniya said.

In Fariida's look there was pride at having undergone an ordeal and survived it. 'I'm the kind of woman whose stomach doesn't blow up much until about the eighth month,' she said, 'but I didn't want to risk it, I didn't want Miski to know until I'd had the baby, and maybe not even then. We already had a strained relationship, you see, Miski and I, following the break-up of her engagement to her fiancé, for which she wrongly blamed me. That's why I didn't let anyone know except Nasiiba, by which time it was too late for me to rid myself of it. Irregular periods play tricks on young women who can't remember whether or not they have taken their pills. My irregular periods were my principal problem.'

'So what exactly did you do?'

'One morning I packed and went, leaving a note on the desk for Miski to find when she got back from Rome. The brief note just said that I had gone away, but that there was no cause for worry, no one need panic. I'd written similar notes for her before when I left of the country, once to Nairobi, another time to Dar es Salaam – on both occasions with Qaasim, who financed our trips. When I became pregnant, I didn't want him to know. We'd enjoyed our illicit affair, every wondrous moment of it, so what was the point regretting? He might have proposed if he'd known I was carrying his child. But I'd said no when he showed interest in marrying me before there was any evidence that I was with child: no, no, no.'

'What made you decide not to marry Qaasim in the first place?'

'Age difference is a major reason, I suppose. Imagine when he's turning seventy, I'll be your age, still young, ready to contract another marriage, fall in love, learn to drive a car, or to swim. No way, I said.'

'Where did it all start?'

'At your place.'

'When?' If Duniya was supposed to feel guilty, she did not. Smiling reminiscently Farrida said, 'I came to deliver a parcel to you from your brother in Rome. Nasiiba wasn't there that day, only you were. Qaasim arrived, we had tea, the three of us. Then he left, only to park within sight of Aw-Cumar's shop, waiting. I knew he was waiting as only women can know such things, and so I, too, left, rather hastily, refusing to stay until Nasiiba returned home. I was eager for adventure. I'd lost my virginity to a boy my age, and was anxious to experiment with older men just for fun. Qaasim took me home. Miski was away and we were alone the best part of that night. That was how it started.'

'You took no precautions?'

'He did.'

'And so how did it happen?'

'I am to blame.'

'How?'

'Let's not go into that now.'

'Did you ever tell him you were having his child?'

'Nasiiba did.'

'And what did he say?'

'He would pay for my abortion if I wanted to get rid of it, that he made clear. What was more, if I were willing he'd take me as his wife. I sent him word through Nasiiba that it was no business of his what I did with myself or the foetus. I had made a mistake, I said, and would pay for it.'

'But why?'

'Maybe because I'd begun atoning for the pain I'd caused Miski.'

'It doesn't make sense.'

'Little in life makes sense,' said Fariida. 'Doesn't it say in a few Koranic verses that one's fate is one's shepherd and one goes where one's destiny is determined to take one. In other words, I decided I am a given. My destiny has its sequences and logic.' She paused to suppress tears welling in her eyes.

'Come, come,' Duniya said, giving Fariida's head a pat, 'the baby was no inconvenience to us – a pleasure in fact.' She stopped herself just in time from telling her what various people had said about the foundling: how Mire had thought of him as a catalyst;

how she and Bosaaso had thought of him as a metaphor. 'How did Miski learn of it all?' Duniya asked.

'It was Qaasim who approached her, proposing that he and I marry. That was the first she knew of my pregnancy. And that caused a bit of a stir. There was total panic, and Nasiiba felt compelled to bring Miski to my hiding-place. You wouldn't believe it, but this occurred a week before you saw me at the clinic. I still have the Number Seventeen token, which I'll keep as a souvenir, to remember all we've gone through.'

'But why didn't you just come and tell me everything?'

'One is never sure what you might do, Duniya,' Fariida said frankly. 'It was too late for you to do anything, anyway, and since we hadn't informed you from the start I thought it best to keep you out of it.'

'What do you think I might have done if you had told me?'

Fariida dimmed her bright eyes. 'We wouldn't be sitting here, talking the way we are, if I had.'

They were silent for a few minutes. Then Nasiiba joined them.

The two girls gossiped for a while about some of their friends. It was when Duniya was ready to leave with Bosaaso that Fariida remembered Miski had given her the keys to the city centre flat, which was Duniya's to move into whenever she pleased.

Bosaaso and Duniya left Nasiiba and Fariida lying beside the pool, in the gathering dusk, talking and smoking together. Duniya was very tired. Swimming had taken a lot of her energy, and listening to Fariida's story had been demanding, too.

When they were moving and on a stretch of good road without traffic or pot-holes, Bosaaso gave Duniya a newspaper neatly folded, a newspaper which felt unread. 'The newspaper you're holding has a long article by Taariq, she said, 'I thought you might like to see it.'

Duniya gave a start, for the image of the dead foundling came floating up in her memory at the mention of Taariq's name. Why was she was beginning to associate Taariq with the dead foundling?

'Is the article any good?' she asked Bosaaso.

He drove cautiously because some children were playing football in the middle of the street. He did not speak until they were in front of Duniya's place. 'Yes, I found it rather good,' he replied.

Getting out of the car, she said, 'I'm too exhausted to entertain anyone, so do you mind if we meet tomorrow? At noon?'

'Of course not.'

His excessive politeness was getting on her taut nerves, but she was too tired to remark on it. 'I hope by then we'll have found two or three cleaning women to mop, dust and prepare the city flat, whose key I have now, for Abshir to use when he arrives.'

'That's a superb idea,' Bosaaso said.

She thought better of a rude remark which called at her mind that very instant. She gave him a kiss, saying, 'Tomorrow then, noon.'

And for the moment was only too glad to be rid of him.

'Sweet dreams,' he said, driving away.

Mataan and Yarey did not come home until a little after midnight. And Duniya was content to lie in bed, propped up with a number of pillows, reading Taariq's article. She had energy only for that.

GIVING AND RECEIVING: THE NOTION OF DONATIONS

by Taariq

Giving is a human instinct, perhaps the oldest, if we are to believe the Adam and Eve story of the paradisiacal apple the serpent offers to the woman who in turn shares it with the man. We give hoping to receive something corresponding to what we've offered. We give in the hope that our gift will express our affection and compassion towards the recipients. We give, as members of a group, to confirm our loyalty to it. We give to meet the demands of a contract, or the obligations and rights others have on our property. We give and may consider this act as part of our penance. We give in order to feel superior to those whose receiving hands are placed below ours. We give to corrupt. We give to dominate. There are a million reasons why we give, but here I am concerned with only one: European and North American and Japanese governments' donations of food aid to the starving in Africa, and why these are received.

Last week, the world ran and Africa starved. Last week, millions of people broke Olympic records. A Sudanese runner flew across the globe to light a torch in New York. Last week, millions of cameras clicked, capturing scenes of rejoicing men and women who breasted the finish ribbon – scenes that were the culmination of media events. The sports activities organized to commemorate the day were a round-the-clock affair, keeping busy radio commentators and TV crews in Western Europe, North America, Japan, South-East Asia and India. In the end, the events were reduced to a compilation of statistics; how many people participated, how much money was collected to aid the starving in Africa? Last week, while the non-starving peoples of the world ran, taking part in the self-perpetuating media exercises of TV performances, Africa waited in the wings, out of the camera's reach, with an empty bowl in hand, seeking alms, hoping that generous donations would come from the governments and peoples of the runners. Empty brass bowls make excellent photographs. Video cameras take shots of them, from every imaginable angle. To starve is to be of media interest these days. Forgive my cynicism, but I believe this to be the truth.

Africa's famine became a story worthy of newspaper headlines when you could sell pictures of faces empty of everything, save the pains of starvation. Jonathan Dimbleby of BBC TV was the first to use the power of the televised message spelling clearly, in letters huge as the politics of drought, the one and only underlying sub-theme of hunger on a massive scale: powerlessness. Dimbleby produced a sensitive programme on the Ethiopian famine in the early 1970s. In this half-hour documentary, he used alternative shots of starving masses and pictures of the world's powerful politicians attending the Emperor's lavish feast at which delicacies like caviar had been served. A few months later, the Emperor was overthrown.

The question is, how come the same story in 1985 and 1986 is used by governments all over the continent in their favour and no heads roll, no despot's regime is overthrown? Unhelped, with no food aid reaching the country, the Emperor was toppled. Can we conclude that if foreign governments stop aiding the African dictators with food hand-outs, then their people will rise against them?

Famine is a phenomenon the African is familiar with. In Somalia, there are people who bear the names of the years of drought. People adjusted the holes in their belts, but they did not beg. They held their heads high, allowing no one to humiliate them, letting no one know that their hearths had remained unlit the previous night. Those who had the people's mandate to rule were united in the belief that he begs who has no self-pride, and he works responsibly who intends to be respected. But we know that a great many of the men at the helm of the continent's power do not have the people's mandate to be there in the first place, and have no self-pride or foresight. We also know that their incompetent five-year plans cannot be executed without the budget being supplemented from foreign sources. Are we therefore up against the proverbial wisdom that people get the government they deserve, and we deserve beggars to be our leaders?

There is a tradition, in Somalia, of passing round the hat for collections. It is called *Qaaraan*. When you are in dire need of help, you invite your friends, relatives and in-laws to come to your place or someone else's, where, as the phrase goes, a mat has been spread. But there are conditions laid down. The need has to be genuine, the person wishing to be helped has to be a respectable member of society, not a loafer, a lazy ne'er-do-well, a debtor or a thief. Here discretion is of the utmost significance. Donors don't mention the sums they offer, and the recipient doesn't know who has given what. It is the whole community from which the person receives a presentation and to which he is grateful. It is not permitted that such a person thereafter applies for more, not soon at any rate. If there is a lesson to be learned from this, it is that emergencies are one-off affairs, not a yearly excuse for asking for more. Now how many years have we been passing round the empty bowl?

Famines awake a people from an economic, social or political lethargy. We've seen how the Ethiopian people rid themselves of their Emperor for forty years. Foreign food donations create a buffer zone between corrupt leaderships and the starving masses. Foreign food donations also sabotage the African's ability to survive with dignity. Moreover, it makes their children feel terribly inferior, discouraging them from eating the emaciated bean sprouts, the undernourished corn-on-the-cob and broken rice. Forgive me for dishing out to you clichés and, if I may beg your indulgence, let me quote a statement made by Hubert Humphrey, who said in 1957, 'I've heard . . . that people may become dependent on us for food. I know this is not supposed to be good news. To me that was good news, because before people can do anything, they have got to eat. And if you are looking for a way to get people to lean on you and to be dependent on you, in terms of their co-operation with you, it seems to me that food dependence would be terrific.' Well put, wouldn't you agree? Now we may continue.

An East African leader, known to be of socialist persuasion, recently granted an interview to a London-based African magazine, in which he said that the developed nations must help Africa. But why *must* they? What makes him think that the African has a proprietory right over the properties of others? Did the country of which he has been a leader the past quarter of a century donate generously to the starving in Ethiopia or Chad? One could understand if this most respected African statesman made his statement in the context of a familiar or tribal society where obligatory or voluntary exchanges of gifts are part of the code of behaviour. In such a context, the exchange is direct. You give somebody something; a year later, when you are in need, today's recipient becomes tomorrow's giver. Does this intellectual statesman foresee the time when Africa will be in a position to donate food to Europe, North America or Japan? Is he aware that he is turning the African into a person forever dependent?

Every gift has a personality – that of its giver. On every sack of rice donated by a foreign government to a starving people in Africa, the characteristics and mentality of the donor, name and country, are stamped on its ribs. A quintal of wheat donated by a charity based in the Bible Belt of the USA tastes different from one grown in and donated by a member of the European Community. You wouldn't disagree, I hope, that one has, as its basis, the theological notion of charity; the other, the temporal, philosophical economic credo of creating a future generation of potential consumers of this specimen of high quality wheat. I have two problems here.

One. It is my belief that a god-fearing Bible Belter knows that publicized charities won't wash with God. The only mileage in it is an earthly sense of vainglory. Second. The European Community bureaucrat need not be told that the donated wheat is but a free sample of items that it is hoped will sell very well when today's starving Africans become tomorrow's potential buyers. There is enough literature to fill bookcases, surveys written up by scholars, following America's policy of donating food aid to Europe, Japan, South-East Asia. I suggest that you walk this well-trodden path in the company of Susan George or Teresa Hayter. But let me deal with the mentality of the receiver and his systems of beliefs and what gifts mean to him.

Most Africans are (paying?) members of extended families, these being institutions comparable to trade unions. Often, you find one individual's fortunes supporting a network of the needs of this large unit. On a psychological level, therefore, we might say that the African is unquestionably accustomed to the exchange of potlachs. Those, who have plenty, give; those who have nothing to give, expect to be given to. In urban areas, there are thousands of strong young men and women who receive 'unemployment benefit' from a member of their extended family, somebody who has a job. Hence, it follows that when the bread-winner's earnings do not meet everyone's needs; when the land isn't yielding, because insufficient work is being put in to cultivate it; when hard currency-earning cash crops are grown and the returns are paid to service debt; and just when the whole country is preparing to rise in revolt against the neo-colonial corrupt leadership: a ship loaded with charity rice, unasked for, perhaps, docks in the harbour – good quality rice, grown by someone else's muscles and sweat. You know the result. Famine (my apologies to Bertold Brecht) is a trick up the powerful man's sleeve; it has nothing to do with the seasonal cycles or shortage of rain.

If I could afford to be cynical, I would say that the African, knowing no better, accepts whatever he is given because it is an insult to refuse what you're offered. If his cousin or a member of the extended family doesn't give, God will or somebody else will. God, as we know Him, has been 'given' to us, together with all the mythological paraphernalia, genealogical truisms that classify us inferior beings, not to forget the Middle Eastern philosophical maxim that God (in a monotheistic sense) is progress. Yes, the truth is our Gods and those of our forefathers, we have been told, do not give you anything; and since they have a beginning, they have an end, too.

Somalis are of the opinion that it is in the nature of food to be shared. If you come upon a group of people eating, you are invited to join them. There is, of course, the prophylactic tendency to avoid the wickedness of the envious eye of the hungry, but this isn't the principal reason why you're offered to partake of the meal being eaten. Linked to the notion of food is the belief regarding the short-lived nature of all perishables. The streets of Mogadiscio are over-crowded with beggars carrying empty bowls, wandering from door to door, begging to be given the day's left-overs. Is it possible, I wondered the other day, to equate the donor governments' food surpluses which are given to starving Africans, to the left-overs we offer to famished beggars? Or am I stretching the point?

When Somalis despair of someone whom they describe as a miser, they often say, 'So-and-So doesn't give you even a glass of water.' So when they hear stories about butter being preserved in icy underground halls, foods kept in temperatures below freezing point, racks and racks of meat shelved, rows and rows of rice and other luxuries kept in a huge cellar colder than the Arctic, it is then that Somalis say, 'But these people are mean.' Press them to tell you why they should be given anything, and they take refuge in generalizations. Ask them why Russia doesn't provide them with food aid, and they become cynical. The only difference between us and Russia, although we eat the same American wheat, is that we pay for it with our begging, and they with their foreign reserves.

Last week the world ran and Africa starved. No doubt, television is a personality creator, and donors have their smiling pictures taken, alternating with scenes of Ethiopian skeletons. For the first time Africa has been given prime time TV coverage, but alas, Africa is speechless, and hungry. In Conrad's *Heart of Darkness*, the one and only moment the African is given a line to speak, the poor fellow is made to employ an incorrect grammatical structure. That was of prime and all-time literary significance. A hundred years later, in a film called *Out of Africa*, directed by an American, based on a book by a Danish woman who lived in Africa and maybe loved the part of the continent she lived in but had no love for its people, this film counted among its actors Somalia's most famous daughter, Iman. Guess what: she has a non-speaking role. Make of all this what you will; but ask yourself, now what? Who gets what, gives what to whom?

I retreat into a skeletal silence: when the world runs and starving Africa starves; when the cameras click and runners catch their breaths, having chested the finish ribbons of a momentary glory. And when the TV-watching public and

> video-producing crews turn and ask me to say something, I feel shy, I am tongue-tied. Like a child to whom an adult has given a gift, who smiles timidly and takes it, and whose mother says, 'Say thank you to Uncle,' I too say, thank you one, thank you all, Uncles Sam, Sung, and Al-Mohamed too.

She put aside the newspaper, delighted that Taariq could still have lucid moments of virtuosity. But why was the article published only now? Did the censors disallow publication when he submitted it, following the week in which the world ran while Africa starved?

Exhausted and yet unable to sleep, she contemplated the world surrounding her with a frown. And the world was a key. By staring at the key to the city flat, the one Fariida had brought from Miski, Duniya had the feeling she was looking at the levers, the carved bends and twists of her own future.

And suddenly, she knew what she was going to do. 'Tomorrow evening,' she said, 'Duniya will spend the night at Bosaaso's to make of her body a gift to him. Tomorrow evening.'

Part IV
Duniya Gives

Chapter Sixteen

Duniya, in a mood of elation, calls at the city-centre flat where three cleaning women are busy preparing; it is in that exalted state of mind that she suggests she and Bosaaso spend the night at his place.

The scene opens in darkness, then a spotlight is directed on a woman standing in a river. As she readies to swim away, an unknown man is saying to her, 'Gum to gum, dust to water, fire to earth, and you are in such a wonderful state of happiness where seven comes before eight, a cot before a baby, the bed before the ring.'

Her splashing arhythmic, the woman swims away, and the spotlight is switched off: end of dream sequence. Soon after a bulb is burning in Duniya's and Nasiiba's room.

Immediately after breakfast, Duniya, her children and Bosaaso went to the city flat – and they all liked it. She had arranged for three hospital cleaning women to perform a moonlighting job, to mop, dust, wash the floors and walls. Bosaaso ferried to and fro getting a plumber to fix the dripping taps and toilets that weren't flushing properly, or a carpenter to repair the creaky garden door that wouldn't shut, or pick up some US-made chemical with which to unblock the sinks and drains.

It was agreed that Abshir would use the city-centre flat, it being more central, more spacious. For his meals he would come to Duniya's; alternatively Nasiiba would move in with him to help him cope, cook if need be. Duniya considered renting a car for the period he was in Mogadiscio, so he would be free to go as and when and where he pleased. Mataan was generous in giving up his spring bed, insisting that he didn't mind sleeping on a mattress on the floor. Nasiiba offered to spend all day in the flat with the three cleaning women, doing as much as them, if not more, her hands and arms dirty to the elbow, her plaited, beaded hair brown with the webbed dust the spiders had spun. Although more of a hindrance than a help, little Yarey washed the midget sink in the kitchen, wasting precious detergent, time and water. Duniya vowed not to take a break until after she had prepared the bedroom, whose french windows overlooked the garden, certain that Abshir would prefer it to the other room facing a hallway. Meanwhile, Bosaaso hired a pick-up truck to bring from Duniya's place Mataan's spring bed, a couple of chairs, tables. A little later, Duniya sent him on a simpler errand: to have the new flat's keys cut.

'Will you be able to stay overnight if need be?' Duniya asked one of the three cleaning women.

'Sure.'

'And no one will worry about you not returning home?'

The second woman said, 'When you are our age, Duniya, you'll discover what it means not to be missed. In any case I live within walking distance from here and can help organize food and mats for my colleagues too.'

'I'll sleep anywhere, even on the bare floor,' said the third cleaner.

Having put in nine hours' labour, Duniya and her entourage returned to her old flat, leaving the new one in the trusted hands of the cleaning women. It was late in the afternoon: tea was made and drunk, and Duniya showered, changed into a house garment and rested. Bosaaso went home to shower, then returned to Duniya's as agreed. He met her, nervous, anxious, but also light-hearted as though his adulthood had provisionally given way to a younger self, brightly glowing in the happy atmosphere their eagerness had brought forth.

When the children's backs were turned the two of them slipped away noiselessly, like naughty adolescents. She had the car keys in her hand and was saying, 'I'll drive.'

The nine-day-old moon led her towards Bosaaso's house.

The sky was starry and spacious. The car stalled now and

then, but this disturbed neither of them, producing only laughter. Doggedly, Duniya restarted the engine whenever the car stopped, both behaving as if they had all the time in the world to cover the distance separating their respective houses.

But wouldn't she be missed, he wondered. Or had she told Nasiiba where she would spend the night? But the twins were so excited at the prospect of Uncle Abshir's visit they might not give their mother's absence a moment's thought, he reasoned.

Now Duniya's feet operated the clutch, brake and accelerator and the car ran smoothly, albeit anxiously, towards Bosaaso's house, as if relying totally on its homing instinct. Duniya's eyes grinned with the joy of anticipation. Bosaaso sat back, envying her calm. He kept his hands to himself; she wouldn't have liked it if he had touched her while she was driving, he knew that.

'I love you,' he said.

Nothing suggested that she had heard his proclamation.

He repeated the words to himself: and then they touched.

The roads were more or less empty of cars, and they were driving through a district in which power had been cut. People, because of this, came out of their houses, poured into the streets where the air was fresher and where there were cage terraces, turning the nuisance of the lack of electricity to their advantage, going for walks by moonlight, or standing, in groups, chatting. At one point, there was a small gathering of men and women engaged in an argument in the centre of a crossroads. With full headlights on, Duniya had come on them without slowing down, causing them to run helter skelter, cursing, speaking all manner of insults, one describing her as a mad woman.

'I'm sorry,' she said, when in a state of mind to speak.

By then, she had eased the vehicle into total submission, and was clearly in a light-hearted euphoria, winged like a griffin. She pressed the accelerator, speeding up more and more. She did this to shorten the distance existing not between her body and Bosaaso's but between herself and her brother, Abshir. Only hours separated them and she wished to spend these in self-abandonment, in Bosaaso's house and company. She wanted several questions about Bosaaso out of the way before she embraced Abshir.

To enrich itself, her memory returned to that ambiguous zone between myth and religion, where griffin-like *buraaqs* rubbed shoulders with jinns eaves-dropping at the gates of heaven; where shooting-stars were said to be aimed at the latter to discourage them; where bored women engage jinns in illicit love affairs; where jinns, out of wickedness, mounted sentry duty at the door to Zubair's sight.

Tonight, Duniya had a deep-seated wish to give herself to him, a wish that had taken days to mature. She was glad he hadn't rushed her. Now the timing was right, and its suddenness lent her decision more power, like unexpected thunder in a season of awaited rains. She wanted to know what he was like in bed; if he snored; what were his quirks; was he fussy about which side of the bed he slept on; was he in a foul mood when he woke in the mornings?

From the way he stirred, she sensed he wished to say something. 'Yes?'

'We'll have time to talk,' she heard, and yet he appeared dead from worry, pale almost, the blood drained out of him. She touched his hand which felt cold, lifeless.

'Say it if it can't wait until we reach your place,' she said.

He hesitated. 'It's just . . .' but he hadn't the courage to finish whatever it was he had intended to say.

She slowed down. He would have to give her directions from then on. But he told her to turn left when he meant her to go to the right. She decided he had a terrible sense of direction, which she attributed to his having lived in a sign-posted city where one had maps and didn't depend on one's instinctive sense of direction. She didn't understand what he was talking about, but she let him talk on and on, because it did him good, reducing the tension considerably. But what exactly did he want to say?

A woman who has brought up three children isn't easily surprised; she can see anxiety on her children's faces, knows what they want long before they speak. As a nurse, she listened to a great many silly questions coming from otherwise intelligent people who, because they're unwell, lose the ability to use their heads wisely.

'Do you know how long Abshir is staying in Mogadiscio?' he asked.

'I've no idea,' she replied.

He is a worrier, she thought. A heart-eating, self-questioning man, with little confidence in himself. He is possibly the kind of man who gets up at day-break to worry about whether or not he will keep his midday appointments.

She was glad when they got to his gate, in front of which she braked. There were lights on in the upper floor of the house, and she could see a balcony badly in need of repair. Was that the balcony from which Yussur and the baby had dropped to their deaths? Duniya, with the engine still running, came out of the car, saying to him, 'You drive it in yourself.'

A night watchman, from the River People, showed her the way with a torch, indicating to her the small side gate by which pedestrians entered Bosaaso's house. But when he had parked his car in its shelter and joined her, in fact, just as he had taken her hand to lead her inside, there was a power cut whose suddenness made her start. The night watchman's faint flashlight provided enough light for them to see the steps to the main door.

'I have a generator and enough diesel to run it,' he said.

'If the rest of the district has no light, why should we?'

'Fair enough,' he said.

As she entered the door which he had held open for her, Duniya saw her shadow severing, in two halves, the moonlight looking in the doorway. She stepped on the tail of her own shadow, as if it were a doormat on which she was meant to wipe her shoes clean. Walking further in, she sensed that the house had something spiritless about it. She walked straight ahead, but stood out of Bosaaso's way, imagining that he would want to look for a box of matches or candles or to pull open curtains or windows. An instant later, however, she could hear the french windows being dragged open scratchily, and he was saying, 'There is an armchair here. Please come.'

'In a moment,' she said.

'Or would you rather we sit in the dark looking out on the moonlight?'

They met midway and embraced. The night was gauze-thin and she had little difficulty penetrating the greyish membrane with which it was wrapped. The moon guided her towards itself, where it occupied the centre of a clearing, and the clouds had stayed back, like a well-behaved crowd of onlookers, giving space and limelight to the principal actor the occasion had crowned. She loved the silence, loved the half-dark, she loved the two of them on their feet, chest to chest, with neither saying anything. Then she lost sight of the moon. But had it gone? She counted up to thirteen, as though it were a lighthouse whose flashing could be timed. Then the outside world began interfering with their inner quietness and peace.

The night watchman called Bosaaso's name.

'Shall I answer?' he said, in a whisper.

Letting go of him, she said, 'You already have.'

His breath was charged with tension, like a frightened lizard's throat. Now that they fell apart, each cast a separate shadow, his shorter than hers. He was clearly upset, but didn't want to shout at the night watchman, poor fellow. He was angry with himself. His voice carried in it a multitude of mixed emotions when he said, 'What is it you want?'

The night watchman stood to the side of the door which Bosaaso had opened. Heard but not seen, he delivered his message, 'Waaberi, your sister-in-law, has been here a number of times.'

Bosaaso was tempted to correct this fool of a night watchman, by reminding him that Waaberi was his *former* sister-in-law. But he let that pass, in deference to Duniya.

'What did she want, did she tell you?'

'She only said she needed to see you urgently.'

'Did she say what about?'

'And there was *that man* with her.'

'What man?'

The night watchman had a Baidoan Somali accent and this began to jar on Bosaaso. He might have lost his self-control had not Duniya come and taken his hand, to kiss it.

'Do you know the name of the man who came with Waaberi?' he asked.

'The one with the car shinier than moonlight,' said the night watchman.

Bosaaso described Kaahin.

'That's him.'

'When did they say they will come back?'

'Some time tonight.'

Bosaaso's voice, when he next spoke, assumed two tones, belonging to two different modes of his being. The first half of the statement was followed by a pause, long enough for him to return Duniya's kiss. He said, 'If either Waaberi or Kaahin comes here tonight . . . my instructions are not to allow either to disturb us.'

'What if they ask when they can see you or where?' said the night watchman.

'Tell them I'll go and see them myself,' Bosaaso said.

When the door closed and they were in the dark, they listened to the receding footsteps of the night watchman.

She said, 'You are so impeccably polite, it puts me to shame, when I think of my rages, fights and tempers. Are we attracted to each other because we're so different?'

'We have many things in common,' he said.

'Of course we do,' she said, 'but it wouldn't upset me at all if you showed your anger now and then.'

Without saying any more, they walked together, hand in hand, towards the french windows.

'You have a beastly temper, you know that?' he said.

'And your politeness is not so much disarming as challenging,' she said, self-censoriously. As they walked on, their hipbones knocked against each other, like a couple dancing the bump.

Finally, they stopped. There was only one armchair. When sitting in it, Duniya's fingers touched something hard, which she worked out to be a pair of binoculars. Since her sense of direction was excellent, it didn't take her long to figure out that the chair was facing west. Did this mean that Bosaaso was a bird watcher? She didn't think he was a voyeur; besides, who was there to pry on?

'I'm a bird watcher,' he volunteered without her asking him.

Then he kissed her. It was so powerful and so sudden that, in an attempt not to lose her balance, Duniya held on to his sleeve.

He said, when he could, before she had the chance to speak, 'I love you.'

She took his hand in both hers and kissed it lightly.

Because she did not say anything, they kissed, this time briefly.

'It would upset me if anything I did or said upset you,' he said.

'I know,' she said.

He sat beside her in the armchair, hoping she could say, 'I love you,' or something as pleasant.

She said, 'Taariq used to say that I'm like most men, in that details bore me. He would argue that it's the general drift of things that fascinate my wild nature, my temperamental mind.'

She pushed aside the book that had been in the armchair. He became curious, wondering what he had been reading the last time he sat there, probably one sleepless dawn. He knew from the feel of it that it was Dostoyevsky's *Brothers Karamazov*.

'I'm a details person, all right; I attend to them rigorously,' he said.

'It's the details of how a person smiles, their nervous tics, how they sleep, where they fall asleep, which side of the bed they prefer: these are the details that interest me,' Duniya replied.

He was restless, like a man on unsafe ground. 'It depends what you mean, knowing a person,' he said.

'Where is the easiest bathroom to get to in the dark?' she asked.

'There's one on the ground floor. Shall I take you there?'

Then he tickled her. She laughed. And laughing, she got to her feet. She thought he was teasing her like a cat that, once hurt by a bigger dog, falls back on its feline alertness, plays with the canine aggressive instinct, holding back a little. His seductive fingers moved up and down her spine, fingers that were ticklishly open like a cat's playful but harmless claws. Suddenly, two of his fingers closed in on the clip of her brassiere and, before she could remember the Akan word for 'breasts', the support was gone and they were throbbing with the warmth of excitement. They kissed, he breathed heavily, his nostrils whistling, like a tyre losing air. She didn't say, 'Don't rush me,' but, 'Where is the bathroom, the one on the ground floor?'

The moon entered, shining their way, showing them where to go. The top landing was awash with moonlight. There were three rooms on this floor. He took the right turning and she followed him. He opened a window. More brightness.

Then she said, 'I'll be with you in a minute.'

Bosaaso approached Duniya's body as if it were a door whose combination locks required the performance of a certain number of feats, before being allowed in. He might have been a lowly-born *Arabian Nights* prince making good. The stakes were too high for him not to perform well. Only when he proved himself to be a charmer, did she let him in.

And then the doors of her body opened wider, and she lay on top of him, the mistress conducting the speed and flow of the river of their common love. Earlier, he had wanted to know if she had taken the necessary precautions. She had said, 'Of course, I have,' making it plain that she wanted no more children, thank you.

He followed the rhythmic dictates of her orchestrated movements, concentrating on the dents on her body, which were like those on stone steps leading to a frequently used door. Her body felt a lot younger than his own, and was undeniably more athletic. For instance, she could sit in a half crouching position for as long as love-making demanded, whereas his back ached.

Loving him was divine. That was clear.

They altered positions. He was on top now, but still thinking, engaging in mental activity because he didn't want to come until much, much later.

'Where are you?' she teased.

He hesitated, not getting her meaning. They were still in the dark, and they were seeing each other's body not by feel alone but by the moon shining in as well. He said, 'I am in tenth heaven.'

'Where the jinns are?' she asked.

'Eaves-dropping.'

'Then I am the shooting-star. Watch me come, hold me.'

He held on to her as she flew away, by-passing all known and unknown planets of the celestial system of joy, light as that proverbial prophet's chariot, the prophet whom some call Ilyaas, some Elijah, some Idris, and whom others describe as descending from Haruun, the brother of Moses; this most revered miracle-maker of a prophet, whom Muslims believe to be Khadr.

'Shall we?' she was saying.

And her body opened wider, and there were many more palaces in it, and Bosaaso realized he owned more keys than had been revealed to him. They swapped positions, but without disengaging, locked to each other by the act of their union. He was enjoying himself. That much was obvious to her.

It was her turn to entertain the thoughts visiting her: she thought of bodies, as he took over the responsibility of conducting the orchestra of their love-making. She felt the marks his trouser belt had left round his waist, body marks that were as prominent as a woman's stretch marks following the delivery of a number of children. He had far too many burns and scars, even for a Somali. Had his mother cauterized every inexplicable complaint, thinking only that curative surgery made any sense?

She went on thinking that the athletics of love is a great sport, if both parties are keen on prolonging it, and are content to live wholly in the present, in the very moment in which everything is taking place. Then love is divine.

She felt embarrassed, because she had been thinking about sin at the very moment he spoke the words 'I love you'. Love is too pedestrian a notion to associate with Allah; he may be merciful, compassionate; human deeds may be worthy of his rage; but he doesn't love. Overwhelmed with these metaphysical self-doubts, her look dropped with the unevenness of a leaf falling down earthwards in the zigzag motion of a serpent hiding in the safety of a bush tree. She thought of Adam and Eve. She thought and commiserated with Eve, whose name is not mentioned in the Koran, not even once.

But she couldn't help reminding herself that even in so-called secular forms of culture such as Western cinema, the notion of sin is very pervasive. Married couples are not shown enjoying sex in the nude, whereas adulterers are shown in celluloid shots yards long, and the same is true of fiction. Why?

Then she ceased thinking, for suddenly his body was on fire and both were giddy with excitement, shouting each other's name. Noisily, joyfully, they reached orgasm.

Neither spoke for a long time. He lay beside her, face down.

Electricity had returned. But only the kitchen light was on. Duniya saw this as emblematic, in keeping with the known facts about Bosaaso's past: his mother had been an excellent cook who had hired out her culinary services and in return received food rather than cash. In the Somali scheme of things, kitchens are associated with women and men are discouraged from setting foot in them.

She got up and, by feel, found a towel on the rack by the entrance. Then she lay beside him, having spread the towel under her. Could a disastrous love-making have ruined their affection for each other, she asked herself. She said, and hoped he was listening, 'Among many African peoples, men do not take as wives a woman until she is already with child. Did you know that?'

He turned to look at her and then lay on his back, in silence.

She sat up. Her smile was now large, taking over her entire face. Her hand touched her hair. She remembered her head-dress dropping off sometime during their love-making. Now she saw it at on the floor at the foot of the bed, entwined with her flimsy underpants. Smiling, she tried with her free hand to scratch a spot in the small of her back. He tried to help her.

'*How* do you sleep?' she asked.

'How or where?' he said, after a quizzical look.

'I'm a very light sleeper, a great asset when you're on night duty at a maternity ward, though I've known it to be a nuisance elsewhere.' Then she added, 'Zubair made a nightmare of noises; Taariq snored heavily, but would none the less confront you with denials when you woke him up. So *how* do you sleep?'

'I normally sleep soundly.'

'You don't somersault in the tumult of the day's memories before falling asleep?' she asked.

'Now and again, yes,' he said.

'Good.'

'There are five spare rooms, with beds in them,' he said, 'if I toss and turn and make your sleep an impossible nightmare.'

'You're not packing me off to one of them, are you?' she teased him.

'No, of course not.'

And so, like a man taking a bitter pill to be placed at the back of the tongue before washing it down with water, Bosaaso's features remained not so much in pain as in suspense. He felt her body with the deliberate slow movements of a masseur working on an athlete's body.

'Do you want me to show you the house, take you round?' he asked.

'What's the point?'

'Won't you want to live in it if you and I marry?'

'I'll certainly not want to live here,' said Duniya.

'Will there be space for me in your new flat, then?'

'You're rushing me,' she said. And she went to the lavatory.

Neither was able to sleep. She started to think of all that had taken place between them, leading to a happy body of events to follow; for his part he thought of the evening as though it were their wedding night. Incapable, somehow, of remaining silent, he said, 'I can't sleep for fear of snoring.'

She gave him a kiss.

A smile, fidgety as a sparrow, alighted on the tip of his nose, which he twitched self-consciously. Then the smile touched his cheeks, first the left one, then the right. For a while, Duniya was unsure where next it would spread. Would it land on the forehead, smoothing the wrinkles? In the end, the smile illuminated his eyes and he squinted.

'You know what I am going to do?' And he sat up.

'What?' she said.

'I am going to sell this house.'

'Shall we sleep?' she said. 'We have a long day tomorrow.'

'You know what I am going to do after I've sold it?'

She grinned. 'But why sell it in the first place?'

'Listen to me, please.'

'Can we go to sleep?' she said. 'Tomorrow is a long day: Abshir is coming and we have to go to the flat to prepare it for his arrival.'

'I'm too stirred up to fall asleep.'

He looked miserable. It would do no good to tell him to cheer up. He was as highly strung as her, but she had the self-control to contain her tension. She was a woman who knew how to accommodate all life's contradictions without going insane. 'Come,' she said. 'Come and lie beside me.'

She stretched out her arm so he could use it as a pillow. She smiled, a smile belt-thin. She listened to him calling her name again and again as though it were the morning's sacred devotions. 'Tell me about Zawadi,' she said.

'What would you like to know?'

'What she's like.'

'She's a lovely person.'

'I didn't think you would have much to do with anyone who wasn't good at heart,' she said. 'Give me a physical description of her.'

'Do you want me to show you photographs of her?' he asked.

She motioned to him to where he had lain before. 'I don't trust cameras as much as I trust your emotive description of her. After all, a person is not only a body, which is what photographs show.'

'That's true,' he agreed.

She encouraged him. 'How would you describe her to someone who has never met her?'

'It's her eyes,' he said, speaking as if under hypnosis.

'What about them?'

'They are almost green.'

'Almost?'

'Like a ginger cat's, each of Zawadi's eyes has a slightly different tint, the left a darker green, the right one almost blue. But you have to get close enough to them to notice.'

'And neither eye is artificial?'

'No.'

'What're her parents' nationalities?' she asked.

'Both her parents were Afro-American.'

'But somewhere along the line, in her genes, perhaps, there is an explanation' she said, feeling he was about to doze off. 'In a place like the US, where almost everybody comes from somewhere else, there's bound to be an explanation.'

His eyes were closed, his breathing even like a sleeper's.

'Would her photographs, the ones you wanted me to see, have shown these differences in the colouring of her eyes?'

There was no answer. He was asleep.

'What do you reckon her reaction will be if she hears you and I are married? Do you think that will upset her? I mean, is she the kind of person who's likely to send us a telegram of congratulations even if she were?'

When there was no reply, she disengaged her body from his. Then something snapped in her head, like a blind snapping open in a room in which dawn, like an egg, broke bright and light-hearted.

She was sad he wasn't awake to hear the decision she had reached.

Chapter Seventeen

In which Duniya wakes up in Bosaaso's house. Later Waaberi, his late wife's younger sister, calls; so do Hibo and Kaahin.

A young woman intimate enough with Duniya speaks in the dream of uptapped wealth to be found at the bottom of a narrow-mouthed well. Would Duniya like to jump in and appropriate it? She thinks for a long while, eventually giving in, plunging head first, brave, adventurous, untouched by fear of death or drowning. Awaiting her, Duniya finds a well-groomed orchard and at its centre a spring.

Somewhere in the house a radio was giving the morning news bulletin, in English. A raft of strange sounds reached Duniya's drowsy sense, in weird sequences. Some of the noises were coming from the kitchen where she assumed Bosaaso was preparing breakfast; some came from the eaves, others from within her own head. She was too exhausted to determine what mysterious waves had washed her ashore, depositing her on such an alien beach. Before taking stock of the externals surrounding her, she listened to the 7 o'clock news:

> It has been announced at a press conference that the US government is donating to Somalia 30 million dollars' worth of aid for three programmes. The first is under the heading The Northwestern Region Reconstruction and Rehabilitation Programme and to this the sum of $12 million has been allocated; the second (to which about $5.5 million has been allocated) is to help ameliorate the overall condition of people from the region which has suffered a civil war; while the third programme comprises reconstruction of all the infrastructure that the war in the area has destroyed.

Thinking: this was no civil war, there was a massacre in the Northern Region of innocent civilians, a will-o'-the-wisp drone deafened Duniya with the suddenness of a shock. It was not so much a din of noises, more the loudness of ugly colours. The colours of the curtains in the room in which she woke, in which she and Bosaaso had made love, clashed with its wall, those of the walls with the ceiling, and the ceiling's with the doors and window. Perhaps it was unfair to pass judgement on other people's taste. In any case, which of the two was responsible: Bosaaso or Yussur? Upon whom would she lay the full blame? And what were the reasons for making these choices? Being of a generous turn of mind, she decided that maybe a number of people's tastes had been accommodated here. But how could he wake in a room like this every morning? The curtain material had a plastic look and feel; the wallpaper was fresh green, bright yellow, flowery, showy. Was it because Bosaaso was a man and so had the enormous capacity to postpone dealing with a domestic problem until some woman came in to tackle it?

It was just as well the lights were off the night before. Would she have stayed, made love and slept here if she had seen all this ugliness? Not likely, although she might have suggested they go to the city flat. Looking up now, she saw a spider spinning the fibre of its own fable. She remembered the warmth of Bosaaso's body, exuding heat much like a radiator.

He slept on his back, right hand placed on his left, both hands resting on his breast, as if performing devout prayers. A smile embellished his lips, his breathing inaudible, his whole body straight, not a bend anywhere. In the body-politic of sleep, he was a handsome man to watch.

Taariq, Duniya reminded herself, used to take up more than his fair share of the bed, and Zubair fell asleep in a tortured posture, like a child whom drowsiness called on in the middle of a convulsive cry. Mataan slept with his mouth half open; wickedly Nasiiba had once splashed a couple of drops of water into it. Could the poor girl have known that in some areas of the Middle East one poured cold water into people's mouths when they died in the belief that this would facilitate their passage to heaven? On the other hand, asleep, Nasiiba's right hand remained half closed in the attitude of someone awaiting something to hold, whereas the fingers of her left hand would be doubled into a fist as if clutching a childhood treasure, a fist compact as a clove of garlic. Yarey would shed all her clothing when asleep, her legs open in a posture Nasiiba would describe as rebellious, not obscene.

She heard quiet footsteps on the stone stairs. Then Bosaaso's head appeared through the door.

'Good morning,' he said, his face expanding with a new smile.

'Good morning.'

'Did you sleep well?' he asked, his hands resting on her belly as his whole body prostrated with the pleasure of giving her a kiss. 'And did you dream sweet dreams?'

'I was too exhausted,' she lied.

He sat on the edge of the bed and took her hand in his. 'I've made an assortment of breakfasts, not knowing what you might like. I realized that it's our first morning together.'

'It is,' she said.

His words were like fresh-cut flowers. He had showered and shaved. His teeth looked whiter than ever as he said, 'Would you like me to bring your breakfast up here or would you prefer to come down and have it with me?'

'What's the time?' she said.

'It's almost eight.'

The world of sleep engulfed her like a fog. 'I'd like to shower first,' she said.

He got up to bring her a towel, opening the cupboard near the window. Then she saw the contrast between his plainness and humble cast of mind and the plastic discomfiture of the furnishings of the room. It was a comfort to let her gaze dwell on him. He was wearing locally-made khaki trousers, a collarless shirt of *maraykaan*-cotton and sandals. He walked back to her with the deference of a waiter.

'If you like, I can go out while you're in the shower, call at the flat in the city centre, collect the key from the cleaning women, pay them off, run other errands like telegraphing New York, if it's possible, and then come back?' he said.

All the other errands struck her as very pedestrian, and it didn't matter to her whether they were done by him or someone else. 'Why telegraph New York?' She actually wanted to ask, 'Telegraph whom in New York?' and suspected she knew the answer.

He was not good at lying. 'I've just remembered it's a friend's birthday,' he said, but his eyes were shifty, evasive.

'Why not postpone going out until we've had breakfast?' she said.

'Very well.'

With the towel dragging behind her, and not a stitch on, she walked past him on her way to the douche. Was she being provocative or deliberately just breaking the Islamic concept of *cawra,* whose primary function is to regulate female-induced chaos, imposing a taboo of ethics on the woman's body? 'See you downstairs,' she said.

Half an hour later, she joined him downstairs.

'Tea? Or would you prefer coffee?' he asked.

'Tea, please.'

He poured her tea into a china cup.

'How much sugar?'

'Two and a half spoons, please.'

Duniya now sensed Yussur's presence more, given that she had died a tragic death. She wondered if the woman's comb lent to her by Bosaaso had been Yussur's and whether she had been disrespectful to Yussur's memory by refusing to be shown round, shown the balcony from which her predecessor fell to her death. But he was selling the house, anyway, wasn't he? People would suspect it was she who had encouraged him to sell it in an effort to start their life afresh, with no sad memories linking them to Yussur.

'How's your omelette?' he asked.

He was a worrier, she decided.

'I can give you something else if you don't like it.'

'It's excellent thanks,' she said.

He felt she wasn't in a mood to talk.

'Could I have a little more sugar, please? For some reason I have a terribly sweet tooth today.'

'You don't mind talking at breakfast, do you? Or do you prefer silence?'

She smiled. 'I don't mind either way, really. I'm just thinking.'

She looked about as they ate, asking herself if the kitchen they were in was wider than the main bedroom in which they had slept. To her the kitchen felt more spacious, and handsomely done up, with tiled walls, two ovens, one run on gas, the other on electricity, two refrigerators and a deep-freeze. Duniya guessed that the sun came in during the day, crouching at one's feet, which it tickled, like a favourite pet. At night, the moon shone in, preceded by particles of light, bright and shiny as gold. When the city power returned, the kitchen was the place in which light first came back. Such was the esteemed position a kitchen held in Bosaaso's thoughts. It seemed to her that he had chosen its decor, leaving Yussur to do what she pleased with the rest of the house. Hence the ugly colours! Bedroom, curtains and all.

'May I share your worries, Duniya?' he said.

It occurred to her she was no longer comfortable with the names each had for the other. She wasn't happy calling him Bosaaso, and Maxmoud lay heavy on her tongue, like yoghurt that has gone bad. She preferred that he choose his own abbreviation of her name. She thought all this as she chewed and then swallowed what she had in her mouth. 'No worries to share, thank you,' she replied.

'What then?'

'I was just thinking about space and kitchens.' He appeared interested; she a little startled, because she didn't know how Taariq's favourite concept 'space' slipped in. Cautious, she said, 'About kitchens, let's say.'

'I've chosen and seen to everything here, including the decor,' he said with pride.

'Why?'

He placed his knife and fork in the shape of a cross, making her think of the two pieces of straw Somalis lay across a milk-vessel, hoping this would discourage jinns from consuming it, or poisoning it for human consumption. He said, 'In my mind kitchens are associated with my mother, not in any pejorative sense, but because in a world in which derogatory terms like Nigger, Woman and Native have become badges of honour, I believe that a woman like my mother afforded me the opportunity to take an appreciative look at the world. On returning home I thought, what better way to commemorate her than build a mausoleum of a kitchen in tribute to her? It was also with this in mind that I paid another tribute to my mother's side of the family – Axmad, the taxi driver and the other cousins in the commune belong to my spindle side of the family, not my father's. But this is neither here, nor there.'

'Surely, you didn't grow up in a setting where space in the home is divided up into living, sleeping, eating and cooking spaces? So how can you think of a kitchen as a mausoleum?'

After a long while he said, 'I would agree with you that men have assigned to themselves all the sacred, powerful, spaces, forbidding women from being visible or present in such places as mosques or at meetings of a council of men reaching decisions which affect the whole community, including women.'

Duniya, agreeing, nodded her head.

'I also agree with you,' he said, following a thoughtful pause, 'that the spaces allotted to women belong to the grey areas of beds, food and the rearing of children.'

Then the bell in the kitchen rang, just when they resumed eating their breakfast in reflective quietness. Bosaaso started. When it rang for the second time, he looked at Duniya for guidance. And when it rang for the third time, he looked up at the bell as if it were a video contraption that would show him on a ten-millimetre screen who wanted to enter.

There was anger in his eyes. But Duniya hoped he could decide whether to answer the bell or no without involving her in his affairs. Who could tell who it might be? Waaberi? Mire? Kaahin? One of Bosaaso's numerous cousins? Or Nasiiba with an urgent message to surprise Duniya?

His mouth was twisted in a grimace.

'I hope that's Waaberi,' he said, in the tone of a man itching for a fight.

They waited for the fourth ring of the bell.

'Did you hear people calling out your name last night?' she asked.

'I'm a heavy sleeper,' he reminded her.

The bell rang for the fourth time. He got up, a man quick to test his own strength against anyone. Leaving in haste, he dropped his napkin on the floor and Duniya bent down to pick it up.

She returned to her omelette and tea, in the quiet comfortable thought that she hadn't pressed him either way. His life was his business and he could do what he pleased with it.

She heard the outside gate creak open and then heard it shut, admitting a woman whose thin voice was explaining to Bosaaso that she had come several times before, but had not found him in. 'Where have you been all this time? I even went to that woman's place this morning, looking for you,' she said.

Bosaaso, voice neutral, said, 'Why don't you come inside?'

I am 'that woman', thought Duniya, smiling.

Bosaaso preceded Waaberi into the kitchen. Duniya sized the woman up as she came in: small, large-mouthed and large-hipped, heavily made up and wearing lipstick, hair singed, dress expensive and belonging to the season's fashion, with a zip in front, and showing enough of her enormous breasts, like a film preview, dark birthmark in the valley and all, bare arms, a bushy armpit, a belt with a pendant, a necklace of amber beads and bracelets for her wrists and anklets as well. Waaberi was so engrossed with thoughts about Bosaaso that she didn't see Duniya who might have been part of the kitchen's furniture. Then, pointing to Duniya, he said, 'You know each other, don't you?'

Not a sound from Waaberi. Only eyes filled with contempt. When next she had an interpretable expression, Duniya thought she might be considering the possibility of turning back whence she had come. But she struggled like a huntswoman caught in the trap she had set.

He offered her a seat, but Waaberi wouldn't take it. 'Would you like to have breakfast with us?' he asked.

'No, thank you,' she said with a touch of nervousness.

Majestically calm, Bosaaso had his hands resting on his hips like a PE instructor watching his trainees rehearse a sequence of exercises, an instructor pleased with the results. 'If you're not sitting down with us and you don't want to have a cup of tea or a glass of water, is there anything we can do for you?' he said to Waaberi.

Speaking with difficulty, she said, 'I've come to see you, yes.'

'Why have you come to see me?' And he looked at Duniya, to see what her reaction to the goings-on might be. Hand under chin. None. 'I haven't much time. So speak up please,' he said.

Waaberi almost whispered, 'May I speak to you privately?'

'No, you may not.'

'It won't take more than a minute,' she promised.

'I haven't a minute to spare. Besides Duniya is no stranger, and there isn't anything I wouldn't discuss in front of her.'

Duniya thought Bosaaso might have been a drama student showing to his teacher what he could do.

Waaberi said, 'My mother has been unwell.'

'Yes?' said Bosaaso and waited.

'And we've just received our electricity, water and other bills, all together.'

'Why bring the bills to me? Or inform me that your mother has been unwell?'

'Because you used to give us a hand in settling some of the bills.'

'Did I only give you a hand or did I settle them all, every cent of your bills?'

Waaberi looked at Duniya for the first time. Then to Bosaaso: 'You used to settle them all. I am sorry,' and her head bowed, of its own accord. 'You've always been generous.'

'Do you recall my words when I last called on your mother,' he said, 'three days ago, as recently as that?'

She spoke after a pause and with difficulty. 'You described yourself as an exploited man, who was being socially blackmailed into giving what he didn't wish to give any more; you asked us to stop presenting you with our bills.'

'What else did I ask of you? You in particular?'

She looked too embarrassed to continue. 'Go on,' Bosaaso urged her.

'You inquired about how much my jewellery cost, how much the dress and shoes I had on cost, and all my other expensive habits, reminding us that although you worked hard for your money, you couldn't afford the clothes I wore, and even if you could, you wouldn't buy them, but would use what you had wisely, care less about external appearances, and not beg.'

'What else did I suggest?' he said.

'That I sell the jewellery to pay the bills.'

'Now whose were they in the first place?'

'Yussur's.'

'Who was?'

'Your former wife.'

'Did she give them to you, all of the pieces?'

'I borrowed some, and she gave me some.'

'And for how long have I been supporting you and your mother and your expensive tastes *after* Yussur's death?'

'One and a half years.'

As though he were counsel for the prosecution rounding up his cross-examination, 'Could you remind me when this conversation took place, Waaberi? Do you remember?'

'Three days ago.'

Duniya sensed that she almost added 'Sir' to her last response.

Bosaaso sat down. He might have been a jubilant barrister celebrating the end of a successful but difficult case. Anyone might have thought him incapable of such a cruel confrontation.

There was silence. Waaberi looked at Duniya. Was Waaberi appealing to her to intervene? It seemed as if they had been joined by a fourth person. Tension was the fourth person in the kitchen, omnipresent, allowing no one to sit still. This wasn't a story of equals having a show-down, thought Duniya; not a Duniya confronting the cruelty of a half-brother; or a Yussur having an all-out fight with her mother. This was more like a donor European or American government having a 'frank talk' (the all-purpose phrase which would appear in the official communiqué) with an African country's representatives, in which the latter were told that they were being immodest in the number of Mercedes and similar extravagances and in the show-pieces they displayed to the rest of the world.

'And you won't give us anything?' Waaberi said. 'Not even this last time?'

'Give your mother my best wishes, that's all.'

Leaving, Waaberi left behind a tension which strangled Duniya and Bosaaso, preventing them from speaking, even after the outside gate had been shut.

Then, after a long silence, he said, 'It's getting late.'

Absent-mindedly, Duniya asked, 'Late for what?'

'I must go and collect the keys from the cleaning women, call at my cousin's commune and arrange that Axmad joins us in his taxi this afternoon to go to the airport.' He paused. He was sure he had forgotten something.

She didn't say anything.

'Are you coming or staying?'

She thought that he had his tension to keep him company; so she said, 'I'll wait for you here, do the washing-up and all that. But could you call at my place on your way back? Just to find out how things are?'

Kissing her lightly, he said, 'Ciao.'

'Ciao!'

Duniya turned a question over and over in her mind, faster and faster, until the words comprising the question ran into each other. Bosaaso had been gone almost half an hour, by which time she had done the dishes. Then the bell in the kitchen rang.

She went to open the door. She was surprised to be greeted by Hibo and Kaahin.

Duniya invited them to come in and walked away, hoping one of them would push the gate shut and then both would follow her. When she didn't hear their footsteps, Duniya turned. Curiously, they were talking in whispers, arguing about something. Now she might not have invited Kaahin into *her* house, but this wasn't hers, and from what she knew of Kaahin's and Bosaaso's relationship, he was welcome in his friend's house. But now she hesitated and was unable to decide what to do. Were Kaahin and Hibo having a very quiet affair and had they come here, assuming to find only Bosaaso who in any case had known of their liaison? She became irritable. 'What's all this? Why won't you come in?' she said to them.

Hibo's eyes moved like a scatter of frightened ants. But Kaahin did not display any nervousness, no deference.

Looking from one to the other, she said, 'If you people aren't coming in, I am going inside to make myself a cup of something and sit in the living-room.'

Unsmiling, Hibo said to Kaahin, 'I'll go in with Duniya, but you sit and wait in the car.'

Duniya knew it wasn't her business to interfere, but said, maybe out of a desire to avoid misunderstanding, 'Come inside, Kaahin.'

He looked like a man who had been dispossessed of all he owned. Duniya thought that Kaahin shared a meagre resemblance with Mataan, in that he too appeared to bloom best when treated like a son. She wondered if this had been the way Zawadi had always treated him, like a son, although he wasn't her junior in years. And his mouth opened just like Mataan's and wouldn't shut; his beady eyes had a glint in them, reflective as silver, when the sun shone on them. 'I don't mind if I wait outside in the car, really,' he said.

'Come, let's all go inside,' Duniya said to Hibo.

'But I've come to talk to you.'

'Let's go inside, all three of us,' insisted Duniya.

She walked away and was relieved to hear the outside gate bang shut and two sets of footsteps following her. If nothing had been going on between them, what were they saying to each other all the time?

When they were in the kitchen, Duniya said, 'Bosaaso isn't here. So what can I offer you? Tea? Coffee?'

Kaahin said, 'We met him in town, running errands. It was he who told us you were here. In fact, I was taking Hibo to your place.' He wore a charming smile.

Duniya decided not to mention that Waaberi had come to see Bosaaso on her own and had not received a warm welcome.

'What's the matter with you? You look like a suttee who's come to take her leave of the world she loves,' she said to Hibo, sitting in her chair wrapped in rags of sadness.

Hibo didn't ask who or what a suttee was, but Kaahin did.

Duniya remembered the explanation Nasiiba had given her, which she repeated, looking not at Kaahin whose question she was answering, but at Hibo who chose to remain silent. 'Suttee is a Hindu custom in which a widow immolates herself on her husband's pyre.'

This made Kaahin so unbearably nervous that he got up as if his chair had instantly turned into an electric one. He said, 'I really must go, to let the two of you talk. Thank you, Duniya. Good luck, Hibo,' and dashed out of the kitchen door, banging into it. Even this didn't stop him. For he shook his head in amazement, grinned and went out as fast as his legs would take him. Soon after, all noises ceased. 'What's ailing you?' Duniya asked Hibo.

Emotionless, Hibo said, 'I think I've killed Gallayr, my husband.'

'You *think* you've killed him?'

'Yes,' said Hibo, her voice empty of sadness.

'Where's his body?'

'At home.'

Duniya remembered the detective novels she had read and said, 'Is he buried under a pile of earth with bushes hiding the mound or is his corpse in the freezer, awaiting a mortician's arrival, soon to be followed by an inspector with an unlit pipe?'

Hibo didn't appreciate Duniya's humour. She said flatly, 'When I left him he was on our bed, grovelling with pain, his face pale and swollen, his eyes bloodshot and all the veins visible.'

'Where did you hide the knife?' asked Duniya.

'I didn't use a knife.'

'And where are your children?'

'They spent the night at a relative's.'

Duniya drew comfort from the news that she wasn't the only one who had spent the night out of her usual bed. For all anyone knew, Waaberi had spent it in Kaahin's place, and was carrying her make-up kit in her handbag that she clutched so tightly during her visit.

'So this was premeditated murder, cold and calculated?' said Duniya.

Not a muscle of Hibo's moved. 'Yes,' she said.

'Where did you throw the gun? Or was this what you and Kaahin were arguing about in whispers by the entrance?' Duniya asked.

'I didn't use a gun.'

'If you didn't a knife or a gun, what did you use – poison?'

Hibo nodded, and for the first time since they started talking about all this, she winced. But she suppressed her tears. Her husband, Gallayr, had done something for which he had to be punished, and she did just that. There was no need to shed a tear.

'Don't you want me to tell you why?' asked Hibo.

'He's given you gonorrhoea and you killed him by poisoning his food,' Duniya said. Hibo had said that she would either kill or commit suicide if her husband gave her gonorrhoea; she had said so on the day an out-patient confessed her own husband had given her the disease. It was a bore to be as predictable as Hibo, Duniya decided.

Hibo then burst into a tiresome explosion of tears and emotions, but there was something shallow, something pretentious, about her weeping. Given a few seconds, Duniya was certain all this crying would peter out like a river ending in a desert.

Hibo was quiet now and asking Duniya, 'What would you do if you were in my place?'

Duniya found it difficult to imagine standing in Hibo's shoes, but she was a very bright woman and so she said, 'If I were you, Hibo, I would go home, and give myself a single effective injection of 2.4 or 4.8 mega units of procaine penicillin.'

'And what would you do about *him*?'

Duniya said to herself that when husbands are reduced to 'him' and wives to 'her', then it is high time the marriage is dissolved, or an illicit affair considered. Being a woman of northerly honour and from Burco where such women are still raised, Hibo contemplated murder. Duniya said, 'It depends if he is dead or still alive and breathing.'

'What do you mean?'

Hibo was formidably calm for someone who had poisoned her husband's food, and Duniya wondered if it was some kind of joke? But she said, 'If he is dead, then you must live with your secret for the rest of your days, telling no one what you've done.'

'Or perform a suttee, is that what you said that Hindu custom is called?'

Duniya marvelled at her own calm; marvelled at the fact that she was behaving as though she knocked off a husband every April Fool's Day, as though it was an annual affair for her. It was so incredible she wished Nasiiba were here, probably the one person who might appreciate such macabre anecdotes.

'Performing suttee is too neat. People here in Somalia have not that subtle an understanding of your kind of motive or death, and we wouldn't wish to waste it on them.'

Hibo pleaded. 'What do I do if he isn't dead?'

'Take him to the hospital and let the doctors decide what chemical antidotes he should be given by telling them what you've put in his food,' Duniya advised.

'The man deserves to be dead,' Hibo said.

'So why ask my opinion if you are already decided?'

'I am his very respectable wife, not some street woman,' Hibo said, 'to whom he may give gonorrhoea and get away unpunished.'

'Let's not get carried away. Forget about all this rhetoric of northern honour and southern dishonour. Gallayr has infected you with poison and by putting poison in his food, you've poisoned him too.' Duniya helped Hibo to her feet. 'There's no time to waste. Go home and take him to the hospital.'

She then escorted her to the gate. There were tears in Hibo's voice as she said. 'You're a very strong woman and I envy you.'

Then Hibo's tongue, thick as a slice of gorgonzola, lay inert in her mouth. Duniya wished her good luck, and they hugged.

Outside they saw Kaahin's car, parked just outside the gate, and Bosaaso was there talking to him. A little later, Duniya and Bosaaso left in great haste for Duniya's place.

The children's chatter stopped when Bosaaso and Duniya walked in. When the ability to speak or to pick up a broom or mop returned, the youngsters went back to work. Bosaaso was treated uniformly by all three as though he were an elder brother. Marilyn and Fariida were there as well, but they were too formal with him for his liking.

Duniya and Bosaaso were offered chairs and asked to relax, as though they had come from a long, physically exhausting journey.

Nasiiba came to report that the city flat had been prepared, or at least Uncle Abshir's room had been readied for use tonight. 'And we're getting a bouquet of flowers,' she added.

Duniya sat up. 'A what?'

'A bouquet of flowers and the whole works.'

'Whose idea is this?' Bosaaso said.

'I'll dress in white, Duniya, gloves and all,' Yarey volunteered.

'But whose idea has this been?'

'Mine,' said Nasiiba.

'We're welcoming him as though he were a visiting head of state,' Yarey continued, repeating something Nasiiba had told her. 'You know, like when a head of another country visits Somalia, a young girl is dressed in white and she gives him a bouquet of flowers. We see that on TV a lot.'

There was energy to Duniya's decision not to argue out the point with either Nasiiba or Yarey, which was why she encouraged them in a gentle way to get back to what they were doing.

'Of course,' said Bosaaso, 'the poor things don't seem to realize not only that this is a neo-colonial tradition, inherited, along with the idea of flags, a state capital and such paraphernalia, but also that embedded in it is a very male notion in which an innocent young virgin dressed in white is offered to a visiting man who happens to be a head of another state. I needn't remind you that in our own tradition a man whose honour is wounded is often rewarded with a maiden as part of the compensation given him. And when male friends visit their own kind in another town, the host provides his guest with a woman to entertain him.'

'Maybe you should tell them,' said Duniya.

'It would probably spoil their fun,' said Bosaaso.

'That's possible,' Duniya agreed.

They both fell silent and solemn, like people entering a place of worship. Both were thinking about Abshir and each was looking forward to being reunited with him. Separated by their thoughts, each held on to a pleasant memory, a keep-sake of tenderness from the night before. For her part, she was proud that she hadn't told him whether she would marry him or not; for his, he took pride in the fact that he wasn't insisting she tell him her decision.

Welcome, Abshir, my darling brother, Duniya said to herself.

Chapter Eighteen

In which Duniya, together with her children, Bosaaso and friends drive in a convoy to welcome Abshir at the airport. The day's party continues late into the night.

Bosaaso's car was at the head of a convoy of three cars, and Duniya was his only passenger. Following, in a taxi driven by his cousin Axmad, were Yarey, Mataan, Fariida and Marilyn. The third vehicle had Qaasim at the wheel, Taariq in the front, and just to be different from the others, Nasiiba, who sat in the back. Axmad had the taxi-driver's ignominious habit of pressing the horn non-stop, which made some passers-by take interest in the convoy. When the traffic slowed down, and the horn kept on sounding, a woman ventured to suggest that a marriage was taking place, this produced curiosity in a number of by-standers and the word 'wedding' occurred in the conversation of those standing on either side of the road. The Chinese whispers finally reached Duniya's and Bosaaso's ears. Then a woman ululated, and another mentioned Duniya's and Bosaaso's names.

Duniya had on a mischievous smile. Bosaaso, however, sat rigidly, his back stiff as an elephant's tail, his eyes looking concentratedly ahead of himself, as though he were driving through patches of fog. 'Shall we all go out for a meal tonight, Duniya?' he said.

'Provided you are my guests,' she said.

'And how many are we?'

'Only family,' she said.

'Let's include Mire, shall we?'

'Yes, let's,' she consented gladly.

'Will Fariida and Marilyn join us as well?'

'I said, only family. Not friends,' Duniya reminded him.

The list of names gave itself to Duniya. She counted the number of invitees several times. She was like the proverbial Arab with ten donkeys for sale, who forgot to count whichever animal he was riding, but got the figure right when he wasn't on a donkey's back.

'Have you thought of a restaurant to go to?' she asked.

'It depends whether we want to eat in a restaurant in the centre or go to a drive-in restaurant outside town,' he said.

'What's your preference?' she asked.

'You decide,' he said.

Here we are, she thought, neither able to make a decision for fear of hurting the other. Will this happen whenever we come to the junction where the road branches into two. Decisively, she said, 'Let's go to Croce del Sud.'

'Fine I'll book a table,' he offered.

With a snap, her eyes shut and opened, so that a momentary darkness was followed immediately by one full of bright sunshine. She was exhausted. Then Qaasim's turning up when Fariida had only just arrived rather complicated matters. The two of them had called at the city flat, which had looked impressively cosy and welcoming. She hoped Abshir would like it.

Now the airport tower came into view, and Bosaaso asked, 'How many of us are coming to dinner, then?'

'I have counted seven,' she said.

'Seven is an ominous number that brings good fortune.'

Then he manoeuvred his way through the narrow entrance to the parking lot. He searched for a place where they could park all three cars side by side. He had just found such a place, when he saw the plane come in to land.

In half an hour, Abshir, her beloved brother, was coming off the plane, the first passenger to do so. Duniya's blood pounded in her ears, thinking not only of Abshir, but also asking herself to whom she would first give the news that she had decided to marry Bosaaso: the bridegroom himself or her brother, a piece of good news with which to welcome him.

Like a chick breaking out of its shock of an outer shell; like an infant's eyes able to see for the first time; like a moth opening its baby wings to fly; like shapes that come, go and return, human forms that have voices, that answer to names if you recall what to call them, human forms that speak one's name 'Duniya'. She remembered that some time in the past, she had felt light like the mythical night journey in the Koran and had flown away; remembered falling asleep some time in the past, and when she had awoken, the foundling had died. Duniya now wondered to herself if she were hallucinating, she was sure she had lost touch with the physical reality surrounding her, and sensed delirium engulfing her, making her feel giddy, the way labour pains desensitize a woman so she cannot feel the pain because there is too much of it.

She was a traveller who had just arrived and was suffering from physical exhaustion. *She* couldn't trust her feet to carry her anywhere, and *her* ears were filled with compressed air, and *her* head was entertaining a thousand and one thoughts which had to wait until the right moment came. *She* was an uncle meeting his nieces and nephews in person for the first time; *she* was a brother meeting his sister Duniya after so many years; *she* was a man encountering his brother-in-law-elect, someone whom he had known before, in another context; *she* was a man meeting two good-looking teenagers. *But then there you are, maybe you are hallucinating!*

Duniya's memory, she would be the first to admit, was fragmentary and full of hiatuses, like a photographer who, while the group of which she was a member posed in front of a camera, adjusted the timing wrongly, giving herself insufficient time before taking her own place in the group portrait.

There is nothing like heightened consciousness to make one's centre shift. Duniya would explain to Bosaaso later that evening that she had suffered from some form of psychic disturbance, of the kind likely to demonstrate itself when one's brain cells receive a greater amount of impressions than they can cope with. She didn't know how else to describe what she had felt.

In spite of all this, everything had gone well. Qaasim had been most helpful in arranging for Abshir to walk through the VIP corridor, and not have to open any of his seven bags for customs. Those present each gave a hand in carrying the bags to the waiting cars. Duniya didn't know much of what happened, not until they got home. By then, all the others had gone, only family remained, and Bosaaso had been accepted as a bona fide member of it.

In her head, Duniya had many unanswered and unasked queries. For instance: How had she introduced Bosaaso? As Abshir's brother-in-law elect? Or just a friend? She was sure Abshir could see that her relationship with Bosaaso deserved to be properly introduced. But did she make a mess of it all? And with whom had Fariida gone? With Qaasim, in his car?

Once Duniya came to, the universe of her imagination was at her beck and call. She could now see Abshir properly, hear his deep voice, remember all his kind gestures, his unlimited generosity. It remained to her a mystery why she always accepted Abshir's gifts, whereas she felt ill at ease receiving other people's.

Abshir was a tall man, with a stoop, whose posture made him appear well over six foot. He was very dark with long limbs, a wide mouth and thick lips. For a man his age, he had a lot of hair, although a few grey hairs showed through. His hands were large, his fingers long. His eyes, when listening, shone with eager expectation. Abshir was a heavy smoker, a cigarette every quarter of an hour, and he had a dry cough. Abshir loved chewing raw garlic, a habit he shared with Nasiiba, and he and his niece were of a similar temperament, although Mataan resembled him more closely.

He had a gentle laugh, very soft, hardly audible. Now he was laughing because someone had told him he had been spared the bouquet-giving ceremony of a niece in white, with a bunch of famished roses.

Having seen the Vespa Mataan had borrowed from Waris's cousin, Abshir offered to buy his nephew a motor scooter if he did well in his exam. When told that Duniya and the children would no longer be living in Qaasim's flat, but in another in the city centre, Abshir asked if it was possible for him to buy a pied-à-terre, for which Duniya would be responsible, or live in. No wonder they had nicknamed him *'Scelaro'*. He was fast.

He, Bosaaso and Mataan were sitting in the courtyard, chatting. The two older men had many friends in common, and each was inquiring of the other about them. Mataan listened attentively, his mouth gaping open, looking admiringly from one to the other. Bosaaso was thrilled to talk about the good times he and Abshir had enjoyed in Rome. How were Abshir's Italian wife and two daughters? Were they still living in Trastevere or had they moved? What about Bosaaso's Australian and South African friends, were they still there, working for the FAO?

'How's Mire?' Abshir asked.

Bosaaso gave Abshir such a quick run-down of what Mire was doing that Mataan wondered if there wasn't more to what

Bosaaso and Mire were up to, coming all the way as they had done from Germany and the USA respectively, and donating their services to their country.

'I would love to see Mire,' said Abshir.

'He's coming to dinner tonight,' said Bosaaso.

Abshir turned to Mataan, 'Where are we having dinner tonight, Mataan?'

'Maybe Mother has organized something, but I don't know.'

'Duniya is inviting us out tonight,' Bosaaso declared.

'Where?' Abshir's eyes lit up eagerly.

After a pause, Bosaaso said, 'Croce del Sud.'

Duniya joined them and stood silently in the parenthesis her arrival opened. Abshir took a loving look at her, then, as his sister sat down beside him said to Bosaaso 'Is Croce still open?'

'It is,' said Bosaaso. 'It has become a bit seedy, but some of the waiters are still there from the days before independence, and they still bow at the appearance of a white-face, because white hands offer better tips than dark ones. But you get excellent service if your dark hand offers a fifteen per cent tip, five per cent higher than the pink hand.'

Reminiscing, Abshir turned to Mataan and Duniya, 'You know, we weren't allowed to go anywhere near Croce del Sud in the fifties, when the Italians were the master race here. Nor were the waiters allowed to wear shoes.'

Duniya felt foolish interrupting the flow of the conversation with a question, but asked, 'Why do Italians believe they are the ones who taught Somalis to wear shoes, as if the whole venture of their so-called higher civilization comprised a gimmicky habit of a pair of feet-covering objects, Abshir?'

'Why, I've never thought of that,' he said, self-censoriously.

'Neither had I,' Bosaaso added.

Then Abshir coughed, his ribs heaving. His chest exploded with a loud cough a second and a third time. He said, 'Don't anyone tell me to stop smoking, because I won't.' And he smiled, wrinkling the corners of his eyes.

'No one will,' Duniya said.

'You mean Shiriye won't?' Abshir queried, surprising everybody.

Duniya, who didn't speak, thought of Abshir as Nasiiba's kindred; but never mind.

After a pause, Abshir said to Duniya, 'How is our half-brother, anyway?'

Duniya's breathing rustled like silk touching rough skin, as she mumbled something brief and unpleasant about Shiriye.

'Do you think Shiriye will give me my share of the bridewealth which he is said to have collected from Zubair for your hand?' Abshir teased her. 'Or half of what he got from Taariq?' He reached for her hand which he held in both his. In fondness.

'I doubt it very much,' said Duniya.

When Abshir coughed his dry cough a few more times, Duniya freed her hand from his hold. She left, excusing herself as though attending to an urgent matter.

'Tell me something about yourself,' Abshir said to his nephew.

'There is nothing to tell really,' Mataan responded shyly.

'How's that?' said Abshir.

'He's excellent at school, the best in mathematics, I've been told,' Bosaaso interjected.

Rather emphatically, Abshir said, 'I see,' as if he knew a lot more than he was willing to give away. Then he continued, 'What do you want to study when you go to university, Mataan?'

'I haven't decided,' said Mataan.

'You have one more academic year to go, haven't you?' said Abshir.

Bosaaso said, 'Plus two years, one in which he must do national service and a second year as an army conscript.'

'How is your Italian?' Abshir asked Mataan.

'Not good enough to study at an Italian university unless I do one of those very intensive courses they give in Perugia.' For Mataan, things were happening too fast. Uncle *Scelaro* was too quick, but he was too slow; even so he was responding with a heightened enthusiasm that suited the occasion.

Abshir said, 'Or would you prefer to go to at an English-speaking university, in the USA or Canada, I mean is your English good enough for you to take a course in mathematics?'

Mataan was not sure if he wished to take a degree in mathematics, but he didn't say that. He was too intimidated and things were happening at a faster rate than he'd been used to.

'We'll talk more then,' Abshir suggested, adding after an appropriate pause and, after looking from Bosaaso to Mataan, 'I trust we can find a way to have him exempted from national and military service?'

'I trust there are ways of doing that,' Bosaaso said.

Abshir suppressed a smile before it subverted the subtlety of a knowing grin which had spread itself all over his face. He said, 'What about Nasiiba?'

Since no one could take upon himself or herself to speak for her, Nasiiba was given a shout, and she came out laden with an armful of clothes which she had taken out of the gift-bags her uncle had brought from Rome for her. She was already wearing a pair of Levi jeans and a matching denim shirt. She said, excited beyond her own measure, 'How did you guess my height, waist and all that, Uncle?'

'Miski gave them to me,' he said.

Nasiiba tripped on some of the dresses she was carrying, as she moved towards them. Yarey was on her heels, and she too was carrying a legion of gifts her uncle had given her. The girls' arrival suddenly turned the place into a noisy one, and Bosaaso got up and said, 'Perhaps I should go now.'

'When do we see you?' Abshir asked him.

'Why don't you come with me and collect the car? Then I won't need to fetch you this evening,' Bosaaso said.

Abshir pondered for a moment, as if unsure where in the world he was, and then said, 'I was meaning to get to the car hire agency as soon as I could. How will you move around if you lend me yours?'

'I have a taxi as my fall-back when I have no transport,' said Bosaaso.

Duniya was called, and she, Bosaaso and Abshir thought about the best way to handle this. The fact that Nasiiba stayed out of this didn't pass unnoticed.

'What do you suggest, Duniya?' Abshir said.

Duniya suggested that Mataan go with them to show Abshir the way back.

'Shall we go for a drive, you and I?' said Abshir. 'When I come back?'

'That's a lovely idea,' said Duniya.

Nasiiba was clearly excited, and she slid in and out of joyous moods. At one point, in fact as soon as she and her mother were let alone, she came out to where Duniya was sitting, wearing a fashionable outfit Abshir had brought her. Sounding high-strung, she spoke what amounted, in her mother's opinion, to be a non-sequitur, saying, 'Have you noticed of late how many dogs there are in any African city? Dogs roaming around the streets in packs, full of menace like wolves let out of a zoo? You see them everywhere, foraging in the very garbage bins the urchins have emptied of everything except the bones they cannot chew; these dogs attack pedestrians minding their own business, especially after dark. Have you any idea where these terrifying beasts come from?'

Duniya didn't seem moved and remained non-committal.

'According to Taariq,' Nasiiba continued, 'most of these dogs at one time or another belonged to Europeans or Americans with plenty of food to spare and human affection to indulge on these beasts that actually live in the same spacious and well-to-do houses as their children. Now the truth is, these dogs received more food and attentive love than most Somalis, and then, between one weekend and the next, the masters went home, leaving behind these spoiled creatures. This has been a pattern, too much love, then with frightening suddenness, homelessness and a hostile Islamic community ready to stone them on the slightest pretext. In short, the dogs are turned into schizoids.'

'What are you driving at, Nasiiba? Please come to the point!' Duniya said.

Then Nasiiba paused for a long while. Finally she said, 'This is that level of reality in which you might discern a certain similarity between dogs and some Third World dictators who receive the pampered approval of their European and American masters until their usefulness has ceased, dictators who are abandoned to the dogs of bad fortune. On a personal level, the Europeans and Americans living in Africa behave in a manner akin to that of their governments on a national level. What I am trying to say . . .'

Duniya's body stiffened. Glaring at Nasiiba, she demanded, 'Do you think I am thick?'

'Why?'

'I am *not* thick!' said Duniya. 'That's all.'

Puzzled, Nasiiba stared at her mother who was leaving the room to prepare herself for the drive with Abshir.

Abshir was at the wheel, driving in an easterly direction, towards the sea. 'You can't imagine how much I missed seeing, swimming in or being near the Indian Ocean,' he said.

She watched him drive. He was a chimney and was smoking out his lungs; and his whole body, now and then, exploded, turning pale like unburied ashes left overnight in a brazier. She began to wonder why Mataan had always reminded her of Abshir, although the two didn't resemble each other physically. She had never seen their own grandfather, but thought that nickname was indicative of a stoop, his nickname being *Tuerre,* meaning the man with the hump. She told herself that certain physical characteristics run in some families, jumping hopscotch-style from one generation to another.

'Tell me a little about Bosaaso,' he said.

'*We*'re thinking of getting married.'

'Is anything in the way?' Abshir asked, as if he wished to get it removed, whatever it was. They both thought about Shiriye, although neither invoked his accursed name.

'He proposed; I asked for time to think it over.'

'Are you still thinking? Or have you decided?'

'I've been turning it over and over in my mind, now the answer is yes, now no, although mostly it has been yes. I am very fond of him, love him actually in my own way,' she qualified. 'He deserves better than I can offer to him. He is too trusting, he has no energy for fighting; I realise I am a bit of a handful.'

'I hope he is aware of what he is in for,' said Abshir with a smile.

'I'm sure he is.'

'He has been rather deferential to me, as in-laws are towards one another. And when we were in his car, taking him home, he suggested I drive. Bosaaso might have been a young man appearing in front of his prospective father-in-law.' Abshir stubbed out a cigarette, only to light another, and continued, 'Love has a certain odour which is seldom smelt, only seen. I scented it on arrival and saw it again when I shook hands with him early this afternoon.'

'The reason I didn't say yes when I could have was that I don't want to give satanic tongues the opportunity to wag like a dog's tail and say that I am marrying him for his money and American Green Card,' Duniya said.

'That's why I spoke to Mataan in his presence, in a sense to assure Bosaaso that your children won't be a financial burden on him. I will make that absolutely clear at the earliest opportunity. Their education, here or abroad, preferably university studies abroad, all these are my responsibility. The poor man has spent a quarter of his life raising other people's offspring.'

Duniya uttered a chuckle, something between a whimper and a worried laugh, and then said, 'Thank you.'

'Let it be understood this in no way should put pressure on you to decide either way. You do what gives you pleasure. You marry if you want to, you don't if you don't wish to. Your destiny is in your hands. But the children's school fees are my responsibility, and mine alone,' he said.

She choked on tears of her rejoicing and couldn't speak for a long time. Finally, she said, 'I've always wondered why it is that I've accepted all the gifts you've given me, when I fret if others come towards me intending to give me something. Can you tell me why?'

'Because when you were less than an hour old,' he answered, 'and you refused to breast-feed and our mother was too unwell to take care of you, it was I who fed you the first drop of milk, a gift you wouldn't take from anyone else, including our father, the midwife or other women of the neighbourhood.' He paused, placing a wedge of a cigarette between his lips, maybe so as not to smile.

'My first conscious moment when I received the first drop of life into my mouth is thirty-five years away,' she said, 'I've been a mother three times, married twice, fallen in love once, or I believe I have. What is it that you have that others don't? There must be something.'

'What about Qaasim: haven't you been accepting to stay in his flat more or less rent free?' asked Abshir.

'Our deal had been based on an understanding, which got pulled down the instant a misunderstanding between me and his wife Muraayo occurred. That's now over and I am moving out of his house and life too.'

'What about your relationship with Bosaaso?'

'He's often been more of a recipient than a giver,' she said.

In the city centre, Abshir was reorienting himself, remembering sights he hadn't seen for a quarter of a century; Duniya was staring at some of these because they had assumed a certain relevance, in that they reminded her of Bosaaso. Abshir was saying that little had changed since he last walked these streets, a taller building here, a semi-developed plot there, but the grid, pattern and mapping of Mogadiscio had stayed unaltered, especially in the centre. It still had its charm and attraction.

'The sea,' he said, 'my love.'

She thought of Bosaaso, but didn't say anything.

'I can smell it,' Abshir said.

Then his face was marked with gridded lines forming a smile. Did love reside in the odour of one? as Abshir had put it. Remembering the Italian film *Profumo di Donna*, Duniya was able to review her life between the blinking of an eye. Then she asked herself whether we wear perfumes to supplement or suppress natural body odours that betray our emotions.

Abshir parked opposite what had once been a fish market. The old post office was somewhere in the vicinity, he remembered. They walked up some steps, and turned left, and then down cobblestones eighty-odd years old, towards the ocean. They touched, they held hands as they strode together, silent.

They stood by the railing, which careless drivers had collided with a great many times, but which had never given way. She reminded herself to be careful: life was a driving-seat and accidents were blind curves, ambushing one. She cheered up, telling herself that dinner-time wasn't that far off and they would all be there, Bosaaso included.

Abshir said, 'But you haven't told me how you've been?' And he lit a cigarette.

'It has been a long journey up and up and up, *here,*' Duniya said, '*here,* here I am, that is,' a pause as if to emphasize a point, 'and *there,* down below, feels like way, way down, and the two stations are separated by a wide gulf, and I am senseless with giddiness whenever I examine how far up I have come, thanks to you, Abshir.'

'Come, come,' he said embarrassed, and wiped his face with a handkerchief. Silent, he waited. She went on, encouraged by his silence. 'To know how I am and how I have fared, you must understand why I resist all kinds of domination, including that of being given something. As my epitaph I would like to have the following written: "Here lies Duniya who distrusted givers".'

'I'll say something, if I may,' said Abshir.

Duniya nodded.

'You are a woman and younger than me,' said Abshir, 'I suppose these facts are central to our gift relationship, yours and mine.'

'And you give because you're guilty?'

He answered in a round-about way, 'If you were a boy, you wouldn't have been married off to a man as old as your grandfather in the first place, and in the second, you might have got a scholarship to a university of your choice, because you were brilliant and ambitious. An injustice had been done. It has been my intention to right the wrong as best I could. I am sorry.'

He indicated that he was ready to go back. It took them a very short time to agree that they should first go to her place and drop her off. He would return to the flat in the city, shower and change, and then come to fetch them himself in Bosaaso's car to go together to Croce del Sud for dinner.

Then they had time to talk about Gisela, Abshir's wife, and the two daughters, Madalena and Annalisa. It was no secret that both girls hated Somalis, to whom they were rude on the phone. On occasion, they would even close the door in a caller's face. But they had welcomed Duniya, when she had visited them, and they got on well. All the same Abshir couldn't help mentioning his family's growing suspicion that he was planning to buy property; and when they learnt that he had taken a few thousand dollars out of his bank account 'as though he would acquire the whole country in one single stroke', his daughters wept for hours on end and peace was made between them only when he promised he was returning to Rome after he had paid a visit to Duniya and their cousins.

'Are you buying property then?' she asked.

'A pied-à-terre, to begin with, in which to house you,' he said, 'and you are free to live in it until you've sorted out your situation. A pied-à-terre small enough for the children to stay in if they choose not to share a house with you and Bosaaso if you happen to marry. And for me to stay in if I visit.'

'Too many ifs,' she said.

'You're a pile of ifs and maybes, if you'll pardon me,' Abshir said.

'Of course,' she said.

Then answering a general question about Bosaaso and herself, Duniya reviewed her own story from the moment it began telling itself, omitting not a single significant detail. Soon after she had finished telling her tale, they reached her place.

He said, 'There is no going back, only forward.'

'Let's hope so,' she said.

By general consent, Mire was seated at the head of a table known to the management of the Croce del Sud as 'Sette', which in their jargon meant the table could seat seven. It had only one end, the other having been pushed against the wall. So three people occupied either side of it, and Mire its only head. Bosaaso had booked the table and arrived earlier than the others, being an anxious type, the kind of man who got to the airport half an hour before the airline people thought necessary. The waiters had set the table under his supervision. While waiting for the other guests to arrive, he had had two long drinks of a fruit concoction, and not a drop of liquor.

Then Duniya and her entourage arrived, all five of them. And before their greeting noises had died down, Mire made his entrance. They all hushed, to let Mire and Abshir greet each other, properly and in total comfort. Duniya saw Mire's eyes burn like a curtain ablaze as he shook with passion Abshir's hand and then hugged him.

A couple of waiters arrived to lead them to their table. People's heads turned to watch them walk past. Duniya had been dressed by Nasiiba in a plain-cut but very attractive print dress, which her favourite seamstress had tailored for an occasion such as this. As Nasiiba had suggested, she wore her hair uncovered, in a bun, making her look almost as tall as Mire, who was a considerable height whilst standing among women. Nasiiba was in a baggy dress, fashionable at the time, and like Yarey, she had on something Abshir had brought them from Italy. The men, all four of them, had changed into something less fancy, no dinner jackets, no ties, in short, nothing quite as impressive as the women's. Duniya's dress didn't feel tight either at the waist or the armpits.

They were all clearly happy to be together and to talk to one another.

Duniya and Bosaaso were the centre-pieces of the gathering, not Abshir. Everyone could see that.

The waiters wouldn't leave until everyone, male and female, young and old, was seated. Bosaaso's eyes turned to Duniya for guidance. Yarey was placed between Duniya and Uncle Abshir, whereas Bosaaso was made to take the chair facing Duniya with Nasiiba sitting next to him, and Mataan opposite Uncle Abshir.

Dispensing with the formality of menus, Mire asked the waiters what they had. There was no point in whetting appetites with a dish listed on the menu but which was most likely not available. They listened to the waiters give a recitation of the dishes that were to be had, providing explanations to queries coming from Yarey, Nasiiba or a gentle 'What's that, Uncle?' from Mataan. Being themselves semi-literate, the waiters were no doubt content to take the orders verbally.

Then a waiter of the older generation, who had worked in Croce del Sud when the Italians were still the master race of Mogadiscio, came, not to serve or take their order, but to pay his respects to Dr Mire who had been his wife's doctor. The waiter was of the River People, with a broad, handsome smile, very smooth skin, growing not a single hair on his chin or upper lip. He half-bowed deferentially towards Duniya and his large eyes make a quick survey of Sette and decided he would take over. He dismissed the two younger waiters with a friendly gesture, and he went round making sure the forks and knives were in their proper places. He apologized again and again, charming Duniya, who placed herself in his experienced hands, as it were, out of which she didn't mind eating.

When he left, the subject of conversation suggested itself to the gathering. Did the older waiter make one feel better and more comfortable because he had been trained by the Italians and had been more adept at his profession than the younger ones who had probably never received as rigorous a training as him? Was this symptomatic of the situation, a regrettable condition in which Somalis were seldom able to run a restaurant proficiently and also profitably? The ball was kicked around, now Mire scored a goal, now Bosaaso and now Abshir. Nasiiba, Yarey and Mataan listened respectfully. Duniya couldn't help remarking to herself how silent Nasiiba had been since Abishir's arrival.

As the others engaged in polite talk, Duniya thought to herself that little is revealed to oneself directly. Revelations are received from out of a mist of doubts, in caves, in the dark, out of a child's mouth, or via the wise utterances of an elderly or mad person. She decided that her own epiphanic instant had occurred at a moment, on a morning, when a story chose to tell itself to her, through her, a story whose clarity was contained in the creative utterance, *Let there be a man*, and there was a story.

Half-attentive to her guests at the table, Duniya looked at Abshir, who had an unlit cigarette in one hand, and a light in the other. And he was saying to Mire, 'Claudia sends her love, and she gave me a parcel for you and a letter. Now here is the letter,' and he gave it to him, 'but the parcel is in Bosaaso's car, but I didn't bring it into the restaurant because it is too bulky to cart around.'

'Thank you,' Mire said, putting the letter in his pocket.

At the mention of Claudia's name, Mire's features seemed too reticent, too unprepared to display emotions in the presence of others. In fact, he appeared uninterested in asking Abshir questions about Claudia. Instead he asked, 'When will you come to dinner at my place?'

'Give me a day or two and I'll be able to know what my plans are,' Abshir replied.

'Take your time.'

Abshir nodded.

Mire said to Abshir: 'How long are you here, by the way?'

'A maximum of ten days.'

Duniya's centres shifted. The skin on her face felt too tight, like that of a woman half-way through washing off her make-up and who receives a visitor. She was thinking that beginning the story had been easy, like extracting a milk-tooth. But how was she to end it?

Here, she paused, for the waiters had come, bringing the food. Looking at the pepper-steak, she told herself that it was not she who had ordered it, but another Duniya. But where was this other Duniya?

She looked around, and everyone seemed to be pleased with what they had been given, and some of those present had started eating, and she heard *bon appetit* said a number of times. Garlic, pervasive as love, permeated the senses, and everyone smelt of it, even those who were not eating dishes which contained he root.

She was asking herself if she was content that her guests could get on with the telling of their respective stories without her. And *the other* Duniya with *her* tale? Then someone was mentioning her name, pairing it with Bosaaso's, and Abshir was raising a glass in a toast. Everyone else was standing up, only Duniya remained seated. Her children were coming round to hug her, and they were saying sweet things in her ears and wishing her well. Mire left his place at the head of the table, and came round to congratulate her, and Abshir responded in a toast, coupling her name with Bosaaso's, but the speech was brief, and in it he gave an elder brother's love and blessings to a younger sister getting married. And Nasiiba broke a glass when she had emptied it, and Mataan said that only a wedding at which something broke was considered lucky. Bosaaso and Duniya were treated as man and wife.

Whom was Bosaaso married to?

Which Duniya?

This or the other?

She wished she knew.

Duniya, the chronicler, is no longer certain how to go on, and nothing short of a much longer pause will enable her to look back on the events as they took place in order for her to describe them accurately.

At one point Nasiiba said to someone, 'Don't all stories end in marriage or the dissolution of such a union?'

Abshir was chain-smoking while speaking; among other things, he was saying that all stories are one story, whose principal theme is love. And if the stories feel different, it is only because the journeys the characters are to undertake take different routes to get to their final destination.

More toasts were drunk, and champagne was offered to those who wanted it.

'All stories,' concluded Abshir, 'celebrate, in elegiac terms, the untapped sources of energy, of the humanness of women and men.' Then Duniya smelt Bosaaso's odour, because he had come round to where she was sitting, and they were kissing while the others toasted them again and again. The world was an audience, ready to be given Duniya's story from the beginning.